Time and the Riddle

Time and the Riddle

Thirty-One Zen Stories

Howard Fast

Houghton Mifflin Company Boston

Library of Congress Cataloguing in Publication Data
Fast, Howard Melvin, date
　Time and the riddle.

　I. Title.
PZ3.F265Ti　1980　[PS3511.A784]　813'.5'2　79-24981
ISBN 0-395-29180-1

Printed in the United States of America

S 10 9 8 7 6 5 4 3 2 1

First published by Ward Ritchie Press 1975. Reprinted by arrangement with the author. Houghton Mifflin Company paperback edition 1980.

Stories from *The General Zapped an Angel,* by Howard Fast © 1969, 1970, and *A Touch of Infinity,* by Howard Fast © 1972, 1973, reprinted by permission of William Morrow & Company, Inc.

For Jerome Fast,

father, mother, brother
and dear friend through
a lifetime.

Contents

Foreword

THERE must be at least half a dozen Howard Fasts. There is the historian-novelist whose *Citizen Tom Paine*, *April Morning*, *The Hessian*, *The American* and *The Crossing* belong in the national archives. There is the reconstructionist who has given new life to ancient lore and legends in *My Glorious Brothers*, *Torquemada*, *Moses*, *Prince of Egypt*, and *Spartacus*. There is the social critic of *Conceived in Liberty* and *Freedom Road*, which has appeared in eighty-two languages and has been read by more than twenty-five million. There is the creator of a most incongruous galaxy of women —*Millie, Margie, Sally, Helen, Lydia, Sylvia, Shirley, Phyllis, Alice, Penelope, Samantha*—all of whom run, and sometimes race, the gamut from the lightest titillations to the darkest terrors, and all of whom owe their origin to the pseudonymous E.V. Cunningham. There is the dramatist of screen and television award-winning plays. And there are probably other Howard Fasts whom I have not yet discovered.

I have not mentioned the Howard Fast who is the author of this collection. The stories included are a balance and sometimes an alternation of fact, fantasy, and science-fiction. I prefer to think of them as speculative fictions. But the speculations transcend categories, for they are tense with electrifying power—a power which makes them frightening and, at times, mantic. The range is from horror to humor. I know of nothing to compare with the dexterity and surprises manifest in these pages.

Among my favorites are "The Hunter," a weird psychological-pathological transmogrification of Hemingway's tragic finale; "The Trap," a vision, or rather a hope, for a new race of men, a more spiritual species of homo sapiens, a breed that might save humanity from what seems to be his built-in drive for destructiveness; the

ix

suspenseful surrealistic farce of "The Hoop"; the vast implications in the little, localized "A Matter of Size"; the deadpan complacency with which the ultimate catastrophe is presented in "Not With a Bang"; the new and devastating twist to the often-tried formula of the time-machine in "The Mind of God"; the hilarious absurdity of "The Talent of Harvey"; the probing and painful bitterness of "Cephes 5"; the purely poetic concept of "The Egg"; the incisive sarcasm of "Cato the Martian"; the paradoxical logic and lingering question of "The Cold, Cold Box," which is both baleful and beautiful; the elaborate ingenuity of "The Martian Shop"; the unbelievably bland nonsense in "The Vision of Milty Boil"; "The Wound," which somehow centers about the old ballad of the son who carries his mother's heart to his sweetheart . . . but these are private predilections.

I have read Howard Fast's stories for years, and I have never failed to be delighted and even dazzled by them, by his gift for capturing, teasing, teaching, terrifying, and generally hypnotizing his audience. Whatever genre he elects to explore, he is unquestionably one of the most varied and vivifying storytellers of our time.

Louis Untermeyer

Introduction

I

WHAT good news—two and a half dozen stories by one of the story-art's modern masters! These tales move along, light, springy, ironic and inventive, skirting the borders of time and space inside and outside of man. Good news, yes; but what exactly is that news, what do these stories tell us and how and why? That itself is another story and, befitting these tales, an unusual one.

First off, when he began to write these unusual stories, Howard Fast allowed them to be called "fantasy and science fiction." This "mistake"—I'm tempted to call it a deception—seems natural enough, since the earliest of this strange breed made their appearance in *The Magazine of Fantasy and Science Fiction* and *Fantastic Universe*; then others were anthologized in collections called "Best Science Fiction" and the like. From the beginning, the stories read well enough as science fiction to take in buffs as well as beginners, even editors, reviewers, publishers, perhaps writers, too. But they are really of their own kind, unique, mutants.

They are Zen stories. Even where they amply contain *both* fantasy and science, as in "The Hoop" and "The Trap," such story-materials are means to an end, friendly clues to an unsolvable puzzle. Or to change the figure slightly, all of the angels and the rockets, the giant ants and midget men, the space flights and time warps—all the lovely, ironic fun and devices—are part of the magician's equipment, the paraphernalia and sleight-of-hand to trick you into at last seeing, to delight you into wisdom. If that claim seems paradoxical, we are on the right track, for Zen is often paradoxical, contradictory, non-logical. It is also intuitive, indirect and playful, qualities we find in abundance here, as you shall see. Science fiction rarely possesses any of these qualities, but like applied science itself, relies on analysis, technology and organization to suggest how life might become. Science fiction is goal-centered and essentially *political*, either utopian or anti-utopian, almost never detached, accepting, tranquil, in the spirit of these stories. Science fiction builds or develops, while Zen strikes—or fails to; science fiction argues its case, while the Zen story hints that there may be no case, then smiles.

Yet, Howard Fast was once the most famous politically-committed writer of fiction in America, possibly the most committed in our history. That a former Marxist and dialectical materialist should ultimately invent the American Zen Story implies a cautionary parable, like one of Zen Buddhism's round-about jokes.

II

Howard Fast's first two novels appeared before his twentieth birthday. By his thirtieth birthday in November of 1944, he had published fifteen books, including such critical and popular successes as *The Unvanquished*, *Citizen Tom Paine* and *Freedom Road*, the latter alone reaching twenty-five million copies in print. Early in 1957, not much beyond his fortieth birthday, he startled the world by announcing that in the previous year he had quit the Communist Party, although he had for years been its best-known advocate. During that important decade of his life, he had gone to prison for defying the now-defunct House Committee on Un-American Activities; he had run for Congress and lost; and he had resorted to publishing his own work when blacklisted (this included *Spartacus*, the only self-published best-seller in recent history). And he had served as a war correspondent, raised a family, produced a newspaper column, delivered countless speeches, written dozens of short stories, many plays for radio and theatre, more novels and several filmscripts. He had also determinedly wrought a "one-man reformation" in the American historical novel: in *The Last Frontier* and *Freedom Road*, he had attacked racial injustice; in *The American* and *Clarkton*, the abuse of the poor and the suppression of labor organization; in *My Glorious Brothers* and his novels of the American revolution, he had exalted man's long fight to be free. Then his political world, the apparent base of his ideas, collapsed. As a writer, he would write his way out of chaos; he would thereby find or make order.

Before his fiftieth birthday (at a time when many thought he was through), he reviewed every historical period he had written on before, returning fictionally to probe the soft spots of his own righteousness. In *Agrippa's Daughter*, he repudiated the concept of just wars in favor of pacifism; in *The Winston Affair*, he rejected political trials and persecution, even of murderous anti-Semites; in *Power*, he dramatized in the labor movement the corruption by power of a good man in a good cause. Not that all his movement was now in reverse. He wrote with renewed feelings of man's quest for peace and justice, with continued aversion to cruelty and violence, with strengthened distrust of rigid institutions. There were some happy new discoveries to move him forward. First, he turned to the wonderful world of women and, as E.V. Cunningham, an imaginary being, he produced the first women's liberation novels written by a man. *Phyllis*, *Alice*, *Shirley*, *Penelope*, each were novels about women who were sane and brave survivors in the lunatic world of men. The successful series grew to more than a dozen volumes wherein Fast added the elements of irony and laughter to his vivid narrative style. Second, he returned to the world of science fiction (his first published short story, at sixteen, had been "straight" science fiction), but, here too, irony and laughter predominated. Both the women's novels and the "science fiction" stories—and their evolving attitudes toward the world of man and the world beyond man—grew out of the most important discovery of all. Howard Fast had found Zen.

III

Now Howard Fast is sixty, a youthful Zen student, the creator of these thirty-one stories. But life is no mere chronicle and summation; it has its interior rhythms and projects its own patterns. These stories were, in a sense, waiting for him his whole life; after so much work and suffering, is it any wonder they are so funny? After all, the alternative was despair. As a group, the stories tell us that the world is full of large disappointments and small, pleasant surprises; that we make the former and it provides the latter. The world itself, the stories say, has meaning apart from us and we must explore our own inner space in order to find our proper place and meaning in that world. As Arthur C. Clarke has observed of Unidentified Flying

Objects: "They tell us absolutely nothing about intelligence elsewhere in the universe; but they do prove how rare it is on earth."

One mental habit that keeps us from connecting with reality, from using our good sense, is the substitution of authority or custom for observation and independent thought. Thus "The Movie House" becomes the modern version of Plato's cave, where people watch shadows flickering on the wall; when young Kiley fashions a key to open the door to the outside, he is condemned as a heretic. Wisdom arrives at the door of those who remain simple, child-like; it is not a matter of "intelligence" and "learning." The authority figures—scientists, generals, businessmen of "The Hoop," "The Trap" and "The General Zapped an Angel"—have little to tell us despite their intelligence, except by the way of horrible example. They have lost all reverence for life, all flexibility or willingness to adapt to its purposes. Even the "normal" central character of "The Large Ant" smashes the strange beast without knowing why ("You killed it because you are a human being"). In "The Insects," the creatures finally rebel because humans "simply take it for granted that anything not human doesn't resent being killed."

So it's a matter of perspective and relativity, of seeing the relatedness of all life, of removing the tragi-comic blinders of ego. In "A Matter of Size," a woman swats a fly and finds it to be a tiny replica of man; shall all its kind, too small and troublesome for our regard, be sprayed with insecticide? Shall other small, troublesome humans (?) likewise be dispatched? "The Egg" offers a reverse perspective, wherein a single, hatching egg, in a future-world bereft of birds, becomes the glory and wonder of the world. In the apocalyptic stories, the world usually ends because something violent, that hides and stirs within us, finally breaks loose. The beast, the monster, the destroyer is never the creature from outer space; it is the general who zaps the angel and the angel who cannot figure out why.

The major opposition is man's ego against nature's indifferent fulfillment. On the planet Cephes 5, the dumping ground of nature's misfits and murderers,

> Every person on the planet spends his life creating an ego structure which subjectively places him at the center of the universe. This ego structure is central to the disease, for given

the sickness that creates the ego, each individual goes on to form in his mind an anthropomorphic superman whom he calls God and who supports his right to kill.

Far better, is it not, to try to enter "the mind of God" as Hitler's would-be assassins attempt in one story. Instead, like the people in "The Interval" and "Not With A Bang," we must accept all, even the finality of death when the world's stage must be emptied, without a whimper. Along the way, we can be sustained by love, by patience and by forgiveness ("we are what we are"), along with the saving grace of humor.

The author has not tried here to create the perfect political state ("The Trap" shows that we would disown it or destroy it), but merely to expand our state of being, to enrich our state of mind. He has combined the parable form of the ancients with the sharp images of the modern cinema. If, in a week, a month, a year from now, your mind flashes whimsical pictures of God's hand flicking off the sun-switch, of garbage pushing up through the cracks of the earth, of a professor surrounded by cloning cats, you will have read these stories right—beginning in delight, ending in surprise, lightly touched by infinity.

Frank Campenni, Ph. D
Department of English
University of Wisconsin, Milwaukee

Time and the Riddle

1
UFO

"**Y**OU never read in bed," Mr. Nutley said to his wife.
    "I used to, you remember," Mrs. Nutley replied. "But then I found it was sufficient simply to lie here and compose my thoughts. To get my head together, as the kids say."
    "I envy you. You never have any trouble sleeping."
    "Oh, I do. At times. To be perfectly honest," she added, "I think women fuss less than men."
    "I don't fuss about it," Mr. Nutley protested, putting aside his copy of *The New Yorker* magazine and switching off his bedside light. "I just find it damned unpleasant. I'm not an insomniac. I just get a notion and it keeps running around in my head."
    "Do you have a notion tonight?"
    "I find Ralph Thompson a pain in the ass, if you can call that a notion."
    "That's certainly not enough to keep you awake. I must say I've always found him pleasant enough—for a neighbor. We could do worse, you know."
    "I suppose so."
    "Why are you so provoked about him?" Mrs. Nutley asked, pulling the covers closer to her chin against the chill of the bedroom.
    "Because I never know whether he's putting me on or not. I find writers and artists insufferable, and he's the most insufferable of the lot. The fact that I drag my butt into the city every day and do an honest day's work makes me what he refers to as a member of the Establishment and an object of what I am certain he regards as his sense of humor."

"Well, you are upset," said Mrs. Nutley.

"I am not upset. Why is it that I must wait at least an hour before I can think of the proper witty rejoinder to the needling of a horse's ass?"

"Because you are a thoughtful and honest person, and I am thankful that you are. What did he say?"

"The way he said it," Mr. Nutley replied. "A kind of a cross between a leer and a snicker. He said he saw a flying saucer come sailing out of the sunset and settle down in the little valley across the hill."

"Indeed! That isn't even witty. You probably fell into his trap and insisted that there was no such thing as a flying saucer."

"I am going to sleep," said Mr. Nutley. He turned over, stretched, wriggled into the bedclothes, and relapsed into silence. After a minute or so he asked Mrs. Nutley whether she was still awake.

"Quite awake."

"Well, I said to him, why didn't you go down there and look at it if you knew where it landed? He told me he doesn't trespass on millionaires' property."

"Does he really think we're millionaires?"

"A man who sees flying saucers can think anything. What's got into this country? No one saw flying saucers when I was a kid. No one was mugged when I was a kid. No one took dope when I was a kid. I put it to you—did you ever hear of a flying saucer when you were a kid?"

"Maybe there were no flying saucers when we were kids," Mrs. Nutley suggested.

"Of course there weren't."

"No. I mean that perhaps there were none then, but there are now."

"Nonsense."

"Well, it doesn't have to be nonsense," Mrs. Nutley said gently. "All sorts of people see them."

"Which proves only that the world is filled with kooks. Tell me something, if there is such a silly thing as a flying saucer, what the devil is it up to?"

"Curiosity."

"Just what does that mean?"

"Well," said Mrs. Nutley, "we are curious, they are curious. Why not?"

2

"Because that kind of thinking is exactly what's wrong with the world today. Wild guesses with no foundation. Do you know that yesterday the Dow dropped ten points because someone made a wild guess and put it on the tape? If people like yourself were more in touch with the world and what goes on in the world, we'd all be better off."

"What do you mean by people like myself?"

"People who don't know one damn thing about the world as it really is."

"Like myself?" Mrs. Nutley asked gently. She rarely lost her temper.

"Well, what do you do all day out here in the suburbs or exurbs or whatever it is sixty miles from New York?"

"I keep busy," she replied mildly.

"It's just not enough to keep busy," Mr. Nutley was off on one of his instructive speeches, which, as Mrs. Nutley reflected, came about once every two weeks, when he had a particularly bad bout of insomnia. "A person must justify his existence."

"By making money. You always tell me that we have enough money."

"I never mentioned money. The point is that when the kids went away to college and you decided to go back and get a doctorate in plant biology, I was all for it. Wasn't I?"

"Indeed you were. You were very understanding."

"That's not the point. The point is that two years have gone by since you got that degree and you do absolutely nothing about it. You spend your days here and you just let them slide by."

"Now you're angry at me," said Mrs. Nutley.

"I am not angry."

"I do try to keep busy. I work in the garden. I collect specimens."

"You have a gardener. I pay him one hundred and ten dollars a week. You have a cook. You have a maid. I was reading an article in the *Sunday Observer* about the aimless life of the upper-middle-class woman."

"Yes, I read the article," said Mrs. Nutley.

"You never let me get to the point, do you?" Mr. Nutley said testily. "We were talking about flying saucers, which you are ready to accept as a fact."

"But now we're talking about something else, aren't we? You're provoked because I don't find a job in some university as a plant biologist and prove that I have a function in life. But then we'd never see each other, would we? And I am fond of you.''

"Did I say one word about you getting a job in some university? As a matter of fact, there are four colleges within twenty miles of here, any one of which would be delighted to have you.''

"That's a matter of surmise. And I do love my home.''

"Then you accept boredom. You accept a dull, senseless existence. You accept—''

"You know you mustn't get worked up at this time of the night,'' Mrs. Nutley said mildly. "It makes it so much harder for you to get to sleep. Wouldn't you like a nice warm glass of milk?''

"Why do you never let me finish any thought?''

"I think I'll bring you the milk. You know it always lets you sleep.''

Mrs. Nutley got out of bed, turned on her bedside light, put on her robe, and went down to the kitchen. There she heated a pan of milk. From a jar in the cupboard she took a tiny packet of Seconal and dropped the powder into a glass. She added the hot milk and stirred. Then she returned to the bedroom. Her husband drank the milk and she watched approvingly.

"You do put magic into hot milk,'' Mr. Nutley said. "It's not getting to sleep that makes me cranky.''

"Of course.''

"It's just that I think of you all alone all day out here—''

"But I do love this old place so.''

She waited until his breathing became soft and regular. "Poor dear,'' she said, sighing. She waited ten minutes more. Then she got out of bed, pulled on old denims, walking boots, shirt and sweater, and moved silently down the stairs and out of the house.

She crossed the gardens to the potting shed, the moon so bright that she never had to use the flashlight hooked to her belt. In the potting shed was the rucksack, filled with the plant specimens she had collected and catalogued over the past three weeks. They were so appreciative of the care with which she catalogued each specimen and the way she wrapped them in wet moss and the way she always left the fungi for the very last day, so they would be fresh and pungent, that she would be left with a warm glow that lasted for days. Not that she wasn't paid properly and sufficiently for her work. Mr. Nutley was absolutely right. A person with a skill should be paid for the skill, and she had an old handbag half full of little

4

diamonds nestling in the drawer of her dressing table. Of course, diamonds were as common in their place as pebbles were here, so she had no guilt about being overpaid.

She slung the rucksack onto her shoulders, left the potting shed, and took the path over the hill into the tiny hidden valley behind it, where the flying saucer lay comfortably hidden from the eyes of the cynical doubters. She walked with a long, easy stride for a woman of fifty, but then outdoor work tended to keep her in good condition, and she couldn't help thinking how beneficial it would be for Mr. Nutley if he could only spend his time out of doors in the country instead of in a stuffy city office.

2
The Hole in the Floor

"YOU must have a lot of clout," Robinson said.

"I haven't any clout. My uncle has clout. He's a friend of the Commissioner."

"We never had anyone in the back seat before."

"Except a perpetrator," said Robinson, grinning. He was a black man with a round face and an infectious smile.

"If I had a brain in my head," McCabe said, "I would be a writer and not a cop. There's this guy out in the L.A. police force, and he's a writer. He wrote this book and it became a best seller, and he's loaded but he still wants to be a cop. Beats the hell out of me. I didn't read the book but I saw the movie. Did you see the movie?"

"I saw it."

"Good movie."

"It was a lousy movie," said Robinson.

"That's your opinion. L.A. isn't New York."

"You can say that again."

"You been to L.A.?" McCabe asked me. He was older than Robinson, in his late thirties and going to fat, with a hard, flat face and small, suspicious blue eyes. I like the way he got along with Robinson; there was an easy give and take, and they never pushed each other.

McCabe took a call, and Robinson stepped on the gas and turned on his siren. "This is a mugging," McCabe said.

It was a purse snatch on 116th Street, involving two kids in their

7

teens. The kids had gotten away, and the woman was shaken and tearful but unharmed. Robinson took down the descriptions of the kids and the contents of the purse, while McCabe calmed the woman and pushed the crowd on its way.

"There are maybe ten thousand kids in this city who will do a purse snatch or a mugging, and how do you catch them, and if you catch them, what do you do with them? You said you been to L.A.?"

"A few times, on and off."

"This is a sad city," Robinson said. "It's hanging on, but that's the most you can say. It's just hanging on."

"What's it like?" McCabe wanted to know.

"Downtown it's like this, maybe worse in some places."

"But in Hollywood, Beverly Hills, places like that?"

"It's sunny. When there's no smog."

"What the hell," said McCabe, "no overcoats, no snow—I got six more years, and then I think I'll take the wife and head west."

We stopped, and Robinson wrote out a ticket for a truck parked in front of a fire hydrant.

"You go through the motions," he said. "I guess that's the way it is. Everyone goes through the motions."

"You ever deliver a baby?" I asked him.

He grinned his slow, pleasant grin and looked at me in the rearview mirror.

"You ask McCabe."

"We did seven of them," McCabe said. "That's just since we been together. I ain't talking about rushing them to the hospital. I'm talking about the whole turn, and that includes slapping them across the ass to make them cry."

"One was twins," Robinson said.

"How did you feel? I mean when you did it, and there was the kid crying and alive?"

"You feel good."

"High as a kite," said Robinson. "It's a good feeling. You feel maybe the way a junkie feels when he can't make a connection and then finally he's got the needle in his arm. High."

"Does it make up for the other things?"

There was a long pause after that before McCabe asked me, "What other things?"

"One son of a bitch," Robinson said slowly, "he put his gun

8

into my stomach and pulled the trigger three times. It don't make up for that."

"Gun misfired," McCabe explained. "Three times. A lousy little Saturday night special—happens maybe once in a thousand times."

"It don't make up for being black," Robinson said.

We cruised for the next ten minutes in silence. Possibly it was the last thing Robinson said; perhaps they resented having me in the back seat. Then they got a call, and McCabe explained that it was an accident in a house on 118th Street.

"It could be anything," Robinson said. "The floors collapse, the ceilings fall down, and the kids are eaten by rats. I grew up in a house like that. I held it against my father. I still hold it against him."

"Where can they go?"

"Away. Away is a big place."

"You can't just write about cops," McCabe said. "Cops are a reaction. A floor falls in and they call the cops. What the hell are we supposed to do? Rebuild these lousy rat-traps?"

We rolled into 118th Street, and there were half a dozen people standing in front of one of the tenements, and one of them told us that it was Mrs. Gonzales who put in the call and that her apartment was in the back, four flights up.

"What happened there?" McCabe wanted to know.

"Who knows? She don't let us in."

We started up the stairs, McCabe and Robinson pushing their coats behind their guns, and myself allowing them to lead the way. A couple of the men outside started to follow us, but McCabe waved them back and told them to clear out. We climbed four flights of stairs, walked to the back of the narrow old-law tenement, and Robinson knocked on the door.

"Who is it?"

"Police," Robinson said.

She opened the door to the length of the safety chain, and Robinson and McCabe identified themselves. Then she let us in, through the kitchen, which is where the door is in most of the old-law tenements. The place was neat and clean. Mrs. Gonzales was a skinny little woman of about forty-five. Her husband, she told us, worked for Metropolitan Transit. Her son worked in a butcher shop on Lexington Avenue. She was all alone in the apartment, and she was on the verge of hysteria.

"It's all right now," McCabe said with surprising gentleness. "Just tell us what happened."

She shook her head.

"Something must have happened," Robinson said. "You called the police."

She nodded vigorously.

"All right, Mrs. Gonzales," Robinson said, "so something happened that shocked you. We know about that. It upsets you, it makes you sick. You feel cold and feel like maybe you want to throw up. Do you feel cold now?"

She nodded.

Robinson took a sweater off a hook in the kitchen. "Put this on. You'll feel better."

She put on the sweater.

"Anyone in there?" McCabe asked, nodding toward the other rooms.

"No," she whispered.

"Got any brandy—whiskey?"

She nodded toward a cupboard, and I went there and found a bottle of rum. I poured a few ounces into a glass and handed it to her. She drank it, made a face, and sighed.

"Now tell us what happened."

She nodded and led the way out of the kitchen, through a room which served as a dining room, clean, rug on the floor, cheap ornate furniture, polished and loved, to the door of the next room, which had two beds that served as couches, a chest of drawers, and a hole in the middle of the floor about three and a half or four feet across.

"Goddamn floor fell in," said McCabe.

"The way they build these places," said Robinson.

"The way they built them seventy-five years ago," I said.

Mrs. Gonzales said nothing, stopped at the door to the room, and would go no further.

"Who lives underneath?" McCabe asked.

"Montez. He is a teacher. No one is home now—except the devil."

Robinson entered the bedroom and walked gingerly toward the hole. The ancient floor creaked under his feet but held. He stopped a foot short of the edge of the hole and looked down. He didn't say anything, just stood there and looked down.

"The building should be condemned," said McCabe. "But then

10

where do they go? You want to write about problems, here's a problem. The whole goddamn city is a problem."

Still Robinson stared silently into the hole. I envisioned a corpse below or the results of some unspeakable murder. I started into the room.

"Take it easy," McCabe warned me. "The floor's rotten. We don't want you down there. What do you think?" he asked Robinson.

Still no answer from Robinson.

I moved carefully in on one side of the room, McCabe following on the other side. We both reached the hole at the same time. Robinson was in front of the hole, his back to the door. McCabe and I stood on either side of him.

Even before my eyes registered what was down there, I was conscious of the smell. It reminded me of the odor of jasmine, yet it was different. It was something I had never known before, as indescribable as it was different, and it came on a slow current of warm air that I can only think of as silver. It's not possible to explain why a breath of air should evoke the image of silver, but there it was.

And then I saw what I saw. I saw what McCabe saw and what Robinson saw, so I did not dream it and I did not imagine it. About ten feet beneath the hole was a grassy sward. Its appearance suggested that it had been mowed, the way an old English lawn is mowed, yet something about it argued that the thick, heavy turf grew that way and had never known a mower's blade. Nor was the grass green the way we know green; it appeared to be overlaid with a glow of lilac.

No one of us spoke. No one suggested that this might be the floor of Mr. Montez's apartment and that the teacher specialized in horticulture; we knew it was not the floor of Mr. Montez's apartment, and that was all we knew. The only sound in the apartment was the gentle sobbing of Mrs. Gonzales.

Then Robinson crouched down, sprawled his huge bulk back from the edge of the hole, and let his head and shoulders hang over, bracing himself with his hands. The rotten floor creaked under him.

"Watch it!" McCabe exclaimed. "You'll be down there on your head."

He was wonderful. He was what only an old New York City cop

11

could be, possessed of a mentality in which there was neither the unexpected nor the impossible. Anything could happen in New York, and it usually did.

"What do you see?" I asked Robinson.

"More of it. Just more of it." He drew himself back and stood up, and he looked from my face to McCabe's face.

"We're four stories high," McCabe said bleakly, his universe finally tilting on edge.

"A lot more of it," said Robinson.

"I'll phone it in. I'll tell them there's a cow pasture on the fourth floor of an old-law tenement."

"It's no cow pasture," Robinson said.

"Then what the hell is it? A mirage?"

"I'm going down there," Robinson said.

"Like hell you are!"

Robinson's round face was no longer jovial, no longer the easy, controlled face of a black cop in New York, who knows how much to push and just when to push. He looked at McCabe, smiling a thin, humorless smile, and he asked him what he thought was down there through the hole to teacher Montez's apartment.

"How the hell should I know?"

"I know."

"My ass, you know!"

"What's down there?" I asked Robinson, my voice shaking. "What did you see?"

"The other side of the coin."

"What the hell does that mean?" McCabe demanded.

"Man," Robinson sighed, "you been white just too goddamn long."

"I'm going to call in," McCabe said. "You hear me, Robinson? I'm going to call in, and then I'm going to get the keys from the super—if there is one in this lousy rat-trap—and I'm going to go through Montez's apartment and I'm going to look right up your ass through that hole, and we'll see who grows grass four stories up. And until I do, you don't go down there. You understand?"

"Sure, man, I understand," Robinson answered softly.

Then McCabe pushed past the sobbing Mrs. Gonzales and slammed the kitchen door behind him. As if his slamming the door had created a current, the perfumed air rose out of the hole and filled the bedroom.

12

"What did you see down there?" I asked Robinson.

"Have a look?" Robinson suggested.

I shook my head. Nothing on earth would persuade me to lie belly down on that creaking floor and hang over the edge the way Robinson had before. Robinson was watching me.

"Afraid?"

I nodded.

"You know what's going to happen when McCabe gets the super and they go into that apartment under us? Just like he said—he'll be standing there looking right up my asshole—then it'll be some kind of optical illusion, and two or three weeks—man, in two, three weeks we won't even remember we saw it."

"It's an illusion," I agreed.

"Smell it!"

"Jesus Christ, you're looking at something that *isn't* there!"

"But you and me, mister, and that lady over there"—he waved one arm in a circle—"that's real. That's no illusion."

"That's real," I said.

He stared at me a long moment, shook his head, then sat down on the edge of the break in the floor, slid down, rolled over, hanging on by his hands, and then dropped, landing in a crouch on the turf. He brought himself erect and turned in a three-hundred-and-sixty-degree circle, his eyes sweeping over what he saw. Like the grass he stood upon, he was bathed in a kind of violet sunshine.

"Robinson!"

He didn't hear me. It was obvious that he didn't hear. He raised his face to where I should have been, his dark skin bathed in the lilac sunshine, and whatever his eyes saw, they did not see me. The strange light turned his dark brown skin into a kind of smoky gold. He looked around again, grinning with delight.

"Hey, man!" he called out. "Hey, man—you still up there?"

"I'm here. Can you hear me?"

"Man, if you're still there, I can't hear you, I can't see you, and you better believe me, it don't bother me one bit!"

Mrs. Gonzales screamed. She screamed two or three times and settled for sobbing.

"Tell McCabe," yelled Robinson. "Tell McCabe to take his prowl car and shove it up his goddamn ass! Tell McCabe—"

I never knew what else he would have told McCabe to do, because at that moment McCabe kicked in the door of Montez's apartment, and then there were two of them, McCabe and Robinson, standing in a litter of broken laths and chunks of plaster, just the two of them, standing in the litter and staring at each other.

McCabe looked up at me and said, "Stay back from the edge, because the whole lousy ceiling's coming down. I called emergency. We're going to empty the building, so tell that Gonzales woman to put on her coat and come downstairs." Then he turned to Robinson. "You had to do it. You couldn't stay up there. You had to show you're an athlete."

To which Robinson said nothing at all.

Back in the prowl car, later, I asked Robinson what he had seen.

"In Montez's apartment? The man has a lot of books. You know, sometimes I say to myself I should have been a teacher instead of a cop. My brother-in-law's a teacher. A principal. He makes more money than I do and he's got some respect. A cop has no respect. You break your back and risk your life, and they spit in your face."

"You can say that again," McCabe said.

"We once pulled four people out of a burning building on One hundred fortieth Street—my own people—and some son of a bitch clipped me with a brick. For what? For saving four people?

"You know what I mean. When you stood there on the grass and looked around you, what did you see?"

"A lousy old-law tenement that should have been torn down fifty years ago," said Robinson.

"You take a car like this," said McCabe, "it's unusual to you. You pull a few strings downtown, and they say, OK, sit in the car and write a story about it. For us it's a grind, day in, day out, one lousy grind." He took a call on the car radio. "Liquor store this time. West One hundred seventeenth, Brady's place. You know," he said to me, "they rip off that place every month, regular as clockwork."

The siren going, we tore up Amsterdam Avenue to 117th Street.

3
General Hardy's Profession

MISS Kanter was not quite certain whether she was in love
with Dr. Blausman or not, but she felt that the privilege of
working for such a man repaid and balanced her devotion, even
though Dr. Blausman never made a pass at her or even allowed her
that peculiar intimacy that many men have with their secretaries. It
was not that Dr. Blausman was cold; he was happily married and
utterly devoted to his work and his family, and brilliant. Miss
Kanter had wept very real tears of joy when he was elected president
of the Society.

In her own right, Miss Kanter was skilled and devoted, and after
five years with Dr. Blausman she had developed a very keen clinical
perception of her own. When she took a history of a new patient, it
was not only complete but pointed and revealing. In the case of
Alan Smith, however, there was a noticeable hiatus.

"Which troubles me somewhat," Dr. Blausman remarked. "I
dislike taking anyone who isn't a referral."

"He has been referred, or recommended, I suppose. He mentioned the air shuttle, which makes me think he is either from
Washington or Boston. Washington, I would say. I imagine that it
would make trouble for him if it got out that he was going into
therapy."

"Trouble?"

"You know how the government is about those things."

"You must have found him very appealing."

"Very good-looking, Doctor. You know, I am a woman." Miss
Kanter seized opportunities to remind Dr. Blausman. "But very

15

desperate for help. If he is government and high government—well, that might be very meaningful, might it not?"

"Still, he refuses to say who recommended him?"

"Yes. But I'm sure you'll get it out of him."

"You told him my fee?"

"Of course."

"Was his face familiar?"

"It was one of those faces that seem to be. But I have no idea who he really is."

Neither did Dr. Blausman have any sure idea of who the new patient was. It was the following day, and across the desk from Dr. Blausman sat a strongly built, handsome man, with pale blue eyes, iron-gray hair, and a square jaw that would have done credit to a Western star of the thirties. He was about forty-five years old, six feet or so in height, and appeared to be in excellent physical condition. He was nervous, but that was a symptom that brought patients into the office in the first place.

"Well, Mr. Smith," Dr. Blausman began, "suppose you tell me something about yourself, what made you seek me out, who referred you to me, your problems—"

"I have only the most rudimentary knowledge of psychoanalysis, Doctor."

"That doesn't matter. It's important that my knowledge should be a little more than rudimentary. Which I hope it is. But for the moment, forget about psychoanalysis. I am a psychiatrist, and I prefer to think of my work as psychotherapy. Does the thought of psychoanalysis disturb you?"

"I suppose it does. The couch and all that—"

"You can lie down if you wish, or you can sit in a chair. That's not important, Mr. Smith. The point is to get at the root of what troubles you and to see whether we can alleviate the pain. We do that by establishing a relationship. So, you see, you have to be rather forthright. It is true that in the course of therapy, even lies can be revealing, but that's not a good way to begin."

"I don't understand you."

"I think you do. I must know who you are. Otherwise—"

"I told you that my name is Alan Smith."

"But it isn't," Blausman said gently.

"How do you know?"

"If I were not adept enough at my discipline to know, you would be making a mistake in coming to me."

"I see." The patient sat in silence for a moment or two. "And if I refuse to give you any other name?"

"Then I am afraid you must seek help elsewhere. There is a sufficient unknown in a person who meets me forthrightly. In one who doesn't—well, it is impossible."

The patient nodded and appeared to reflect on the doctor's words. "How confidential is your treatment?"

"Totally."

"Do you make tapes?"

"No."

"Do you take notes?"

"In most cases, yes. If there were sufficient reason not to keep notes, I would forgo it." When the patient still hesitated, Dr. Blausman said, "Perhaps you would prefer to think about it and return tomorrow?"

"No, that won't be necessary. I also pride myself on being a judge of character, and I think I can trust you. My name is Franklin Hardy. General Franklin Hardy. I am a three-star general, second in command at the War Board. A three-star general who is second in command at the War Board does not consult a psychoanalyst."

"Have you thought of resigning or taking a leave of absence, General Hardy?"

"I have thought of it—yes. My pride will not allow me to resign, and the situation today is too grave for me to take a leave of absence. Also, I don't think I am unable to perform my duties. My country has a large investment in me, Dr. Blausman. I don't feel it is my right to play fast and loose with that."

"And how did you come to me? You are stationed in Washington, are you not?"

"At the Pentagon."

"So if we were to have three sessions a week—and I am afraid that would be minimal—you would have to do a good deal of commuting. Isn't that a burden?"

"I want this kept secret, and that might be impossible with a local man."

"But why me?"

"I read a paper of yours and I was very impressed by it. Your monograph on the Amnesia Syndrome."

17

"Oh? But surely you don't feel you have amnesia?"

"Perhaps—I don't know."

"Very interesting." Dr. Blausman stared at the General thoughtfully. "Since you read my paper, you are aware that there is an enormous variety of amnesia, loss of identity being most common in the public mind. You obviously do not suffer that. There are childhood amnesias, adolescent amnesias, traumatic amnesias, and a hundred other varieties, due to shock, brain injury, drugs, senility—well, I could go on and on. Why do you feel you suffer from amnesia?"

The General considered this for a while, and then he spoke flatly and abruptly. "I am not sure I know who I am."

Dr. Blausman smiled slightly. "Most interesting indeed. But in what sense? I have many young patients who feel a desperate need to know who they are. But that is in a religious, philosophical, or teleological sense. What meaning has their presence on earth?"

"Not exactly."

"You told me that you are General Franklin Hardy. I could ask you to show me your papers, but that's hardly necessary."

"Not at all." The general went into his pocket and revealed a series of identity cards. He smiled a very engaging smile. "Of course, they are not my only source of information. I have been with the army for twenty-seven years, and there are no gaps in my memory. I have served in World War Two, in Korea, and in Vietnam. As you may recall."

Dr. Blausman nodded. "I read the papers." He waited a long moment. "Go on, sir."

"All right, let me be specific. Three nights ago, I awakened. I am not married, Doctor. As I said, I awakened about four o'clock in the morning, and I was not General Hardy."

"You are sure you were awake?"

"Absolutely sure. I was not dreaming. I got out of bed, and I was someone else."

"In a strange place? I mean, was your bedroom strange to you? Was it completely dark?"

"No, I could see. I don't draw the blinds, and there was moonlight. Was it strange to me?" He frowned and closed his eyes. "No—not entirely. I appeared to have a vague memory of a room that should have been completely familiar. I wondered what I was doing there. I felt that I should know."

18

"And then?"

"And then I was myself again, and it was over. But I couldn't get back to sleep. I was terribly shaken. I am not a man with poor nerves. I cannot remember being so shaken before."

Dr. Blausman glanced at his watch. "I'm afraid our time is over for today. Can you come back on Wednesday, the same time?"

"Then you will—?"

"Help you? Treat you? Yes, however you wish to see it."

When the doctor took his break for lunch, he said to his secretary, "You can make up a new history for Mr. Smith, Miss Kanter. He'll be back on Wednesday."

"Did you crack the mystery?"

"If you think of it that way. He's General Franklin Hardy."

"What!"

"Yes, General Hardy."

"And—and you—hell, it's none of my business."

"Exactly. I am not a moralist or a jurist, Miss Kanter. I am a physician."

"But, my God, Vietnam is not just a war. You know his record."

"What would you say if he came here bleeding, Miss Kanter? Would it be proper to put a tourniquet on him? Or would it be more moralistic to allow him to bleed to death?"

"Are you asking me, Doctor?"

"No, I am telling you, Miss Kanter."

"You don't have to get angry. Mine is a normal, human reaction. Anyway, it is a comfort to know that he has flipped out."

"He has not, as you put it, flipped out. Furthermore, this is to be absolutely confidential. He asked for my confidence, and I gave it to him. No one is to know that he is a patient of mine, not your father, not your mother, not your boyfriend—no one. Do you understand?"

"Loud and clear." Miss Kanter sighed.

Sitting opposite Dr. Blausman in a comfortable chair, his legs stretched out, General Hardy remarked that he had not thought of therapy in just this manner.

"It's the end product that counts, General—to find out why. Do you dream a great deal?"

"As much as the next one, I suppose. I don't remember them."

19

"I'd like you to take notes. Keep a pencil and pad next to your bed. Now the night this happened—it was not the first time?"

"No, not the first time."

"When was the first time?'

"Two years ago, in Vietnam. We had been set back on our heels by Charlie's big offensive, and we had taken some pretty heavy losses. There was a lot of loose talk, and at one of our meetings the use of tactical atomic weapons was put on the agenda. Against my will, mind you. No sane or reasonable man can even think of tactical atomic weapons without going into a cold sweat, but since they were determined to talk about them, I decided to let them talk and get it out of their systems. After all, they could do nothing without my vote. I listened to the discussion, and there was one idiot there—who shall be nameless—who was all for using the tacticals and ending the war in hours. Of course it wouldn't have ended the war—no way—but he was off on a laboratory kick, that we'd never know how they worked until we worked them, and this was the one place it made sense to experiment. I kept my mouth shut, because there is nothing to defeat an argument like its own loopholes, and then it happened."

"What happened?"

"I was no longer General Hardy. I was someone else, and I was listening to this featherbrain and laughing inside at his whole proposition."

"Laughing? In what way?"

"Not contempt, not disapproval—I was laughing the way you laugh at a kid who has a new toy and has gone hog-wild with it. I was amused and—" He broke off.

"What were you going to say?"

The General remained silent.

"I am not a Congressional Committee," Blausman said softly. "I am not the public. I am a physician. I am not here to confront you or expose you, but to help you. If you don't want that help—well, the door is open."

"I know the damn door is open!" the General cried. "Do you think I'd be here if I could live with this? I was going to say that I was amused and delighted."

"Why didn't you say it?"

"Because the *I* is a lie. Not me. Not Franklin Hardy. The other one."

20

"Why do you say the other one?" Blausman asked. "Why not the other man?"

"I don't know."

"You have read about possession? By evil entities?"

"Yes."

"It has interesting psychological references. Do you have the feeling—I only speak of the feeling—that you were possessed?"

"No!"

"You appear very certain."

"I am certain," the General said emphatically.

"Why?"

"Because this is myself. Because the syndrome—as you call it—is not being possessed or used or manipulated, but simply remembering. I remember who I am."

"Who?"

"That's the damn trick. It passes too quickly."

"At this meeting, how long did this memory last?"

"A minute. A little more, a little less."

"And as I understand it," Dr. Blausman said carefully, "during that time you were delighted and amused at the thought of using atomic tactical weapons. Will you accept that?"

"You're asking me do I have the guts to?" the General said harshly. "All right, I do. I accept it as the man who was amused."

"Whom you insist is yourself?"

"Yes. Do you understand now why I commute from Washington each day to see a psychiatrist?"

"What was the outcome of the meeting?"

"You know that. Atomic weapons are not firecrackers. We squashed the whole notion."

On his next visit, Dr. Blausman returned to the night-time incident, asking the General whether he had been awakened from sleep at other times.

"Yes."

"How many times?"

Hardy thought for a while. "Fourteen—or thirteen."

"Always the same time?"

"No. Sometimes earlier, sometimes later."

"Does one occasion stand out more than any other?"

"Yes." Then the General clamped his square jaw shut, and his pale blue eyes avoided the doctor's. The doctor waited.

21

"But you don't want to talk about it," Blausman said at last. "Why?"

"God damn you to hell, must you know everything?"

"Not everything. I don't ask you who you are sleeping with, or for the secret plans of the War Board, or what your golf score is," Blausman said gently. "If you had a piece of shrapnel in your left arm, I would not be fussing over your right foot. By the way, were you ever wounded?"

"No."

"Amazing luck, with your experience. Now let's go back to this waking up at night. That one occasion you don't want to talk about. It is nothing you are afraid of."

"How do you know?"

"You get disturbed but not frightened. There's a difference. What happened that night, General?"

"I woke up, and I was someone else."

"You were someone else. What makes that night stand out?"

"You won't let go, will you?"

"Otherwise I am taking your money under false pretenses," Blausman said gently. "So you might as well tell me about that night."

"All right. I woke up. It was last May, and I was still in Vietnam. It was almost dawn. I was myself—not Hardy—and God almighty, I felt good. I felt like I had swallowed ten grains of Dexedrine and put down a pint of bourbon without getting drunk. Christ, what power, what sheer physical strength and joy! I wanted to run, to leap, to use my strength, as if I had been in a straitjacket for years. I felt that I was complete."

"For how long?"

"Two or three minutes."

"You went outside?"

"How did you know?" the General asked curiously. "Yes, I went outside in my robe. It was like walking on air, the sun just coming up, the kind of clean, cool, wonderful morning you get sometimes in that part of Vietnam. There was an iron fence in front of my quarters. Pointed bars, like a row of spears, an inch thick. I reached out and bent one of them, like I might bend rubber."

"You're a strong man."

"Not that strong. Well—then it was gone. I was Franklin Hardy again."

22

"Why hesitate to tell me?" Blausman asked.

"I don't know."

"Do you remember what you said a moment ago? You said that when you woke up, you were yourself, not General Hardy. That's rather odd, isn't it?"

"Did I say that?"

"Yes."

"It is odd," Hardy admitted, frowning. "I always said I was someone else, didn't I?"

"Until now."

"What do you make of it?"

"What do you make of it, General? That's the important thing."

When the General had left, Dr. Blausman asked Miss Kanter whether Alexander the Great had ever been wounded.

"I was a history dropout. They let me substitute sociology. Does the General think he's Alexander the Great?"

"How about Napoleon?"

"Was he wounded? Or does the General think he's Napoleon?"

"I want you to hire a researcher," Dr. Blausman said. "Let him pick up the three hundred most important military leaders in history. I want to know how many died in battle and how many were wounded."

"Are you serious?"

"Deadly so."

"As long as you pay for it," Miss Kanter said.

In the next session, Dr. Blausman asked the General about dreams. "You have been taking notes?"

"Once."

"Only once?"

"It appears that I dreamed only once. Or remembered only once long enough to get the notebook."

"Tell me about it."

"As much as I can remember. I was driving a truck."

"What kind of a truck? I want you to be very specific and to try to remember every detail you can."

"It was a tank truck. I know that. It was a shiny metal tank truck, strong motor, six speeds forward—" He closed his eyes and then shook his head.

"All right, it was a tank truck. Oil—milk—chemicals—chocolate syrup—which one? Try to think, try to visualize it."

The General kept his eyes closed. His handsome face was set and intent, his brow furrowed. "It was a tank truck, all right, a big, gutsy son of a bitch. The gearing was marked on the shift bar, but I knew it. I didn't have to be coached. I got out of it once, walked around it. Pipes—"

"What kind of pipes?"

"Black plastic, I guess. Beautiful pumping equipment. I remember thinking that whoever built that job knew what he was doing."

"Why did you get out of it?"

"I thought I had to use it."

"For what?" Blausman insisted. "For what?"

He shook his head, opened his eyes now. "I don't know."

"Fire truck?"

"No—never."

"Then you got back in the truck?"

"Yes. I started off again. In low gear, she whined like some kind of mad cat."

"Where were you? What was the place like?"

"A dead place. Like desert, only it wasn't desert. It was a place that had once been alive, and now it was dead and withered."

"Withered? Do you mean there were trees? Plants?"

The General shook his head. "It was desert. Nothing grew there."

"You started the truck again. Where were you going?"

"I don't know."

"Think about it. What were you?"

"What do you mean, what was I?"

"What was your profession?"

"I told you I was driving a truck."

"But was that your profession?" Blausman pressed him. "Did you think of yourself as a truck driver?"

After a moment of thought, the General said, "No. I didn't think of myself as a truck driver."

"Then what?"

"I don't know. I just don't know. What damn difference does it make?"

"All the damn difference in the world." Blausman nodded. "A man is what he does. Did you ever notice the way kids talk about what they are going to be when they grow up? They will be what

24

they do. A man is his profession, his work. What was the profession
of the man who was driving the truck?''

"I told you I don't know."

"You were driving the truck. Who were you? Were you General
Hardy?''

"No."

"How were you dressed? Did you wear a uniform?"

Again General Hardy closed his eyes.

"Did you bring your notes with you?" the doctor asked.

"I know what was in my notes."

"Then you wore a uniform?"

"Yes," Hardy whispered.

"What kind?"

Hardy frowned and clenched his fists.

"What kind of a uniform?" Blausman persisted.

Hardy shook his head.

"Try to remember," Blausman said gently. "It's important."

Blausman took him to the door, and as it closed behind him,
Miss Kanter said, "God, he's handsome."

"Yes, isn't he?"

"I wonder what it's like to be a General's wife?"

"You're losing your moral principles, Miss Kanter."

"I am simply speculating, which has nothing to do with
morality."

"What about the research?"

"My goodness," said Miss Kanter, "you only told me about it
the day before yesterday."

"Then this is the third day. What have you got?"

"I gave it to Evelyn Bender, who is a friend of mine and teaches
history at Hunter College, and she was absolutely enthralled with
the idea and she's going to charge you a hundred and fifty dollars."

"I said, what have you got?"

"Now?"

"Right now. Call her up."

Miss Kanter started to argue, looked at Dr. Blausman, and then
called Evelyn Bender at Hunter College. Blausman went back to his
office and his next patient. When the patient had left, Miss Kanter
informed Dr. Blausman, rather tartly, that Mrs. Bender had only
begun the project.

25

"She must have some indications. Did you ask her that?"

"Knowing you, I asked her. She's a scholar, you know, and they hate to guess."

"But she guessed."

"She thinks that perhaps ninety percent died in bed. She indicated that very few wounds are recorded."

"Keep after her."

There was a noticeable difference about General Hardy when he came back for his next visit. He sat down in the comfortable armchair that substituted for the couch, and he stared at Dr. Blausman long and thoughtfully before he said anything at all. His blue eyes were very cold and very distant.

"You've been thinking about your profession," Blausman said.

"Whose profession? This time you say my profession."

"I was interested in what your reaction would be."

"I see. Do you know how I spent the weekend?"

"Tell me."

"Reading up on schizophrenia."

"Why did you do that?" the doctor asked.

"Curiosity—reasonable curiosity. I wondered why you had never mentioned it."

"Because you are not schizophrenic."

"How do you know?"

"I have been in practice twenty-three years, General Hardy. It would be rather odd if I could not spot schizophrenia."

"In anyone?"

"Yes, in anyone. Certainly after the second visit."

"Then if I am not schizophrenic, Dr. Blausman, what explanation do you have for my condition?"

"What explanation do you have, General?"

"Well, now—the neurotic finds his own source, uncovers his own well of horror—is that it, Doctor?"

"More or less."

"Dreams are very important in the Freudian scheme of things. Are you a Freudian analyst, Doctor?"

"Every analyst is more or less a Freudian, General. He developed the techniques of our discipline. We have perhaps changed many of his techniques, modified many of his premises, but we remain Freudians, even those of us who angrily repudiate the label."

"I was speaking of dreams."

"Of course," Blausman agreed calmly. "Dreams are important. The patient uses them to deal with his problems. But instead of the realities of his waking world, he clothes his problem in symbols. Sometimes the symbols are very obscure indeed. Sometimes they are not. Sometimes they are obvious."

"As in my dream?"

"Yes, as in your dream."

"Then if you understood the symbols, why not tell me?"

"Because that would accomplish nothing of consequence. It is up to you to discover the meaning of the symbols. And now you know."

"You're sure of that?"

"I think so, yes."

"And the truck?"

"An exterminator's truck, obviously. I see you have remembered who you are."

"I am General Franklin Hardy."

"That would make you schizophrenic. I told you before that you are not schizophrenic."

"You say you have been in practice twenty-three years. Have you ever had a case like mine before, Doctor?"

"In a non-schizophrenic? No."

"Then does it make medical history of sorts?"

"Perhaps. I would have to know more about it."

"I admire your scientific detachment."

"Not so scientific that I am without very ordinary curiosity. Who are you, sir?"

"Before I answer that, let me pose a question, Doctor. Has it never occurred to you that in the history and practice of what we call mankind, there is a certain lack of logic?"

"It has occurred to me."

"What do you make of it?"

"I am a psychiatrist, General. I deal with psychosis and neurosis, neither of which is logical. Understandable, yes. Logical, no."

"You miss the point."

"Do I?" Blausman said patiently. "Then what is the point?"

"The point is fantastic."

"There is very little that astonishes me."

27

"Good. Then allow me to put it to you this way. The earth is a beautiful, rich, and splendid planet. It has all things that man desires, but none of these things is limitless, not the air, not the water, not even the fertility of the land. Let us postulate another planet very similar to earth—but used up, Doctor, used up. There are men on this planet as there are men here, but somewhat more advanced technologically. Like many men, they are selfish and self-seeking, and they want the earth. But they want the earth without its human population. They need the earth for their own purposes. I see you doubt me."

"The notion is certainly ingenious."

"And from that you conclude that madmen are ingenious. Let me go on with my premise, and since you have assured me that I am not schizophrenic, you can ponder over the precise quality of my madness."

"By all means," Blausman agreed.

"They could attack the earth, but that would mean grave losses and even the possibility of defeat—no matter how small that possibility is. So some time ago, they hit upon another plan. They would train men for a particular profession, train them very well indeed, and then they would bring these men to earth, put them into positions of great power, and then induce a conditioned amnesia. Thus, these men would know what they had to do, what they were trained to do, yet be without the knowledge of why they do what they must do."

"Absolutely fascinating," Blausman said. "And in your case, the amnesia broke."

"I think it is a limited thing in every case. A time comes when we remember, but more clearly than I remembered. We know our profession, and in time we remember why we have been trained to this profession."

"And your profession?" Blausman asked.

"Of course, we are exterminators. I thought you understood that from the dream. So, Doctor, you would say I am cured, would you not?"

"Ah—there you have me," Blausman smiled.

"You don't believe me? You really don't believe me?"

"I don't know. What are your intentions, General? Are you going to kill me?"

"Why on earth should I kill you?"

"You defined your profession."

"One small, overweight New York psychiatrist? Come, come, Dr. Blausman—you have your own delusions of grandeur. I am an exterminator, not a murderer."

"But since you have told me what you are—"

Now it was the General's turn to smile. "My dear Dr. Blausman, what will you do? Will you take my story to the mayor, the governor, the President—the FBI, the press? How long would you maintain your professional status? Would you tell a story about little green men, about flying saucers? No, there is no need to kill you, Doctor. How inconvenient, how embarrassing that would be!" He rose to leave.

"This does not negate your bill," Blausman said. He could think of nothing else to say.

"Of course not. Send it to me in Washington."

"And just for my own parting shot, I don't believe one damn word you've said."

"Precisely, Doctor."

The General left and the doctor pulled himself together before he strode into the outer office and snapped at Miss Kanter: "Get his history and put it in the files. He won't come back."

"Really? Evelyn Bender just called and said she can have the survey by Wednesday."

"Tell her to tear it up, and send her a check. Cancel the rest of my appointments today. I'm going home."

"Is anything wrong?"

"No, Miss Kanter—not one damn thing. Everything is precisely the way it has always been."

4
Echinomastus Contentii

P ROFESSOR Timothy Melrick loved cacti. He also grew cacti and felt, as many others do, that there was no plant quite as intriguing. That was his avocation. He earned a modest living as a Professor of Chinese Philosophy at a small California college, where he could share his adoration of Chuang Tzu with the handful of students who were interested enough in Chinese Philosophy to maintain his tenure. He was also, somewhat apologetically, a Zen Buddhist.

His wife, Barbara, who was inclined to blame Zen for his lack of ambition, frequently took him to task on this score.

"I happen to be a Presbyterian," she would say to him. "I don't apologize when someone asks me why I am a Presbyterian."

"Well, you can explain that, you know," he would reply gently. "Your mother and father were Presbyterians."

"Yours were certainly not Zen Buddhists."

"No, they weren't."

"And what you are you can't even explain to me."

"It's not very easy to explain you know. Old Tozan said 'when I am hungry I eat, when I am thirsty I drink, and when I am tired, I sleep'."

"Who was Tozan?" Barbara asked.

"He was an old Zen monk who lived long ago."

"He sounds like some kind of wino. You are probably the lowest-paid full professor in all California, and I know one thing."

"Yes?"

"I'll never own a Mercedes, not even a used one. So much for you and what you call contentment!"

Professor Melrick loved his wife. He thought of this as he retreated to his garden, where he was trying to cross two very improbable cousins, *Echinomastus macdowellii* with *Echinopsis longispina,* both of which resembled sick and confused porcupines until they came into flower. Their flowers were beautiful indeed. He hardly blamed his wife, and while the reference to the Mercedes —a very high priced automobile made in Germany—might have seemed a non sequitor to an outsider, it was quite understandable to the professor. Of course, he lived in Glendale, which is only a short distance from Beverly Hills, and, as the Mercedes Company knows full well, there are more Mercedes per capita in Beverly Hills than in any city in the world except Bel Air, which flanks Beverly Hills to the west, and which has an even higher per-capita income.

It was not simply proximity or envy that had reduced Barbara to a perpetual state of bitterness and frustration. It was her brother, recently deceased. Her brother was the Gordon Tymon of Interlock Industries. He had owned an eleven-acre estate in Bel Air, and he was rich beyond probability. Soon after the explosion of the first atom bombs toward the end of World War II, Gordon Tymon determined that his was not to go the way of all flesh—whereupon he undertook the ultimate in atom bomb shelters at his Bel Air estate.

For twenty-five years an army of contractors labored on this project in an out-of-the-way corner of the estate. It did no good for Professor Melrick to warn him that the Santa Monica Mountains, threaded as they were with earthquake faults, were an unlikely place for an atom bomb shelter, or to propose a philosophical attitude toward man's future; in fact, as Barbara often pointed out to her husband, he so alienated the tycoon that Gordon cast off his sister, even as a recipient of small gifts.

Year after year, more and more of the atom bomb shelter emerged—or did not emerge, since shelters are sheltered—and a great cavern grew in the ground. Airlocks, elevators, generators, hidden tanks of oil and gasoline, vitamins by the thousands, dehydrated food, film-projectors, films for amusement, water tanks—only name it and rest assured that it was there. Meanwhile, Gordon's wife, Zelda, played tennis. Whatever else she did was unseen; the tennis was public. Between his financial interests and the atom bomb shelter, he had little time for her. He had become a fanatical pioneer for survival, one of that handful of fortunate beings in America who would survive a direct hit.

In March of 1970, Gordon was on his way from his thirty-two room mansion to the bomb shelter. He often took the little path that led from the one to the other, that he might look upon his recently completed work and find it good. Halfway there, one of those tremendous rainstorms that douse Southern California in March exploded upon him. He quickened his pace, slipped, fell, fractured his skull, and died. They found him there the following day.

Two weeks after the funeral, after the reading of the will which left everything to her and not one penny to Barbara, Zelda married the tennis pro at her club. The happy couple then took off for the south of France, where for years Gordon had maintained a splendid villa which he never had time to visit. And since anything and everything grows like mad in Southern California, the bomb shelter was soon covered by a heavy blanket of Moorish Ivy—forgotten of the world and especially of Zelda, who had never given the atom bomb a second thought.

All this Professor Melrick reflected upon as he made his way from the house to the garden, where he grew his cacti. There were, perhaps, elements of cosmic justice in Gordon's fate, if one desires to believe in so silly a business as cosmic justice—which, Timothy Melrick, for one, did not—but the bitter nut of the matter was that three elegant Mercedes had been standing idle in Gordon's—now Zelda's—garage for five years. How could he blame Barbara for bitterness, frustration, anger? He had never even been able to afford a Buick and, even worse, had never even desired a Buick—the trouble with being a Zen person in a very non-Zen environment.

He turned with a sigh to that marvelous diversion, the cacti. He, for one, had never accepted the theory that the cactus was a primitive plant—a holdover from the early time of life on earth. Quite otherwise; he saw the cacti as plants faced with that same threat of extinction that the environmentalists forecast for all of mankind these days. An earth once wet and rich now dried up; where once were seas, deserts appeared, and where once were cloudy skies and cool winds, there was a burning sun, never shaded. The plants were faced with the imperative of life. Adapt—or perish. In musing over this, he thought of a story told recently in the faculty dining room. It would seem—according to this little tale—that the Russians had exploded a very large atom bomb at the North Pole. The Polar icecap began to melt at a rate that would raise the seas above all the land masses of the earth. One by one, the heads of nations informed their people that human life was doomed, that they must prepare to perish—that is with the exception of the Prime Minister of Israel. She said to her handful of people: "Fellow Jews—we have three months to learn to breathe under water."

Not so different from what the plants faced, the professor mused, when the land turned into desert. Their life-giving leaves shriveled under the burning sun, whereupon they shed their leaves, abandoned their dry stems and trunks, and instead grew stems of green, rich in chlorophyl. When the sun attacked these new recepticles of life, the plants thickened their skin until it resisted the worst the sun could do. When animals found these thick, juicy stems very much to their taste, the plants proceeded to grow long, sharp spines, and when the insects they needed so desperately for cross pollination began to avoid the hot desert, the plants developed flowers of such beauty and color as the world had not seen before. Not at all a bad recommendation for the power and resourcefulness of life, the professor decided, looking with affection at his garden of strange shapes, needle-like spikes and gorgeous blooms; not at all. And looking at them, he felt that his affection was being returned, that these marvelous plants knew his feelings and reciprocated them.

And then something new caught his eye. His strange new cactus, the result of his crossing *Echinomastus macdowellii* with *Echinopsis longispina* had suddenly flowered with one great, lovely bloom: white petals that yellowed at the tips, with a heart that contained a few brilliant pink pistils in a mass of white stamens so heavily crowned with a yellow pollen that they could barely stand erect. For moments that grew into minutes, he stood there regarding it, with pleasure, love and deep aesthetic appreciation. Then, after sufficient homage, he did a very curious thing, moved by something he found difficult to account for later; he wet his finger, reached out and touched the pollen, and then put it to his lips. As his tongue licked it, the reaction was immediate and wonderful. He experienced what Zen people call *satori*, or, as others say, enlightenment.

He knew it, because one always does. He could not explain it or describe it, because one never can. He looked at the world around him with understanding and joy and compassion. It was all right. It would be all right.

Now the professor had a cat. He had the cat, not out of his choice but out of the cat's choice. It was a mean cat. It was a plain old gray and white alley cat that in its lifetime had suffered such a succession

34

of indignities and hurts that it could only display hate and suspicion. It was a nasty cat, a hate-filled, wretched angry cat. And at this moment, the cat was watching the professor with interest, suspicion, and hunger. The cat had been absent for two days, catting around as cats do, which accounted for the hunger.

Again, the professor wet his finger and picked up a bit of the yellow pollen, which he rubbed off into the center of his palm. Then he bent down and offered his hand to the cat.

Slowly, dubiously, watchfully, the cat advanced. The professor was patient; the cat was suspicious. The professor had fed the cat for a full two years, and still the cat was suspicious. But the cat was also hungry, and step by step he approached the professor's hand. He was at the hand. He sniffed. He looked at the professor, and then he sniffed again. And then he licked the yellow pollen out of the professor's palm.

And then he looked at the professor—as once in a while, very rarely, a cat will look at a man. Then he mewed.

The professor reached down and picked up the cat in his hands and then nestled him in his arms. The cat licked the professor's face and mewed. After a minute or so, the professor put down the cat and went into the house. The cat followed him. The professor went into the kitchen and opened a can of cat food. Purring with pleasure, the cat ate it.

"What on earth are you doing in the kitchen?" his wife called to him.

"Feeding the cat."

"Why you don't get rid of that ugly, wretched cat, I will never know."

"I'm rather fond of him," the professor replied.

Then he went into his study and meditated for a while, sitting cross-legged on a small cushion. He had quite a problem facing him, and while meditation offered no solution for such problems, it did at least allow him to stop thinking about it. He had been meditating for some ten minutes or so when his wife came into the room, looked at him, and said:

"Oh." She had a way of saying it, a remarkable way. "You do look ridiculous when you sit like that. I mean, a grown man."

He smiled apologetically.

"That cat of yours is acting very strangely."

"Yes. How?"

"Dinner is ready."

"You were saying about the cat?"

"He purred."

"Cats do purr."

"He purred pleasantly."

"I'll be with you in a moment," the professor said. "I'll just wash up."

He took a tiny plastic envelope from his desk, and went out to the garden, musing over a name. He was neither proud nor obsessed with any desire for immortality, even in the small botonist's world of the cactus, and he decided that *Echinomastus contentii* would serve very satisfactorily. The cat came after him mewing with delight as the professor shook a little of the yellow pollen into the plastic envelope.

"I do wonder how the world appears to you," he said to the cat.

Apparently the cat, purring with pleasure, understood him completely.

"What a beautiful, incredible thing you are!" he said to the cactus.

From the house, his wife called to him. "What on earth are you up to out there? Who are you talking to?"

"A cactus," he replied as he came back into the house.

"I don't think that's funny. If we could eat one meal where the food doesn't sit around and get cold while you fuss over God knows what to get yourself to the dinner table, I would be a very happy woman. Anyone else can come to dinner when dinner is ready, not you. You always have five things that must be done."

"I'm afraid so," the professor agreed.

"And I don't want that miserable cat in the room while we eat."

The cat understood. He regarded his mistress plaintively, and then he marched reluctantly out of the room.

Barbara served the chicken and rice, and then informed him that she had run into Clair Maguire at the shopping center.

"Did you? I do hope you gave her my very best. And to her husband. He's a gifted man."

"They're making him the head of Oriental Studies at U.C.L.A."

"That's just wonderful," the professor replied.

"It's more than just wonderful. It's forty thousand dollars a year."

The professor nodded with appreciation.

"I don't think you ever hear me, Timothy," Barbara said. "I said forty thousand a year."

"Yes. Yes, of course. It's a handsome wage."

"They're moving. Do you want some more rice?"

"No, thank you."

"To Westwood."

"Oh? Well, that will be nice. He can walk to the college."

"They bought a ninety thousand dollar house. With a swimming pool."

The professor smiled and nodded.

"Timothy, Timothy," his wife said, her voice as soft and beguiling as she could make it under the circumstances. "I'm trying to tell you something. Bob Maguire will be the head of the department. They will have an empty chair in Oriental Philosophy, and Clair said he is thinking of you. It's thirty thousand dollars a year. Thirty thousand dollars."

"That's very thoughtful of him."

"Is that all you can say? It's double what you make now."

"Well, a small college has its own problems."

"But they're not your problems."

"I just don't know whether I would be very happy at U.C.L.A. It's such an enormous place."

"Well, I do know that I would be very happy in Westwood or Brentwood and driving a decent car instead of that miserable Pinto, and just once, just once in my life being able to take some friends for lunch to the Bistro and not thinking twice about the check—"

"What is the Bistro?" the professor asked curiously.

"You ass!" Barbara exploded. "You fool!"

"I'm terribly sorry."

"Like hell you are! You wouldn't accept it—not even if Bob Maguire got down on his knees and pleaded."

The professor was thinking of how he could possibly move his cactus garden. Some of the plants were twenty years old. There was no way he could imagine transferring them to another area. And as if she were reading his mind, Barbara snapped at him, "It's those damn ugly plants of yours, isn't it!"

He was trying to formulate some answer to this when suddenly Barbara burst into tears, leaped to her feet, and ran into the bedroom.

The professor sat at the table for a few minutes, lost in thought. Then he poured a cup of coffee, took out the plastic envelope of pollen, shook it into the coffee, and stirred. He brought the coffee into the bedroom, where Barbara was sprawled on the bed.

"Barbara," he said gently.

She didn't move.

"Barbara, please look at me. Please."

She sat up, presenting him with a tear-stained face, and the professor observed that she was a very handsome woman indeed, quite as attractive in her forty-ninth year as on the day he had married her. Even her frown of anger and disgust could not hide it.

"What do you want?" she asked coldly.

"I thought we might talk about this."

"Why?"

"Well, it's not open and shut, is it? I brought you a cup of coffee. Please drink it. You'll feel better."

He touched her most tender spot. Coffee was an elixir to Barbara She reached for the coffee, tasted it and then drained the cup. She took a deep breath and then stared curiously at her husband.

"Of course, you couldn't move the cactus garden, could you," she said finally.

"I could move the smaller plants, certainly. That's no great task."

"But the big ones?"

"They'd have to stay."

"Oh, no—no."

"It's no great loss."

"But you love them. They mean so much to you."

"Really not," the professor said. "Not at all. They're there. I don't own them. A plant is a living thing. It has a life and existence of its own."

"I never thought about it that way."

"Well, most people don't. We're so used to owning things."

"Then it's not the cactus garden," said Barbara.

"I don't think so. Look dear, why don't we go outside and talk about this. It's a fine evening."

He took her by the hand and led her out into the garden. The cat joined them. They sat down on the bench under an enormous hibiscus, and the cat leaped into Barbara's lap and curled up there, purring with pleasure.

"Whatever has gotten into this cat?" Barbara wondered.

"He seems very content."

"Oh, I was so angry with you," she said, stroking the cat. "Isn't

38

there something we could do to improve his coat—I mean vitamins or something—he really is a handsome cat.''

"I'm sure. I'll have to ask the vet.''

"I don't know why I was so angry.''

"You had reason enough.''

"I can't think of any reason. Thirty thousand dollars is a lot of money. We could do things for the kids.''

"The kids are very independent.''

"They are. Do you know, I think they resent gifts.''

"That's understandable,'' the professor agreed.

"It's nice to think about living in Westwood, but I do love this old house. And our friends are here.''

"I could commute. It's not a long drive on the freeway.''

"You'd hate it.''

"Well, not really. But I do have half a dozen students who are very dear to me. I don't know whether that's worth giving up such an enormous increase.''

"Timmey,'' she said, "we are not starving.''

"No—'' He reached out and touched her cheek. "Do you know how long it is since you called me Timmey?''

"Is it that long?''

"I can get two more years out of my Volkswagen. We could turn in the Pinto and get you one of those big Chevies, what with the rebate and all that.''

"A gas guzzler? Not on your life. I am perfectly content with the Pinto. Anyway, I don't want to talk about cars. Look how the light strikes the cactus now. I never realized how beautiful they are.''

"People don't, because they are strange and different. We're so afraid of anything different.''

"Come to bed,'' she said suddenly.

"It's only nine o'clock.''

"Come to bed.''

"Shall we do the dishes first?''

"The hell with the dishes,'' Barbara said. "Come to bed.''

Barbara was asleep when the professor awakened in the morning. He lay there for a while, watching her. No doubt about it, she was quite as attractive as the day they met, and he reflected upon the singular joy of sex between two people who were without rancor, without selfishness, without frustration and very much in love.

39

He got out of bed quietly and dressed without awakening his wife, and then he went out to wish a good morning to *Echinomastus contentii,* who had survived the night quite well, and whose lovely petals glistened with a drop or two of the morning dew.

The cat joined him, rubbing contentedly against his leg, which prompted the professor to say, "Cat, there are more things in heaven and earth than I have ever dreamt of, which is hardly original but very much to the point. What are we going to do about it? I really don't approve of people who interfere, and here I've interfered with three of us."

Then he sighed, climbed into his aged Volkswagen, and drove to the college.

Since he had skipped breakfast at home, he went first to the faculty dining room, and joined two of his colleagues. One of them was Professor Roscoe Martin, widely known as dean of the P.O.D. Society, P.O.D. meaning "prophets of doom," who stood by his flat statement—on television talk shows as well as in scholarly magazines—that mankind would not be around in 1985, considering the rate at which we were destroying the environment. The other was Professor Hallis Grundy, business administration, corporate management, etc. They waved to Melrick, and he sat down at their table and ordered his orange juice, eggs, and toast, and then smiled with pleasure for their company.

"You are disgustingly content," Grundy said. "You sit down with two of the nastiest malcontents on this miserable faculty, who are even more ridden with dissatisfaction and jealousy than our average unattractive colleague, and you act as though you were convening a caucus of saints. That's a stinking attitude."

"I agree," said Martin.

"Well, it is a lovely day," Melrick said.

"Did you notice the smog or didn't you?" Martin snapped at him. "It's lying against the mountains like a stinking yellow blanket. By the day after tomorrow, we'll have the worst reading in the history of Los Angeles County. In L.A. County alone, this week should bring us 83.14 smog-associated deaths."

"Is the point-one-four a child?" Melrick asked mildly.

"I marvel at people like you," Grundy said to Melrick. "Here we are in one of the worst depressions in history, runaway inflation, more business failures per week than ever in history, and you smile."

"Not to mention," Martin added quickly, "the pollution of the sea. That's the killer. We may stop spray cans and supersonic flights in time to save the ozone layer, but as far as the sea is concerned, we've passed the point of no return."

"Now hold on," said Grundy. "Don't go into that lecture of yours on the oil companies."

"This man," Martin responded, directing a finger at Grundy, "is paid four times what any of us earn because he sits in a chair established by the so-called Energy Council, a front for the international oil trusts—"

"You can't prove that," Grundy said cheerfully.

"You will go with the rest of us," Martin said comfortably. "You, me, the oil executives, old, young—there are no lifeboats on spaceship earth."

"I wonder," Melrick said, looking up from his scrambled eggs, which were very tasty indeed, "whether you ever thought about the cactus?"

"That is a non sequitor, if I ever heard one," Grundy snorted.

"Oh, no. No, indeed. Very much to the point. You know, the seas dried up. The rain stopped, and the plants had to adapt. They became cacti."

"They were plants."

"People are very adaptable, you know," Melrick said.

"Sheer nonsense."

"Perhaps," Melrick said. "But this doom that is facing us—it's the result of greed, isn't it? A lust for money, for power, riches, things, baubles, man's discontent with himself as he is, envy of one's neighbor, desire—"

"That's putting it rather harshly."

"Are you going to change man?" Martin demanded.

"Man is always changing, you know. Otherwise, he could not conceivably endure this thing we call civilization. Now just suppose—just suppose we were to find some miracle drug that would rid man of greed, aquisitiveness, envy, the desire for power, for things?"

"Ambition?" Grundy demanded.

"What we call ambition—yes, indeed."

"God save us from that."

"Why?" Melrick wondered.

"Discontent is the only thing that makes it work."

"Your way."

"What other way is there, Melrick?"

"I like to think that there's another way."

"As much as it pains me, I must agree with Grundy," Martin said.

"Yes—but suppose one did come up with such a drug. What would happen?"

"They would destroy the drug and kill its inventor."

"They?" asked Melrick. "Who are they?"

"Myself, to begin with," Grundy stated emphatically. "Any community leader with an ounce of responsibility. Any executive of a large corporation. Any political leader. Any man who values civilization."

"Do you agree with him?" Melrick asked Martin.

"I'm afraid I do. You're talking about something a hundred times worse than heroin. Just think of what it would do to our tenure."

Melrick sighed. It was time for his first class, and as he walked across the campus, he wondered what Chuang Tzu would have made of his predicament. He mused over it through the day, and he was relieved, when he returned home, to be greeted with an enveloping embrace from his wife.

"Dinner in a half hour," she said to him. "I cooked Mexican. I know how you love it."

"It's fattening."

"Devil take the calories tonight!"

"I'll be in the garden," he said.

In the garden, he observed with delight the appearance of a second flower. The evening breeze was beginning to blow the pollen, and his first impulse was to reach down and pick the flower. Then he stopped, and for quite a while he just stood there and observed the two lovely blooms.

The cat approached. He saw it from the corner of his eye coming toward him, slowly, tentatively. He bent and reached out his hand toward the cat. It arched, hissed and struck, and there were four claw marks on the back of his hand.

He was licking the back of his hand when Barbara came out of the house and joined him.

42

"What happened?"

"I'm afraid our cat has reverted back to his true nature."

"What a pity!"

"Well—perhaps. Perhaps not."

"You have another flower on that beautiful thing!" she exclaimed with delight.

"Oh, yes."

"Your new species, isn't it?"

"Well, it's a cross breed of sorts, but whether it will breed true or breed at all, that's hard to say. Some cross breeds are sterile, you know. "We'll let mother nature decide. The old lady is very wise about such things."

"Dinner?"

He turned to her, took both her hands, and said, "My dear Barbara, I love you very much. I always have. An act of love is something we create within us, and, if we are lucky, we nurture it."

"I like that," Barbara said. "I'll remember it."

"We both will, and we'll try as hard as we can, won't we?"

"What an odd thing to say! Of course we'll try. You're very strange tonight."

Then he put his arm around her waist, and they went in to dinner.

5
Tomorrow's *Wall Street Journal*

A T precisely eight forty-five in the morning, carrying a copy of tomorrow's *Wall Street Journal* under his arm, the devil knocked at the door of Martin Chesell's apartment. The devil was a handsome middle-aged businessman, dressed in a two-hundred-dollar gray sharkskin suit, forty-five dollar shoes, a custom-made shirt, and a twenty-five-dollar iron-gray Italian silk tie. He wore a forty-dollar hat, which he took off politely as the door opened.

Martin Chesell, who lived on the eleventh floor of one of those high-rise apartments that grow like mushrooms on Second Avenue in the seventies and eighties, was wearing pants and a shirt, neither with a lineage of place or price. His wife, Doris, had just said to him, "What kind of nut is it at this hour? You better look through the peephole."

Knowing a good tie and shirt when he saw them, Martin Chesell opened the door and asked the devil what he wanted.

"I'm the devil," the devil answered politely. "And I am here to make a deal for tomorrow's *Wall Street Journal.*"

"Buzz off, buster," Martin said in disgust. "The hospital's over by the river, six blocks from here. Go sign yourself in."

"I am the devil," the devil insisted. "I am really the devil, scout's honor." Then he pushed Martin aside and entered the apartment, being rather stronger than people.

"Martin, who is it?" his wife yelled—and then she came to see. She was dressed to go to her job at Bonwit's, where she sold dresses until her feet died—every day about four-twenty—and she saw enough faces in a day's time to smell the devil when he was near her.

"Ask your wife," the devil said pleasantly.

"It wouldn't surprise me," said Doris. "What are you peddling, mister?"

"Tomorrow's *Wall Street Journal,*" the devil repeated amiably. "Everyman's desire and dream."

"It's an old, tired saw," Martin Chesell said. "It's been used to death. Not only have a dozen bad stories been written to the same point, but the *New Yorker* ran a cartoon on the same subject. A tired old bum looks down, and there's tomorrow's *Wall Street Journal* at his feet."

"That's where I picked up the notion." The devil nodded eagerly. "Basically, I am conservative, but one can't go on forever with the same old thing, you know." He walked sprightly into their living room, merely glancing into the bedroom with its unmade bed, and measuring with another glance the cheap, tasteless furniture, and then spread the paper on the table. Martin and Doris followed him and looked at the date.

"They print those headlines in a place on Forty-eighth Street," Doris said knowingly.

"Ah! And the inside pages as well?" The devil riffled the pages.

"Suppose you let me have a look at the last page?" Martin said.

"Ah—that costs."

"Mister, go away. There is no devil and you're some kind of a nut. My wife has to go to work."

"But you don't? No job. Bless your hearts, what does a devil do to prove himself. My driving license? Or this?" Blue points of fire danced on his fingernails. "Or this?" Two horns appeared on his forehead, glistened a moment, and then disappeared. "Or this?" He held up finger and thumb and a twenty-dollar antique gold piece appeared between them. He tossed it to Martin, who caught it and examined it carefully.

"Tricks, tricks," said the devil. "Look into your own heart if you doubt me, my boy. Do we deal? I sell—you buy—one copy of tomorrow's *Wall Street Journal.* Yes?"

"What price?" Doris demanded, precise, businesslike, and to the point, while her husband stared bemused at the coin.

"The usual price. The price never changes. A human soul."

"Why?" Martin snapped, holding out the coin.

"Keep it, my son," the devil said.

"Why a human soul? What do you do with them? Collect them? Frame them?"

"They have their uses, oh yes, indeed. It would make for a long, complicated explanation, but we value them."

"I don't believe I have a soul," Martin said bluntly.

"Then what loss if you sell it to me? To sell what you do not own without deceiving the purchaser, that is good business, Martin—all profit and no loss."

"I'll sell mine," Doris said.

"Oh? Would you? But that won't do."

"Why not?"

"No—it just wouldn't do." He looked at his watch, a beautiful old pocket watch, gold and set with rubies and with little imps crawling all over it. "You know, I don't have all the time in the world. You must decide."

"For Christ's sake," Doris said, "sell him your damn soul or do we spend the rest of our lives in this lousy three-room rathole? Because if that's the case, you spend them alone, Marty boy. I am sick to death of your sitting around on your ass while I work my own butt off. You're a loser, sweety, and this is probably the last chance."

"Good girl," the devil said approvingly. "She has a head on her shoulders, Martin."

"How do I know—"

"Martin, Martin, what do you have to lose?"

"My soul."

"Whose existence you sensibly doubt. Come, Martin—"

"How?"

"Old-fashioned but simple. I have the contract here, all very direct and legal. You read it. A pinprick, a drop of blood on your signature, and tomorrow's *Wall Street Journal* is yours."

Martin Chesell read the contract. A pin appeared like magic in the devil's hand. A thumb was pricked, and Martin found himself smearing a drop of blood across his signature.

"All of which makes it legal and binding," the devil said, smiling and handing Martin the paper. Doris forgot her job and Martin forgot his erstwhile soul, and they flung the paper open with trembling hands, riffled to the last page, where the New York Stock Exchange companies and prices were printed, and scanned the list.

The devil watched this with benign amusement, until suddenly Martin whirled and cried:

"You bastard—this is a rotten day. Everything is down."

"Hardly, Martin, hardly," the devil replied soothingly. "Everything is never down. Some are up, some are down. I will admit that today is hardly the most inspiring of days, but there is a surprise or two. Just look at old Mother Bell."

"Who?"

"American Telephone," the devil said. "Look at it, Martin."

Martin looked. "Up four points," he whispered. "That makes no sense at all. American Telephone hasn't jumped four points in a day since Alexander Graham Bell invented it."

"Oh, it has, Martin. Yes, indeed. You see, until two o'clock today, it will just dilly-dally along the way it does every other day, and then at two precisely the management will announce a two-for-one split. Yes, indeed, Martin—two for one. Just read those prices again, and you will see that it touches a high of five dollars and seventy-five cents over the two o'clock price, even though it closes at a profit of only four points. So you see, Martin, if you sell at the high, you can clear five dollars and better, which is a very nice return for an in-and-out deal. No reason at all why you shouldn't be a very rich man before today is over, Martin. No reason at all."

"Marty," Doris shouted, "we're going to do it. We're going to make it, Marty. This is the big one, the big red apple—the one we've been waiting for. Oh, Marty, I love you, I love you, I love you."

The devil smiled with pleasure, put on his forty-dollar hat, and departed. They hardly noticed that he had gone, so eager were they to be properly dressed to make a million. Doris tied Martin's tie—something she had not done for a long time. Martin admired the dress she changed into and quietly agreed when she snapped at him:

"You keep that newspaper in an inside pocket, Marty. Nobody sees it—and I mean nobody."

"Right you are, baby."

"Marty, what do we go for? Five dollars a share—is that it?"

"That's it, baby. Suppose we pick up twenty thousand shares—that's one hundred thousand dollars, baby. One hundred thousand bright, green dollars."

48

"Marty, have you lost your mind? This is it—the one and only—and you talk about one hundred thousand dollars. We pick up a hundred thousand shares, and then we got half a million. Half a million dollars, Marty. Beautiful, clean dollars."

"All right, baby. But I'm not sure you can buy a hundred thousand shares of a stock like American Tel and Tel without influencing the price. If we drive the price up—"

"We can't drive the price up, Marty."

"How do you know? What makes you such a goddamn stock market genius?"

"Marty, maybe I don't know one thing about the market—but I know how it closes today. Honey, don't you see—we have tomorrow's *Wall Street Journal*. We know. No matter how many shares of that stock you buy, it is going to stay put until two o'clock and then it's going to go up to five dollars and seventy-five cents. Isn't that what he said?"

Marty opened the paper and concentrated on it. "Right!" he cried triumphantly. "Says so right here—no movement until two o'clock—and then zoom."

"So we could buy two hundred thousand shares and make a cool million."

"Right, baby—oh, you are so right!"

"Two hundred thousand shares then—right, Marty?"

"I hear you, kid."

They took a cab downtown to the brokerage office of Smith, Haley and Penderson on Fifty-third Street. When you have it, you spend it. "Lunch today at the Four Seasons?" Doris asked him. "Right, baby. Right, baby." Rich people are happy people. When he and Doris marched up to the desk of Frank Gibson, their poise and pleasure were contagious. Frank Gibson had gone to college with Martin and had supervised his few unhappy stock market transactions, and while he did not consider Martin one of his more valuable contacts, he found himself smiling back and telling them that it was good to see them.

"Both of you," he said. "Day off, Doris?"

Doris indicated that days off were the farthest things from her mind, and Martin outlined his purpose with that superior and secure sense that the buyer in quantity always has. But instead of leaping with joy, Gibson stared at him unhappily.

"Please sit down," Gibson said.

They sat down.

"If I understand you, Marty, you want to buy two hundred thousand shares of American Telephone. You're putting me on."

"No. We're dead serious."

"Even if you're serious, you're putting me on, Marty," Gibson said. "This kind of goofing—well, someone gets upset. Someone gets angry."

"Look, Frank," Martin said, "you are a broker. You are a customer's man. I am a customer. I come to buy, and you tell me politely to go take a walk."

"Marty," Gibson said patiently, "that much American Telephone adds up to over ten million dollars. That means you have to have at least six million, give or take a few, to back it up. So what's the use, Marty? Take the gag somewhere else."

"Then you won't take my order?"

"Marty—Marty, no one will take your order. Because you got to be some kind of nut to even talk that way when I know that you and Doris between you—you got maybe twenty cents."

"That's a hell of a thing to say!"

"Is it true?"

"For heaven's sake, Marty," Doris put in, "come clean with him and get the thing on the road. Here it is, Frank. We got inside dope that Telephone is going up five points this afternoon. At two o'clock today they are going to announce a stock split—and it will go."

"How do you know?"

"We know."

"Nobody knows. That rumor has been around for months. Telephone is the blandest, dullest piece of action on the market. You are asking for a day sale, and this firm would not stand for even a little one. It's out of the question."

"You mean you won't sell me stock?"

"A hundred shares of Telephone—sure. You have an account with us. Buy a hundred shares. Don't be greedy—"

They stalked out while Gibson was talking. The next stop was Doris' brother, who was a lawyer and made a good living out of it and could have gone on living if he never saw Martin Chesell again.

"I should underwrite six million of credit for you? You got to be kidding."

"I'm not kidding, I'm dead serious," Martin replied, telling himself, "You, you son of a bitch, what a pleasure it would be to toss you out on your fat ass if you came pleading to me. Time—just give me time."

"Am I permitted to ask what for?" his brother-in-law said.

"To make an investment in the market," Martin said. "I am desperate. It is eleven o'clock. This is the first real chance I ever had. Please," he pleaded, "do you want me to get down on my knees?"

"It would be an interesting position for a snotty guy like you," the brother-in-law said. "I should be happy to underwrite seventy-five cents for you, Martin. For a whole buck, I write it off immediately."

"You may be my brother," Doris said, "but to me you are a louse. May I spell it—l-o-u-s-e."

It was eleven-thirty when they got to the branch of the Chase Manhattan on upper Madison. Martin had been in college with the son of the present manager, and once he had introduced himself and Doris, the manager listened politely.

"Of course, we would be happy to lend you the money," he agreed. "In any amount you wish—providing you offer acceptable collateral."

"Would American Telephone stock be acceptable collateral?" Doris asked eagerly.

"The very best. And I think we might even lend you up to eighty percent of the market value."

"See, Marty!" Doris exclaimed. "I knew we'd do it! Now can we get the money immediately?"

"I think so—at least within fifteen minutes. Do you have the stock with you?"

Doris' face fell, while Martin explained that they were going to use the money to buy the stock.

"Well, that's a little different, isn't it? I am afraid it makes the loan impossible—unless you have sufficient stock already in your possession. It doesn't have to be American Telephone. Any listed security—"

"You don't understand," Martin pleaded, watching the clock on the wall. "We got to buy that stock before two o'clock."

"I am sure you have good reason to. But we can't help you."

"Lousy crumb," Martin said when they got outside. "He stinks!

The whole lousy Chase Manhattan stinks! You got a friend at Chase
Manhattan, you don't need enemies. You know what I'd like to
do—go in there up to the window and—stick 'em up!—that's what
I'd like to do."

Neither First National City nor Chemical New York proved any
more flexible on the question of collateral, nor was Merrill Lynch
disposed to open an account and plunge into a massive day sale.
One forty-five P.M. found them back at the offices of Smith, Haley
and Penderson, pleading anew with Frank Gibson.

"I got a job," Gibson told them. "You may not believe me, but
being a customer's man just happens to be a job. I don't interfere
with you, so just let me do my job."

"It's a quarter to two," Martin begged him.

"Oh, Jesus—show him the damn *Wall Street Journal,*" Doris
snapped.

"Why don't you drop dead?"

"Why don't you get one little brain in your head? It's ten
minutes to two. Show him the paper."

Martin took out the paper and shoved it at Gibson. "There—
tomorrow's *Wall Street Journal.* All markets—complete closing
prices."

"You're both out of your minds. What do I have to do? Make a
scene? Call the cops?"

"Just look at the date? Am I asking so much? Jesus God, if I was
drowning would you stretch out a hand for me? I'm asking you to
look at the date."

"O.K.—so I look at the date." Gibson picked up the paper and
looked at the date. Then he stared at the date. Then he turned the
paper around and looked at the date on the back ·page. Then he
opened it.

"Marty, where did you get this?"

"Now you believe me. Now Marty's not a lousy creep any more.
Now Marty's your buddy boy. Now will you buy the goddamn
stock?"

"Marty, I can't. Even if I thought this paper wasn't phony—"

"Phony! Do you know—"

His voice died away. Gibson was staring at the screened flash
news at the front of the office, where suddenly the news had
appeared that the directors of American Telephone had decided
upon a two-for-one stock split, pending approval of stockholders.

52

"Will you buy the stock?" Martin whimpered. "Oh, dear Jesus, will you please buy the stock?"

"Marty—I can't."

"It's up two points already," Doris said. "Why don't I kill myself? Oh, no—I couldn't jump in front of a subway train or anything like that. No sir—not me. I had to marry Chesell."

At three-thirty, when the market closed, American Telephone was four points over its opening price. At four-fifteen, the Chesells had one of their minor fights. If they had not been so done in with the day, it might have been a major fight. As it was, there was nothing physical, only a few recriminations, one word leading to another. Doris began the peroration by concluding:

"Drop dead—that's all."

"So long as you understand the feeling is mutual."

"Lovely—and I have had it, ducky. Words cannot portray my feelings for you. You disgust me. You also turn my stomach. You also stink—and now I intend to have a nap. So just get out of here!"

Martin went into the living room, and she slammed the door behind him—and there was a gentle knock at the door to the apartment. Martin opened the door, and there was the devil.

"Greetings, my lad," he said with a great good nature.

"You got one hell of a nerve!" Martin exclaimed. "You miserable son of a bitch—after what you did to me, to come back here!"

"What I did? Martin, Martin, you are understandably angry—but that kind of wild talk—not good."

"You tricked me into that."

"Martin, my boy," the devil said kindly, "did we or did we not make an honest trade, a bargain in kind, merchandise given, merchandise taken? Did we not?"

"You knew what would happen."

"And just what did happen, Martin? Why get so upset? I gave you the *Wall Street Journal* for tomorrow and you found yourself not unexpectedly short of cash. Lesson number one—money makes money. How easily learned—and you complain."

"Because I blew my one lousy chance," Martin said. "One lousy chance out of a whole lifetime, and I blew it. One chance to come out on top, and I threw it away."

"Martin."

"No, it doesn't matter to you. Well—me, I am sick and tired of you, so out. Just get the hell out!"

"Martin," the devil said placatingly.

"Out!"

"Really, Martin."

"Are you trying to tell me you didn't know what would happen?"

"Martin, of course I knew what would happen. I have been at this so long, and people are so wretchedly predictable. But what happened today is of no importance."

"No importance?"

"None whatsoever. The really important thing is that you sold me your soul, Martin. That's the nitty-gritty of it. Riches? No problem. Wealth, power, success? No problem, Martin. It all follows. Once you have sold your soul to me, everything comes to you—everything, Martin. Dear lad—you look so blue, so morbid. Cheer up. The *Wall Street Journal*—who needs it? Do you want a tip for tomorrow? Cimeron Lead—four dollars a share. It will close at seven. Buy a few shares; pin money, but buy a few shares."

"With what?" Martin asked sourly.

"Money—dear Martin, there is money wherever you look. For example, you have a bit of insurance on your wife, don't you?"

"We each have a policy for twenty thousand."

"Very nice beginning money, Martin. Fortunes have been built on less. And you don't really like her at all, do you?"

"Why wouldn't you make a deal for her soul this morning?" Martin asked suddenly.

"Dear Martin—her soul is worthless. In the five years of your marriage you have shriveled it to nothing. You have a talent for destruction, Martin. Her soul is almost nonexistent, and she's not very pleasant to be with, is she, Martin?"

Martin nodded.

"And she's so despondent today—it would be understandable that she should leap from an eleventh-story window. Poor girl, but some win and some lose, Martin."

"I wouldn't collect on the insurance for ten days," Martin said.

"Good thinking. I like that. Now you are using your head, lad. Rest assured, I have a better tip for next week. Tips, opportunities, good liquor, rich food, uncomplaining women, and money—so much money. Dear Martin, why do you hesitate?"

54

Martin went into the bedroom, closing the door behind him. There were the sounds of a short scuffle—and then a long, awful scream. When Martin came out of the bedroom, the devil sighed and said, "Poor boy, you'll be despondent tonight. We must dine together. You will be my guest—of course. And to console you—"

He took out of his inside breast pocket a neatly folded copy of the *Wall Street Journal*.

"For a week from Wednesday—ten days," he said.

6
A Matter of Size

MRS. HERBERT COOKE—Abigail Cooke—was a woman with a social conscience and a sense of justice. She came from five generations of New Englanders, all of whom had possessed social consciences and devotion to justice, qualities not uncommon in New England once the burning of witches was gotten over with. She lived in a lovely old Colonial house on fifteen acres of land in Redding, Connecticut; she forbade any spraying of her trees, and she gardened ecologically. She believed firmly in mulch, organic fertilizers, and the validity of the New Left; and while she herself lived quietly with her teen-age children—her husband practiced law in Danbury—her heart and small checks went out to a multitude of good causes. She was an attractive woman, still under forty, an occasional Congregationalist, and a firm advocate of civil rights. She was not given to hysterics.

She sat on her back porch—unscreened—on a fine summer morning and shelled peas and saw something move. Afterward she said that it appeared to be a fly, and she picked up a flyswatter and swatted it. It stuck to the flyswatter, and she looked at it carefully; and then she began to have what amounted to hysterics, took hold of herself, thanked heaven that her children were at day camp, and, still unable to control her sobbing, telephoned her husband.

"I've killed a man," she said to him.

"You what? Now wait a minute," he replied. "Get hold of yourself. Are you all right?"

"I'm all right."

"Are the children all right?"

"They're at day camp."

"Good. Good. You're sure you're all right?"

"Yes. I'm a little hysterical—"

"Did I hear you say that you killed a man?"

"Yes. Oh, my God—yes."

"Now please get hold of yourself, do you hear me, Abby? I want you to get hold of yourself and tell me exactly what happened."

"I can't."

"Who is this man you think you killed? A prowler?"

"No."

"Did you call the police?"

"No. I can't."

"Why not? Abby, are you all right? We don't have a gun. How on earth could you kill someone?"

"Please—please come home. Now. Please."

In half an hour Herbert Cooke pulled into his driveway, leaped out of his car, and embraced his still shivering wife. "Now, what's all this?" he demanded.

She shook her head dumbly, took him by the hand, led him to the back porch, and pointed to the flyswatter.

"It's a flyswatter," he said impatiently. "Abby, what on earth has gotten into you?"

"Will you look at it closely, please?" she begged him, beginning to sob again.

"Stop crying! Stop it!"

Convinced by now that his wife was having some kind of nervous breakdown, he decided to humor her, and he picked up the flyswatter and stared at it. He stared at it for a long, long moment, and then he whispered, "Oh, my God—of all the damn things!" And then, still staring, he said to her, "Abby, dear, there's a magnifying glass in the top drawer of my desk. Please bring it to me."

She went into the house and came back with the magnifying glass. "Don't ask me to look," she said.

Herbert placed the flyswatter carefully on the table and held the magnifying glass over it. "My God," he whispered, "my God almighty. I'll be damned. A white man, too."

"What difference does that make?"

"No difference—none at all. Only—my God, Abby, he's only half an inch tall. I mean if he were standing up. Perfectly formed, the blow didn't squash him, hair, head, features—naked as the day he was born—"

"Must you carry on like that? I've killed him. Isn't that enough?"

"Honey, get a grip on yourself."

"I though it was a fly. I saw it out of the corner of my eye. I saw it and swatted it. I'm going to throw up."

"Stop that. You didn't kill a human being. A human being isn't half an inch tall."

"I'm going to throw up."

She raced into the house, and Herbert Cooke continued to study the tiny object under the magnifying glass. "Of all the damn things," he muttered. "It's a man all right, five fingers, five toes, good features, blond hair—handsome little devil. I can imagine what the flyswatter felt like, like being trapped under one of those iron blasting mats. Squashed him a bit—"

Pale, but more in command of herself, Abigail returned to the porch and said, "Are you still looking at that dreadful thing?"

"It's not a dreadful thing, Abby."

"Can't you get rid of it?"

Herbert raised his head from the magnifying glass and stared at his wife thoughtfully. "You don't mean that, Abby."

"I do."

"Abby, this is the strangest damn thing that ever happened to us, possibly to anyone. I mean, there simply is no such thing as a human being half an inch tall."

"Except on that flyswatter."

"Exactly. We can't just throw him away. Who is he?"

"What is he?"

"Exactly," Herbert agreed. "What is he? Where did he come from? Or where did it come from? I think you understand my point," he said patiently and gently.

"What is your point?" she asked, a note of coldness coming into her voice.

"I'm a lawyer, Abby. I'm an officer of the court. That's my life, that's not something I forget."

"And I'm your wife, which is something you appear to have forgotten."

"Not at all. You have done nothing wrong. Nothing. I will stake my legal life on that."

"Go on."

"But we have a body here. It's only half an inch long, but it's still a body. We have to call the police."

"Why? It's done. I killed the poor thing. I have to live with that. Isn't that enough?"

"My dear, let's not be dramatic. We don't know what it is. You swatted an insect. For all we know, it is some kind of an insect."

"Let me look through that magnifying glass."

"Are you sure you want to?"

"I'm perfectly all right now."

He handed her the magnifying glass, and she peered through it. "It's not an insect," she said.

"No."

"What will the children say? You know how they are—when you wanted to put out poison for the rabbits that were eating the lettuce."

"The children don't have to know anything about it. I'll call Chief Bradley. He owes me a favor."

Herbert and Bradley sat in the chief's office and stared at the flyswatter. "Couldn't bring myself to take it off the flyswatter," Herbert said. "But I forgot to bring the magnifying glass."

The chief slowly and deliberately took a magnifying glass from his desk drawer and held it over the flyswatter. "I'll be damned," he murmured. "Never thought I'd see one of them things. It's a man, sure enough, isn't it?"

"Men are not a half inch tall."

"How about pygmies?"

"Four feet. That's forty-eight inches, just ninety-six times as tall."

"Well—"

"What did you mean when you said you never thought you'd see one of them things? You don't seem one bit surprised."

"Oh, I'm a little bit surprised, Herb."

"Not enough."

"Maybe it's harder for a cop to show surprise, Herb. You get to expect anything."

"Not this."

"All right, Herb. Truth is, Abigail ain't the first. I never saw one before, but we been getting the reports. Frightened kids, housewives, old Ezra Bean who still farms his place up in Newtown,

60

a frightened old lady in Bethel—she said her dog ate a mess of them—another lady over in Ridgefield, said her dog sniffed some out and they shot his nose full of little arrows, quarter of an inch long, had to take them out with tweezers. Of course, none of them really believed what they saw, and nobody else believed it either." He stared through the magnifying glass again. "Don't know what I believe myself."

"Bows and arrows?"

"Little bugger has no clothes on. Kind of hard to believe."

"Bows and arrows mean intelligence," Herbert Cooke said worriedly.

"Ahh, who knows? Might have poked his nose into a bramble bush."

"Abigail's pretty upset. Says she killed a man."

"Baloney."

"Can I tell her she's clear, in a legal sense?"

"Of course. It was an accident anyway."

"What are you going to do with that?" Cooke asked, nodding at the flyswatter.

"Pick it off and put in in formaldehyde. You want the flyswatter back?"

"I don't think Abby would welcome it. You can't just leave him swimming in formaldehyde?"

"No, I don't suppose so. Maybe it's a case for the FBI, although I ain't heard nothing about this outside of Connecticut. Maybe I'll run over and see Judge Billings. He might have some ideas on the subject. You tell Abby not to worry."

"That's not easy," Herbert said. He himself was far from satisfied. Like several million other Americans, he had been brooding over the question of war and murder and Vietnam, and he had even thought seriously of switching his affiliation from the Congregational Church to the Quakers. It would be harder for Abigail, who came from many generations of Congregationalists, but they had discussed it, and he felt secure in his position as a man of conscience.

"Well, you tell her not to worry, and I'll have a talk with Judge Billings."

When Herbert Cooke returned to his home the following day, he was met by a wife whose face was set and whose eyes were bleak.

"I want to sell the house and move," she announced.

"Oh, come on, come on, Abby. You know you don't mean that. Not our house."

"Our house."

"You're upset again."

"Not again. Still. I didn't sleep all night. Today Billy got a splinter in his toe."

"It happens. The kids run around barefoot."

"I want to show you the splinter. I saved it." She led him to his desk, unfolded a piece of paper, and handed him the magnifying glass. "Look at it."

He peered through the glass at a tiny sliver of wood, less than a quarter of an inch long.

"Good heavens!"

"Yes."

"Incredible."

"Yes," his wife repeated.

"Barbed head—it could be metal. Looks like it."

"I don't care whether it's metal. I don't care what it looks like. I want to sell the house and get out of here."

"That's simply an emotional response," he assured her in his calmest and most legalistic tone of voice.

"I'm emotional."

"You're reacting to an unprecedented event. Outside of *Gulliver's Travels,* this has never happened to anyone before, and if I am not mistaken, Gulliver's people were three or four inches tall. A half inch is very disturbing."

"It's also very disturbing to live with the fact that you've killed a man with a flyswatter."

A few days after this conversation, Abigail read an editorial in the Danbury paper. In properly light and mocking tones, it said: "Is it true, as the song puts it, that there are fairies at the bottom of our gardens? A number of otherwise sober citizens have been muttering that they have seen very small people. How small? Anywhere from half an inch to three-quarters of an inch, a diminution of size that puts Gulliver to shame. We ourselves have not encountered any of the little fellows, but we have an Irish grandmother who reports numerous such encounters in the Old Country. We might say that Irish Dew, taken in sufficient quantities, will produce the same effect in any locale."

Since the children were present, Abigail passed the paper to her husband without comment. He read it, and then he said:

"I asked Reverend Somers to stop by."

"Oh?"

"It's a moral question, isn't it? I thought it might put your mind to rest."

Their daughter watched them curiously. There are no secrets from children. "Why can't I play in the woods?" Billy wanted to know.

"Because I say so," Abigail answered, a tack she had never taken before.

"Effie Jones says there are little people in the woods," Billy continued. "Effie Jones says she squashed one of them."

"Effie Jones is a liar, which everyone knows," his sister said.

"I don't like to hear you call anyone a liar," Herbert said uncomfortably. "It's not very nice."

"We're such nice people," Abigail told herself. Yet she was relieved when Reverend Somers appeared later that evening. Somers was an eminently sensible man who looked upon the world without jaundice or disgust, not at all an easy task in the 1970s.

Somers tasted his sherry, praised it, and said that he was delighted to be with nice people, some of the nicest people.

"But like a doctor," Herbert said, "your hosts are never very happy."

"I don't know of any place in the Bible where happiness is specified as a normal condition of mankind."

"Last week I was happy," Abigail said.

"Let me plunge into some theology," Herbert said bluntly. "Do you believe that God made man in His own image?"

"Anthropomorphically—no. In a larger sense, yes. What is it, Herbert? The little people?"

"You know about them?"

"Know. Heard. It's all over the place, Herbert."

"Do you believe it?"

"I don't know what to believe."

"Believe it, Reverend. Abby swatted one. With the flyswatter. Killed it. I brought it over to Chief Bradley."

"No."

"Yes," Abigail interjected bitterly.

"What was it?" the Reverend asked.

"I don't know," Herbert replied unhappily. "Under the

magnifying glass, it was a man. A complete man about as big as a large ant. A white man."

"Why must you keep harping on the fact that it was a white man?" Abigail said.

"Well, it's just a matter of fact. It was a white man."

"You appear quite satisfied that it was a man."

"I thought it was a fly," Abigail interjected. "For heaven's sake, the thing was not much bigger than a fly."

"Absolutely," Herbert agreed.

"What you both mean," Somers said slowly, "is that it looked like a man."

"Well—yes."

"Where is it now?"

"Chief Bradley put it into formaldehyde."

"I should like to have a look at it. We say it looks like a man. But what makes man? Is it not above all things the possession of a soul?"

"That's debatable," said Abby.

"Is it, my dear? We know man in two ways, as he is and as he is divinely revealed to us. Those two aspects add up to man. All else is of the animal and vegetable kingdom. We know man as a creature of our size. Divinely revealed, he is still a creature of our size."

"Not from outer space," Abby said.

"What does that mean?" her husband demanded.

"It means that from one of those wretched spaceships, the earth is the size of an orange, and that doesn't make man very big, does it?"

"For heaven's sake," Herbert said, "you are really blowing things out of proportion. You're talking about perspective, point of view. A man remains the same size no matter how far out into space you get."

"How do you know?" she asked with the reasonable unreasonableness of an intelligent woman.

"My dear, my dear," Somers said, "you are upset, we all are upset, and probably we shall be a good deal more upset before this matter is done with. But I think you must keep a sense of proportion. Man is what God made him to be and what we know him to be. I am not an insensitive person. You know I have never wavered in my views of this wretched war in Vietnam—in spite of the difficulties in holding my congregation together. I speak to you, not as some Bible Belt fundamentalist, but as a person who believes in God in an indefinable sense."

"If He's indefinable, He's still rather large, isn't He? If He goes out into space a million light-years, how big are we to Him?"

"Abby, you're being contentious for no reason at all."

"Am I?" She unfolded a piece of paper and held it out to Somers with a magnifying glass. He peered at it through the glass and said words to the effect that the sliver of wood that it contained looked like an arrow.

"It is an arrow. I took it out of Billy's toe. No, he didn't see what shot at him, but how long before he does? How long before he steps on one?"

"Surely there's some explanation for this—some new insect that appears remarkably manlike. Monkeys do, apes do, but one doesn't leap to the conclusion that they are men."

"Insects with blond hair and white skin and two arms and two legs who shoot arrows—really, Reverend Somers."

"Whatever it is, Abby, it is a part of the natural world, and we must accept it as such. If some of them are killed, well, that too is a part of our existence and their existence, not more or less than the natural calamities that overtake man—floods, earthquakes, the death of cities like ancient Pompeii."

"You mean that since they are very small, a flyswatter becomes a natural calamity."

"If you choose to put it that way—yes, yes, indeed."

Aside from a small squib in *The New York Times* about the strange behavior of some of the citizens of upper Fairfield County, the matter of the little people was not taken very seriously, and most of the local residents tended to dismiss the stories as the understandable result of a very hot summer. The Cookes did not sell their house, but Abigail Cooke gave up her habit of walking in the woods, and even high grass gave her pause. She found that she was looking at the ground more and more frequently and sleeping less well. Herbert Cooke picked up a field mouse that fairly bristled with the tiny arrows. He did not tell his wife.

Judge Billings telephoned him. "Drop by about four, Herb," he said. "A few people in my chambers. You'll be interested."

Billings had already indicated to Herbert Cooke that he considered him an excellent candidate for Congress when the present incumbent—in his middle seventies—stepped aside. It pleased Cooke that Billings called him Herb, and he expected that the summons to his chambers would have something to do with the coming elections. Whereby he was rather surprised to find Chief Bradley already there, as well as two other men, one of them a Dobson of the FBI and the other a Professor Channing of Yale, who was introduced as an entomologist.

"Herb here," the judge explained, "is the young fellow whose wife swatted the thing—the first one we had. Now we got a round dozen of them."

Channing took a flat wooden box out of his pocket—about six inches square. He opened it and exhibited a series of slides, upon each of which one of the tiny folk was neatly pressed. Cooke glanced at it, felt his stomach rise, and fought to control himself.

"In addition to which," the judge continued, "Herb has a damn good head on his shoulders. He'll be our candidate for the House one of these days and a damn important man in the country. I thought he should be here."

"You must understand," said the FBI man, "that we've already had our discussions on the highest level. The Governor and a number of people from the state. Thank God it's still a local matter, and that's what we're getting at here."

"The point is," said Channing, "that this whole phenomenon is no more than a few years old. We have more or less mapped the beginning place of origin as somewhere in the woods near the Saugatuck Reservoir. Since then they've spread out six or seven miles in every direction. That may not seem like a lot, but if you accept their stride as a quarter inch compared to man's stride of three feet, you must multiply by one hundred and forty-four times. In our terms, they have already occupied a land area roughly circular and more than fifteen hundred miles in diameter. That's a dynamic force of terrifying implications."

"What the devil are they?" Bradley asked.

"A mutation—an evolutionary deviation, a freak of nature—who knows?"

"Are they men?" the judge asked.

"No, no, no, of course they're not men. Structurally, they appear to be very similar to men, but we've dissected them, and internally there are very important points of difference. Entirely different relationships of heart, liver, and lungs. They also have a sort of

66

antenna structure over their ears, not unlike what insects have."

"Yet they're intelligent, aren't they?" Herbert Cooke asked. "The bows and arrows—"

"Precisely, and for that reason very dangerous."

"And doesn't the intelligence make them human?" the judge asked.

"Does it? The size and structure of a dolphin's brain indicate that it is as intelligent as we are, but does it make it human?"

Channing looked from face to face. He had a short beard and heavy spectacles, and a didactic manner of certainty that Herbert Cooke found reassuring.

"Why are they dangerous?" Cooke asked, suspecting that Channing was inviting the question.

"Because they came into being a year or two ago, no more, and they already have the bow and arrow. Our best educated guess is that they exist under a different subjective time sense than we do. We believe the same to hold true of insects. A day can be a lifetime for an insect, even a few hours, but to the insect it's his whole span of existence and possibly subjectively as long as our own lives. If that's the case with these creatures, there could be a hundred generations in the past few years. In that time, from their beginning to the bow and arrow. Another six months—guns. How long before something like the atomic bomb does away with the handicap of size? And take the question of population—you remember the checkerboard story. Put a grain of sand on the first box, two grains on the second, four grains on the third, eight grains on the fourth—when you come to the final box, there's not enough sand on all the beaches to satisfy it."

The discussion went on, and Herbert Cooke squirmed uneasily. His eyes constantly strayed to the slides on the table.

"Once it gets out . . ." the judge was saying.

"It can't get out," the FBI man said flatly. "They already decided that. When you think of what the kids and the hippies could do with this one—no, it's a question of time. When? That's up to you people."

"As soon as possible," Channing put in.

"What are you going to do?" Herbert asked.

"DDT's been outlawed, but this will be an exception. We've already experimented with a concentration of DDT—"

"Experimented?"

"We trapped about eighteen of them alive. The DDT is incredibly effective. With even a moderate concentration, they die within fifteen minutes."

"We'll have forty helicopters," the FBI man explained. "Spray from the air and do the whole thing between three and four A.M. People will be asleep, and most of them will never know it happened. Saturation spraying."

"It's rough on the bees and some of the animals, but we have no choice."

"Just consider the damn kids," Chief Bradley pointed out to Herbert. "Do you know they're having peace demonstrations in a place like New Milford? It's one thing to have the hippies out every half hour in New York and Washington and Los Angeles—but now we got it in our own backyard. Do you know what we'd have if the kids got wind that we're spraying these bugs?"

"How do they die?" Herbert asked. "I mean, when you spray them, how do they die?"

"The point is, Herb," Judge Billings put in, "that we need your image. There have been times when it's been a damn provoking image—I mean your wife riding around with that *Mother for Peace* sticker on her bumper and holding the vigils and all that kind of thing, not to mention that petition she's been circulating on this ecology business—it's just dynamite, this ecology thing—so I'll be frank to tell you it has been a mighty provoking image. But I suppose there's two sides to every coin, and I'm the first one to say that you can't wipe out a whole generation of kids; damn it, you can't even lock them up. You got to deal with them, and that's one of your virtues, Herb. You can deal with them, you have the image, and it's an honest image and it's worth its weight in gold to us. There'll be trouble, but we want to keep it at a low level. Those crazy Unitarians are already stirring up things, and I'm a Congregationalist myself, but I could name you two or three Congregationalist ministers who would stir up a hornet's nest if they were sitting here. There are others too, and I think you can deal with them."

"I was just wondering how they die when you spray them," Herbert said.

"That's just it," Channing said eagerly. "There may not be

68

much explaining to do. The DDT appears to paralyze them almost instantly, even when it's not direct, even when it's only a drift. They stop movement and then they turn brown and wither. What's left is shapeless and shriveled and absolutely beyond any identification. Have a look at this slide.''

He took one of the slides and held a magnifying glass over it. The men crowded close to see, and Herbert found himself joining them.

"It looks like last season's dead cockroach," said Bradley.

"We want you to set the time," Dobson, the FBI man, told them. "It's your turf and your show."

"What about the dangers of DDT?"

"Overrated—vastly overrated. We sure as hell don't recommend a return to it. The Department of Agriculture has put its foot down on that, but the plain fact of the matter is that we've been using DDT for years. One more spray is not going to make a particle of difference. By the time the sun rises, it's done with."

"The sooner the better," Chief Bradley said.

That night Herbert Cook was awakened by the droning beat of the helicopters. He got up, went into the bathroom, and looked at his watch. It was just past three o'clock in the morning. When he returned to bed, Abigail was awake, and she asked him:

"What's that?"

"It sounds like a helicopter."

"It sounds like a hundred helicopters."

"Only because it's so still."

A few minutes later she whispered, "My God, why doesn't it stop?"

Herbert closed his eyes and tried to sleep.

"Why doesn't it stop? Herb, why doesn't it stop?"

"It will. Why don't you try to sleep? It's some army exercise. It's nothing to worry about."

"They sound like they're on top of us."

"Try to sleep, Abby."

Time passed, and presently the sound of the helicopters receded into the distance, faded, and then ceased. The silence was complete—enormous silence. Herbert Cooke lay in bed and listened to the silence.

"Herb?"

"I thought you were asleep."

"I can't sleep. I'm afraid."

"There's nothing to be afraid of."

"I was trying to remember how big the universe is."

"To what end, Abby?"

"Do you remember that book I read by Sir James Jean, the astronomer? I think he said the universe is two hundred million light-years from end to end—"

Herbert listened to the silence.

"How big are we, Herb?" she asked plaintively. "How big are we?"

7
Show Cause

U NDERSTANDABLY, it was couched in modern terms; in the United States, on the three great networks in radio and in television, in England on BBC, and in each country according to its most effective wavelength. The millions and millions of people who went burrowing into their Bibles found a reasonable facsimile in Exodus 32, 9 and 10: "And the Lord said unto Moses, I have seen this people and behold, it is a stiff-necked people: now therefore let me alone, that my wrath may wax hot against them, and that I may consume them."

The radio and television pronouncement said simply, "You must show cause why the people of Earth shall not be destroyed." And the signature was equally simple and direct: "I am the Lord your God."

The announcement was made once a day, at eleven A.M. in New York City, ten o'clock in Chicago, seven in Honolulu, two in the morning in Tokyo, midnight in Bangkok, and so forth around the globe. The voice was deep, resonant, and in the language of whatever people listened to it, and the signal was of such intensity that it preempted whatever program happened to be on the air at the moment.

The first reaction was inevitable and predictable. The Russians lashed out at the United States, holding that since the United States, by their lights, had committed every sin in the book in the name of God, they would hardly stop short at fouling up radio and television transmission. The United States blamed the Chinese, and the Chinese blamed the Vatican. The Arabs blamed the Jews, and

71

the French blamed Billy Graham, and the English blamed the Russians, and the Vatican held its peace and began a series of discreet inquiries.

The first two weeks of the daily pronouncement were almost entirely devoted to accusation. Every group, body, organization, sect, nation that had access to power was accused, while the radio engineers labored to find the source of the signal. The accusations gradually perished in the worldwide newspaper, television, and radio debate on the subject, and the source of the signal was not found. The public discussions during those first two weeks are a matter of public record; the private ones are not, which makes the following excerpts of some historical interest:

THE KREMLIN

REZNOV: "I am not a radio engineer. Comrade Grinowski is a radio engineer. If I were Comrade Grinowski, I would go back to school for ten years. It is preferable to ten years in Siberia."

GRINOWSKI: "Comrade Reznov speaks, I am sure, as an expert radio engineer."

BOLOV: "Insolence, Comrade Grinowski, is no substitute for competence. Comrade Reznov is a Marxist, which allows him to penetrate to the heart of the matter."

GRINOWSKI: "You are also a Marxist, Comrade Bolov, and you are also Commissar of Communications. Why haven't you penetrated to the heart of the matter?"

REZNOV: "Enough of this bickering. You have every resource of Soviet science at your disposal, Comrade Grinowski. This is not merely a matter of jamming our signals; it is an attack upon our basic philosophy."

GRINOWSKI: "We have used every resource of Soviet science."

REZNOV: "And what have you come up with?"

GRINOWSKI: "Nothing. We don't know where the signals originate."

REZNOV: "Then what do you suggest, Comrade Bolov—in the light of Comrade Grinowski's statement?"

BOLOV: "You can shoot Comrade Grinowski or you can invite in the Metropolitan or both. The Metropolitan is waiting outside."

REZNOV: "Who asked the Metropolitan here?"

GRINOWSKI: (*with a smile*) "I did."

THE WHITE HOUSE

THE PRESIDENT: "Where's Billy? I told him we start at two o'clock. Where is he?"

THE SECRETARY OF STATE: "I called him myself. We might hear from Professor Foster of MIT meanwhile."

THE PRESIDENT: "I want Billy to hear what Professor Foster has to say."

PROFESSOR FOSTER: "I have a very short statement. I have several copies. I can give a copy to Billy or I can read it again."

THE ATTORNEY GENERAL: "I say CBS is at the bottom of the whole matter. CIA agrees with me."

THE FEDERAL COMMUNICATIONS COMMISSIONER: "CBS is not at the bottom of it. I think we ought to hear from Professor Foster. He has been working with our people."

THE PRESIDENT: "Why in hell isn't Billy here?"

THE SECRETARY OF DEFENSE: "We might as well hear it from Professor Foster. If his statement is short, he can read it again for Billy."

THE PRESIDENT: "All right. But he reads it again for Billy."

(*The door opens. Enter Billy.*)

BILLY: "Greetings, everyone. God bless you all."

THE ATTORNEY GENERAL: "Are you sure you speak for Him?"

THE PRESIDENT: "Professor Foster has a statement. He has been meeting for the past week with my ad hoc committee of scientists. Would you read your statement, Professor?"

PROFESSOR FOSTER: "Here is our statement. In spite of all our efforts, we cannot ascertain the source of the signal."

THE PRESIDENT: "Is that all?"

THE ATTORNEY GENERAL: "Well, damn it to hell, sir, you must know where the signal comes from. Does it come from outer space? From the earth? From Russia?"

PROFESSOR FOSTER: "I stand by my statement."

THE PRESIDENT: "Well, here we are, faced with a show cause order. Billy, I don't expect anything from the Russians or the Chinese. Can we show cause?"

BILLY: "I have been thinking about that."

THE PRESIDENT: "Yes or no?"

[*Silence*]

73

JERUSALEM

THE PRIME MINISTER: "At the suggestion of Professor Goldberg, I have invited Rabbi Cohen to this meeting."

THE FOREIGN MINISTER: "Why? To complicate this hoax?"

THE PRIME MINISTER: "Suppose we hear from Professor Goldberg."

PROFESSOR GOLDBERG: "Not only have we been working on it day and night, but we have been in touch with the Americans. As in our case, they can find no source for the signal. I think we ought to hear from Rabbi Cohen."

THE PRIME MINISTER: "What the Gentiles will do, Rabbi, is their problem. Ours is more personal, since when you come right down to it, our people have been faced with this problem before. We are presented with a show cause order. Can we show cause?"

RABBI COHEN: (*sadly*) "I am afraid not."

WHITEHALL

CHIEF OF INTELLIGENCE: "I've put four of our best men on it. We're running them north of the Afghan border."

THE CHIEF MINISTER: "What do you hear from them?"

CHIEF OF INTELLIGENCE: "We've lost touch with them."

THE PRIME MINISTER: "I think you ought to get in touch with the Archbishop."

CHIEF OF INTELLIGENCE: "I'll put one of my best men on it."

(*Thoughtful silence*)

THE VATICAN

FIRST CARDINAL: "I can't believe it. After two thousand years of effort."

SECOND CARDINAL: "Backbreaking effort."

FIRST CARDINAL: "No word of appreciation. Just show cause."

SECOND CARDINAL: "Have you spoken to the legal department?"

FIRST CARDINAL: "Oh, yes—yes indeed. He's within His rights, you know."

The above excerpts are just a sampling of what went on in the upper circles of every government on earth. Both the Vatican and Israel, due to the singular nature of their antecedents, attempted to probe for a time limit, and at least four times they were given the use of the broadcasting facilities of the Voice of America, both medium wave and short wave; but their frantic pleas of "How much time do we have?" were simply ignored. Day after day the resonant and majestic voice, same hour, same minute, called upon the people of the earth to show cause.

By the third week, Russia and China and their client countries joined in a public statement, denouncing the voice as a tasteless bourgeois prank, directed at the moral integrity of the peace-loving nations; and while they admitted that the source of the signal was not yet apparent, they stated that it was only a matter of time before they pinned it down. But Moscow's efforts to jam the voice continued to result in failure, and China accused Moscow of being a part of the Western conspiracy to foist their primitive and anthropomorphic concept of a Biblical God upon the civilized world.

Meanwhile, the various sectors of the human race reacted in the entire spectrum of reaction, from hooting disdain to indifference to anger and to riot and panic; and the President of the United States had a long and earnest talk in his study with his friend, Billy. Knowing only the results of this talk, one has to deduce its content, but one can safely presume that it went somewhat in this fashion:

"I've read your bill of particulars, Billy. It's not very convincing," the President said.

"No? Well, I didn't think too highly of it myself."

"I think you could have done better."

"Oh? Perhaps. Perhaps not. I never liked show cause orders—I was never wholly convinced that they are constitutional."

"They're constitutional," the President assured him. "I had a long talk with the Chief Justice about this. He says it's quite constitutional."

"I meant in a general sense. We must not become too parochial about this."

"One falls into the habit," the President confessed. "You must admit that we've always been on God's side."

"The question is—is He on our side?"

"You're not losing faith, Billy?"

"It's just the problem of making a case for us."

"He must be on our side," the President insisted. "Take the very fact of show cause. Our country has pioneered the legal field in the use of show cause orders. We were putting an end to subversive strikes with show cause orders before the rest of the world even thought of the device. And as far as a case for us—where else in the world has a nation provided as free and abundant a life as the American way?"

"I'm not sure that's to the point."

"Billy, I've never seen you like this before. I would have said you're the most confident man on earth. Do you want me to take this out of your hands and give it to the Attorney General? He has a damn good legal staff, and if they put their heads together, they'll come up with something that will hold up in court."

"That's not it. He asks a question point-blank. It's a moment of truth."

"We've had our moments of truth before, and we've lived through them."

"This one's different."

"Why?"

Billy looked at the President, and the President looked at Billy, and after a long, long moment of silence, the President nodded.

"Hopeless?"

"I thought of something," Billy said.

"What? I'll put every resource of the country at your disposal."

"When you come right down to it," Billy said, "it's the showing cause that breaks our back. It's one thing to preach in the big stadium at Houston; but when you say your piece at the United Nations, for example, it doesn't hold water."

"The hell it doesn't."

"Well, with England and Guatemala, but where's the plain majority we had ten years ago?"

"We're no worse than any other country and a damn sight better than the Reds."

"That's the crux of it," Billy said.

"You said you thought of something."

"I did. Let's take that big computer you have down at Houston. Suppose we start programming it. We'll throw everything into it, the good and the bad—get the best men in the field to program it, and keep throwing facts into it—say for a week or ten days."

76

"We don't know how much time we have."

"We have to presume that He knows what we're doing. And so long as He knows that we're working on the show cause order, He'll wait."

"Isn't that a calculated risk, Billy?"

"I'd say it's more of an educated guess. Good heavens, He's got all the time in the world. He invented it."

"Then why don't we bring IBM into it? They can throw together a set of computers that will make the thing down in Texas—that's where the big one is—look like a kiddy toy."

"If the government will foot the bill. I'm not sure that the IBM folk will see it just our way."

More or less in that fashion the IBM project came into being. Since they had a free hand to call on their own computer centers as well as what they had set up for the Department of Defense, it was no more than two weeks before they began the programming. Day and night, facts were fed into the giant complex of computers, day after day, not by a single person but by over three hundred computer experts; and precisely thirty-three days after they began, the job was done. The computer complex was the repository of all the facts available concerning the current role of the human species on the planet Earth.

It was three o'clock in the morning when the last fact was fed into the humming machine. At Central Control, a sleepless President and his Cabinet and some two dozen local luminaries and representatives of foreign countries waited. Billy waited with them. And the world waited.

"Well, Billy?" the President asked.

"We've given it the problem and the facts. Now we want the answer." He turned to the Chief Engineer of IBM. "It's your move now."

The Chief Engineer nodded and touched a button. The gigantic complex of computers came alive and hummed and throbbed and blinked and flashed, took a full sixty seconds to digest the information that had been fed to it, and then took ten seconds more to imprint the information on a piece of tape.

No one moved.

The President looked at Billy.

"It's up to you, sir," Billy said.

The President moved slowly toward the machine, tore off the six inches of tape that protruded from it, read it, then turned to Billy and handed it to him silently.

On the tape was printed: "Harvey Titterson."

"Harvey Titterson," Billy said.

The Attorney General came over and took the tape from Billy. "Harvey Titterson," he repeated.

"Harvey Titterson," the President said. "A billion dollars into the biggest computer project the world ever saw, and what do we have?"

"Harvey Titterson," said the Secretary of State.

"Who is Harvey Titterson?" asked the British Ambassador.

Who indeed? Two hours later the President of the United States and his friend, Billy, sat in the White House, facing the bulldog visage of the aging director of the Federal Bureau of Investigation.

"Harvey Titterson," said the President. "We want you to find him."

"Who is he?" asked the aging director of the Federal Bureau of Investigation.

"If we knew who he was, you would not have to find him," the President explained slowly and respectfully, for he was always respectful when he exchanged ideas with the aging director of the Federal Bureau of Investigation.

"Is he dangerous? Do we take him alive or dead?"

"You don't take him, sir," Billy explained respectfully, for like everyone else, he was always respectful when he spoke to the aging director of the Federal Bureau of Investigation. "We simply want to know where he is. If possible, we don't want him to be alarmed or disturbed in any way; as a matter of fact, we would prefer that he should be unaware of any special supervision. We only desire to know who he is and where he is."

"Have you looked in the telephone book?"

"We've been in touch with the telephone company," the President replied. "You must understand, we had no intention of bypassing you. But knowing the heavy load of work your department carries, we thought the telephone company might be able to simplify our task. Harvey Titterson does not have a telephone."

"It might be an unlisted number."

"No. The telephone company was very cooperative. It's not even an unlisted number."

"You'll have results, Mr. President," said the aging director of the Federal Bureau of Investigation. "I'll put two hundred of my best agents on it."

"Time is of the essence."

"Yes, sir. Time is of the essence."

It is a tribute to the Federal Bureau of Investigation and to the acumen of its aging director that in three days a report was placed upon the President's desk. The folder was marked "Confidential, top secret, restricted and special to the President of the United States."

The President called Billy into his office before he even opened the folder. "Billy," he said grimly, "this is your dish of tea. I've dealt with Russia and Red China, but this is a piece of diplomacy you have to make your own. We'll read it together."

Then he opened the folder, and they read:

"Special secret report on Harvey Titterson, age twenty-two, son of Frank Titterson and Mary (Bently) Titterson. Born in Plainfield, New Jersey. Educated at Plainfield High School and at the University of California at Berkeley. Majored in Philosophy. Arrested twice for possession of marijuana. Sentence suspended in the first instance. Thirty days in jail in the second instance. Presently living at 921 East Eighth Street in New York City. Present occupation unknown."

So that's Harvey Titterson," the President said. "He works in strange ways."

"I wouldn't blame Him," said Billy. "Harvey Titterson came out of the IBM machine."

"I want you to take this, Billy," the President said. "I want you to carry on from here. I have given you top clearance. *Airforce 1* is at your disposal if you need it. Also my personal helicopter. It's your mission, and I don't have to say what rides on its success or failure."

"I'll do my best," Billy promised.

Two hours later a chauffeur-driven black government limousine drew up in front of 921 East Eighth Street, an old-law cold-water tenement, and Billy got out of the car, climbed four flights of stairs, and tapped at the door.

"Enter, brother," said a voice.

Billy opened the door and entered a room whose contents consisted of a table, a chair, a single bed, a rug, and on the rug a young man in ancient blue jeans and a T-shirt, sitting cross-legged. He had a russet beard and moustache, russet hair that fell to his shoulders, and a pair of bright blue eyes; and Billy couldn't help noticing his resemblance to his own mentor.

Billy stared at the young man, who stared back and said pleasantly, "You're sure as hell not fuzz and you're not the landlord, so you got to have the wrong place."

"Are you Harvey Titterson?" Billy asked.

"Right on. At least there are times when I believe I am. The search for identity is no simple matter."

Then Billy identified himself, and the young man grinned appreciatively. "Man, you are with it," he said.

"Let me come to the point," said Billy, "because time is of the essence. I have come to you on the question of our basic dilemma."

"You mean the war in Vietnam?"

"No, I mean the show cause order."

"Man, you confuse me. What show cause order?"

"Don't you read the newspapers?" Billy asked in amazement.

"Never."

"Surely you listen to radio—to television?"

"Don't own one."

"You meet people. At work. Everyone's talking—"

"I don't work."

"What do you do?"

"Man, you're direct," said Harvey Titterson. "I smoke a little grass and I meditate."

"How do you live?"

"Affluent parents. They tolerate me."

"But this has been going on for weeks. Surely you've been out of here?"

"I been on a long meditation trip."

"Are you a Jesus Freak?" Billy asked, drawing on his knowledge of the vernacular, a note of respect in his voice.

"No, hardly. I got my own way."

"Then let me bring you up to date. Some weeks ago, at precisely the same time all over the world, a voice took over the major

80

broadcasting channels and spoke these words: 'You must show cause why the people of Earth shall not be destroyed. I am the Lord your God.' Those were the words."

"Cosmic," Harvey said. "Absolutely cosmic."

"It repeats every day. Same voice, same words."

"Absolutely cosmic."

"You can imagine the results," Billy said.

"It must have been a hassle."

"China, Russia—all over the world."

"Out of sight," said Harvey.

"The President is a friend of mine—"

"Oh?"

"The point is, I convinced him that there was no simple answer. He depends on me for this kind of thing. It's a great honor, but this was too big."

"Absolutely cosmic," Harvey said.

"So I came up with an idea and sold it to him. We put together the biggest computer the world ever saw, and we fed it all the information there is. Everything. And then, when we put the question to it, it came up with your name."

"You're putting me on."

"You have my word of honor, Harvey."

"That shakes me."

"So you see what it means to us, Harvey. You're the last hope. Can you show cause?"

"Heavy—very heavy."

"Maybe you want time to think about it?"

"You don't want to think about it," Harvey said. "If it's there, it's there."

Harvey Titterson closed his eyes for a long moment, and then he looked up at Billy and said simply:

"We are what we are."

"What?"

"We are what we are."

"Just that?"

"Man, it's your thing. Just think about it."

"Exodus three, fourteen," Billy said. " 'And God said unto Moses, I am what I am.' "

"Right on."

81

Billy looked at his watch. It was three minutes before eleven o'clock. With hardly a thank you, he bolted out of the room and down the stairs and into the big black limousine.

"Turn on the radio!" he shouted at the chauffeur. "Eight eighty on the dial."

The chauffeur fiddled nervously.

"Eight eighty—what's holding you?"

"This is the Columbia Broadcasting Company," the radio crackled, "CBS radio in New York City. At this time we have been leaving the air for a special announcement." Then silence. Silence. Minute after minute went by, and still silence.

Then the voice of the announcer, "Apparently we are not to be interrupted today—"

On the fourth floor of the tenement, Harvey Titterson rolled a joint, had a toke, and then laid it aside.

"Crazy," he said softly.

And then he composed himself to continue his meditation trip.

8
The Martian Shop

T HESE are the background facts given to Detective Sergeant
Tom Bristol when he was instructed to break down the door
and go into the place. It is true that the locksmiths at Centre Street
have earned the reputation of being able to open anything that has
been closed; and that reputation is not undeserved. But this door
was an exception. So Bristol went to break down the door with two
men in uniform and crowbars and all the other tools that might be
necessary. But before that he studied a precis of the pertinent facts.

It had been established that three stores had been opened on the
same day and the same hour; and more than that, as an indication
of a well-organized and orderly mind, the space for each of the
stores had been rented on the same day, the leases signed on the
same hour. The store in Tokyo was located in the very best part of
The Ginza. The space had been occupied by a fine jewelry and
watchmaking establishment, perhaps the second or third best in all
Japan; they vacated the premises, refusing to give the press any
explanation whatsoever at the time. Later, however, it was revealed
that the price paid to the jewelry establishment for the purchase of
its lease consisted of fifty diamonds of exactly three carats each, all
of them so perfectly matched, so alike in their flawlessness, that
diamond experts consider the very existence of the collection—
hitherto unknown—to be a unique event in the long history of
jewels.

The store in Paris was, of course, on Faubourg St. Honore. There
were no stores vacant at the time, and the lease of a famous

couturier was purchased for forty million francs. The couturier (his name is omitted at specific request of the French government) named the price facetiously, for he had no intention of surrendering his place. When the agent for the principal wrote out a check on the spot, holding him to his word, he had no choice but to go through with the deal.

The third store was on Fifth Avenue in New York City. After thirty years on the Avenue, the last ten increasingly unprofitable, the old and stodgy firm of Delbos gave up its struggle against modern merchandising. The store it had occupied was located on the block between 52nd and 53rd Street, on the east side of the street. The property itself was managed by Clyde and Abrahams, who were delighted to release Delbos from a twenty-five year lease that had been signed in 1937, and who promptly doubled the rent. The Slocum Company, acting as agents for the principals—who never entered into the arrangements at all, either with Clyde and Abrahams or subsequently with Trevore, the decorating firm—made no protest over the increased rent, signed the lease, and then paid a year's rent in advance. Arthur Lewis, one of the younger partners in the Slocum Company, conducted the negotiations. Wally Clyde of Clyde and Abrahams, remarked at the time that the Slocum Company was losing its grip. Lewis shrugged and said that they were following instructions; he said that if he had bargaining power himself, he would be damned before he ever agreed to such preposterous rent.

Lewis also conducted the negotiations with Trevore, turning over to them detailed plans for the redesigning and decoration of the store, and agreeing to the price they set. He did make it plain, however, that his specific instructions from his principal were to agree to all prices asked and to deal only with the firms he was told to deal with. He pointed out to Trevore that such practices were abhorrent to the Slocum Company and were not to be anticipated under any circumstances in the future.

When the information for this precis was gathered, Mr. Samuel Carradine of the Trevore Company produced the original plans for the remodeling and decoration of the store, that is the plans turned over to him by Mr. Lewis. They are hand-drawn on a fine but strong paper of pale yellow tint. Two paper experts, one of them chief chemist for Harlin Mills, have already examined these plans, but they are unable to identify the paper, nor have they seen similar paper before. They do assert that the paper has neither a pulp nor a rag base. Part of the paper is at present undergoing chemical analysis at Crestwood Laboratories.

From this point onward, the history of the three stores is sufficiently general for the data on the Fifth Avenue store to suffice. In all three cases, rental and alteration were managed under similar circumstances; in all three cases the subsequent progress of events was the same, making due allowance for the cultural patterns of each country. In each case, the decoration of the store was in excellent taste, unusual, but nevertheless artfully connected with the general decor of the particular avenue.

Trevore charged over a hundred thousand dollars for alteration and decoration. The storefront was done in stainless steel panels, used as tile. Window-space was enlarged, and a magnificient bronze-veneered door replaced the ancient oak portal of Delbos. The interior was done in tones of yellow, and the display cases and platforms were of bronze and glass. Decorators whose opinions have been sought all concur in the assessment of results. Without doubt the three stores were done in excellent, if not superb, taste—the decoration bold, unique, but never vulgar or distressing. It must be noted, however, that Mr. Ernest Searles, who heads the decor department of the Fifth Avenue Association, pointed out certain angular—that is, unfamiliar degree angles—concepts never used before by American decorators.

On Fifth Avenue, as in the other cases, the center focus of the decorating scheme was the crystal replica of the planet Mars, which was suspended from the ceiling in each shop, and which revolved at the same tempo as Mars itself. It has not yet been determined what type of mechanism activates these globes. The globes, which display a unique and remarkable map of Mars's surface, were installed by the principals, after Trevore had completed the overall alteration and decoration. While the Fifth Avenue storefront is striking, it was done with the type of expensive modesty that would do credit to Tiffany's. The last thing installed was the name of the shop itself, MARS PRODUCTS, in gold letters, each letter a half-inch in relief and five inches high. It has since been determined that these letters are cast out of solid gold.

The three shops opened their doors to the public at ten A.M., on the tenth of March—in local time and day. In New York, the letters spelling out MARS PRODUCTS had been displayed for eight days, and a good deal of curiosity had been aroused, both among the public and the press. But until actual opening, no information had been offered.

During those days, four objects had been on display in the shop windows. No doubt the reader of this precis has seen or examined these objects, each of which stood upon a small crystal display stand, framed in black velvet, for all the world like precious jewels, which in a sense they were. The display consisted of a clock, an adding machine, an outboard motor and a music box, although only the clock was recognizable through its appearance, a beautiful precision instrument, activated as a number of clocks are by the variation in atmospheric pressure. Yet the workmanship, materials and general beauty of this clock outdid anything obtainable in the regular market.

The adding machine was a black cube, measuring slightly more than six inches. The covering is of some as yet undetermined synthetic or plastic, inlaid with the curious hieroglyphs that have come to be known as the Martian script, the hieroglyphs in white and gold. This machine is quickly and easily adjusted or sensitized to the sound of an individual voice, and it calculates on the basis of vocal instruction. The results emerge through a thin slit in the top, printed on paper similar to that mentioned before. Theoretically, such a calculator could be built today, but, so far as we know, by only two shops, one in Germany and the other in Japan, and the cost would be staggering; certainly, it would take years of experimental work to develop it to the point where it would deal with thirteen digits, adding, subtracting, multiplying and dividing entirely by vocal command.

The outboard motor was an object about the size of a small electric sewing machine, fabricated of some blue metal and weighing fourteen pounds, six ounces and a fraction. Two simple tension clips attached it to any boat or cart or car. It generated forty horsepower in jet propulsion, and it contained, almost microcosmically, its own atomic generator, guaranteed for one thousand continuous hours of operation. Through a muffling device, which has so far defied even theoretical solution, it produced less sound than an ordinary outboard motor. In each shop, this was explained, not as a muffling procedure, but as a matter of controlled pitch beyond the range of the human ear. Competent engineers felt that this explanation must be rejected.

In spite of the breathtaking implications of this atomic motor, it was the music box that excited the most attention and speculation. Of more or less the same dimensions as the adding machine, it was of pale yellow synthetic, the hieroglyphs pricked out in dark gray. Two slight depressions on the top of this box activated it, a slight touch of one depression to start it, a second touch on the same depression to stop it. The second depression, when touched, changed the category of the music desired. There were twenty-two categories of music available—symphonic music in three chronological sections, chamber music in three sections, piano solo, violin solo with and without accompaniment, folk music for seven cultures, operatic in three sections, orchestra, full cast and orchestra, that is the complete opera, and selected renderings, religious music, divided into five religious categories, popular songs in national sections, instrumental music in terms of eighty-two instruments, jazz in five categories and three categories of children's music.

The salespeople in each of the three shops claimed that the music box had a repertoire of eleven thousand and some odd separate musical selections, but this, of course, could not be put to the test, and varying opinions on this score have been expressed. Also the use of vocal instruction to set the sound and pitch—which was not inferior to the best mass-produced high fidelity—was poo-pooed as fakery. But Mr. Harry Flannery, consulting sound engineer for the Radio Corporation of America, has stated that the music box could be compiled out of available technical knowledge, especially since the discovery of transistor electronics. As with the adding machine, it was less the technical achievement than the workmanship that was unbelievable. But Mr. Flannery admitted that a content of eleven thousand works was beyond present day knowledge or skill, providing that this enormous repertoire was a fact. From all witnesses interrogated, we have compiled a list of more than three hundred works played by the shop's demonstration music box.

These were the four objects displayed in the windows of each of the three stores. The same four objects were available for examination and demonstration inside each of the stores. The clock was priced at $500.00, the adding machine at $475.00, the outboard motor at $1620.00 and the music box at $700.00—and these prices were exactly the same, at the current exchange, in Tokyo and Paris.

Prior to the opening—that is, the previous day—quarter-page advertisements, in the *New York Times* only, stated simply and directly that the people of the Planet Mars announced the opening, the following day, of a shop on Fifth Avenue, which would display, demonstrate, and take orders for four products of Martian industry. It explained the limited selection of offerings by pointing out that this was only an initial step, in order to test the reactions of Earth buyers. It was felt, the advertisement stated, that commercial relations between the Earth and Mars should be on the friendliest basis, and the Martian industrialists had no desire to upset the economic balance of Earth.

The advertisement went on to say that orders would be taken for all of the products, and that delivery was guaranteed in twelve days. The advertisement expressed the hope that this would mark the beginning of a cordial and fruitful and lasting relationship between the inhabitants of both planets.

This advertisement was hardly the first word in the press concerning the Martian shops. Already, every columnist had carried an item or two about what was, without question, one of the most imaginative and novel publicity schemes of the space age. Several columnists had it on the best authority—for rumors were all over the city—that General Dynamics was behind the Martian shops. They were also credited to General Electric, the Radio Corporation, and at least a dozen of large industrial enclaves. Again, a brilliant young merchandiser was named, a Paris dress designer, and a Greek shipping magnate. Still others spoke of a scheme by German industrialists to break into the American market in force, and of course there were hints that the Soviet Union was behind the method of destroying capitalism. Engineers were willing to grant Russia the skill, but interior decorators refused to acknowledge the ability of the Russians to produce original and tasteful decor. But until the shops actually opened and the working capabilities of the machines were actually demonstrated, no one was inclined to take the matter too seriously.

On the tenth of March, the shops opened in each of the three cities. The tenth of March was a Monday in New York. The shops remained open until Friday, and then they closed down for good—so far as we know.

But in those five days, thousands of people crowded into the Fifth Avenue store. The machines were demonstrated over and over. Thousands of orders were taken, but all deposits and prepayment were refused. The New York shop was staffed by one man and five tall, charming and efficient women. What they actually looked like is a matter of dispute, for they all wore skin-tight masks of some latex-like material; but rather than to make them repulsive, the effect of the masks was quite pleasant. Gloves of the same material covered their hands, nor was any part of their skin anywhere exposed.

John Mattson, writing in the *News* the following day, said, "Never did the inhabitants of two planets meet under more promising circumstances. Having seen the Martian figure and having had a touch of the Martian charm, I am willing to take any chances with the Martian face. Uncover, my lovelies, uncover. Earth waits with bated breath."

Professor Hugo Elligson, the famous astronomer, visited the shop for *Life*. His report says in part, "If the masked people in this shop are Martians, then I say, Space must be conquered. I know it is strange for an astronomer to dwell on shapely legs and muted, rippling accents, yet I know that from here on my wife will eye me strangely whenever I look at the Red Planet. As to the relationship of an excellent publicity scheme to the Planet Mars, common intelligence orders me to withhold comment—"

Perhaps the Soviet Union thought different; for on the second day of the shop's business, two gentlemen from the Russian Embassy were known to enter and offer a cool million United States dollars for the demonstration sample of the atomic outboard. The Martians were polite but firm.

By Wednesday, Mars Products occupied more space in the New York press than international news. It crowded out the crises in the Middle East, and Formosa was relegated to page seventeen of the *Times*. A dozen authorities were writing scholarly opinions. Traffic on Fifth Avenue was impossible, and one hundred extra police were detailed to maintain order and make it possible for any of the Fifth Avenue stores to do business. The Fifth Avenue Association decided to apply for an injunction, on the grounds that Mars Products disrupted the ordinary practice of business.

Much the same was happening on Faubourg St. Honore, and on the Ginza.

Also on Wednesday, American industry awoke and panicked. Boards of Directors were convened all over the nation. Important industrial magnates flew to Washington, and the stock of electronic, business-machine and automobile companies sent the Dow-Jones averages down twenty-six points. The largest builder of systems and

89

calculating machines in America saw its stock sell ten minutes ahead of the ticker, down one hundred and eighty points for the day. So also on the London, Paris and Tokyo exchanges.

But the intelligence service was not perturbed until Thursday, when it sent formal requests to the F.B.I. and to the New York City Police Department to determine who and what the principals behind Mars Products were—and to ascertain where these machines had been manufactured, whether they had been imported, and whether duty had been paid. The Sureté and the Tokyo Police were by then taking similar steps.

Without going into the details of this investigation, it suffices to say that in every case, the investigating authorities were baffled. All three bank accounts were the result of large cash deposits by very commonplace men who were no different from thousands of other average men. The acting agents were given, by mail, full power of attorney as well as instructions. The investigations were not completed until Friday evening.

By Friday, each of the three shops was under surveillance by various government and police agencies. In New York, city detectives put a twenty-four hour watch on Mars Products Wednesday evening, even before any instructions or requests came from Washington. But no member of the staff left the shop after closing hours, or at any other time. Curtains were drawn across the windows, blocking off the display products. At ten A.M., the curtains were drawn back.

During Friday, in New York and Washington, discussions were held on the advisability of issuing injunctions or search warrants. At the same time, there was understandable hesitancy. If this was a publicity scheme of some industrial group, whatever agency acted could be the laughing stock of the nation—as well as opening itself to considerable liability, if legal action was taken by the injured party. Plainclothesmen had been in and out of the shop a hundred times, searching for some violation. None had been found. No loophole had been detected.

Friday night, the shop on Fifth Avenue closed as usual. The curtains were drawn. At eleven P.M., the lights went out. At three A.M., the door of the shop opened.

At that time on Saturday morning, Fifth Avenue was deserted. The shop was then being observed by four city detectives, two federal agents, two members of Central Intelligence, and three

90

private operatives hired by the National Association of Manufacturers. The eleven men made no attempt at concealment. There was only one store entrance. Across the avenue, four cars waited.

When the door of Mars Products opened, the five members of the staff walked out. They all carried packages. At precisely the same moment, a large black automobile drew up at the curb in front of the shop. The man opened the back door of this car, and all five staff members entered. Then the door closed and they drove away. They were followed by the four cars. The agents who were watching them had instructions not to interfere, to make no arrests, but to follow any member of the staff to his or her destination and to report along the way by radio.

We have an exact description of the automobile. Shaped somewhat like a Continental, it was at least a foot longer, though no broader. It had a strange hood, more rounded than a stock car; but it was larger than any known sport car.

It headed uptown, well within the speed limits, turned into Central Park, emerged at 7th Avenue and 110th Street, proceeded north and then beneath 155th Street to the Harlem River Speedway. When it reached the Speedway, two police cars had joined the caravan behind it. Toward the George Washington Bridge approachramp, it began to pick up speed, and when it passed the ramp, continuing on the deserted Speedway, it was already doing eighty miles an hour. The police cars opened their sirens, and by radio, additional police cars were instructed to set up a roadblock at Dyckman Street.

At that point, the black car put out wings, at least seven feet on either side, and went over to jet power. It left the pursuing cars as if they were standing still. It is impossible to arrive at any accurate estimate of its ground speed then, but it was certainly well over a hundred and thirty miles an hour. It was airborne in a matter of seconds, gained altitude quickly, and disappeared, by its sound, eastward. It was picked up twice by radar at an altitude of twenty thousand feet, moving at very high speed, even for jet power. The airforce was immediately notified and planes took off within minutes, but there is no report of the black car—or plane—being sighted again, nor was it again raised with radar.

It is sufficient to note that the progress of events in Tokyo and Paris was more or less identical. In no case was the staff of the shop interfered with or taken.

Such was the precis that Detective Sergeant Bristol reviewed before he went uptown to break in the door of Mars Products. It told him nothing that he did not already know, and in all truth, he knew a great deal more. His own specialty was *entry and search,* but like almost every other citizen of New York, he had speculated during the past days on the intriguing problem of Mars Products. He was well trained in the art of rejecting any conclusions not founded on facts he could test with sight, touch or smell; but in spite of this training, his imagination conjured up a host of possibilities behind the locked door of Mars Products. He was still young enough to view his work with excitement, and all during this day, his excitement had been mounting.

Both the city police and the F.B.I. had decided to wait through Saturday before opening the shop, and these decisions were communicated to Tokyo and Paris. Actually, the New York shop was opened a few hours later than the others.

When Bristol arrived at 52nd Street and Fifth Avenue, at least a dozen men were waiting for him. Among them were the police commissioner, the mayor, General Arlen Mack, the Chief of Staff, a colonel in Military Intelligence and several F.B.I. officials. There were also at least a hundred onlookers, held back by policemen. The police commissioner was irritated and indicated that Bristol was the type to be late at his own funeral.

"I was told to be here at seven o'clock sir," Bristol said. "It is still a few minutes before seven."

"Well, don't argue about it. Get that door open!"

It was easier said than done. When they ripped off the bronze plate, they found solid steel underneath. They burned through it and hammered off the bolted connection. It took almost an hour before the door was open—and then, as had been the case in Tokyo and Paris, they found the store empty. The beautiful crystal reproduction of the Planet Mars had been pulverized; they found the shards in a waste basket, and it was taken to Centre Street for analysis. Otherwise, none of the decorations had been disturbed or removed, not even the solid gold letters on the store front—a small fortune in itself. But the eight products, the four from the window and the four used in the shop as demonstrators, were gone.

The high brass prowled around the place for an hour or so, examining the decorations and whispering to each other in corners. Someone made the inevitable remark about fingerprints, and the commissioner growled, "People whose skin is covered don't leave fingerprints." By nine o'clock, the brass had left, and Bristol went to work. Two F.B.I. men had remained; they watched the methods of the three men from Centre Street in silent admiration.

Bristol's specialty was, as we noted, *entry and search*. He had four children, a wife he adored, and he was soberly ambitious. He had long since decided to turn his specialty into a science and then to develop that science to a point unequaled elsewhere. First he brought in lights and flooded the store with three thousand additional watts of illumination. Since there was only the main room and a small office and lavatory behind it, it brightened the space considerably. Then he and his two assistants hooked portable lights into their belts. He told the F.B.I. men:

"The first element of search is find it."

"Do you know what to look for?"

"No," Bristol said. "Neither does anyone else. That makes it easier in a way."

First they removed all drapery, spread white sheets, brushed the drapery carefully on both sides, folded it and removed it. The dust was collected and labeled. Then they swept all the floors, then went over them a second time with a vacuum cleaner. The dust was sifted, packaged and labeled. Then, fitting the vacuum cleaner with new bags each time, they went over every inch of space, floor, walls, ceiling, molding and furniture. Again, the bags were packaged and labeled. They took the upholstered furniture apart, bit by bit, shredding the fabric and filling. The foam rubber in the cushions was needled and then picked apart. Once again, everything was labeled.

"This is more or less mechanical," Bristol explained to the government men. "Routine. We do the chemical and microscopic analysis downtown."

"Routine, eh?"

"I mean for this type of problem. We don't get this kind of problem in terms of search more than two or three times a year."

At two o'clock in the morning, the government men went to buy coffee and sandwiches. They brought back a box of food for the city men. By four A.M., the carpeting had been taken down to Centre Street, the toilet walls stripped of tile, the plumbing removed and checked, the toilet and sink entirely dismantled. At six o'clock on Sunday morning, in the cold gray light of dawn, Bristol was supervising the taking apart of every piece of bonded wood or metal in the shop.

He made the find in a desk, a modern desk of Swedish design that had been supplied by the decorators. Its surface was of polished birch and there was a teak strip across the front. When this strip was removed, Bristol found a bit of film, less than an inch long and about three millimeters in width. When he held it up to the light with tweezers and put a magnifying glass on it, it was discovered to be film strip. It contained sixteen full frames and part of a seventeenth frame.

Minutes later, he was in a car with the government men, racing down to Centre Street; and only then did he permit himself the luxury of a voiced opinion.

"They must have been editing that film," he remarked. "I have been reading how orderly and precise they are. But even an orderly person can lose something. Even a Martian," he finished doubtfully.

Strangely enough, the government men made no comment at all.

Bristol is remembered, and it has been said in many places that he will go far. He has already been promoted, and without question he will be mentioned by historians for years to come. He was an honest and thorough man, and he had an orderly mind to match other orderly minds.

Professor Julius Goldman will also be remembered. The head of the Department of Semitic Languages at Columbia University, he was also the leading philologist in the Western Hemisphere, if not the world; and to him as much as to any other goes the credit for breaking through the early Cretan script. He pioneered the brilliant—if again failing—recent Etruscan effort. Along with Jacobs of Oklahoma, he is the leading authority on American Indian languages, specializing there in the Plains dialects. It is said that there is no important language on earth, living or dead, that he cannot command fluently.

This is possibly an exaggeration, but since he was reached by the White House that same Sunday, flown to Washington, put at the head of a team of five of the Country's finest philologists—and since he accomplished what was expected of him in thirty-two hours, it might be said that his reputation was deserved.

Yet by the grace of God or whatever force determines our destiny, he was given a "Rosetta Stone," so to speak. Without it, as he was the first to point out, the Martian script would not have been broken, not now and possibly not ever. The "Rosetta Stone"—

which, you will recall, originally enabled philologists to break the mystery of the Egyptian hieroglyphs by providing them, on the same stone tablet, with translations in known tongues—was in this case a single frame of the film strip, containing both an English and Martian inscription. Acting on the possibility that one was a translation of the other, Professor Goldman found an opening for the attack. Nevertheless, it remains perhaps the most extraordinary case of reconstruction in all the history of language.

That Tuesday, the Tuesday after the store had been broken into, the President of the United States held an enlarged meeting of his cabinet at the White House. In addition to the regular members of the cabinet, some forty-two other persons were present, Julius Goldman among them; and it was not Goldman alone who appeared haggard from want of sleep. Each of the men present had a precis—somewhat enlarged—that was not too different from the one presented here. Each of them had read it and pondered it. Opening the meeting, the President reviewed the facts, mentioned some of the opinions already gathered from experts, and then said:

"What are we to think, gentlemen? Our own halting probes into outer space have removed the starry realm from the province of fiction writers and gullible fools. As yet we have not firm conclusions, but I do hope that at the end of this meeting, we will formulate a few and be able to act upon them. I need not repeat that some of the keenest minds in America still consider the Martian shops to be a remarkable hoax. If so, a practical joke costing its originator a great many millions in dollars, has been played out to no point. In all fairness, I reject this conclusion, nor can I, at this point in my knowledge, support any arguments that we have seen a great publicity campaign. I have come to certain conclusions of my own, but I shall withhold them until others have been heard.

"As most of you know, through the energy and resourcefulness of the New York City police department, we found a tiny bit of film strip at the Fifth Avenue shop. Nothing of any value was found either in Paris or Tokyo. Nevertheless, I have invited the Japanese and French ambassadors to be present tonight, since their countries have been chosen, even as ours was. I do not say that their interest is higher than that of other nations, for perhaps—"

The President hesitated then—and shrugged tiredly. "Well at this point, I will turn the meeting over to Professor Julius Goldman of Columbia University, our greatest philologist, whose contribution to the unravelling of this problem cannot be overestimated.

Professor Goldman said quietly that, for the record, he had made no contribution not shared equally by his colleagues, who were not present this evening. They had, all six of them, prepared an affidavit, which he would read in the name of the entire team. First, he would like the people assembled to see the film strip for themselves.

The room was darkened. The first frame appeared on a prepared screen at one end of the room. It was covered with vertical lines of what had already come to be called the Martian Hieroglyphic. So with the second and the "Rosetta Stone." At the top, in English block letters:

"Compound for white males—16 to 19 years of age."

And directly beneath, again in English, "General warning. Any discussion of escape or resistance will be met by permanent stimulation of the tri-geminal nerve."

And beneath that, "Feeding room—yellow-skinned females, 7-10 years of age."

And as a final line in English, "Much have I travelled in the realms of gold."

Beneath these English lines were a number of vertical hieroglyph columns.

The voice of Professor Goldman explained, "This frame gave us our key, but we do not claim any clear knowledge of what these inscriptions mean. Medical authorities consulted have suggested that a certain type of irritation of the tri-geminal nerve can result in the most trying pain man knows. The line from Keats is utterly meaningless, so far as we can determine; the reason for its inclusion remains to be explained in the future, if ever. The remaining frames, as you see, are in the hieroglyph."

The lights went on again. Professor Goldman blinked tiredly, wiped his glasses, and said, "Before I present our affidavit, I must ask your indulgence for a few words concerning language. When we philologists claim to have cracked the mystery of some ancient tongue, we do not talk as a cryptographer who has broken a code. Philology and Cryptography are very different sciences. When a code is broken, its message is known. When a language is broken, only the first step in a long and arduous process is taken. No single man or single group of men has ever revealed an ancient language; that is an international task and must of necessity take generations to complete.

"I say this because perhaps your hopes have been raised too high. We have very little to work from, only a few words and numerals; we are dealing with an unrelated tongue, totally alien; and we have had only a few hours to grapple with the problem. Therefore, though we have been able to extract some meaning from two of the frames, there are many blank spaces and many perplexities. In our favor are these facts: first—all language, possibly anywhere in the universe, appears to have a developmental logic and relationship; secondly, these frames deal with life on earth; and finally, it is our good fortune that this is an alphabetic form of writing, consisting, so far as we can determine, of forty-one sound signs, at least thirty of them consonantal. These consonantal forms suggest a vocal arrangement not unlike our own—that is in physical structure, for sounds are to a large extent determined by the physical characteristics of the creature producing them. My colleagues agree that there is no indication of any relationship between this alphabet and language and any known language of Earth. For my part, I will make no comment on the origin of this language. It is not my field—nor is it my purpose."

The President nodded. "We understand that, Professor Goldman."

Goldman continued: "The affadavit itself will be projected on the screen, since we consider it more effective for the partial translation to be read rather than heard."

The room was then darkened again, and the following appeared on the screen:

"A tentative and partial translation of the first two frames of a film strip, given to the undersigned for translation purposes:

"——greedy lustful—[dedicated?] [practicing?] mass [murder?] [death?] — [time] generations [of?] murder — [docile?] [willing?] O when shown pleasure ——— [titled?] [self styled?] [boastful self styled?] man [or humanity?] —— [compare to?] [equate with?] disease [or plague or rust] on face of [fair?] [rich?] planet [or globe] ————"

The voice of Professor Goldman cut in, "That is the first frame. As you see, our translation is tentative and incomplete. We have very little to work from. Where the word is within brackets and coupled with a question mark, we are making what might be called a calculated surmise, not a guess, but a surmise from too few facts. Now the second frame.

97

"Force [or violence] understood [or reacted to]—man [or humanity]——primitive [or number 1] development of atomic [force or power or engine]——— [space station or small planet]—[non-possession-relating possibly to space station]— —[outer space?] [void?] negative [long-arm?] [weapon?]————— [superstition?] [ignorance?] [mindless]— —"

The inscription remained on the screen, and Goldman's voice, flat, tired and expressionless, explained:

"When we bracket a number of words, one after another, we are uncertain as to which is preferable. Actually, only a single word is being translated—"His voice faded away. The names of the six philologists appeared on the screen. The lights went on, but the silence was as deep and lasting as the darkness before it. Finally, the Secretary of State rose, looked at the President, received his nod, and said to Professor Goldman:

"I desire your opinion, Professor. Are these faked? Do they originate on earth? Or are we dealing with Martians? That's not a dirty word. Everyone is thinking it; no one will say it. I want your opinion."

"I am a scientist and a scholar, sir. I form opinions only when I have sufficient facts to make them credible. This is not the case now."

"You have more facts than anyone on earth! You can read that outlandish gibberish!"

"No more than you can, sir," Goldman replied softly. "What I have read, you have read."

"You come to it as a philologist," the Secretary of State persisted.

"Yes."

"Then as a philologist, is it your opinion that this language originated on earth?"

"How can I answer that, sir? What is my opinion worth when fashioned out of such thin stuff?"

"Then tell us—do you detect any relationship to any known Earthly language?"

"No—no, I do not," Goldman answered, smiling rather sadly.

And then there was silence again. Now one of the President's secretaries appeared, and distributed copies of the affadavit to everyone present. A longer silence now, while the affidavits were studied. Then the French ambassador asked for the floor.

"Mr. President," he said, "members of the cabinet and gentlemen—many of you know that my own government discussed this same problem yesterday. I am instructed, if the occasion should so determine, to make a certain request of you. I think the occasion does so determine. I request that you send immediately for the Soviet Ambassador."

No one was shocked or surprised by the suggestion. The Soviet Ambassador was sent for. He had evidently been waiting, for he arrived within minutes; and when he stated immediately that he would also represent the People's Republic of China or take his leave, the President of the United States suppressed a smile and nodded. He was given a precis and a copy of the affidavit, and after he had read both, the meeting began. It went on until three o'clock on Wednesday morning, during which time thirty-two technical specialists arrived, gave opinion or testimony, and departed. Then the meeting was suspended for five hours—and came together again with the representatives of India, China, Great Britain, Italy and Germany in attendance. At six o'clock Wednesday evening, the meeting was adjourned, and the following day an extraordinary session of the Assembly of the United Nations was called. By that time, Professor Goldman, with the assistance of Japanese, Chinese and Russian philologists, had completed a tentative translation of the film strip. Before this complete translation was published in the international press, it was made available to all delegates to the United Nations Assembly.

On Saturday, only a week after Detective Sergeant Bristol had forced the door of the Fifth Avenue shop, the Premier of India arose to address the Assembly of the United Nations.

"It is more than ironic," he said with some sadness, "that we who have been so savagely condemned by another planet, another culture and people, can find more than a little truth in the accusations. How close we have come, time and again, to accomplishing the destruction outlined by these people from outer space! And how unhappy it is to know that our own fitful dream of a peaceful future must be laid aside, perhaps forever! Shall it be some consolation that we must join hands to fight another enemy rather than each other? I pray so, for it is not without deep grief that my country lays aside the slim shield of neutrality it has clung to so desperately. Gentlemen, India is yours; its teeming millions will labor in the common defense of our mother earth. Its

99

inadequate mills and mines are at the world's disposal, and I hope with all my heart that we have time to build more."

Then Russia spoke, then the United States. China and eight other countries were admitted to the United Nations without a veto; but this was only the beginning of a series of actions which led, within the month, to the creation of World Spaceways—an international plan for the building of four great space stations circling the earth, a mighty fleet of atomically powered space-ships, and the construction of a military defense base on the moon, under the control of the United Nations. A three-year plan for the defense of Earth was put into operation; and, as so few had anticipated, the beginnings of world government in terms of actual sovereign power, came with a comprehensive world general staff.

Within three months after Detective Sergeant Bristol's discovery, the first world code of law was drafted and presented to the General Assembly. The antiquated and rusting ships of the navies of earth, the discarded and useless artillery, the already archaic guided missiles, the laughable small arms—all of them bore witness to the beginning of world government.

And in less than a year, Culpepper Motors, one of the largest industrial complexes on earth, announced that they had duplicated the Martian outboard atomic motor. The people of earth laughed and flexed their arms. When they looked up at the sky, at the tiny red orb of Mars, it was with growing confidence and lessening fear.

For they had discovered a new name for themselves; they had discovered that they were a nation of mankind. It was a beginning—rough and fumbling and uneasy in many of its aspects, but nevertheless a beginning. And all over the earth, this *beginning* was celebrated in a variety of ways.

At the home of Franklin Harwood Plummer, its eighty-three rooms nestled securely in the midst of an eleven hundred acre estate in New York's Putnam County, it was celebrated in a style befitting the place and circumstances. Mr. Plummer could and did give dinners that were large and important and unnoticed by the press—a fact not unrelated to his control of a great deal of the press, among other things. But even for his baronial halls, this evening's gathering was large and unique, three hundred and twenty-seven men and women, apart from Mr. Plummer himself and his eighteen colleagues who composed the Board of Directors of Culpepper Motors.

At fifty-eight, Mr. Plummer was president of Culpepper. Culpepper Motors had a net value of fifteen billion dollars, a private industrial worth exceeded, in all the world, only by American Tel and Tel; but if one were to trace the interlocking and various influences of the nineteen board members, the question of worth became so large as to be meaningless. As the nominal lord of this giant enterprise, Mr. Plummer was best defined by his history. He had started, thirty-five years before, as a lathe operator in the old Lewett Shop, and he had fought and smashed and cut his way to the eventual top. In the recent history of America, there have been a few cases like his, but not more than you could count on the fingers of one hand.

Even in his own circles, he was not loved; feared and respected he was, but without family or university, he remained a strange, violent and unpredictable interloper. He was tall and broad and red-faced and white-haired; and as he stood at one end of the great dining room in his over-large and over-furnished home, he made reference to the fact that he did not even play golf. His three hundred and twenty-seven guests and his eighteen colleagues permitted themselves to smile slightly at that.

"No," Mr. Plummer continued, "no golf, no tennis, no sailing—I have been what most of you would call a preoccupied man, and my preoccupation has been the making of money. If I have ever laved my conscience with any sop, it was to recollect that single witty remark of a man who was otherwise remarkably humorless, Calvin Coolidge—who gave folk like myself grace by stating that the business of the United States was business."

Mr. Plummer grinned. He had an infectious grin—the smile of a man who has made it beyond belief, who drives back to the old home town in a chrome-plated Cadillac.

"I enjoy making money," he said simply. "I am accused of lusting for power. Hogwash! I lust for a naked and nasty word—profit; always have and I always will. It embarrasses my eighteen colleagues, sitting here on either side of me, for me to be as blunt and ignoble as this; but I thank whatever gods may be that I have never been inhibited by breeding. I also make a double point. Firstly, the question of profit—I succeeded. Not only have I been able to insure and secure the future existence of Culpepper Motors; not only have I developed a situation where its profits will increase every year—perhaps double every five years, which makes

101

our stock a pretty good investment for any of you—but I have been able to bring together under this roof as fine a collection of human beings as mankind can provide. I will not try to explain what that means to me—what it has meant to know and work with each of the three hundred and twenty-seven people here. I think you can guess.

"Secondly, I said what I said to ease the feelings of those among you who have cooperated in our enterprise and have been paid for their cooperation—as against those who would accept no pay. Those who have been paid may feel a certain guilt. To that I say—nonsense! No one does anything strictly for money; there are always other factors. I know. I went into this for dollars and cents—plain and simple, and so did my holier than God colleagues on my Board of Directors. We have all changed in the process. My colleagues can stop wishing me dead. I love them for what they are now. I did not love them for what they were when we began this enterprise two years ago.

"Sitting among you, there is one Jonas Wayne, of Fort Fayette, Kentucky. He is an old-fashioned blacksmith, and possibly the finest hand worker in metal in America. Our enterprise would have been more difficult, if not impossible, without him. Yet he would not take a dollar from me—not even for expenses. He is a God-fearing man, and he saw himself as doing God's work, not mine. Perhaps so. I don't know. At the same table with him is M. Orendell, the Ambassador of France. He is far from being a rich man, and his expenses have been paid. We have no secrets here. We live and die with our knowledge, as a unique fraternity. Professor Julius Goldman—would you please stand up, Professor—was, as you know, central to our whole scheme. If it was painless for him to decipher the Martian script, it was far from painless for him to devise it—a task that took more hours of work than the building of the motor. He would take no money—not because he is religious but because as he puts it, he is a scientist. Komo Aguchi, the physicist—he is at the table with Dr. Goldman, accepted one hundred thousand dollars, which he spent in an attempt to cure his wife, who is dying of cancer. Shall we judge him? Or shall we put cancer on the immediate agenda?

"And what of Detective Sergeant Tom Bristol? Is he an honest cop or a dishonest cop? He accepted four hundred shares of Culpepper Motors—a hundred for each of his children. He wants them to go to college, and they will. Miss Clementina Arden, possibly the finest decorator here or on Mars, charged us forty thousand dollars for her contribution to the decor. The price was reasonable. She is a hard-headed business woman, and if she does not look after herself, who will? Yet she has turned down other jobs. She didn't turn down this one—

"Well, my good friends, ladies and gentlemen—we will not meet again, ever. My father, a working man all his life, once said that perhaps if I opened a store, even a small store, I would no longer have my life subject to the crazy whim of this boss or that. Maybe he was right. Finally, with your good help, I opened three stores. The total cost, if you are interested, was twenty-one million dollars, more or less—and a shrewd investment, I don't mind saying. Culpepper Motors will add five times that sum to its profits over the next three months. And our three stores, I do believe, have accomplished a little something that wiser men have failed to do.

"That is all I have to say. Many of you may regret that no monuments will enshrine our work. I wish we could change that, but we can't. For myself, I feel that when a man's wealth reaches a certain point of large discomfort, he does better to remain out of the public's eye. So guard our secret—not because you will be believed if you reveal it, but because you will be laughed at . . ."

As time passed, the question arose as to the disposition of the one thing of value left by the "space merchants" as they came to be called—the solid gold letters. Finally, those from the Fifth Avenue shop were set in a glass display case at the United Nations. So visitors to the national museum of France or Japan—or to the United Nations—have always before them to remind them, in letters of gold:

MARS PRODUCTS

9
The Pragmatic Seed

F OUR, five, six billion years ago the seed drifted through space. Then the seed was simply a seed, and it had no knowledge of itself. It rode the electronic and magnetic winds of the universe, and neither time nor space existed for the seed. It was all chance, for the seed had absolutely no idea of what it required or what its ultimate destiny was. It moved throughout a starry, incredible universe, but it also moved through empty space, for the stars and the galaxies were only pinpoints of illumination in infinity.

The professor and the priest were old, good friends, which made their talks easy and not terribly argumentative. The one taught physics, the other taught religion. They were both in their middle years, beyond most passions, and they savored simple things. On this particular fall day, they met after an early dinner and strolled across the campus. It was a cool, delightful October evening, the sun still an hour before setting, the great maples and oaks robed in marvelous rust and amber—as the priest remarked, an evening to renew one's faith.

"I had always thought," said the professor, "that faith was an absolute."

"Not at all."

"How can it be otherwise? Of course," the professor added, "I speak as a man of little faith."

"More's the pity."

"But some little knowledge."

"I am glad you qualify it."

"Thank you. But aren't we both in the same boat? If your faith needs periodic renewing, and can be influenced by so commonplace an event as the action of certain chemicals in the leaves of deciduous trees, then it is as relative as my small store of knowledge."

Lost in his thoughts for a minute or so, the priest admitted that the professor raised an interesting point. "However," he said, "it is not my faith but myself that wants renewing. Just as God is absolute, so is my faith absolute."

"But God, if you choose to believe in Him, is not knowable. Is your faith also unknowable?"

"Perhaps—in a manner of speaking."

"Then thank heavens science does not depend on faith. If it did, we should all be back in the horse-and-buggy era."

"Which might not be the worst thing in the world," the priest speculated.

In the infinity of space, however, the laws of time and chance cease to exist, and in a million or a billion years—one being as meaningless as the other—the winds of space carried the seed toward a galaxy, a great pinwheel of countless blazing stars. At a certain point in space, the galaxy exerted its gravitational pull upon the seed, and the seed plunged through space toward the outer edge of the galaxy. Closer and closer it drove, until at last it approached one of the elongated arms of the pinwheel, and there it was trapped into the gravitational field of one of the countless stars that composed the galaxy. Blindly obedient to the laws of the universe, the seed swung in a great circle around the star, as did other bits of flotsam and jetsam that had wandered into the gravitational field of the star. Yet while they were all similarly obedient to the laws of chance, the seed was different. The seed was alive.

"No, it might not be the worst thing in the world," the professor admitted, "but as one who has just recovered from an infection that might well have killed him had it not been for penicillin, I have a bias toward science."

"Understandably."

"And some mistrust of a faith that renews itself with the beauty of a sunset." He pointed toward the wild display of color in the west.

106

"Nevertheless," the priest said gently, "faith is more constant and reliable than science. You will admit that?"

"By no means."

"Surely you must. Science is both pragmatic and empirical."

"Naturally. We experiment, we observe, and we note the results. What else could it be if not pragmatic and empirical? The trouble with faith is that it is neither pragmatic nor empirical."

"That's not the trouble with faith," said the priest. "That's the basis of faith."

"You've lost me again," the professor said hopelessly.

"Then you get lost too easily. Let me give you an example that your scientific mind can deal with. You've read St. Augustine?"

"I have."

"And if I say that the core of my faith is not very different from the core of St. Augustine's faith, you would accept that, would you not?"

"Yes, I think so."

"You have also read, I am sure, The *Almagest* of Claudius Ptolemy, which established the earth as the center of the universe."

"Hardly science!" the professor snorted.

"Not at all, not at all. Very good science, until Copernicus overturned it and disproved it. You see, my dear friend, empirical knowledge is always certain and absolute, until some other knowledge comes along and disproves it. When man postulated, thousands of years ago, that the earth was flat, he had the evidence of his own eyes to back him up. His knowledge was certain and provable, until new knowledge came along that was equally certain and provable."

"Surely more certain and provable. Even your fine Jesuit mind must accept that."

"I am a Paulist, if it matters, but I accept your correction. More provable. More certain. And vastly different from the earlier theory. However, the faith of St. Augustine can still sustain me."

The life within the seed and the structure of that life gave it a special relationship to the flood light and energy that poured out of the star. It absorbed the radiation and turned it into food, and with food it grew. For thousands and thousands of years the seed circled the star and drank in its endless flood of radiation, and for thousands and thousands of years the seed grew. The seed became a fruit, a plant, a being, an animal, an entity, or perhaps simply a fruit—since all of these words are descriptive of things vastly different from the thing that grew out of the seed.

The professor sighed and shook his head. "If you tell me that a belief in angels has not been shattered, then you remind me of the man who grew wolfsbane to keep vampires off his place. He was eminently successful."

"That's hitting pretty low, for a man of science."

"My dear fellow, you can still maintain the faith of St. Augustine because it requires neither experiment, observation, nor a catalogue of results."

"I think it does," the priest said, almost apologetically.

"Such experiments perhaps as walking in this lovely twilight and feeling faith renewed?"

"Perhaps. But tell me—is medicine, that is, the practice of medicine, empirical?"

"Far less so than once."

"And a hundred years ago? Was medicine empirical then?"

"Of course, when you talk of medicine," the professor said, "and label it empirical, the word becomes almost synonymous with quackery. Obviously because human lives are at stake."

"Obviously. And when you fellows experiment with atomic bombs and plasma and one or two other delicacies, no human lives are at stake."

"We are even. Touché."

"But a hundred years ago, the physician would be just as certain of his craft and cures as the physician today. Who was that chap who removed the large intestine from half a hundred of his patients because he was convinced that it was the cause of aging?"

"Of course science progresses."

"If you call it progress," the priest said. "But you chaps build your castles of knowledge on very wet sand indeed. I can't help thinking that my faith rests on a firmer foundation."

"What foundation?"

The shape of the thing that the seed became was a sphere, an enormous sphere, twenty-five thousand miles in circumference, in human terms; but a very significant sphere in terms of the universe.

It was the third mass of matter, counting out from the star, and in shape not unlike the others. It lived, it grew, it became conscious of itself, not quite as we know consciousness, but nevertheless conscious of itself. In the course of the aeons that it existed, tiny cultures appeared upon its skin, just as tiny organisms thrive upon the skin of man. A wispy aura of oxygen and nitrogen surrounded it and protected its skin from the pinpricks of meteors, but the thing that grew from the seed was indifferent, unaware of the cultures that appeared on and disappeared from its skin. For years eternal, it swam through space, circling the star that fed it and nourished it.

"The wisdom and the love of God," the priest replied. "That's a pretty firm foundation. At least it is not subject to alteration every decade or so. Here you fellows were with your Newtonian physics, absolutely certain that you had solved all the secrets of the universe, and then along came Einstein and Fermi and Jeans and the others, and poof—out of the window with all of your certainties."

"Not quite with all of them."

"What remains when light can be both a particle and a wave, when the universe can be both bounded and boundless, and when matter has its mirror image, antimatter?"

"At least we learn we deal with realities—"

"Realities? Come now."

"Oh, yes. The reality changes, our vision is broadened, we do push ahead."

"In the hope that at least your vision will match my faith?" the priest asked, smiling.

The thousands of years became millions and the millions billions, and still the thing that was the seed circled the sun. But now it was ripe and bursting with its fullness. It knew that its time was coming to an end, but it did not resist or protest the eternal cycle of life. Vaguely it knew that its own beginning seed had been flung out of the ripened fruit, and it knew that what had been must occur again in the endless cycle of eternity—that its purpose was to propagate itself: to what end, it neither knew nor speculated. Full to bursting, it let be what must be.

The day was ending. The sun, low on the horizon now, had taken refuge behind a lacework of red and purple and orange clouds, and against this the golden leaves of the trees put to mock the art of the best jewelers. A cool evening wind made a proper finish for a perfect day.

No other words. "What a perfect day," the priest said.

"Now that's odd."

They had come to the edge of the campus, where the mowed, leaf-covered lawns gave way to a cornfield.

"Now that's odd," said the professor, pointing to the cornfield.

"What is odd?"

"That crack over there. I don't remember seeing it yesterday."

The priest's eyes followed the pointing hand of the professor, and sure enough, there was a crack about a yard wide running through the cornfield.

"Quite odd," the priest agreed.

"Evidently an earth fault. I didn't know there were any here."

"It's getting wider, you know," the priest said.

And then it got wider and wider and wider and wider.

10
The Trap

Bath, England
October 12, 1945

Mrs. Jean Arbalaid
Washington, D.C.

My dear Sister:

I admit to lethargy and perhaps to a degree of indifference—although it is not indifference in your terms, not in the sense of ceasing to care. I care for you very much and think about you a good deal. After all, we have only each other, and apart from the two of us, our branch of the Feltons has ceased to exist. So in my failure to reply to three separate letters, there was no more than a sort of inadequacy. I had nothing to say because there was nothing that I wanted to say.

You knew where I was, and I asked Sister Dorcas to write you a postcard or something to the effect that I had mended physically even if my brain was nothing to shout about. I have been rather depressed for the past two months—the doctors here call it melancholia, with their British propensity for Victorian nomenclature—but they tell me that I am now on the mend in that department as well. Apparently, the overt sign of increasing mental health is an interest in things. My writing to you, for example, and also the walks I have taken around the city. Bath is a fascinating town, and I am rather pleased that the rest home they sent me to is located here.

They were terribly short of hospitals with all the bombing and with the casualties sent back here after the Normandy landing, but

111

they have a great talent for making do. Here they took several of the great houses of the Beau Nash period and turned them into rest homes—and managed to make things very comfortable. Ours has a garden, and when a British garden is good, it has no equal anywhere else in the world. In fact, it spurred me to make some rather mawkish advances to Sister Dorcas one sunny day, and she absolutely destroyed my budding sexual desires with her damned understanding and patience. There is nothing as effective in cutting down a clean-cut American lad as a tall, peach-skinned, beautiful and competent British lady who is doubling as a nurse and has a high-bridged nose in the bargain.

I have been ambulant lately, pottering around Bath and poking my nose into each and every corner. The doctor encourages me to walk for the circulation and final healing of my legs, and since Bath is built up and down, I take a good deal of exercise. I go to the old Roman baths frequently, being absolutely fascinated by them and by the whole complex that is built around the Pump Room—where Nash and his pals held forth. So much of Bath is a Georgian city, perhaps more perfect architecturally than any other town in England. But there are also the baths, the old baths of the Middle Ages, and then the Roman baths which date back before that. In fact, the doctors here have insisted that I and other circulatory-problem cases take the baths. I can't see how it differs from an ordinary hot bath, but British physicians still believe in natural healing virtues and so forth.

Why am I a circulatory problem, you are asking yourself; and just what is left of old Harry Felton and what has been shot away and how much of his brain is soggy as a bowl of farina? Yes indeed—I do know you, my sister. May I say immediately that in my meanderings around the town, I am permitted to be alone; so apparently I am not considered to be the type of nut one locks away for the good of each and everyone.

Oh, there are occasions when I will join up with some convalescent British serviceman for an amble, and sometimes I will have a chat with the locals in one of the pubs, and on three or four occasions I have wheedled Sister Dorcas into coming along and letting me hold her hand and make a sort of pass, just so I don't forget how; but by and large, I am alone. You will remember that old Harry was always a sort of loner—so apparently the head is moderately dependable.

112

It is now the next day, old Jean. October 13. I put the letter away for a day. Anyway, it is becoming a sort of epistle, isn't it? The thing is that I funked it—notice the way I absorb the local slang— when it came down to being descriptive about myself, and I had a talk with Sister Dorcas, and she sent me to the psychiatrist for a listen. He listens and I talk. Then he pontificates.

"Of course," he said to me, after I had talked for a while, "this unwillingness to discuss one's horrors is sometimes worn like a bit of romantic ribbon. You know, old chap—a decoration."

"I find you irritating," I said to him.

"Of course you do. I am trying to irritate you."

"Why?"

"I suppose because you are an American and I have a snobbish dislike for Americans."

"Now you're being tactful."

The psychiatrist laughed appreciatively and congratulated me on a sense of humor. He is a nice fellow, the psychiatrist, about forty, skinny, as so many British professionals are, long head, big nose, very civilized. To me, Jean, that is the very nice thing about the English—the sense of civilization you feel.

"But I don't want you to lose your irritation," he said.

"No danger."

"I mean if we get to liking and enjoying each other, we'll simply cover things up. I want to root up a thing or two. You're well enough to take it—and you're a strong type, Felton. No schizoid tendencies—never did show any. Your state of depression was more of a reaction to your fear that you would never walk again, but you're walking quite well now, aren't you? Yet Sister Dorcas tells me you will not write a word to your family about what happened to you. Why not?"

"My family is my sister. I don't want to worry her, and Sister Dorcas has a big mouth."

"I'll tell her that."

"And I'll kill you."

"And as far as worrying your sister—my dear fellow, we all know who your sister is. She is a great scientist and a woman of courage and character. Nothing you can tell her would worry her, but your silence does."

"She thinks I've lost my marbles?"

"You Americans are delightful when you talk the way you

113

imagine we think you talk. No, she doesn't think you're dotty. Also, I wrote to her a good many months ago, telling her that you had been raked by machine-gun fire across both legs and describing the nature of your injuries.''

"Then there it is.''

"Of course not. It is very important for you to be able to discuss what happened to you. You suffered trauma and great pain. So did many of us.''

"I choose not to talk about it,'' I said. "Also, you are beginning to bore me.''

"Good. Irritation and boredom. What else?''

"You are a goddamn nosey Limey, aren't you?''

"Yes, indeed.''

"Never take No for an answer.''

"I try not to.''

"All right, doc—it is as simple as this. I do not choose to talk about what happened to me because I have come to dislike my race.''

"Race? How do you mean, Felton—Americans? White race? or what?''

"The human race,'' I said to him.

"Oh, really? Why?''

"Because they exist only to kill.''

"Come on now—we do take a breather now and then.''

"Intervals. The main purpose is killing.''

"You know, you are simply feeding me *non sequiturs*. I ask you why you will not discuss the incident of your being wounded, and you reply that you have come to dislike the human race. Now and then I myself have found the human race a little less than overwhelmingly attractive, but that's surely beside the point.''

"Perhaps. Perhaps not.''

"Why don't you tell me what happened?''

"Why don't you drop dead?'' I asked him.

"Or why don't you and I occupy ourselves with a small pamphlet on Americanisms—if only to enlighten poor devils like myself who have to treat the ill among you who inhabit our rest homes?''

"The trouble is,'' I said, "that you have become so bloody civilized that you have lost the ability to be properly nasty.''

"Oh, come off it, Felton, and stop asking for attention like a seven-year-old. Why don't you just tell me what happened—

114

because you know, it's you who are becoming the bore."

"All right," I agreed. "Good. We're getting to be honest with each other. I will tell you—properly and dramatically and then will you take your stinking psychiatric ass off my back?"

"If you wish."

"Good. Not that it's any great hotshot story for the books—it simply is what it is to me. I had a good solid infantry company, New York boys mostly; some Jews, some Negroes, five Puerto Ricans, a nice set of Italians and Irish, and the rest white Protestants of English, Scotch, North of Ireland and German descent. I specify, because we were all on the holy mission of killing our fellow man. The boys were well trained and they did their best, and we worked our way into Germany with no more casualties or stupidities than the next company; and then one of those gross and inevitable stupidities occurred. We came under enemy fire and we called our planes for support, and they bombed and strafed the hell out of us."

"Your planes?"

"That's right. It happened a lot more often than anyone gave out, and it was a wonder it didn't happen twice as much. How the hell do you know, when you're way up there and moving at that speed? How do you know which is which, when one and all are trying to cuddle into the ground? So it happened. There was an open farm shed, and one of my riflemen and I dived in there and took cover behind a woodpile. And that was where I found this little German kid, about three years old, frightened, almost catatonic with fear—and just a beautiful kid."

I must have stopped there. He prodded me, and pointed out that the war had drawn small distinction between children and adults, and even less distinction between more beautiful and less beautiful children.

"What did you do?"

"I tried to provide cover for the child," I explained patiently. "I put her in my arms and held my body over her. A bomb hit the shed. I wasn't hurt, but the rifleman there with me—his name was Ruckerman—he was killed. I came out into the open with the kid in my arms, warm and safe. Only the top of her head was gone. A freak hit. I suppose the bomb fragment sheared it clean off, and I stood there with the little girl's brains dripping down on my shoulder. Then I was hit by the German machine-gun burst."

115

"I see," the psychiatrist said.

"You have imagination then."

"You tell it well," he said. "Feel any better?"

"No."

"Mind a few more questions, Felton? I am keeping my promise to take my ass off your back, so just say No, if you wish."

"You're very patient with me."

He was. He had put up with my surliness and depression for weeks. Never lost his temper, which was the principal reason why he irritated me so.

"All right. Question away."

"Now that you've told this to me, do you feel any different?"

"No."

"Any better?"

"No."

"That's good."

"Why is it good?" I asked him.

"Well, you see—the incident outraged you, but not in a traumatic sense. Apparently it doesn't hurt or help very much to recall it."

"It's not blocked, if you mean that. I can think about it whenever I wish to. It disgusts me."

"Certainly. As I said, I believe your depression was entirely due to the condition of your legs. When you began to walk, the depression started to lift, and they tell me that in another few weeks your legs will be as good as ever. Well, not for mountain climbing —but short of that, good enough. Tell me, Felton, why were you so insistent upon remaining in England for your convalescence? You pulled a good many strings. You could have been flown home, and the care stateside is better than here. They have all sorts of things and conveniences that we don't have."

"I like England."

"Do you? No girl awaited you here—what do you like about us?"

"There you go with your goddamn, nosey professional touch."

"Yes, of course. But, you see, Captain, you made your indictment universal. Man is a bloody horror. Quite so. Here, too. Isn't he?"

"Oh, do get off my back," I said to him, and that ended the interview; but by putting it down, "he said," "I said," etc., I am able, my dear Jean, to convey the facts to you.

116

You ask whether I want to come home. The answer is No. Not now, not in the foreseeable future. Perhaps never, but never is a hairy word, and who can tell?

You say that my share of mother's estate brings me over a hundred dollars a week. I have no way to spend any of it, so let the lawyers piddle with it just as they have been doing. I have my own dole, my accumulated pay and a few hundred dollars I won playing bridge. Ample. As I said, I have nothing to spend it on.

As to what I desire—very little indeed. I have no intentions of resuming the practice of corporate law. The first two years of it bored me, but at least I brought to them a modicum of ambition. Now the ambition is gone, and the only thing that replaces it is distaste. No matter what direction my thinking takes, I always return to the fact that the human race is a rather dreadful thing. That is, my dear, with the exception of yourself and your brilliant husband.

I am better able to write now, so if you write to me and tell me what brilliance and benevolence you and your husband are up to now, I shall certainly answer your letter.

Thank you for bearing with me through my boorish months.

Harry.

2

Washington, D.C.
October 16, 1945

Captain Harry Felton
Bath, England

My dear Harry:

I will not try to tell you how good it was to hear from you. I never was terribly good at putting my feelings down on paper, but believe me I have read and reread your letter, oh, I should say, at least half a dozen times, and I have done little but think of you and what you have been through and your situation at this moment. I am sure you realize, Harry, better than anyone else, that this is not a time for bright words and happy cliche's. Nothing I say at this moment is going to make very much difference to you or to your state of mind or, of course, to your state of health. And nothing I offer at this moment in the way of philosophical argument is going to change any of your attitudes. On my part, I am not sure that changing them at this moment is very important. Far more important is Harry Felton, his life and his future.

I have been talking about that to Mark and thinking about it a great deal myself. Harry, we've both of us engaged on a most exciting project which, for the moment, must remain surrounded with all the silly United States Army attitudes of secrecy and classification. Actually, our project is not military and there are no military secrets concerned with it. But at the moment we are operating with Army money and therefore we are surrounded with all sorts of taboos and rules and regulations. Nevertheless, Harry, rest assured that the project is fascinating, important and, quite naturally, difficult. We need help—I think specifically the kind of help you might provide. And at the same time, I think we can give you what you need most at this moment of your life—a purpose. We cannot give you a profession, and, when you come right down to it, we cannot ask you to be much more than an exalted messenger-boy—reporter. However, the combination of the two will give you a chance to travel, perhaps to see some of the world that you have not yet seen, and, we think, to ask some interesting questions.

Truthfully, our mission requires a very intelligent man. I am not apple-polishing or trying to cheer you with compliments. I am simply stating that we can make you a fairly decent offer that will take your mind off your present situation and at least give you an interest in geography.

At the moment we can pay you only a pittance, but you say in your letter that you are not particularly concerned with money. We will pay all expenses, of course, and you may stay at the best places if you wish.

Just as an indication of the kind of wheels we presently are and the kind of weight we can throw around, Mark has completed your discharge in England; your passport is on its way via diplomatic pouch, and it will be handed to you personally either before this letter arrives or no more than a day later.

118

The bit in your letter about your legs was reassuring, and I am sure by now you are even further improved. What I would like you to do, at our expense, is to pick up a civilian outfit. If you can buy the clothes you need in Bath, good; if not, you'd better run up to London and buy them there. You will want, for the most part, tropical lightweight stuff since the wind is up for us in the Far East. Though you will travel as a civilian, we are able to offer you a sort of quasi-diplomatic status, and some very good-looking papers and cards that will clear your way whenever there is a difficulty about priorities. I'm afraid that priorities will remain very much in the picture for the next six months or so. We are short of air-travel space as well as a number of other things. But, as I said before, we are very large wheels indeed, and we envisage no trouble in moving you wherever we desire to. That's a dreadful thing to say, isn't it, and it almost places you outside of the picture as a human being with any volition of your own. Believe me, Harry, like your charming British psychiatrist, I am combining irritation with love. No, I know how easy it would be for you to say No, and I also know that a sharp negative will be absolutely your first and instinctive reaction. By now, of course, simply reading my letter you have said No half a dozen times, and you have also asked yourself just who the devil your sister thinks she is. My dear, dear Harry, she is a person who loves you very much. How easy it would be for me to say to you, "Harry, please come home immediately to the warmth of our hearts and to the welcome of our open arms." All too easy, Harry, and as far as I can tell, thinking the matter through, it would do you absolutely no good. Even if we could persuade you to come back stateside, I am afraid that you would be bored to tears and frustrated beyond belief. I think that I can understand why you do not want to come home, and I think that at this moment in your existence, it is a very proper decision for you to make. That is to say, I agree with you: you should not come home; but, at the same time, you must have something to do. You may feel, Harry, that this messenger-boy business is not the most creative thing in the world, but I think that rather than attempt to explain to you in advance what we are up to and what you will encounter, you should allow yourself to be drawn into it. You need make no absolute commitments. You will see and you will understand more and more, and at any point along the way you are free to quit, to tell us to go to the devil—or to continue. The choice is always yours; you have no obligation and you are not tied down.

On the other hand, this is not to say that we do not very much want you to accept the assignment. I don't have to tell you what Mark's opinion of you is. You will remember—and believe me it has not changed—he shares my love for you, and you command his very great respect along with mine.

Harry, if you are able to accept my offer, cable me immediately. I would like you to be ready to move out in the next day or two after cabling.

Meanwhile, you have all our love and all our best and deepest and most sincere wishes and prayers for a complete recovery. I do love you very much, and I remain,

Your most devoted sister,
Jean.

3

By cable:

MRS. JEAN ARBALAID
WASHINGTON, D.C.
OCTOBER 19, 1945

THAT YOU SHOULD EVEN APOLOGIZE. I ACCEPT YOUR OFFER WITH UNEQUIVOCAL DELIGHT. ENTIRE OUTFIT AVAILABLE AT BATH WHERE THE MEN'S HABERDASHERY SHOPS ARE VERY GOOD INDEED. OUTFITTING UP LIKE A VERY PUKKA EAST INDIAN TYPE. READY TO LEAVE WHENEVER YOUR SPECIFIC INSTRUCTIONS ARRIVE. THIS IS THE FIRST TOUCH OF PLEASURE OR EXCITEMENT THAT I HAVE EXPERIENCED IN A GOOD MANY DREARY MONTHS. YOU AND MARK DEAR SISTER ADMIRABLE PSYCHOLO-GISTS. THANK YOU BOTH. LOVE AND KISSES. I AWAIT INSTRUCTIONS.

HARRY FELTON

By cable:

HARRY FELTON
BATH, ENGLAND
OCTOBER 21, 1945

THANK YOU HARRY AND OUR BLESSINGS WITH YOU. AIR TRANSPORT FROM LONDON AIRPORT ON 23 OCTOBER. SPECIAL PRIORITIES TO CALCUTTA INDIA. AT CALCUTTA PROCEED TO CALCUTTA UNIVERSITY AND SEE THE INDIAN ANTHROPOLOGIST PROFESSOR SUMIL GOJEE. QUESTION HIM. GET ALL DETAILS INDIAN CHILD SUPPOSEDLY STOLEN AND RAISED BY WOLVES VILLAGE OF CHANGA IN ASSAM. STORY ASSOCIATED PRESS REPORTER OCTOBER 9, 1945. ASSOCIATED PRESS STORY HAS PROFESSOR GOJEE DEEPLY INVOLVED. PLEASE GET ALL DETAILS AND WRITE FULL REPORT AS SOON AS POSSIBLE.

JEAN ARBALAID

4

By airmail:

Calcutta, India
November 4, 1945

Mrs. Jean Arbalaid
Washington, D.C.

My dear Sister:

First of all, I want you to know that I have taken your mission very seriously. I have never been contented with errand-boy status, as you will remember if you look back through the years of my life. Therefore, I decided to bring to the problem you set before me an observing eye, a keen ear, an astute mind, and all the skills of a poor lawyer. In any case, the mission has been completed, and I think that to some degree I have fallen in love with India. What a

121

strange and beautiful place it is, especially now in November! I am told that in the summer months it is very different and quite unbearable. But my experience has been of a congenial climate and of a people as hospitable and gentle as I have ever known.

I arrived in Calcutta and saw the Indian anthropologist, Professor Gojee. We had a number of meetings, and I discussed this case with him quite thoroughly. I found him charming, intelligent and very perceptive, and he has been kind enough to have me at his house for dinner on two separate occasions, and to introduce me to his family. Let me tell you, indeed let me assure you, my dear sister, that in Bengal this is no small achievement.

But before I go into my discussions with Professor Gojee and the conclusions we came to, let me give you the general background of the matter.

The original Associated Press story seems to have been quite accurate in all of its details—so far as I can ascertain—and I have done my detective work thoroughly and assiduously. I went personally to the small village of Changa in Assam. It is not an easy place to get to, and requires plane, narrow-gauge train and ox cart. At this time of the year, however, it was a fairly pleasant trip. The village itself is a tiny, rather wretched place, but in Indian terms it is by no means the worst place in the world. It has what very few Indian villages have, especially in this part of Bengal—a tiny schoolhouse. It also has a school-teacher and a number of people who are literate. This helps a great deal in the process of tracking down any historical data or events connected with the life and history of the village.

The village schoolmaster, whose name is Adap Chaterjee, was very helpful, since his English was excellent and since he knew all the participants in the particular event, and, indeed, was at the village when the child was originally lost. That was twelve years ago.

I am sure, Jean, that you know enough about India to realize that twelve is very much an adult age for a girl in these parts—the majority of them are married by then; and there is no question, none at all, about the age of the child. I spoke to the mother and the father, who originally identified the child by two very distinctive birthmarks. I saw these birthmarks myself in Calcutta, where the child is kept at the university. She has there at the university the best of care, kindness, and all the attention she demands. Of

122

course, at this moment we cannot say how long the university will be able to keep her.

However, everything the mother and father told me about the child in the village of Changa seemed to be entirely compatible with the circumstances. That is, wherever their stories and the statements of other villagers could be checked, this checking proved that they had been telling more or less the truth—considering, of course, that any truth loses some of its vividness over a twelve-year period.

The child was lost as an infant—at eight months—a common story in these parts. The parents were working in the field. The child was set down and then the child was gone. Whether the child crawled at that age or not, I can't say, nor can I find any witness who will provide that particular information. At any rate, all agree that the child was healthy, alert and curious—a fine and normal infant. There is absolutely no disagreement on that point.

Now, I know full well that most European and American scientists regard the whole mythology of a child being raised by wolves or some other animal under jungle conditions as an invention and a fiction. But a great many things that Western science has regarded as fiction are now proving to be at least the edge of a fact if not the fact itself. Here in India, the child raised in the jungle is regarded as one of the absolutes of existence. There are so many records of it that it seems almost impossible to doubt it. Nor, as you will see, is there any other conceivable explanation for this child.

How the child came to the wolves is something we will never know. Possibly a bitch who had lost her own cubs carried the infant off. That is the most likely story, isn't it? But I do not rule out entirely any act of animosity against the parents by another villager. The child could have been carried off and left deep in the jungle; but, as I said, we will never have the truth on this question.

These wolves here in Assam are not *lupus,* the European variety, but *pallipes,* its local cousin. *Pallipes* is nevertheless a most respectable animal in size and disposition, and not something to stumble over on a dark night. When the child was found, a month ago, the villagers had to kill five wolves to take her, and she herself fought like a devil out of hell. At that point, the child had lived as a wolf for eleven years. This does not mean, however, that *pallipes* is a vicious animal. I recall reading a book not too long ago concerning the Canadian variety of *lupus,* the wolf. The naturalist commented on the fact that *lupus,* raised with a family as a dog might be raised, is, contrary to common legend, even more dependable and gentler than almost any house dog. The same naturalist goes on to say that all of the stories of *lupus* running in packs, viciously tearing down his prey, killing his fellow wolf in wolf-to-wolf fights—that all of this is invention, and not very pleasant invention. This naturalist said that there are absolutely no cases of interpack fighting among wolves, that they do not kill each other, and that they have taught each other and taught their offspring as great a responsibility as can be found in any species.

Personally, I would include man in that statement. My being here on this mission has led me to do a great deal of investigation and reading on wolves, and it all comes down to the fact that at this moment Harry Felton is ready to regard the wolf as an animal quite equal to, if not superior to, man in all moral and ethical behavior—that is, if you are willing to grant ethics to a wolf.

To get back to the problem we have here—namely, the story of this child's life among the wolves—will the whole story ever emerge? I don't know. To all effects and purposes she is a wolf. She cannot stand upright, the curvature of her spine being beyond correction. She runs on all fours and her knuckles are covered with heavy calluses.

One day at the university, I watched her run. They had put a heavy leather belt around her waist. From it a chain extended to a cable which, in turn, was anchored high up on two opposite walls of a room about twenty feet wide. While I observed her, this time for a period of about fifteen minutes, she ran back and forth the length of the cable, on all fours, using her knuckles as front paws. She ran back and forth in that swaying, horrible, catatonic manner that a caged animal comes to assume.

My first reaction to this was that they were being unduly cruel. Later I learned better. The fact of the matter is that, if anything, they were overly tender, overly gentle and thoughtful with her. It is in the nature of the educated Indian to have enormous reverence for all forms of life. The people at the university combine such reverence with great pity for this child and her fate. If you will remember, my dear Jean, your readings in Buddhism—specifically in the type of Buddhism that is practiced in Bengal—you will recollect that it teaches, among other things, the doctrine of reoccurrence.

124

This means that this poor damned child is caught in an eternal wheel, destined to live this senseless, awful fate of hers over and over for eternity—or at least so they believe. And it evokes their great pity.

They have been trying for days to teach her to use her hands for grasping and holding, but so far unsuccessfully. We are very glib when we talk of what man has done with a thumb in opposition to four fingers; but I assure you that in so far as this wolf-child is concerned, the thumb in opposition to her four fingers is utterly meaningless. She cannot use her thumb in conjunction with her fingers, nor can she properly straighten her fingers or use them in any way for any kind of manipulation—even for the very simple manipulation that her teachers try to lead her into.

Did I mention that she must be naked? She tears off any clothes they dress her in, and there are times when she will attack her leather belt with a kind of senseless ferocity. They attempted to put a cloth sleeping pad in the room, but in this they were unsuccessful, since she promptly tore to pieces each pad they placed there. They were equally unsuccessful in their attempts to teach her to defecate in toilet or chamber pot; in fact, any puppy is more easily house-broken than this child. Eleven years have given her a rigidity of action—or a mechanicality, as the university people here prefer to call it—which appears to preclude any kind of training.

However, the people at the university do not despair, and they hope that in time she will be able to master at least some elements of civilized behavior.

At this point, however, she has not been able to grasp even the meaning of speech, much less make any progress herself in the art of conversation or communication. The problem of communication with this child is absolutely staggering.

The Indian anthropologist, Professor Sumil Gojee (the man you had been in communication with), is very highly regarded both here and in Bombay, where he has been a guest lecturer on one occasion or another. He is a social anthropologist, you know, and he is recognized as a great authority on village life in Bengal. He has been working with the wolf-child for a week now, and during the past four days he has been joined by Professor Armen Ranand from the University of Bombay. Both of them have been very kind to me and have given me unstintingly of their time, which I want you to know is an achievement on my part, since I was unable to explain to them in any coherent fashion just what you are up to and after. That comes back to the fact that I am entirely ignorant of what you are up to and after, and have been able only to guess and to form some rather silly theories of my own which I will not bore you with.

At this point, both men have little hope that any real communication will ever be possible. In our terms and by our measurements, the wolf-child is a total idiot, an infantile imbecile, and it is likely that she will remain so for the rest of her life. This prognosis of mental rigidity puzzled me, and I discussed it at some length with both Professor Gojee and Professor Ranand.

Our first discussion took place while we were observing the child in her room, which has become for the most part her habitat. Do not think that she is held prisoner there in some heartless manner. She is taken for walks, but that is not easy; she is a rather savage little animal, and a great many precautions must be taken every time she is removed from her room. The room is equipped with one of those mirrors that enable you to look into it without being perceived from the inside. The mirror is placed high enough on the wall not to bother the child, and so far as I know she has never become aware of either the mirror or its two-way quality. Watching her on this occasion, Professor Gojee pointed out to me that she was quite different from a wolf.

I said to him, "I would think that being so unhuman she would at least be wolflike in most ways."

"Not at all," Gojee replied. "In the first place, she is twelve years old, which is very old indeed for a wolf. Do you understand? She has spent a lifetime, a wolf lifetime among the wolves, during which her wolf companions have matured and, I imagine, in many cases gone to their deaths. She, however, remained through that period a child. Now you must not believe for a moment that she could have been unaware of her difference from the wolves. She was most aware of the difference, and indeed the wolves were also aware of this difference. The fact that they accepted her, that they fed her, that they took care of her, does not mean that they were foolish enough to mistake her for a wolf. No, indeed! They knew that they were dealing with a very nonwolf type of child; and I am inclined to believe that within the limitations of their mentality the wolves had some hazy notion that this was a human child. This could only have meant that she would be treated differently from the rest of the wolves, and the result of this different treatment would be a series of traumas. In other words, a wolf brought up in a normal wolf environment would, we could expect, be fairly free from neuroses. Now, this is probably a very silly use of terminology. We do not know whether neuroses exist among wolves, and we are not absolutely certain as to the nature of neuroses in the human being. However, we can with some certainty make a case for the neurosis of this child. Whether she is pathological, I am not certain, but certainly her emotional structure has been deformed beyond repair, and her intellectual powers have been stunted beyond belief and deprived of any ability to mature.''

"Then what exactly is she?" I asked him.

He turned to Dr. Ranand and, with a rather sad smile, repeated my question. Dr. Ranand, the professor from Bombay, shrugged his shoulders.

"How can I possibly answer that? She is not human; she is not a wolf. If we were to approach her in terms of her intelligence, then certainly we would say that she is closer to the wolves. But a wolf's intelligence is a completed thing; in other words, a wolf is just as intelligent as a wolf should be. Whether she is as intelligent as a wolf should be, I don't know. Presumably a wolf with her cranial capacity would be capable of a great deal of learning. She, on the other hand, is not capable of the kind of learning we would expect from this theoretical but non-existent wolf with a super-large cranial capacity. What, then, is the poor child? A human being? No, I don't think she is a human being. A wolf? Quite obviously she is not a wolf.'' His voice trailed away here. He looked at Professor Gojee helplessly.

"We can conclude this," Professor Gojee said, "she has been denied the opportunity to become a human being.''

The next day, a Dr. Chalmers, a British public-health officer, joined us for a period of observation. Like myself, he had been to the village of Changa, investigating her background. He bore out what I had learned there, that there was absolutely no history of imbecilism in her background. Afterwards, he was able to examine the child very carefully. I must say here, Jean, that in order for him to make this examination the child had to be put to sleep. Ether was used, and every care was taken. An anaesthetist from the General

127

Hospital here administered the anaesthesia—under difficult conditions, I will admit. Then the child was unchained and was taken to a medical examination room where Dr. Chalmers conducted his physical examination under the supervision of both Professor Gojee and Professor Ranand. He found absolutely no physical elements to account for the child's mental condition: no malformation of the cranial area and no signs of imbecilism. His findings bore out my own in Changa; that is, the fact that everyone in the village had attested to the normalcy—indeed, alertness and brightness—of the infant. Both Dr. Chalmers and Professor Gojee made a special point of the alertness and adaptability that the infant must have required to enable it to begin its eleven years of survival among the wolves. The child responds excellently to reflex tests, and neurologically, she appears to be sound. She is also strong—beyond the strength of most adults—very wiry, quick in her movements, and possessed of an uncanny sense of smell and hearing.

I watched while the doctor examined the wolf marks upon her—that is, the specific physical idiosyncrasies that were the result of her life among four-legged animals. Her spine was bent in a perpetual curvature that could not be reversed—even with an operation. Her calluses were well developed and most interesting; evidently she ran mostly, if not always, on all fours. Her teeth were strong and there were no signs of decay, although the incidence of tooth decay is rather high in the native village. While Dr. Chalmers is not a psychiatrist, his experience in the Public Health Service has been long and very varied; and, in his opinion, the prognosis for this child is not hopeful. Like Professor Gojee, he does not believe that she will ever progress to a point where she can master even the simplest use of language.

Professor Ranand believes that eventually the child will die. He has examined records of eighteen similar cases. These eighteen cases were selected from several hundred recorded in India during the past century. Of these several hundred recorded cases, a great many could be thrown aside as fiction. These eighteen cases Professor Ranand chose to study carefully were cases which he believed had been documented beyond a possibility of doubt. In every case, he says, the recovered child was an idiot in our terms—or a wolf in objective terms.

"But this child is not a wolf, is she?" I asked him.

"No, certainly not, by no means. The child is a human child."

"An imbecile?" I asked him. "Would you call the child an idiot? Would you call the child a moron? If you did, would you give her any number on the scale of intelligence we use?"

Professor Ranand was upset by this kind of thing and he brushed it aside, and he had some very harsh things to say about our Western methods of measuring intelligence.

"Of course the child is not an idiot," he said; "neither is the child an imbecile. You cannot call the child an imbecile any more than you would call a wolf an idiot or an imbecile because the wolf is not capable of engaging in human actions."

"But the child is not a wolf," I insisted.

"Of course not. We went over that before. The child is not a wolf, not by any means. Then you must ask what the child is and that, too, we have gone over before. It is impossible to state what this child is. This child is something that nature never intended. Now, to you, to you Westerners, this is a clinical point of view, but to us it is something else entirely. You do not recognize any such things as intentions on the part of nature. In so far as your Western science is concerned, nature moves blindly and mechanically with neither purpose nor intent nor direction. I think you have all driven yourselves into blind alleys with your concepts of the origin of the species. I am not arguing with Darwin's theories; I am only saying that your use of Darwin's theories has been as blind as your overall attitude toward the world and the life of the world."

Two days have passed since I wrote that section of my report which you have just read. Yesterday the wolf-child came down with some sort of amoebic dysentery. She seems entirely unable to fight the disease and she is obviously growing weaker. I will send you news as her condition changes.

Meanwhile, I am putting together all of the notes and the verbatim records of conversations that I have taken down concerning the wolf-child. When I have them in some proper and understandable form, I will send them to you. I don't know why this whole experience has depressed me as it has. My spirits were quite high when I arrived in India, and the whole business around this poor child has been, from my own selfish point of view, consistently interesting. At the same time, I made some good friends here, and the people at the university, the native Indian professors as well as the British here, could not have been kinder to me. I have every reason, my dear sister, for saying that I have enjoyed my stay in Bengal—but, at the same time, I feel a terrible sense of tragedy around this child, a sense of tragedy that goes far beyond her own pitiful fate and her own personal tragedy. Perhaps when I work this out in my mind, I will be able to turn it into something constructive.

In any case, be assured that I am your errand boy for as long as you desire. I am intrigued by this matter, and I spend the pre-sleep hour each night guessing what you are up to, what your purpose is, and what you and Mark have in those cunning little scientific minds of yours. I have made some absolutely fascinating guesses, and if you are very nice to me perhaps I will pass them on to you.

Love and kisses,
Harry.

5

By cable:

MRS. JEAN ARBALAID
WASHINGTON, D.C.
NOVEMBER 7, 1945

TODAY AT TWO O'CLOCK OUR TIME HERE THE WOLF-CHILD DIED. THE DIRECT CAUSE OF HER DEATH WAS THE DYSENTERY. THAT IS THERE WAS NO WAY TO STOP THE DEHYDRATION OF THE CHILD WHICH CONTINUED TO A POINT WHERE SHE COULD NO LONGER SUSTAIN HER LIFE. HOWEVER DR. CHALMERS WHO IS BY NO MEANS A MYSTIC BUT A VERY PRACTICAL BRITISH PRACTITIONER FEELS THAT ALMOST ANY INFECTIOUS DISEASE WOULD HAVE LED TO THE SAME RESULT. SHE HAD BEEN DIVESTED OF ANY DESIRE TO LIVE AND IN HER OWN WAY HAD BEEN IN VERY DEEP DEPRESSION SOMETHING I RECOGNIZE AND SYMPATHIZE WITH WHOLLY. I AM SENDING THIS CABLE COLLECT AND AM MAKING NO EFFORT TO ECONOMIZE WITH WORDS. I AM SURE YOU CAN AFFORD IT. WHAT NOW? I AWAIT WORD FROM YOU AT THE HOTEL EMPIRE CALCUTTA.

HARRY FELTON

130

By cable:

HARRY FELTON
HOTEL EMPIRE
CALCUTTA, INDIA
NOVEMBER 9, 1945

YOU HAVE DONE SUPERBLY HARRY AND WE ARE DEEPLY APPRECIATIVE. HOWEVER YOUR REPORTS ARE TOO MODEST. WE LOOK UPON YOU AS AN INTELLIGENT AND WELL-INFORMED PERSON AND WE ARE VERY EAGER FOR YOUR OWN REACTION. PLEASE REMAIN IN INDIA AT HOTEL EMPIRE FOR TIME BEING AND WRITE US IMMEDI-ATELY AIRMAIL YOUR REACTION TO THE CHILD AND YOUR EXPLANATION OF WHAT HAPPENED TO THE CHILD. THIS IS TO BE ABSOLUTELY YOUR OWN EXPLANATION AND IF POSSIBLE NOT TEMPERED OR BIASED IN ANY WAY BY THE SPECIALISTS YOU HAVE DISCUSSED THE CASE WITH.

JEAN ARBALAID

6

By airmail:

Calcutta, India
November 10, 1945

Mrs. Jean Arbalaid
Washington, D.C.

My dear Jean:

I am flattered by your interest in my opinion. On the other hand, I am not going to negate the value of such an opinion. I think I agree with you that professional people, specialists in one branch or another of the various sciences, tend to have a narrow point of view where they have either a background of experimental evidence or specific existing evidence upon which to base their assertions and conclusions. This is a very admirable and careful method in so far as it goes, but I am afraid it will achieve only what the facts at hand— that is, the provable facts—allow it to achieve.

131

I can guess that by now you have consulted every available specialist on the question of human children being raised by animals. I am sure you have discussed this thoroughly with the bigwigs at the National Geographic Society and with all the various specialists who know more about animals than the animals know about themselves. Do they all agree that no human child was ever reared by so-called beasts? Do they all agree that the whole thing is a sort of continuing invention, a fiction that each generation perpetuates to confuse itself? If they do, they are in agreement with your Western naturalists here in Calcutta. I have spoken to three of them—two Englishmen and a Frenchman—and they are all absolutely certain of the scientific and historical ground they stand on. The wolf-girl is a fraud; she was not raised by the wolves; she is an idiot child who ran away from the village and spent perhaps weeks, perhaps months, wandering in the forest, deranged and developing calluses where the calluses are. And the odd thing, my dear Jean, is that I cannot prove differently. So much for evidence.

Now, as to my own conclusion which you asked for: I told you in the previous letter that I had been deeply depressed by the incident of this child and by her condition. I have been attempting to understand the origin of this depression in myself and to deal with it—if only to repay an obligation and a promise to a skinny British psychiatrist who pulled me out of the doldrums back in Bath. I think I have found the source of the depression—a sort of understanding of what the girl was afflicted with. I believe she was afflicted simply with the loss of humanity. Now you have every right to say that the loss of humanity is a widespread disease that afflicts most of the human race; and there I cannot argue with you. But regardless of how much or often we turn into killers, mass murderers, sadists, etc., we seem always to preserve some sense of our origin, some link with our beginnings. We are at least recognizable as Homo sapiens. This child, poor thing, cut all her connections. She is no longer recognizable as Homo sapien. Having the form of a human being, she is less than a human being, less indeed than what nature intended her to be.

I am quite impressed by the outlook of Professor Gojee and his associates. I think I must agree with their opinion of Western science. The sad fact is that, while the East is ahead of us in many ways, they have lagged behind in scientific method and discoveries; and therefore, the great intuitive feelings that they have and which they incorporate into some of their religion, concerning the meaning and the destiny of mankind, have remained disassociated from any wide discipline of fact and investigation.

For myself, I tend to agree with them that there must be some purpose to human existence. I am hesitant to ascribe such purpose to the presence of God. I think that their definition and concept is as limited by our intelligence and as constrained by our outlook as most of our other theories. But, speaking only for myself, I have never been truly aware of the essence of humanity until I was present here at a case where humanity was extracted from a human being. We are too pat with our descriptions, designations and accusations of those whom we consider devoid of humanity. I don't really believe that anyone is devoid of humanity in the sense that this poor little wolf-child was. But then that leads me to another question. What is your human being? What is the essence of being human?

I have not been quick to embrace the all-encompassing theories of environment that have come out of the democratic movement of the nineteenth century. Too often I have felt that theories of environment have been used to prove political points and to make for political ammunition. At the same time, heredity is possibly less important than many people imagine it to be. I think that to create a human being, you need the presence, the society and the environment of other human beings. Directly to answer the question you put to me—What happened to the child?—I would say that she was deprived of her humanity. Certainly, she is not a human being, and neither is she a wolf. A wolf society can produce wolves; a human society can produce human beings. A human being trapped in a wolf society is a good deal less than a human being and perhaps not as much as a wolf. So I would say that this child occupied a sort of limbo on the scale, or in the current, of evolution. She is not a part of development; she is not a thing in herself; she is something that had been destroyed by a set of circumstances; she is a spoiled mechanism that continued to function in a limited sort of way. Do you find that a rather dreadful definition—a spoiled mechanism? Perhaps the word "mechanism" is wrong. Would a spoiled bit of life be better? I don't know, but there are my opinions for what they are worth.

I have found a charming young lady, Miss Edith Wychkoff by name, who is the daughter of the colonel of an old Indian regiment.

The whole thing is a cliché except that she is charming and blue-eyed, and will make the hours here, while I wait for your reply and for your instructions, much more endurable.

Please allow me to continue as your free-wheeling, theorizing errand boy. As the above demonstrates, my state of mind is infinitely better. I send my love to both of you, and await your reply.

Harry.

7

By cable:

HARRY FELTON
HOTEL EMPIRE
CALCUTTA, INDIA
NOVEMBER 14, 1945

THANK YOU FOR EVERYTHING HARRY. YOU HAVE DONE NOBLY AND YOUR CONCLUSIONS HAVE BEEN READ AND REREAD AND DISCUSSED SERIOUSLY AND WITH THE GREATEST OF INTEREST. A SIMILAR CASE HAS CROPPED UP IN PRETORIA UNION OF SOUTH AFRICA AT GENERAL HOSPITAL THERE UNDER DR. FELIX VANOTT. WE HAVE MADE ALL ARRANGEMENTS WITH AIR TRANSPORT AND YOU WILL BE WHISKED THERE BEFORE YOU CAN SAY JACK ROBINSON. DREADFULLY SORRY TO END ROMANCE WITH THE COLONEL'S DAUGHTER BUT IF YOU ARE VERY SERIOUS ABOUT IT AND DESPERATE TO CONTINUE IT WE WILL ARRANGE FOR YOU TO PICK IT UP LATER. MEANWHILE ON TO PRETORIA.

JEAN ARBALAID

8

By airmail:

Pretoria, Union of South Africa
November 18, 1945

Mrs. Jean Arbalaid
Washington, D.C.

134

My dear Sister:

You are evidently very big wheels, you and your husband, and I wish I knew just what your current experiment adds up to. I suppose that in due time you'll see fit to tell me. Meanwhile, my speculations continue.

But in any case, your priorities command respect. A full colonel was bumped, and I was promptly whisked away to South Africa, a beautiful country of pleasant climate and, I am sure, great promise.

I saw the child, who is still being kept in the General Hospital here; and I spent an evening with Dr. Vanott, an entire day at the hospital, and another evening with a young and attractive Quaker lady, Miss Gloria Oland, an anthropologist working among the Bantu people for her doctorate. Her point of origin is Philadelphia and Swarthmore College, so I was able to play upon all the bonds that unite countrymen (I will have something to say about that later). But I think that my acquaintance with Miss Oland has been fruitful, and, all in all, I will be able to provide you with a certain amount of background material.

Superficially, this case is remarkably like the incident in Assam. There it was a girl of twelve; here we have a Bantu boy of eleven (an estimate). The girl was reared by a variety of wolf; the boy in this case was reared by baboons—that is, supposing that here, as in India, we can separate fact from fiction, and come to a reasonable assumption that the child actually was stolen and reared by baboons. Let me say at this point that I have done some investigating, and I have been able to add to my notebook over twenty cases of African children stolen by baboons or by some other kind of baboonlike ape and reared by said baboons and apes. Now these cases are by no means researched; they have not been tracked down; they have not been proven: so along with their interest as background material must go the assumption that most, if not all of them, belong to the mythology. However, if I have been able to turn up this number of cases in so short a time, and by asking as few questions as I did and of as few people, then it seems to me that this kind of thing must be fairly widespread throughout South Africa. Even if the overwhelming majority of stories belong to the mythology, any such mythology must have some basis in fact, however small.

The child was rescued from the baboons by a white hunter, name of Archway—strong, silent type, right out of Hemingway. Unfortunately, unlike most of his fictional counterparts, this Ned Archway is a son of a bitch with a nasty temper and a thoroughgoing dislike for children. So when the boy understandably bit him—for which the boy can only be praised—the white hunter whipped the child to within an inch of his life.

"Tamed him," as Mr. Archway put it to me in one of the local bars over a tall mint julep. Archway is a thoroughgoing gentleman when he is with his betters, and, as much as I dislike that kind of talk, namely, "his betters," it is the only kind that fits. Back home, a sensitive person would catalogue Archway as poor white trash. I think that describes him better than several pages of words.

I asked him for some of the details of the capture and Archway swore me to silence, since evidently his actions were somewhat illegal. He loves to shoot baboons; it proves him "a target master," as he puts it.

"Shot twenty-two of the bloody beasts," he said to me.

"You're a very good shot," I said to him.

"Would have shot the black bastard too," he added. "However, he awakened my curiosity. Nimble little creature. You should have seen him go. You know, I have one of your jeeps—marvelous car, marvelous for the brush country, kind of car that might have been made for this part of Africa. Well, I was in the car and I had with me two of your American women, two of your very rich women— you know the type: brown as smoked goose, long legs drawn hard and thin, and just couldn't wait for the war to be over to get out here on safari. They enjoyed the chase no end. Ran the thing down in the jeep. You know, I don't think I would have ever gotten him if it weren't that the jeep threw a bad scare into him, and he froze. Animals do that, you know."

"He is not an animal," I ventured.

"Oh, of course he is. The Kaffirs are not so different from the baboons anyway, when you come right down to it."

This and a lot more. My conversation with the white hunter was not pleasant, and I don't enjoy repeating it.

May I say that at the hospital here they have a more humane, if not a more egalitarian, point of view. The child is receiving the very best of care and reasonable scientific affection. I asked them at the hospital whether there was any way to trace him back to his point of origin, that is, to his parents or to the village where he originated. They said No, there was no way at all of doing so, not in a thousand years. Evidently these Basutoland baboons are great travelers, and there is no telling where they picked up the child. It might be several hundred or a thousand miles away.

Putting his age at eleven years is a medical guess, but nevertheless reasonable. That he is of Bantu origin there is no doubt; and if I were to put him up as a physical specimen alongside of the white hunter, there is no doubt in my mind who would come out best. The child is very handsome, long-limbed, exceedingly strong, and with no indication of any cranial injury. His head is narrow and long, and his look is intelligent. Like the girl in Assam, he is—in our terms—an idiot and an imbecile, but there is nevertheless a difference. The difference is the difference between the baboon and the wolf. The wolf-child was incapable of any sort of vocalization. Did I mention that at moments of fear she howled? In her howling she was able to give an almost perfect imitation of a wolf's howl—that is, the howl of the local wolf whose habitat is Assam. Aside from this howl, her vocalization was limited to a number of wolf sounds—barks, whines and that sort of thing. Here we have something different indeed.

The vocalization of this eleven-year-old Bantu boy is the vocalization of a baboon. Strangely enough, at least here in Pretoria, there is no indication of any local scientific and serious work being done on the question of baboon vocalization. Again, all we have is a variety of opinion based on mythology. Some of the Kaffirs here will swear that the baboons have a language. Others claim to know a little of the baboon language, and I have had some of the Kaffir hunters make an assortment of sounds for me—after I had paid them well—and proceed to state their own interpretations of what these sounds meant. I think this is less a tribute to the speech abilities of the baboon than to the ingenuity of the local Kaffir when it comes to extracting money from a white man. Miss Oland pooh-poohs any suggestion that the baboons have a language, and I am inclined to go along with her.

There is one reasonably well informed naturalist at the local college with whom I had a short chat over the luncheon table. He, too, derides the notion that there is a language among the baboons. He raises an interesting point, however. He believes that the ability to talk is the motivating factor for man's becoming man, and he also believes that certain frontal sections of the brain are absolutely necessary before a species can engage in conversation. He says that the only species on earth that has any sort of conversational powers whatsoever is man, and he proceeded to break down for me various theories that bees and other insects and some of the great apes can talk to each other. He said that there is a very strong myth in gorilla country that the gorillas are able to talk to each other, but this, too, he rejects unconditionally.

He does admit that there is a series of specific sounds that the gorillas use; but these sounds are explosive grunts used entirely for situations of danger. Each and every one of these sounds relates to some area of fear, and my naturalist cannot include them in what we understand as language. He is willing to admit, however, that the baboons have a series of squeaks and grunts that may communicate, in addition to situations of fear, situations of affection. I am inclined to agree with this, for there seem to be some indications that this Bantu child will in time learn at least some elements of speech.

In that way he differs from the wolf-girl, and he also differs from her in that he is able to use his hands to hold things and to examine things. He also has a more active curiosity, but that, I am assured by the naturalist, is the difference between the wolf and baboon. The baboon is a curious creature, endlessly investigative, and he handles an endless number of objects. So the boy's curiosity and his ability to grasp things with his hands are an indication of his relationship to baboons, I think, more than an indication of his relationship to mankind.

As with the wolf-child, he too has a permanent curvature of the spine. He goes on all fours as the baboons do, and the backs of his fingers, specifically the area of the first knuckle joint, are heavily callused. After tearing off his clothes the first time, he accepted them. This too, is quite different from the case in India, and here again we have a baboon trait. Miss Oland told me of cases where baboons have been trained to wear clothing and to do remarkable tricks. Miss Oland has great hope for the boy's progress in the future, but Dr. Vanott, who has worked with him and tested him in the hospital, doubts that the child will ever talk. How much Dr. Vanott is influenced by local attitudes toward Negroes, I leave for you to decide. Incidentally, in those numerous reports of human children raised by animals, which Professor Ranand of Bombay

University professed to believe, there is no case where the child was able subsequently, upon being recovered and brought back into the company of human beings, to learn human speech.

So goes my childhood hero, Tarzan of the Apes, and all the noble beasts along with him. Poor Lord Graystroke. He would have been like this Bantu child—trembling with fear, never released from this fear, cowering into a corner of his cage, staring at his human captors with bewilderment and horror. Has it been said to you that animals do not experience fear in the sense that we human beings do? What nonsense! Fear appears to be woven into the fabric of their lives; and the thing that is most heartbreaking in both of these cases is the constant fear, the fear from which neither child was apparently free, even for a moment.

But the most terrifying thought evoked by this situation is this: What is the substance of man himself, if this can happen to him? The learned folk here have been trying to explain to me that man is a creature of his thought, and that his thought is, to a very large extent, shaped by his environment; and that this thought process— or mentation as they prefer to call it—is based on words. Without words, thought becomes a process of pictures, which is on the animal level and rules out all, even the most primitive, abstract concepts.

In other words, man cannot become man by himself: he is the result of other men and of the totality of human society and experience. I realize that I am putting this forward rather blandly, but it is all new to me; and newcomers tend to simplify and (as you would say, my dear sister) vulgarize a science of which they possess some small knowledge.

Yet my thinking was borne out to some degree during a very pleasant dinner I had with Miss Oland. It was not easy to get her to have dinner with me. You see, I don't think she liked me very much, although I am presuming to say that she likes me a little better now. But in the beginning, her attitude was very much shaped by my objective and somewhat cold investigative attitude toward what had happened to the little boy.

Miss Oland, may I say, is a very intelligent young lady, an attractive young lady, and a very devout Quaker. She takes her religion with great seriousness, and she lives it. It was a nice and perhaps constructive blow to my ego to realize that she looked down upon me with a mixture of dislike and pity. I think, however, that

Miss Oland and people like her look down upon most of the human race. I put this surmise of mine to her, and she denied it very hotly. In fact, she was so annoyed by the thought that I wonder whether she will agree to spend another evening with me.

However, there is no doubt in my mind but that people like Miss Oland occupy the role of the outsider. They watch the human race, without actually belonging to it. I have noticed this same attitude in a number of well-educated Jews I have met. But Miss Oland is the first Quaker with whom I ever discussed these things. I would hardly be surprised if her attitude were shared by other Quakers of sensitivity and thoughtfulness.

Miss Oland regards me as a barbarian—less a barbarian, of course, than such an obvious creature as the white hunter Ned Archway. But only by contrast with him do I become admirable, and at that only slightly admirable. As Miss Oland put it to me:

"You profess your superiority to the white hunter, Mr. Felton, and you look down on him as a rather uncivilized sort of man, but for what actually do you condemn him? For shooting the baboons for the fun of it or for beating the child?"

"For both," I replied.

"But he kills only animals, and surely the child will recover from the beating."

"And do you see virtue in killing animals for fun, as you put it?" I asked her.

"No virtue indeed, Mr. Felton, but I see less evil in it than in the slaughter of human beings."

"By that, just what do you mean, Miss Oland?"

"I mean that, like Ned Archway, you have been a hunter. You hunted men."

"What do you mean, I hunted men?"

"You told me you were an infantry captain, didn't you? What other purpose would an infantry captain have but the hunting down and the slaughter of human beings?"

"But that was different."

"How was it different, Mr. Felton?"

"My goodness, I don't have to go into all that, do I? You're not going to trap me with that old, old saw? You lived in the world that Adolf Hitler was remaking. You inhabited the same world that contained the concentration camps, the abattoirs, the gas ovens, the slaughter pits. How can you ask me such an absurd question?"

140

"Of course the question is absurd," she nodded. "Any question, Mr. Felton, becomes absurd when it is new to you or irritating to you or outside of your particular sphere of mental agreement. My question disturbed you; therefore, it becomes absurd."

"But surely you are not going to defend the Nazis."

"Now that indeed becomes rather absurd, doesn't it, Mr. Felton? You know that I would not defend the Nazis. How could you conceivably think that under any circumstances I would?"

"You're right. I could not conceivably think that. I admit it."

"I am not objecting, Mr. Felton, to your attitude toward the Nazis. I am simply objecting to your attitude toward killing. Obviously, you resent the pointless and witless killing of baboons, but you do not resent the equally pointless and witless slaughter of human beings."

"I like to think, Miss Oland, that I was fighting for the survival of human civilization and human dignity, and that whatever killing I was forced to do was neither thoughtless nor witless."

"Oh come now, Mr. Felton, we are both a little too old for that sort of thing, aren't we? Were you fighting for man's dignity? And by what process did you know that whatever German soldier you happened to kill was not equally aware of what was demanded by man's dignity? Did you know whether he opposed Hitler, if he did not oppose Hitler, how he agreed with Hitler or whether he agreed or disagreed with Hitler? You knew nothing of that; and certainly you knew enough of military structure to know that, like yourself, he had no choice but to face you and fight you."

"He could surrender," I said.

"Could he really, Mr. Felton? Now I am going to ask you a question. Did you shoot first and ask questions afterwards? Or did you ask questions first and shoot afterwards? I have never been on a battlefield, but I have a good imagination, and I have read many stories about what goes on on a battlefield. Could he have surrendered, Mr. Felton?"

"No," I admitted, "you're quite right. In most cases he couldn't have surrendered. There were cases where he could and maybe he did, but in most cases he could not have surrendered. Certainly, as an individual, he could not have surrendered. So you are absolutely right there, and I will not argue it. Nevertheless, I also will not relinquish my belief that there was a virtue in our cause in World

War II, a virtue in what we fought for and what so many of us died for."

"Then why don't you say that there was virtue in what you killed for, Mr. Felton?"

"I don't like to put it that way because I have never regarded myself as a killer."

"But the plain and naked fact of the matter, Mr. Felton, is that you are a killer. You have killed human beings, haven't you?"

"I have," I admitted weakly.

"I am not trying to pin you down to something nasty, Mr. Felton. I am not trying to derogate you, please believe me. It is only that no man takes any action without some sort of justification. He would go out of his mind if he did, wouldn't he? You ask me to prefer you to Mr. Archway, but I find that very hard to do. Really, I know this hurts you and I know I am not being polite, but from my point of view you and Archway inhabit the same world."

"And you don't inhabit that world, Miss Oland?" I wanted to know.

"No, not really. I am a Quaker, Mr. Felton. I think that my culture, the culture of my family, the culture of my people, has been different for many generations. We live among you but not with you. Your world is not our world. It really isn't, Mr. Felton, and you might do well to think about that. You seem very seriously interested in what has happened to this poor child. Maybe thinking about what I have just said would give you some clue as to what happens when a human child must live in a baboon's world."

"And at the same time," I said to her, "you have your little triumph and great, great satisfaction of righteousness."

She did not argue that point. "Yes," she said, "I suppose I am righteous, Mr. Felton. I wish I knew how to be otherwise, and perhaps in time I will learn. For the moment I am young enough to feel righteous and disgusted as well. You have no idea how frequently I am disgusted, Mr. Felton."

So, you see, I can fail her for politeness and score her very low as regards hospitality, she having been in Pretoria at least six months longer than I. At the same time, even though she is a woman I will not remember fondly, I have to admire her, and, in the last analysis, I have to admit that she was speaking the truth.

All of which leads me to ask some very pertinent questions, sister mine. The man raised by the wolf is no longer a man, and the man

142

raised by the baboons is no longer a man, and this fate is inevitable, isn't it? No matter what the man is, you put him with the apes and he becomes an ape and never very much more than that. My head has been swimming with all sorts of notions, some of them not at all pleasant. My dear sister, what the hell are you and your husband up to? Isn't it time you broke down and told old Harry, or do you want me to pop off to Tibet and hold converse with the lamas? I am ready for anything; I will be surprised by nothing, and I am prepared to go anywhere at all to please you. But, preferably, hand me something that adds up to a positive sum and then put a few words of explanation with it.

Your nasty killer brother,
Harry.

9

By airmail:

Washington, D.C.
November 27, 1945

Mr. Harry Felton
Pretoria, Union of South Africa

Dear Harry:

You are a good and sweet brother, and quite sharp, too. You are also a dear. You are patient and understanding and you have trotted around dutifully in a maze without trying to batter your way out.

Now it comes down to this Harry: Mark and I want you to do a job for us which will enable you to go here and there across the face of the earth, and be paid for it, too. In order to convince you, and to have your full cooperation and your very considerable creative abilities as well, we must spill out the dark secrets of our work—which we have decided to do, considering that you are an upright and trustworthy character. But the mail, it would seem, is less trustworthy; and since we are working with the Army, which has a constitutional dedication to top-secrecy and similar nonsense, the information goes to you via diplomatic pouch.

As of receiving this, that is, providing that you agree, you may consider yourself employed. Your expenses will be paid—travel, hotel and per diem—within reason, and there will be an additional eight thousand a year, less for work than for indulgence. In fact, as I write it down here, it makes so absolutely intriguing a proposition that I am tempted to throw over my own job and take yours instead.

So please stay put at your hotel in Pretoria until the diplomatic pouch arrives. I promise you that this will be in not more than ten days. They will certainly find you—that is, the diplomatic courier will.

Love, affection and respect,
Jean.

10

By diplomatic pouch:

Washington, D.C.
December 5, 1945

Mr. Harry Felton
Pretoria, Union of South Africa

Dear Harry:

Consider this letter the joint effort of Mark and myself. The thinking is ours and the conclusions are also shared. Also, Harry, consider this to be a very serious document indeed.

You know that for the past twenty years we have both been deeply concerned with child psychology and child development. There is no need to review our careers or our experience in the Public Health Service. Our work during the war, as part of the Child Reclamation Program, led to an interesting theory, which we decided to pursue. We were given leave by the head of the service to make this our own project. The leave is a sort of five-year sabbatical, with the option given to us at the end of five years to extend the leave for five years more, and a third five years then, if necessary. Recently, we were granted a substantial amount of Army funds to work with. In return for this, we have agreed to put our findings at the disposal of the Government.

Now to get down to the theory, which is not entirely untested. As you know, Mark and I have behind us two decades of practical work with children. When I say practical, I cover a good deal of ground. Since we are both physicians, we have worked with children as pediatricians. We have done hospital work with children. We have operated on children as surgeons; and, under certain conditions (as for example, during emergencies in the early years of the war), we have pioneered surgical work with children simply because we were placed in a position which left us no other choice. From this vast experience, we have come to some curious conclusions. I would put it better if I said that we have come to a great many conclusions, but have now focused our interest on one conclusion in particular, namely this: Mark and I have come to believe that within the rank and file of Homo sapiens is the beginning of a new race.

Call this new race "man-plus"—call it what you will. The people who constitute this new race of men are not of recent arrival; they have been cropping up among men—Homo sapiens, that is—for hundreds, perhaps for thousands, of years. But they are trapped in the human environment; they are trapped in the company of man, and they are molded by the company of man and by the human environment as certainly and as implacably as your wolf-girl was trapped among the wolves or your Bantu child among the baboons. So, you see, the process is quite certain.

Everything that you discovered in Assam and in South Africa tended to bear out our own conclusions. Just as the little Assamese girl was divested of her humanity, deprived of her membership in the human race, by being reared among the wolves, so is our theoretical man-plus deprived of his racehood, of his normal plus-humanity, by living among men. Perhaps your Bantu boy would be a closer parallel to what we mean. I will not at this point try to explain more fully. Later on in this letter we will go into other details of our theory; and if you agree to work with us, as your work progresses, so will your understanding of exactly what we are after.

By the way, your two cases of animal child-rearing are not the only attested ones we have. By sworn witness, we have records of seven similar cases: one in Russia, two in Canada, two in South America, one in West Africa and, just to cut us down to size, one in the United States of America. This does not mean that all seven of these cases are wholly authenticated. If we were to turn to each in succession and apply to it the kind of severe interviewing and testing that you have applied to the two cases you investigated, we might find that of the seven cases perhaps all are fictional, perhaps one is based on reality, perhaps all are based on reality. We might come to any one of these conclusions. *A priori,* we are not able to do more than accept the facts and apply to these facts our own judgment.

You may add to this the hearsay and folklore of three hundred and eleven parallel cases which cover a period of fourteen centuries. We have in fifteenth-century Germany, in the folio manuscript of the monk Hubercus, five case histories he claims to have observed personally. In all these cases, in the seven cases witnessed by people alive today, and in all but sixteen of the hearsay cases, the result is more or less precisely what you have seen and described yourself; that is, the child reared by the wolf is divested of humanity.

We have yet been unable to find a case, mythological or otherwise, in which the child reared by the wolf is able subsequently to learn man's speech. Mythology adds up to a little—of course, very little. But speaking in mythological terms, we can find over forty such cases that survived from great antiquity in the mythologies of one nation or another.

But of course, Harry, we are not attempting to prove that animals can rear a human child, or that human children have been so reared, or that any of the facts connected with human children so reared are true. We are merely attempting to use these cases of the rearing of human children by animals as indications of what may face superior-man reared by man. You see, our own work adds up to the parallel conclusions: the child reared by a man is a man. And what is a man? In the broadest historical sense, a man is a creature who builds social organizations, the major purpose of such organizations being man's own destruction. If what I have just written were an ethical or moral judgment, it could certainly be challenged and perhaps successfully; however, it is not by any means a judgment; it is simply an historical conclusion. If one examines the history of man with total objectivity, one can only come to the conclusion that man's existence as a social being has been mainly for the purpose of war. All that he has achieved, all that he has built, has been achieved and has been built in the intervals between wars, thereby creating a social organism that can function during a war and in the act of war. This is by no means a judgment, nor is it an historical observation upon man as an individual. Man as an individual would have to be described quite differently. But we must not for one moment forget that we have just come through a holocaust that has consumed fifty million human lives. I refer to World War II, in which we all played our parts. We have now calculated that the toll of human life internationally in World War II was above fifty million men, women and children. This is larger than the entire human population of the earth at the time of the Roman Empire. We are used to large numbers today; it puts a little different light on the figure when we observe to ourselves that we have just succeeded in destroying in a period of less than five years more human beings than existed upon the entire face of the earth two thousand years ago. That is one to think about, isn't it, Harry? But the observation—the historical observation of the role of man—is made here in a purely clinical sense and in terms of man-plus.

You see, if man-plus exists, he is trapped and caged as certainly as any human child reared by animals is caged. In the same way the incipient man-plus is divested of whatever his potential is. The wolf dealing with our little Assamese girl would hardly be able to calculate or even to guess what she might have been in her own civilization. The wolf can only see her as the product of a wolf society. If man-plus exists, we see him and we have always seen him as a product of man's society. Of course, we have no proof that he exists. We have simply created a supposition that he exists, and we have enough evidence at our disposal for us to support this proposition. This of course, is a usual procedure among scientists. Einstein's conception of the shape of the universe and of the curvature of light was hypothetical to begin with; it originated as a creative idea. After he had formulated the hypothesis, he set about proving it in physical terms. And we shall follow a similar method.

Why do we think the super-child exists? Well, there are many reasons, and we have neither the time nor the space here to go into all of them, or into much detail. However, here are two very telling and important reasons:

Firstly, we have gathered together the case histories of several hundred men and women who as children had IQ's of 170 or above. Since these men and women are now adults, their testing goes back to the early days of the Binet-Simon method, and it is by no means reliable—that is if any intelligence testing, any system of IQ, is reliable. We do not operate on the presumption that IQ testing has any objective reliability; we simply use it as a gauge and in lieu of anything better. In spite of the enormous intellectual promise as

147

children of these several hundred men and women, less than ten percent have succeeded in their chosen careers. Considering how small the whole group is, their record of disaster and tragedy deserves attention in itself.

Another ten percent, roughly speaking, have been institutionalized as mental cases beyond recovery—that is, as pathological cases on the path to disintegration. About fourteen percent of the group have had or now require therapy for mental health problems; in this fourteen percent, roughly half have been in psychoanalysis or are in psychoanalysis or some similar therapy. Nine percent of the group have been suicides. One percent are in prison. Twenty-seven percent have had one or more divorces, nineteen percent are chronic failures at whatever they attempt—and the rest are undistinguished in any important manner. That is to say, they have not achieved even nominal success in the lines of endeavor they finally chose to follow. All of the IQ's have dwindled—and the dwindling of these IQ's, when graphed, bears a relationship to age. About four percent of the group studied have gone under the hundred or normal mark and are now in the condition of social morons.

Since society has never provided the full potential for such a mentality—that is, a mentality such as this group seemed to have had as children—we are uncertain as to what this potential might be. We have no valid, provable reasons to imagine that this group or a similar group would achieve more under other conditions; but against that we have every reason of logic and common sense to suppose. Our guess is that this group has been reduced to a sort of idiocy, an idiocy that puts them on the level with what we call normalcy. But having been put on that level, they could not become men any more than your Assamese child could become a wolf. Unable to live out their lives, unable to become men, they were simply divested of their destiny, biological and otherwise, and in that sense destroyed. So much for the first reason, Harry.

The second reason we put forward is this: we know that man uses only a tiny part of his brain. Extensive testing enables us to put this forward as a provable fact, but we have no idea what blocks the human ego from using the rest of the human brain. We have to ask why nature has given man equipment that he cannot put to use—not atrophied equipment such as the appendix, but equipment that marks or is definitive of the highest life form ever produced by evolution. We must ask why nature has done this. We must also ask whether society, human society, prevents human beings from breaking the barriers that surround their own potential. In other words, have human beings themselves created a cage which prevents them from ever being more than human beings?

There, in brief, are the two reasons I spoke about before. Believe me, Harry, there are many more—enough for us to have convinced some very hard-headed and unimaginative Government people that we deserve a chance to release super-men. Of course, history helps— in its own mean and degraded manner. It would appear that we are beginning another war, this time with Russia; a cold war, as some have already taken to calling it. Among other things, it will be a war of intelligence—a commodity in rather short supply these days, as some of our local mental giants have been frank enough to admit.

Our new breed of computer warriors licked their lips when we sounded them out. They can't wait to have at another blood bath with all their new gimmicks; they have fed their tapes into the machines, and they have come out with new and enticing methods of human destruction. They look upon our man-plus as a secret weapon, little devils who will come up with death rays and super-atom-bombs and all sorts of similar devices when the time is ripe. Well, let them think that way. It is inconceivable to imagine a project like ours, a project so enormous and so expensive, under benign sponsorship. The important thing is that Mark and I have been placed in full charge of the venture—millions of dollars, top priority, the whole works. We are subject to no one; we must report to no one; we have complete independence. We can requisition what we wish within reason, and we have a long period of time— that is, five years with an extension of an additional five years, and the very real possibility of another extension after that.

But nevertheless, Harry, the project is secret. I cannot stress this enough. This secrecy is not simply the childish classification business that the Army goes into; we support them on the question of secrecy. It is as important to us as to the Army, and I simply cannot stress this sufficiently or make it sound more serious than it actually is.

Now, as to your own job—that is, if you want it. And somehow or other, at this point I cannot envision you saying No. The job will develop step by step, and it is up to you to make it. First step: in

Berlin, in 1937, there was a Professor Hans Goldbaum. He was half Jewish. He lectured on child psychology at the university, and he was also the head of the Berlin Institute for Child Therapy. He published a small monograph on intelligence testing in children, and he put forward claims—which we are inclined to believe—that he could determine a child's IQ during its first year of life, in its pre-speech period. The use of the term "IQ" is mine, not his. Professor Goldbaum had no use for the intelligence-quotient system that was developed by the Binet-Simon people, and he rejected it entirely. Instead, he devised his own method of intelligence testing, a very interesting method indeed.

He presented some impressive tables of estimations and subsequent checked results; but we do not know enough of his method to practice it ourselves. In other words, we need the professor's help.

In 1937, Professor Goldbaum vanished from Berlin. All of our efforts, combined with the very generous investigatory help of Army Intelligence, have convinced us that he was not murdered by the Nazis but that in some manner he escaped from Berlin. In 1943, a Professor Hans Goldbaum, either the same man in whom we are interested or someone of the same name, was reported to be living in Cape Town. This is the last address we have for him, and I am enclosing the address herewith. Now, as for you, Harry, here goes your job. You should leave for Cape Town immediately. Somehow or other, find the Professor Goldbaum reported to be in Cape Town. Find out whether he is our Professor Goldbaum. If he is not there, but has left, then follow him. Follow him wherever he has gone. Find him. I am not telling you how and, in turn, I do not expect you to ask us how. It is up to you. Find him! Naturally, all expenses will be paid. Of course, he may be dead. If that is the case, inform us immediately.

At this point I am no longer asking whether or not you will take the job. Either you will take it or I cease to be your sister, and I will curse your name and strike it out of all the family journals, etc. We love you and we need your help; in fact, we need it desperately, and at this moment I know of no one else who could substitute for you.

Jean.

11

By airmail:

Cape Town, South Africa
December 20, 1945

Mrs. Jean Arbalaid
Washington, D.C.

My dear Sister:

I could write a book about my week in Cape Town. This is a city I am not in love with, and if I get out of here alive I have no desire to return ever. The days have been very interesting indeed, as you will see, and the nights have been occupied with nightmares about your hare-brained scheme for super-man. Instead of sleeping peacefully, I dream of rows of little devils preparing all sorts of hideous death rays for your Army partners. What are you up to? No, I am not quitting. I am not walking out. A job is a job, and I remain your faithful employee.

Let me tell you something about the professor. Evidently, in one way or another he was important to the Nazis—that is, important enough for them to desire to eliminate him. There was a very considerable organization of the Nazi bully boys here in Cape Town when the war began, and they had Herr Goldbaum on their list. A few days after he arrived, an attempt was made on his life. He received a superficial bullet wound, but it became infected and he had a rather bad time of it. The Jewish community took care of him and hid him, but then things got a little hot, and they turned him over to some friends they had in the Kaffir compound. I was following the trail, an old and stale trail, but one that became the path of duty and all that. Leave it to your brilliant brother Harry. I did not meet up with any revanchist Nazis who had survived the war and were hiding out for *der Tag,* whenever it might come. No indeed. I simply followed this cold trail into the Kaffir compound, and thereby was picked up by the police and tossed into jail. They had me tagged for a Communist; can you imagine? I thought that just about everything had happened to me, but this was it. It took two days of argument and the efforts of the American Consul General as well, to prove that I was the very conservative and rather thoughtless brother of one of our most eminent Americans. I am a little tired

151

of the weight your name carries, but thank heavens it carried enough weight to take me out of one of the most uncomfortable jails I have ever occupied or ever read about. It was crawling with bugs—huge, terrifying South African bugs.

After I got out of jail, I did the sensible thing that I should have done in the beginning. I sought an interview with the head of the Jewish community here, a Rabbi Anatole Bibberman. Bibberman, it seems, is an amateur Assyriologist—and, if I do not make myself entirely plain, Assyriologists are a small group who devote their spare time to the study of ancient Assyria. I imagine a good many of them devote full time to the subject and become pros. Rabbi Bibberman, however, is a spare time Assyriologist; and it turns out that Professor Goldbaum shared his interest. They spent long hours, I am told, discussing ancient Assyria and Babylon and things of that sort.

The Rabbi told me something that he thought everyone knew— that is, everyone who is interested in Professor Goldbaum. He told me that in 1944 the people in London (and by people I suppose he meant scientists or physicians or something of that sort) discovered that Professor Goldbaum was holed up in Cape Town. They needed him for something or other, and he took off for London. I am leaving for London myself as soon as I finish this letter, and goodbye to Cape Town. As you plan my itinerary for the future, I would appreciate your eliminating Cape Town from the list.

Your ever-loving brother,
Harry.

12

By cable:

MRS. JEAN ARBALAID
WASHINGTON, D.C.
DECEMBER 25, 1945

PERHAPS YOUR TRUST MISPLACED SINCE I TAKE GLEEFUL AND CHILDISH PLEASURE IN SENDING LONG LONG CABLES COLLECT WHICH THE UNITED STATES ARMY PAYS FOR. LIKE ANY OTHER MAN WHO HAS SERVED ANY LENGTH OF TIME IN THIS HIDEOUS WAR WE HAVE JUST

FINISHED I SEEM TO HAVE AN UNSHAKABLE BIAS AGAINST
THE UNITED STATES ARMY. BE THAT AS IT MAY I HAVE
FOUND THE PROFESSOR. IT WAS ABSURDLY EASY AND IN
A LETTER TO FOLLOW I WILL GIVE ALL THE DETAILS. HE IS
A CHARMING AND DELIGHTFUL LITTLE MAN AND LAST
NIGHT I TOOK HIM FOR A CHRISTMAS EVE DINNER TO
SIMPSON'S. IT TURNED OUT THAT HE IS A VEGETARIAN.
CAN YOU IMAGINE A VEGETARIAN AT SIMPSON'S ON
CHRISTMAS EVE? I SUPPOSE AT THIS POINT I SHOULD PUT
IN A STOP JUST TO INDICATE THAT I AM QUITE AWARE
THAT I AM SENDING YOU A CABLE BUT I HAVE HEARD IT
TOLD ON RELIABLE AUTHORITY THAT THE NEW YORK
TIMES REPORTERS CABLE THOSE ENDLESS STORIES OF
THEIRS IN FULL AND NOT IN CABLESE SO I PRESUME OF
THIS TIDBIT. MAY I SAY THAT THE PROFESSOR IS IN-
TRIGUED BY THE LITTLE I HAVE TOLD HIM. I DID NOT
KNOW HOW MUCH TO TELL HIM OR HOW HARD TO PUSH.
JUST WHAT DO YOU WANT ME TO DO WITH HIM? WHAT
SHALL I ASK HIM? WHAT SHALL I TELL HIM? YOU CAN SEE
THAT SINCE THIS IS A PUBLIC CABLE I AM USING
GUARDED CIRCUITOUS AND SOMETIMES RATHER SILLY
LANGUAGE. I TRUST YOU UNDERSTAND ME MY DEAR
JEAN. WHAT NOW?

HARRY FELTON.

13

By diplomatic pouch:

Washington, D.C.
December 26, 1945

Mr. Harry Felton
London, England

Dear Harry:

While I am delighted that your spell of depression has disappeared,
you are beginning to worry me just a wee bit with your silliness. I
try to remember whether you were always as light-headed as you

now appear to be, and I keep telling myself and Mark that the war has changed you. In any case, you are our man on the spot, and we must go along with you. The truth is, I'm teasing. We do trust you, dear, but please be more serious. Our project is dead serious. We believe that despite protestations of your own limitations, you have enough sense and good instincts to gauge Professor Goldbaum's method. Talk to him. Unless you believe he is a complete fraud—and from the little you say, I doubt that—we want you to sell him on this venture. Sell him! We will give him whatever he asks—that is, in the way of financial remuneration. A man like Professor Goldbaum, according to all my past experience with such men, should be more or less indifferent to money; but even if he is, Harry, I want you to set his fee and to set it generously. We want to make an arrangement whereby he will continue to work with us for as long as we need him. If it must be less than that, try to specify some contractual terms, at least a year. As far as his future is concerned, I repeat that we are able to take care of his future; we will take care of it financially, and we will take care of it in terms of citizenship. If he desires American citizenship, we can arrange that with no trouble whatsoever. If he wishes to continue as a British national—I presume that is his status now—then we will smooth the way. No difficulty will be encountered.

I am sure that when you discuss the matter with him he will have a number of questions of his own, and he will desire to be enlightened more fully than we have enlightened you. Perhaps we should have briefed you more completely before now; but the truth of the matter is that we had not yet completed our own preparations, nor were we exactly decided on what our procedure would be. At this point we are.

We have been allocated a tract of eight thousand acres in northern California. The eight thousand acres are very attractive. There is a stand of sequoia forest, a lovely lake, and some very beautiful and arable meadowland. There is also a stretch of badland. All in all, it is a variegated and interesting landscape. Here we intend to establish an environment which will be under military guard and under military security. In other words, we propose to make this environment as close to a self-contained world as perhaps ever existed. In the beginning, in the first years of our experiment, the outside world will be entirely excluded. The environment will be exclusive and it will be controlled as absolutely as anything can be controlled within the present world and national situation.

Within this environment, we intend to bring forty children to maturity—to a maturity that will result in man-plus. But please understand, Harry, and convey this to the professor, that when I state something as a positive I am proceeding on a theoretical hypothesis. Man-plus does not exist and may never exist. We are making an experiment based on a presumption. Always come back to that, Harry; never talk as if we were dealing with certainties.

As to the details of the environment—well, most of it will have to wait. I can tell you this: We shall base its functioning on the highest and the gentlest conclusions of man's philosophy through the ages. There is no way to put this into a few sentences. Perhaps I might say that instead of doing unto others as we would have them do unto us, we will attempt to do not unto others as we would not have them do unto us. Of course that says everything and anything, and perhaps nothing as well; but in due time we will tell you the details of the environment as we plan it, and the details of its functioning. The more immediate and important problem is finding the children. We need a certain type of child—that is, a superior child, a very superior child. We would like to have the most extraordinary geniuses in all the world; but, since these children are to be very young, our success in that direction must always be open to question. But we are going to try.

As I said, we intend to raise forty children. Out of these forty children, we hope to find ten in the United States of America; the other thirty will be found by the professor and yourself—outside of the United States.

Half are to be boys. We want an even boy-girl balance, and the reasons for that, I think, are quite obvious. All of the children are to be between the ages of six months and nine months, and all are to show indications of an exceedingly high IQ. As I said before, we would like to have extraordinary geniuses. Now, you may ask me how, how is this location of infant genius going to work? Well, Harry, there's where the professor comes into the picture, as your guide and mentor. How we are going to accomplish the problem at home, we have not fully worked out. But we believe that we have some methods, some hints, some directions that will ultimately lead us to success. In your case, we are depending upon the professor's method—that is, if his method is any good at all. If it is not—well, there are a dozen points where we can fail, aside from his methods.

We want five racial groupings: Caucasian, Indian, Chinese, Malayan and Bantu. Of course, we are sensible to the vagueness of these groupings, and you will have to have some latitude within them. As you know, racial definitions are at worst political and at best extremely imprecise. If you should find, let us say, three or four or five Bantu children who impress you as extraordinary, naturally we want to include them. Again, when we say Bantu we are not being literal. You may find in South Africa a Hottentot child who commands your attention. By all means include the Hottentot child.

The six so-called Caucasian infants are to be found in Europe. We might suggest two Northern types, two Central European types and two Mediterranean types; but this is only a suggestion and by no means a blueprint for you to follow. Let me be more specific: If you should by any chance find seven children in Italy, all of whom are obviously important for our experiment, you must take all seven children, even though only six children are suggested from Europe.

Now the word "take" which I have just used—understand this: no cops and robbers stuff, no OSS tactics, no kidnapping. If you find the most marvelous, the most extraordinary, infant of your entire search, and the parents of that infant will not part with it, that ends the matter right there. This is not simply an ethical point that I am raising, Harry. This is integral to the success of our program, and I think that in time you will understand why.

Now, where will the children come from? We are going to buy children. Let us be brutally frank about it. We are in the market for children. Where will they come from? Unfortunately for mankind but perhaps fortunately for our narrow purpose here, the world abounds with war orphans—and also in parents so poor, so desperate, that they will sell their children if the opportunity arises. When you find a child in such a situation and you want the child and the parents are willing, you are to buy. The price is no object. Of course, I must add here that you should exercise a certain amount of common sense. When I say price is no object, I mean that if you have to pay a hundred thousand or a hundred and fifty thousand dollars for a child, you are to pay the price. If, on the other hand, a price is in the neighborhood of a million dollars, you are to think it

156

over very carefully. This is not to say that we will not pay as high as a million dollars if the necessity arises; but at that price, I want you to be very certain of what you are doing. We have enormous backing and an enormous amount of money to work with; but regardless of how enormous our resources are at this moment, they are going to be spent eventually, and there are limitations. I am afraid that we must work within these limitations.

However, I will have no maudlin sentimentality or scruples about acquiring the children, and I would like you and the professor to share my point of view. We are scientists, and sentimentalism rarely advances science; also, in itself, I find sentimentalism a rather dreadful thing. Let me state emphatically that these children will be loved and cherished as much as it is possible for those who are not blood parents to love and cherish children; and in the case of these children that you acquire by purchase, you will be buying not only a child but, for that child, a life of hope and promise. Indeed, we hope to offer these children the most wonderful life that any child could have.

When you find a child that you want and you are ready to acquire that child, inform us immediately. Air transport will be at your disposal. We are also making all arrangements for wet nurses—that is to say, if you find a nursing infant who should continue to nurse, we will always have wet nurses available. Rest assured that all other details of child care will be anticipated. We will have a staff of excellent pediatricians whom you can call on anywhere on earth. They will fly to where you are.

On the other hand, we do not anticipate a need for physicians. Above all things, we want healthy children, of course within the general conditions of health in any given area. We know that an extraordinary child in certain regions of the earth may well have the most discouraging signs of poor health, undernourishment, etc. But I am sure that you and Professor Goldbaum will be able to measure and assess such cases.

Good luck to you. We are depending on you, and we love you. We do wish that you could have been here with us for Christmas Day; but, in any case, a Merry Christmas to you, and may the future bring peace on earth and good will to all men.

Your loving sister,
Jean.

14

Copenhagen, Denmark
February 4, 1946

Mrs. Jean Arbalaid
Washington, D.C.

Dear Jean:

I seem to have caught your top-secret and classified disease, or perhaps I have become convinced that this is a matter wanting some kind of secrecy. That seems hard to believe in such a down-to-earth, practical and lovely place as Copenhagen. We have been here for three days now, and I am absolutely charmed by the city and delighted with the Danes. I set aside today, in any case a good part of today, to sum up my various adventures and to pass on to you whatever conclusions and opinions might be of some profit to you.

From my cables, you will have deduced that the professor and I have been doing a Cook's Tour of the baby market. My dear sister, this kind of shopping spree does not set at all well with me; however, I gave my word, and there you are. I will complete and deliver. I might add that I have also become engrossed with your plans, and I doubt that I would allow myself to be replaced under any circumstances.

By the way, I suppose I continue to send these along to Washington, even though your "environment," as you call it, has been established? I will keep on doing so until otherwise instructed.

As you know, there was no great difficulty in finding the professor. Not only was he in the telephone book, but he is quite famous in London. He has been working for almost a year now with a child reclamation project, while living among the ruins of the East End, which was pretty badly shattered and is being reclaimed only slowly. He is an astonishing little man, and I have become fond of him. On his part, he is learning to tolerate me.

I think I cabled to you how I took him to dinner at Simpson's only to learn that he was a vegetarian. But did I say that you were the lever that moved him, my dear sister? I had no idea how famous you are in certain circles. Professor Goldbaum regarded me with awe, simply because you and I share a mother and a father. On the other hand, my respect for unostentatious scientific folk is growing. The second meeting I had with Dr. Goldbaum took place on the terrace of the House of Commons. This little fellow, who would be lost so easily in any crowd, had casually invited three Members of Parliament and one of His Majesty's Ministers to lunch with us. The subject under discussion was children: the future of children, the care of children, the love of children and the importance of children.

Whatever you may say about the Government here, its interest in the next generation is honest, moving, and very deep and real. For the first time in British history, the average Englishman is getting a substantial, adequate and balanced diet. They have wonderful plans and great excitement about the future and about children's role in the future. I think it was for this purpose (to hear some of the plans) that Goldbaum invited me to be there. I am not sure that he trusts me—I don't mean this in a personal sense, but rather that I, being simply what I am, and he, being a sensitive man who recognizes what I am—well, why should he trust me? In that sense, he is quite right not to trust me.

At this lunch he drew me into the conversation, explaining to the others that I was deeply interested in children. They raised their eyebrows and inquired politely just where my interest derived from and where it was directed.

Believe me, my only claim to a decent standing in the human race was the fact that I was Mrs. Jean Arbalaid's brother; and when they heard that I was your brother their whole attitude toward me changed. I passed myself off as a sort of amateur child psychologist, working for you and assisting you, which is true in a way, isn't it? They were all very polite to me, and none of them questioned me too closely.

It was a good day, one of those astonishing blue-sky days that are real harbingers of spring, and that come only rarely in London in February. After the luncheon, the professor and I strolled along Bird Cage Walk, and then through Saint James's Park to the Mall. We were both relaxed, and the professor's uncertainty about me was finally beginning to crumble just a little. So I said my piece, all of it, no holds barred. To be truthful, I had expected your reputation to crumble into dust there on the spot, but no such thing. Goldbaum listened with his mouth and his ears and every fiber of his being. The only time he interrupted me was to question me about the Assamese girl and the Bantu boy; and very pointed and meticulous questions they were.

"Did you yourself examine the child?" he asked me.

"Not as a doctor," I replied, "but I did examine her in the sense that one human being can observe another human being. This was not a calm little girl, nor was the Bantu boy a calm little boy; they were both terror-stricken animals."

"Not animals," Goldbaum corrected me.

"No, of course not."

"You see," Goldbaum said, "that point is most important. Animals they could not become; they were prevented, however, from becoming human beings."

There he hit upon the precise point that I had come to and which Professor Gojee had underlined so often. When I had finished with my whole story, and had, so to speak, opened all my cards to Professor Goldbaum's inspection, he simply shook his head—not in disagreement, but with sheer excitement and wordless delight. I then asked him what his reaction to all this was.

"I need time," he said. "This is something to digest. But the concept, Mr. Felton, is wonderful—daring and wonderful. Not that the reasoning behind it is so novel. I have thought of this same thing; so many anthropologists have thought of it. Also, throughout the ages it has been a concept of many philosophies. The Greeks gave their attention to it, and many other ancient peoples speculated upon it. But always as an imaginative concept, as a speculation, as a sort of beautiful daydream. To put it into practice, young man—ah, your sister is a wonderful and a remarkable woman!"

There you are, my sister, I struck while the iron was hot, and told him then and there that you wanted and needed his help, first to find the children and then to work in the environment.

"The environment," he said. "You understand, that is everything, everything. But how can she change the environment? The environment is total, the whole fabric of human society, self-deluded and superstitious and sick and irrational and clinging to the legends and the fantasies and the ghosts. Who can change that?"

I had my answer ready, and I told him that if anyone could, Mrs. Jean Arbalaid could.

"You have a great deal of respect for your sister," he said. "I am told that she is a very gentle woman."

"When she is not crossed," I agreed. "But the point is this,

Professor: Will you work with us? That is the question she wants me to put to you?"

"But how can I answer it now? You confront me with perhaps the most exciting, the most earth-shaking notion of all of human history—not as a philosophical notion but as a pragmatic experiment—and then you ask me to say Yes or No. Impossible!"

"All right," I agreed, "I can accept that. How long do you want to think about it?"

"Overnight will be enough," he said. "Now tell me about California. I have never been there. I have read a little about it. Tell me what the state is like and what sort of an environment this would be in a physical sense; I would also like to know something more specific about your sister's relations to what you call 'the Army.' That phrase you use, 'the Army'—it seems quite different from what we understand in European terms or even in British terms."

So it went. My anthropology is passable at best, but I have read all your books. My geography and history are better, and if my answers were weak where your field was concerned, he did manage to draw out of me a more or less complete picture of Mark and yourself, and as much sociological and political information concerning the United States Government, the United States Army, and the relationship of the Government and the Army to subprojects, as I could have provided under any circumstances. He has a remarkable gift for extracting information, or, as I am inclined to regard it, of squeezing water from a rock.

When I left him, he said that he would think the whole matter over. We made an appointment for the following day. Then, he said, provided he had agreed to join us, he would begin to instruct me in his method of determining the intelligence of infants.

By the way, just to touch on his methods, he makes a great point of the fact that he does not test but rather determines, leaving himself a wide margin for error. Years before, in prewar Germany, he had worked out a list of about fifty characteristics which he had noted in infants. All of these characteristics had some relationship to factors of intelligence and response. As the infants in whom he had originally noted these characteristics matured, they were tested regularly by standard methods, and the results of these tests were compared with his original observations. Thereby he began to draw certain conclusions, which he tested again and again during the next fifteen years. Out of these conclusions and out of his tests, his checking, his relating testing to observation, he began to put together a list of characteristics that the pre-tested (that is, the new) infant might demonstrate, and he specified how those characteristics could be relied upon to indicate intelligence. Actually, his method is as brilliant as it is simple, and I am enclosing here an unpublished article of his which goes into far greater detail. Suffice it to say he convinced me of the validity of his methods.

I must note that subsequently, watching him examine a hundred and four British infants and watching him come up with our first choice for the group, I began to realize how brilliant this man is. Believe me, Jean, he is a most remarkable and wise man, and anything and everything you may have heard about his talents and knowledge is less than reality.

When I met him the following day, he agreed to join the project. Having come to this conclusion, he had no reservations about it. He seemed to understand the consequences far better than I did, and he told me very gravely just what his joining meant. Afterwards I wrote it down exactly as he said it:

"You must tell your sister that I have not come to this decision lightly. We are tampering with human souls—and perhaps even with human destiny. This experiment may fail, but if it succeeds it can be the most important event of our time—even more important and consequential than this terrible war we have just been through. And you must tell her something else. I once had a wife and three children, and they were put to death because a nation of men had turned into beasts. I personally lived through and observed that transition, that unbelievable and monstrous mass transition of men into beasts—but I could not have lived through it unless I had believed, always, that what can turn into a beast can also turn into a human being. We—and by we I mean the present population of the earth—are neither beast nor man. When I speak the word 'man,' I speak it proudly. It is a goal, not a fact. It is a dream, not a reality. Man does not exist. We are professing to believe that he might exist. But if we go ahead to create man, we must be humble. We are the tool, not the creator, and if we succeed, we ourselves will be far less than the result of our work. You must also tell your sister that when I make this commitment as I do today, it is a commitment without limitation. I am no longer a young man, and if this experiment is to be pursued properly, it must take up most, perhaps

162

the rest, of my life. I do not lightly turn over the rest of my existence to her—and yet I do."

There is your man, Jean, and as I said, very much of a man. The words above are quoted verbatim. He also dwells a great deal on the question of environment, and the wisdom and judgment and love necessary to create this environment. He understands, of course, that in our work—in our attempt to find the children to begin the experiment with—we are relying most heavily upon heredity. He does not negate the factor of heredity by any means, but heredity without the environment, he always underlines, is useless. I think it would be helpful if you could send me a little more information about this environment that you are establishing. Perhaps Professor Goldbaum could make a contribution toward it while it is in the process of being created.

We have now sent you four infants. Tomorrow we leave for Rome, and from Rome for Casablanca. We will be in Rome for at least two weeks and you can write or cable me there. The Embassy in Rome will have our whereabouts at any time.

More seriously than ever and not untroubled.

Harry.

15

by diplomatic pouch:

Via Washington, D.C.
February 11, 1946

Mr. Harry Felton
Rome, Italy

Dear Harry:

Just a few facts here—not nearly as many as we would like to give you concerning the environment, but at least enough for Professor Goldbaum to begin to orient himself. We are tremendously impressed by your reactions to Professor Goldbaum, and we look forward eagerly to his completing his work in Europe and joining us as a staff member here in America. By the way, he is the only staff member, as such, that we will have. Later on in this letter, I will make that clear. Meanwhile, Mark and I have been working night and day on the environment. In the most general terms, this is what we hope to accomplish and to have ready for the education of the children:

The entire reservation—all eight thousand acres—will be surrounded by a wire fence, what is commonly known as heavy tennis fencing or playground fencing. The fence will be eleven feet high; it will be topped by a wire carrying live current, and it will be under Army guard twenty-four hours a day. However, the Army guards will be stationed a minimum of three hundred yards from the fence. They will be under orders never, at any time under any circumstances, to approach the main fence nearer than three hundred yards. Outside of this neutral strip of three hundred yards, a second fence will be built—what might be thought of as an ordinary California cow fence. The Army guards will patrol outside of this fence, and only under specific and special circumstances will they have permission to step within it into the neutralized zone. In this way, and through the adroit use of vegetation, we hope that, for the first ten years, at least, people within the reservation will neither see nor have any other indication of the fact that outside of the reservation an armed guard patrols and protects it.

Within the reservation itself we shall establish a home; indeed, the most complete home imaginable. Not only shall we have living quarters, teaching quarters, and the means of any and all entertainment we may require; but we shall also have machine shops, masonry shops, wood-carving shops, mills, all kinds of fabrication devices and plans—in other words, almost everything necessary for absolute independence and self-maintenance. This does not mean that we are going to cut our relationships with the outside. There will certainly be a constant flow of material from the outside into the environment, for we shall require many things that we shall not be able to produce ourselves.

Now for the population of the environment: We expect to enlist between thirty and forty teachers or group parents. We are accepting only young married couples who love children and who will dedicate themselves entirely to this venture. This in itself has become a monumental task, for enlistment in this project is even more of a commitment than enlistment in the Army was five years ago. We are telling those parents who accept our invitation and who

164

are ready to throw in their lot with the experiment that the minimum time they will be asked to spend with us is fifteen years, and that the maximum time may well be a lifetime. In other words, the people who accept our invitation and come with us to be a part of the environment are, in actuality, leaving the planet Earth. They are leaving their friends and they are leaving their relatives, not for a day, a week, a month, or a year, but in a manner of speaking, forever. It is as if you were to approach twenty married couples and suggest to them that they emigrate from Earth to an uninhabited planet with no possibility of a return.

Can you imagine what this is, Harry? Can you imagine how keenly these people must believe? You might well suppose that nowhere could we find people who would be willing to join us in our venture; but that is far from the case. It is true that we are going all over the world for the parents, just as we are going all over the world for the children. However, we have already enlisted twelve couples, superb people, of several nationalities. We are excited and delighted with every step forward we take. Remember, it is not enough to find couples willing to dedicate themselves to this venture; they must have unique additional qualifications; and the fact that we have found so many with these qualifications is what excites us and gives us faith in the possibility that we will succeed.

Even to begin the experiment, we must dedicate ourselves to the proposition that somewhere in man's so-called civilized development, something went tragically wrong; therefore, we are returning to a number of forms of great antiquity. One of these forms is group marriage. That is not to say that we will cohabit indiscriminately; rather, the children will be given to understand that parentage is a whole, a matter of the group—that we are all their mothers and their fathers, not by blood but by a common love, a common feeling for protection and a common feeling for instruction.

As far as teaching is concerned, we shall teach our children only the truth. Where we do not know the truth, we shall not teach. There will be no myths, no legends, no lies, no superstitions, no false premises and no religions. There will be no gods, no bogeymen, no horrors, no nameless fears. We shall teach love and compassion and cooperation; and with this we shall demonstrate, in our lives and in every action we take, the same love and compassion —hoping, trusting and fighting for all of this to add up to the fullest possible measure of security. We shall also teach them the knowledge of mankind—but not until they are ready for that knowledge, not until they are capable of handling it. Certainly we shall not give them knowledge of the history of mankind or what mankind has become in the course of that history until they have completed the first eight years of their lives. Thus they will grow up knowing nothing of war, knowing nothing of murder, knowing nothing of the thing called patriotism, unaware of the multitude of hatreds, of fears, of hostilities that has become the common heritage of all of mankind.

During the first nine years in the environment, we shall have total control. We have already installed a complete printing press, a photo-offset system; we have all the moving-picture equipment necessary, and we have laboratories to develop the film we take, projection booths and theaters. All the film we need we shall make. We shall write the books; we shall take the film; we shall shape the history as history is taught to them in the beginning—that is, a history of who they are and what they are within the environment. We shall raise them in a sort of Utopia—God willing, without all the tragic mistakes that man has always made in his Utopias. And, finally, when we have produced something strong and healthy and beautiful and sturdy—at that point only will we begin to relate the children to the world as it is. Does it sound too simple or presumptuous? I am almost sorry, Harry, that I cannot make it more complicated, more intriguing, more wonderful, yet Mark and I both agree that the essence of what we are attempting to do is simple beyond belief; it is almost negative. We are attempting to rid ourselves of something that mankind has done to itself; and, if we can rid a group of children of that undefined something, then what will emerge just might be exciting and wonderful and even magnificent beyond belief. That is our hope; but the environment as I describe it above, Harry, is all that we can do—and I think that Professor Goldbaum will understand that full well and will not ask more of us. It is also a great deal more than has ever been done for any children on this earth heretofore.

So good luck to both of you. May you work well and happily and complete your work. The moment it is completed we want Professor Goldbaum to join us in the United States and to become a part of our group and our experiment. I am not asking you to become a part of it, Harry, and I think you can understand why. I don't want to put you in a position of having to make the choice. By now I can

166

well understand how deeply you have committed yourself to our experiment. Mark and I both realize that you cannot spell out such a commitment, but, dear Harry, I know you so well and I know what has happened inside of you. If I asked you to join us, you would not allow yourself to say No; but, at the same time, I don't think that your road to happiness consists of taking off for another planet. However you might feel about it, Harry, you are far too attached to the reality of the world as it is. You have not yet found the woman that you must find, but when you do find her, Harry, she and you will have your own way to find.

Your letters, in spite of your attempt to make them highly impersonal, do give us a clue to the change within you. Do you know, Harry, everyone associated with this experiment begins a process of change—and we feel that same curious process of change taking place within us.

When I put down simply and directly on paper what we are doing now and what we intend to do in the future, it seems almost too obvious to be meaningful in any manner. In fact, when you look at it again and again, it seems almost ridiculously simple and pointless and hopeless. What are we doing, Harry? We are simply taking a group of very gifted children and giving them knowledge and love. Is this enough to break through to that part of man which is unused and unknown? We don't know, Harry, but in time we shall see. Bring us the children, Harry, and we shall see.

With love,
Jean.

16

One day in the early spring of 1965, Harry Felton arrived in Washington from London. At the airport he took a cab directly to the White House, where he was expected.

Felton had just turned fifty; he was a tall and pleasant-looking man, rather lean, with graying hair. As president of the board of Shipways, Inc.—one of the country's largest import and export houses, with offices in London and in New York—Felton commanded a certain amount of deference and respect from Eggerton, who was then Secretary of Defense. A cold, withdrawn, and largely unloved man, Eggerton frequently adopted an attitude of immediate superiority, or, if that failed to impress, of judicious and controlled hostility; but he was sufficiently alert and sensitive not to make the mistake of trying to intimidate Felton.

Instead, he greeted him rather pleasantly—that is, pleasantly for Eggerton. The two of them, with no others present, sat down to talk in a small room in the White House. Drinks were served and a tray of sandwiches was brought in case Felton was hungry. Felton was not hungry. He and Eggerton drank each other's good health, and then they began to talk.

Eggerton proposed that Felton might know why he had been asked to Washington.

"I can't say that I do know," Felton replied—a little less than truthfullly; but then, Felton did not like Eggerton and did not feel comfortable with him.

"You have a remarkable sister."

"I have been aware of that for a long time."

Felton seemed to take a moment to think about what he had just said, and then he smiled. Whatever made him smile was not revealed to Eggerton who, after a moment, asked him whether he felt that his statement had been humorous.

"No, I didn't feel that," Felton said seriously.

"You are being very careful here, Mr. Felton," the Secretary observed, "but you have trained yourself to be a very close-mouthed person. So far as we are able to ascertain, not even your immediate family has ever heard of man-plus. That's a commendable trait."

"Possibly and possibly not. It's been a long time," Felton said coldly. "Just what do you mean by 'ascertain'? How have you been able to ascertain whether or not I am close-mouthed? That interests me, Mr. Secretary."

"Please don't be naïve, Mr. Felton."

"I have practiced being naïve for a lifetime," Felton said. "It's really not very sensitive on your part to ask me to change in a moment sitting here in front of you. I find that a degree of naivete fits well with close-mouthedness. What did it come to, Mr. Secretary? Was my mail examined?"

"Now and then," the Secretary admitted.

"My offices bugged?"

"At times."

"And my home?"

"There have been reasons to keep you under observation, Mr. Felton. We do what is necessary. What we do has received large and

168

unnecessary publicity; so I see no point in your claiming ignorance."

"I am sure you do what is necessary."

"We must, and I hope that this will not interfere with our little conversation today."

"It doesn't surprise me. So, in that direction at least, it will not interfere. But just what is this conversation and what are we to talk about?"

"Your sister."

"I see, my sister," Felton nodded. He did not appear surprised.

"Have you heard from your sister lately, Mr. Felton?"

"No, not for almost a year."

"Does it alarm you, Mr. Felton?"

"Does what alarm me?"

"The fact that you have not heard from your sister in so long?"

"Should it alarm me? No, it doesn't alarm me. My sister and I are very close, but this project of hers is not the sort of thing that allows for frequent social relations. Add to that the fact that my residence is in England, and that, while I do make trips to America, most of my time is spent in London and Paris. There have been long periods before when I have not heard from my sister. We are indifferent letter writers."

"I see," Eggerton said.

"Then I am to conclude that my sister is the reason for my visit here?"

"Yes."

"She is well?"

"As far as we know," Eggerton replied quietly.

"Then what can I do for you?"

"Help us if you will," Eggerton said just as quietly. He was visibly controlling himself—as if he had practiced with himself before the meeting and had conditioned himself not to lose his temper under any circumstances, but to remain quietly controlled, aloof and polite. "I am going to tell you what has happened, Mr. Felton, and then perhaps you can help us."

"Perhaps," Felton agreed. "You must understand, Mr. Eggerton, that I don't admire either your methods or your apparent goal. I think you would be wrong to look upon me as an ally. I spent the first twenty-four years of my life in the United States. Since then I have lived abroad with only infrequent visits here. So, you see, I am not even conditioned by what you might think of as a patriotic frame of mind. I am afraid that, if anything, I am a total internationalist."

"That doesn't surprise me, Mr. Felton."

"On second thought, I realize that it wouldn't. I am sure that you have investigated my residences, my frame of mind, my philosophy, and I would also guess that you have enough recordings of my conversations with my most intimate friends to know exactly what my point of view is."

The Secretary of Defense smiled as if to exhibit to Felton the fact that he, the Secretary of Defense, possessed a sense of humor. "No, not quite that much, Mr. Felton, but I must say that I am rather pleased by the respect you have for our methods. It is true that we know a good deal about you and it is also true that we could anticipate your point of view. However, we are not calling upon you in what some might term a patriotic capacity; we are calling upon you because we feel that we can appeal to certain instincts which are very important to you."

"Such as?"

"Human beings, human decency, the protection of mankind, the future of mankind—subjects that cross national boundaries. You would agree that they do, would you not, Mr. Felton?"

"I would agree that they do," Felton said.

"All right then; let us turn to your sister's project, a project which has been under way so many years now. I don't have to be hush-hush about it, because I am sure that you know as much concerning this project as any of us—more perhaps, since you were in at its inception. At that time, you were on the payroll of the project, and for a number of months you assisted your sister in the beginnings of the project. If I am not mistaken, part of your mission was to acquire certain infants which she needed at that stage of her experiment?"

"The way you say 'infants'," Felton replied, smiling, "raises a suspicion that we wanted them to roast and devour. May I assure you that such was not the case. We were neither kidnappers nor cannibals; our motives were rather pure."

"I am sure."

"You don't say it as if you were sure at all."

"Then perhaps I have some doubts, and perhaps you will share my doubts, Mr. Felton, when you have heard me out. What I intended to say was that surely you, of all people, realize that such a

170

project as your sister undertook must be regarded very seriously indeed or else laughed off entirely. To date it has cost the Government of the United States upwards of one hundred and fourteen million dollars, and that is not something you laugh off, Mr. Felton."

"I had no idea the price was so high," Felton said. "On the other hand, you may have gotten a hundred and fourteen million dollars' worth for your money."

"That remains to be seen. You understand, of course, that the unique part of your sister's project was its exclusiveness. That word is used advisedly and specifically. Your sister made the point again and again and again—and continues to make it, I may say—the point that the success of the project depended entirely upon its exclusiveness, upon the creation of a unique and exclusive environment. We were forced to accept her position and her demands— that is, if we desired the project at all; and it seems that the people who undertook to back the project did desire it. I say we, Mr. Felton, because 'we' is a term we use in government; but you must understand that was a good many years ago, almost twenty years ago, and I myself, Mr. Felton, did not participate in its inception. Now, in terms of the specifications, in terms of the demands that were made and met, we agreed not to send any observers into the reservation for a period of fifteen years. Of course, during those fifteen years there have been many conferences with Mr. and Mrs. Arbalaid and with certain of their associates, including Dr. Goldbaum."

"Then, if there were conferences," Felton said, "it seems to me that you know more about my sister than I do. You must understand that I have not seen my sister almost since the inception of the project."

"We understand that. Nevertheless, the relationship differs. Out of these conferences, Mr. Felton, there was no progress report that dealt with anything more than general progress and that in the most fuzzy and indefinite terms. We were given to understand that the results they had obtained in the reservation were quite rewarding and exciting, but little more, very little more indeed."

"That was to be expected. That's the way my sister works; in fact, it's the way most scientists work. They are engaged in something that is very special to them, very complicated, very difficult to explain. They do not like to give reports of the way stations they

171

may arrive at. They like to complete their work and have results, proven results, before they report."

"We are aware of that, Mr. Felton. We honored our part of the agreement, and at the end of a fifteen-year period we told your sister and her husband that they would have to honor their part of the agreement and that we would have to send in a team of observers. We were as liberal, as flexible, as people in our position could be. We advised them that they would have the right to choose the observers, that they could even limit the path of the observers—limit what the observers would see and the questions the observers could ask—but that we would have to send in such a team."

"And did you?" Felton asked him.

"No, we did not. That's a tribute to the persuasive powers of your sister and her husband. They pleaded for an extension of time, maintaining that it was critical to the success of the entire program, and they pleaded so persuasively that in the end they did win a three-year extension. Some months ago, the three-year period of grace was over. Mrs. Arbalaid came to Washington and begged for a further extension. I was at the meeting where she was heard, and I can tell you, Mr. Felton, that never before in my life had I heard a woman plead for something with the fervor, the insistence, with which Mrs. Arbalaid pleaded for this further extension."

Felton nodded. "Yes, I imagine my sister would plead with some intensity. Did you agree?"

"No. As I said, we refused."

"You mean you turned her down completely—entirely?"

"Not as completely perhaps as we should have. She agreed—when she saw that she could not move us—that our team could come into the reservation in ten days. She begged the ten-day interval to discuss the matter with her husband and to choose the two people who would make up the observation team. The way she put it, we had to agree to it; and then she returned to California."

Eggerton paused and looked at Felton searchingly.

"Well," Felton said, "what happened then? Did my sister select competent observers?"

"You don't know?" Eggerton asked him.

"I know some things. I'm afraid I don't know whatever you're interested in at this moment. I certainly don't know what happened."

"That was three weeks ago, Mr. Felton. Your sister never chose observers; your sister never communicated with us again; in fact, we know nothing about your sister or her reactions or what she said to her husband because we have not heard from her since."

"That's rather curious."

"That is exceedingly curious, Mr. Felton, far more curious than you might imagine."

"Tell me, what did you do when ten days went by and you didn't hear from my sister?"

"We waited a few days more to see whether it was an oversight on her part, and then we tried to communicate with her."

"Well?"

"We couldn't. You know something, Felton? When I think about what I'm going to tell you now I feel like a damn fool. I also feel a little bit afraid. I don't know whether the fear or the fool predominates. Naturally, when we couldn't communicate with your sister, we went there."

"Then you did go there," Felton said.

"Oh, yes, we went there."

"And what did you find?"

"Nothing."

"I don't understand," Felton said.

"Didn't I make myself plain, Mr. Felton? We went there and we found nothing."

"Oh?"

"You don't appear too surprised, Mr. Felton."

"Nothing my sister did ever really surprised me. You mean the reservation was empty—no sign of anything, Mr. Eggerton?"

"No, I don't mean that at all, Mr. Felton. I wish to God I did mean that. I wish it were so pleasantly human and down to earth and reasonable. I wish we thought or had some evidence that your sister and her husband were two clever and unscrupulous swindlers who had taken the Government for a hundred and fourteen million dollars. That would have been a joy, Mr. Felton. That would have warmed the cockles of our hearts compared to what we do have and what we did find. You see, we don't know whether the reservation is empty or not, Mr. Felton because the reservation is not there."

"What?"

"Precisely. Exactly what I said. The reservation is not there."

"Oh, come on now," Felton smiled. "My sister is a remarkable woman, but she doesn't make off with eight thousand acres of land. It isn't like her."

"I don't find your humor entertaining at this moment, Mr. Felton."

"No. No, of course not. I'm sorry. I realize that this is hardly the moment for humor. Only a thing is put to me and the thing makes no sense at all—how could an eight-thousand-acre stretch of land not be where it was? Doesn't that leave a damn big hole?"

"It's still a joke, isn't it, Mr. Felton?"

"Well, how do you expect me to react?" Felton asked.

"Oh, you're quite justified, Mr. Felton. If the newspapers got hold of it, they could do even better."

"Supposing you explain it to me," Felton said. "We're both guessing, aren't we? Maybe we're both putting each other on, maybe we're not. Let's be sensible about it and talk in terms that we both understand."

"All right," the Secretary said, "suppose you let me try, not to explain—that's beyond me—but to describe. The stretch of land where the reservation is located is in the Fulton National Forest: rolling country, some hills, a good stand of sequoia—a kidney-shaped area all in all, and very exclusive in terms of the natural formation. It's a sort of valley, a natural valley, that contains within itself areas of high land, areas of low land, and flat areas as well. Water, too. It was wire-fenced. Around it was a three-hundred-yard wide neutral zone, and Army guards were stationed at every possible approach. I went out there last week with our inspection team: General Meyers; two Army physicians; Gorman, the psychiatrist; Senator Totenwell of the Armed Services Committee; and Lydia Gentry, the educator who is our present Secretary of Education. You will admit that we had a comprehensive and intelligent team that represented a fine cross-section of American society. At least, Mr. Felton, that is my opinion. I still have some veneration for the American society."

"I share your admiration, Mr. Secretary, if not your veneration. I don't think that this should be a contest between you and me, *re* our attitudes toward the United States of America."

"No such contest intended, Mr. Felton. Let me continue. We crossed the country by plane and then we drove the final sixty miles to the reservation. We drove this distance in two Government cars.

174

A dirt road leads into the reservation. The main guard, of course, is on that dirt road, and that road is the only road into the reservation, the only road that a vehicle could possibly take to go into the reservation. The armed guard on this road halted us, of course. They were merely doing their duty. The reservation was directly before us. The sergeant in charge of the guard approached the first car according to orders; and, as he walked toward our car, the reservation disappeared."

"Come on now," Felton said.

"I am trying to be reasonable and polite, Mr. Felton. I think the very least you could do is attempt to adopt the same attitude towards me. I said, 'The reservation disappeared'."

"Just like that?" Felton whispered. "No noise—no explosion—no earthquake?"

"No noise, no explosion, no earthquake, Mr. Felton. One moment a forest of sequoia in front of us—then a gray area of nothing."

"Nothing. Nothing is not a fact, Mr. Secretary. Nothing is not even a description; it's simply a word and a highly abstract word."

"We have no other word for this situation."

"Well, you say 'nothing.' What do you mean? Did you try to go in? If there was nothing in front of you did you try to go through this nothing?"

"Yes, we tried. You can be very certain that we tried, Mr. Felton, and since then the best scientists in America have tried. I do not like to speak about myself as a brave man, but certainly I am not a coward. Yet believe me, it took a while for me to get up enough courage to walk up to that gray edge of nothing and touch it."

"Then you touched it?"

"I touched it."

"If it was nothing, it seems to me you could hardly touch it. If you could touch it, it was something, certainly not nothing."

"If you wish, it was something. It blistered these three fingers."

He held out his hand for Felton to see. The first three fingers of his right hand were badly blistered.

"That looks like a burn," Felton said.

"It is a burn. No heat and no cold, nevertheless it burned my hand. That kind of thing sets you back, Felton."

"I can appreciate that," Felton said.

"I became afraid then, Mr. Felton, I think we all became afraid.

We continue to be afraid. Do you understand, Mr. Felton? The world today represents a most delicate and terrible balance of power. When news comes to us that the Chinese have developed an atomic weapon, we become afraid. Out of necessity, our diplomatic attitude must reflect such fear and our attitude toward the Chinese must change. When the French began their atomic stockpile, our attitude toward the French changed. We are a pragmatic and a realistic administration, Mr. Felton, and we do not lie about fear or abjure power; we recognize fear and power, and we are very much afraid of that damn thing out there in California."

"I need not ask you if you tried this or that."

"We tried everything, Mr. Felton. You know, I'm a little ashamed to say this, and it is certainly damned well not for publication—I trust you will honor my request in that direction, Mr. Felton—?"

"I am not here as a reporter for the press," Felton said.

"Of course, yet this is very delicate, very delicate indeed. You asked whether we tried this or that. We tried things. We even tried a very small atomic bomb. Yes, Mr. Felton, we tried the sensible things and we tried the foolish things. We went into panic and we went out of panic and we tried everything we have and it all failed."

"And yet you have kept it a secret?"

"So far, Mr. Felton, we have kept it a secret," the Secretary agreed. "You cannot imagine what wire-pulling that took. We threw our weight here and there, and we threw our weight heavily, and we kept the secret—so far, Mr. Felton."

"Well, what about airplanes? You couldn't bar access to it from the air, could you? You couldn't cut off so wide a lane of air visibility that it would not be seen?"

"No, we immediately observed it from the air; you can be sure we thought of that quickly enough. But when you fly above it you see nothing. As I said, the reservation is in a valley, and all you can see is what appears to be mist lying in the valley. Perhaps it is mist—"

Felton leaned back and thought about it.

"Take your time," the Secretary said to him. "We are not rushing you, Mr. Felton, and believe me we are not pressuring you. We want your cooperation and, if you know what this is, we want you to tell us what it is."

176

Finally Felton asked him, "What do your people think it is?"

Eggerton smiled coldly and shook his head. "They don't know. There you are. At first, some of them thought it was some kind of force field. I have since learned that *force field* is a generic term for any area of positive action not understood too well. But when they tried to work it out mathematically, the mathematics wouldn't work. When they put it on the computers, the mathematics still refused to work. I don't know the math, Mr. Felton. I'm not a physicist and I'm not a mathematician, so I'm merely reporting what I have been told. And, of course, it's cold, and they're very upset about the fact that it's cold. It seems to confuse them no end. Terribly cold. Don't think only I am mumbling, Mr. Felton. As I said, I am neither a scientist nor a mathematician, but I can assure you that the scientists and the mathematicians also mumble. As for me, Mr. Felton, I am sick to death of the mumbling. I am sick to death of the double-talk and the excuses. And that's why we decided that you should come to Washington and talk with us. We thought that you might know about this thing that bars us from the reservation, and you might be able to tell us what it is or tell us how to get rid of it."

"I haven't the vaguest idea what it is," Felton said, "but even if I had, what on earth makes you think that I would tell you how to get rid of it?"

"Surely you don't think it's a good thing."

"How can I say whether it's a good thing or a bad thing?" Felton asked him. "I haven't the faintest notion of what it is, and I'm not sure that I know, in today's scheme of things, what is good or what is bad."

"Then you can't help us at all?"

"I didn't say that either. I just might be able to help you."

For the first time, Eggerton emerged from his lethargy, his depression. Suddenly he was excited and patient and overly cordial. He tried to force another drink on Felton. When Felton refused, he suggested that champagne be brought. Felton smiled at him, and the Secretary admitted that he was being childish.

"But you don't know how you have relieved me, Mr. Felton."

"I don't see why the little I said should relieve you. I certainly didn't intend to relieve you, and I don't know whether I can help you or not. I said I might help you."

Felton took a letter out of his pocket.

"This came from my sister," he said.

"You told me you had no letter from her in almost a year," the Secretary replied suspiciously.

"Exactly. And I have had this letter for almost a year." There was a note of sadness in Felton's voice. "I haven't opened it, Mr. Secretary, because when she sent it to me she enclosed it in a sealed envelope with a short letter. The letter said that she was well and quite happy, and that I was not to open or read the enclosed letter until it was absolutely necessary to do so. My sister is like that. We think the same way. I think that it's necessary now, don't you?"

The Secretary nodded slowly but said nothing. His eyes were fixed on Felton. Felton scanned the letter, turned it over, and then reached toward the Secretary's desk where there was a letter opener. The Secretary made no move to help him. Felton took the opener, slit the letter and took out a sheaf of onionskin paper. He opened this sheaf of paper and he began to read aloud.

17

June 12, 1964

My dear Harry:

As I write this, it is twenty-two years since I have seen you or spoken to you. How very long for two people who have such love and regard for each other as we do! And now that you have found it necessary to open this letter and read it, we must face the fact that in all probability we will never see each other again unless we are most fortunate. And Harry, I have watched so many miracles occur that I hesitate to dream of another. I know from your letters that you have a wife and three children, and I have seen their photographs. So far as I can tell, they are wonderful people. I think the hardest thing is to know that I will not see them or come to know them and watch them grow, and at least be some sort of sister to your wife.

Only this thought saddens me. Otherwise, Mark and I are very happy—perhaps as happy as two human beings have any right to be. As you read this letter I think you will come to understand why.

Now, about the barrier—which must exist or you would not have opened the letter—tell them that there is no harm to it and that no hurt will be caused by it. The very worst that can happen is that if one leans against it too long, one's skin may be badly blistered. But the barrier cannot be broken into because it is a negative power rather than a positive one, an absence instead of a presence. I will have more to say about it later, but I don't think I will be able to explain it better. My physics is limited, and these are things for which we, as human beings, have no real concepts. To put it into visual terms or understandable terms for a layman is almost impossible—at least for me. I imagine that some of the children could put it into intelligible words. But I want this to be my report, not theirs.

Strange that I still call them children and think of them as children—when in fact we are the children and they are the adults. But they still have the quality of children that we know best: the innocence and purity that vanishes so quickly with the coming of puberty in the outside world.

Now, dear Harry, I must tell you what came of our experiment—or some of it. Some of it, for how could I ever put down the story of the strangest two decades that man ever lived through? It is all incredible and, at the same time, it is all commonplace. We took a group of wonderful children and we gave them an abundance of love, security and truth—but I think it was the factor of love that mattered most, and because we were able to give them these three very obvious things—love, security and truth—we were able to return them to their heritage, and what a heritage it is, Harry!

During the first year we weeded out those couples who showed less than a total desire to love the children. I mention this because you must not think that any stage of this was easy or that any part of it ran smoothly. We went into the reservation with twenty-three couples; six of them—that is twelve people—failed to meet our test, and they had to go, but they were still good people and they abided by the necessity for silence and security.

But our children are easy to love, and they were easy to love from the very beginning. You see, I call them our children, Harry, because as the years passed they became our children—in every way. The children who were born to the couples in residence here simply joined the group. No one had a father or a mother; we were a living, functioning group in which all the men were the fathers of all the children and all the women were the mothers of all the children.

Now this is very easy to state as a fact, Harry; it is easy to project as a concept; but its achievement was far from easy. Its achievement was something that tore us to pieces. We had to turn ourselves inside out, totally reexamine ourselves, to achieve this. This among ourselves, Harry, among the adults who had to fight and work and examine each other inside and outside again and again and again—and tear out our guts and tear our hearts out—so that we could present ourselves to the children as something in the way of human beings. I mean a quality of sanity and truth and security embodied in a group of adult men and women. Far more spectacular achievements than this were accomplished, Harry—but perhaps nothing more wonderful than the fact that we, the adults, could remake ourselves. In doing so, we gave the children their chance.

And what did the chance amount to? How shall I tell you of an American Indian boy, five years old, composing a splendid symphony? Or of the two children, one Bantu, one Italian, one a boy, one a girl, who at the age of six built a machine to measure the speed of light? Will you believe that we, the adults, sat quietly and respectfully and listened to these six-year-olds explain to us a new theory of light? We listened, and perhaps some of us understood, but most of us did not. I certainly did not. I might translate it and repeat it in these terms—that since the speed of light is a constant anywhere, regardless of the motion of material bodies, the distance between the stars cannot be mentioned or determined in terms of the speed of light, since distance so arrived at is not, and has no equivalence to, distance on our plane of being. Does what I have said make any sense to you? It makes just a little to me. If I put it poorly, awkwardly, blame my own ignorance.

I mention just this one small thing. In a hundred—no, in a thousand—of these matters, I have had the sensations of an uneducated immigrant whose beloved child is exposed to all the wonders of school and knowledge. Like this immigrant, I understand a little of what the children achieve, but very little indeed. If I were to repeat instance after instance, wonder after wonder—at the ages of six and seven and eight and nine—would you think of the poor tortured nervous creatures whose parents boast that they have an IQ of 160 or of 170 and, in the same breath, bemoan the fate that did not give them normal children? Do you understand me, Harry? These children of ours, in your world, would have been condemned to disaster—not to simple disaster but to the specific, terrible disaster that befalls the super-knowing, the super-sensitive, the super-intelligent who are ground down, degraded and destroyed just as that Assamese child raised by the wolves was destroyed. Well, our children were and are normal children. Perhaps they are the first truly normal children that this world has seen in a long time—in many thousands of years. If just once you could hear them laugh or sing, you would know how absolutely true my statement is. If only you could see how tall and strong they are, how fine of body and movement. They have a quality that I have never seen in children before.

I suppose, dear Harry, that much about them would shock you just as it would shock most of the population of the outside world. Most of the time, they wear no clothes. Sex has always been a joy and a good thing to them, and they face it and enjoy it as naturally as we eat and drink—more naturally, for we have no gluttons in sex or food, no ulcers of the belly or the soul.

Our children kiss and caress each other and do many things that the world has specified as shocking, nasty, forbidden, dirty, obscene. But whatever they do, they do it with grace and they do it with joy, and they have no guilt nor any knowledge whatsoever of guilt. *Guilt* as a word or fact is meaningless to them.

Is all this possible? Or is it a dream and an illusion? I tell you that it has been my life for almost twenty years now. I live with these children, with boys and girls who are without evil or sickness, who are like pagans or gods, however you would look at it.

But the story of the children and of their day-to-day life is one that will some day be told properly in its own time and place. Certainly I have neither the time nor the ability to tell it here, Harry. You will have to content yourself with the bits and snatches that I can put down in this letter to you. All the indications that I have put down here add up only to great gifts and great abilities. But, after all, this was inherent in the children we selected. Mark and I never had any doubts about such results; we knew that if we created a controlled environment that was predicated on our hypothesis, the children would learn more than children do on the outside.

Naturally, this part of it came about. How could it have been otherwise—unless, of course, Mark and I had flubbed the whole thing and acted like fools and sentimentalists. But I don't think that there was much danger of that. Without being egotistical I can say that we, and of course Professor Goldbaum (who was with us through all the most difficult years), and our associates—we knew what we were doing. We knew precisely what we were doing and we knew pretty well how to do it.

In the seventh year of their lives, the children were dealing easily and naturally with scientific problems normally taught on the college level or on the postgraduate level in the outside world. But, as I said, this was to be expected, this was normal and we would have been very disappointed indeed if this development had not taken place. It was the unexpected that we hoped for, prayed for, dreamed of and watched for. A flowering, a development of the mind of man that was unpredictable and unknowable, which we could comprehend only negatively by theorizing that a block to such development is locked in every single human being on the outside.

And it came. Originally, it began with a Chinese child in the fifth year of our work. The second incident occurred in an American child, and the third in a Burmese child. Most strangely, it was not thought of as anything very unusual by the children themselves. We did not realize what was happening until the seventh year, that is, two years after the process had begun; and by that time it had happened already in five of the children. The very fact that it took place so gently, so naturally, so obviously, was a healthy symptom.

Let me tell you how we discovered what was happening. Mark and I were taking a walk that day—I remember it so well, a lovely, cool and clear northern California day—when we came upon a group of children in a meadow. There were about a dozen children gathered together in the meadow. Five of the children sat in a little circle, with a sixth child in the center of their circle. The six heads were almost touching. They were full of little giggles, ripples of mirth and satisfaction. The rest of the children sat in a group about ten feet away—watching intently, seriously, respectfully.

As we came closer the children were neither alarmed nor disturbed. The children in the second group put their fingers to their lips, indicating that we should be quiet. So we came rather close, and then we stood and watched without speaking.

After we were there about ten minutes, the little girl in the center of the circle of five children leaped to her feet, crying out ecstatically:

"I heard you! I heard you! I heard you!"

There was a kind of achievement and delight reflected in the sound of her voice that we had not experienced before, not even from our children. Then all of the children there rushed together to kiss and embrace the girl who had been in the middle of the group of five. They did a sort of dance of play and delight around her. All this we watched with no indication of surprise or even very great curiosity on our part. For even though this was the first time anything like this—anything beyond our expectation or comprehension—had ever happened, we had worked out what our own reaction should be to such discoveries and achievements on the part of the children. We had made up our minds that whatever they accomplished, our position would be that it was perfectly natural and completely expected.

When the children rushed to us for our congratulations, we nodded and smiled and agreed that it was all indeed very wonderful.

"Whose turn is it now?" Mark asked.

They called all the men "Father," the women "Mother." A Senegalese boy turned to me and said excitedly, "Now, it's my turn, Mother. I can do—well, I can almost do it already. Now there are six to help me, and it will be much easier."

"Aren't you proud of us?" another child cried.

"So proud," I said. "We couldn't be more proud."

"Are you going to do it now?" Mark asked him.

"Not now, we're tired now. You know, when you go at it with a new one, it's terribly tiring. After that, it's not tiring. But the first time it is."

"Then when will you do it?" I asked.

"Maybe tomorrow."

"Can we be here? I mean would you want us here when you do it or does it make it harder?"

"No harder," one of them said.

"Of course you can be here," another answered. "We would like you to be here."

"Both of us?" Mark asked.

"Of course, both of you and any other mother or father who wants to come."

We pressed it no further, but that evening at our regular staff meeting, Mark described what had happened and repeated the conversation.

"I noticed the same thing a few weeks ago," Mary Hengel, our semantics teacher, said. "I watched them, but either they didn't see me or they didn't mind my watching them."

"Did you go up close to them?" I asked her.

"No, I was a little uncertain about that. I must have stayed about forty or fifty yards away."

"How many were there then?" Professor Goldbaum asked Mary Hengel. He was very intent on his question, smiling slightly.

"Three. No there was a fourth child in the center—the three had their heads together. I simply thought it was one of their games—they have so many—and I walked away after a little while."

"They make no secret about it," someone else observed.

"Yes," I said, "we had the same feeling. They just took it for granted that we knew what they were doing, and they were quite proud of what they were doing."

"The interesting thing is," Mark said, "that while they were doing it, no one spoke. I can vouch for that."

"Yet they were listening," I put in. "There is no question about that; they were listening and they were listening for something, and finally, I imagine, they heard what they were listening for. They giggled and they laughed as if some great joke were taking place—you know the way children laugh about a game that delights them."

"Of course," said Abel Simms, who was in charge of our construction program, "of course they have no knowledge of right and wrong in our terms, and nothing they do ever seems wrong to them, just as nothing they do ever seems right to them; so there is no way to gauge their attitude in that sense toward whatever they were doing."

We discussed it a bit further, and it was Dr. Goldbaum who finally put his finger on it. He said, very gravely:

"Do you know, Jean—you always thought and hoped and dreamed too that we might open that great area of the human mind that is closed an blocked in all human beings. I think they found out how to open it. I think they are teaching each other and learning from each other what is to them a very simple and obvious thing—how to listen to thoughts."

There was a rather long silence after that, and then Atwater, one of our psychologists, said uneasily, "I am not sure I believe it. You know, I have investigated every test and every report on telepathy ever published in this country, and as much as I could gather and translate of what was published in other parts of the world—the Duke experiments and all the rest of it. None of it, absolutely none

184

of it, was dependable, and absolutely none of it gave any provable or reliable or even believable evidence or indication that such a thing as mental telepathy exists. You know, we have measured brain waves. We know how tiny and feeble they are—it just seems to me utterly fantastic that brain waves can be a means of communication."

"Hold on there," said Tupper, an experimental physicist. "The seemingly obvious linkage of brain waves with telepathy is rather meaningless, you know. If telepathy exists, it is not a result of what we call brain waves of the tiny electric pattern that we are able to measure. It's quite a different type of action, in a different manner on a wholly different level of physical reality. Just what that level is, I have no idea. But one of the things we are learning more and more certainly in physics is that there are different levels of reality, different levels of action and interaction of force and counterforce, so we cannot dispose of telepathy by citing brain waves."

"But how about the statistical factor?" Rhoda Lannon, a mathematician, argued. "If this faculty existed, even as a potential in mankind, is it conceivable that there would be no recorded instance of it? Statistically it must have emerged not once but literally thousands of times."

"Maybe it has been recorded," said Fleming, one of our historians. "Can you take all the whippings and burnings and hangings of history, all the witches, the demigods, the magicians, the alchemists, and determine which of these were telepaths and which were not? Also, there is another way of looking at it. Suppose one telepath alone is totally impotent. Suppose we need two telepaths to make it work, and suppose there is a limited distance over which two telepaths can operate. Then the statistical factor becomes meaningless and the accident becomes virtually impossible."

"I think that all in all I agree at least to some extent with Dr. Goldbaum," Mark said. "The children are becoming telepaths. It seems to me there is no question about that; it is the only sensible explanation for what Jean and I witnessed. If you argue, and with reason, that our children do not react to right and wrong and have no real understanding of right and wrong, then we must also add that they are equally incapable of lying. They have no understanding of the lie, of the meaning of the lie or of the necessity of the lie. So, if they told me that they heard what is not spoken, I have to believe them. I am not moved by an historical argument or by a statistical argument, because our concentration here is the environment and the absolute singularity of our environment. I speak of an historical singularity. There is no record in all of human history of a similar group of unusual children being raised in such an environment. Also, this may be—and probably is—a faculty of man which must be released in childhood, or remain permanently blocked. I believe Dr. Haenigson here will bear me out when I say that mental blocks imposed during childhood are not uncommon."

"More than that," Dr. Haenigson, our chief psychiatrist, stated. "No child in our history escapes the need to erect mental blocks in his mind. Without the ability to erect such blocks, it is safe to say that very few children in our society would survive. Indeed, we must accept the fact—and this is not theoretical or hypothetical, this is a fact, a provable fact which we have learned as psychiatrists—that whole areas of the mind of every human being are blocked in early childhood. This is one of the tragic absolutes of human society, and the removal—not the total removal, for that is impossible, but the partial removal—of such blocks becomes the largest part of the work of practicing psychiatrists."

Dr. Goldbaum was watching me strangely. I was about to say something, but I stopped and I waited, and finally Dr. Goldbaum said:

"I wonder whether we have begun to realize what we may have done without even knowing what we were doing. That is the wonderful, the almost unbearable implication of what may have happened here. What is a human being? He is the sum of his memories and his experience—these are locked in his brain, and every moment of experience simply builds up the structure of these memories. We do not know as yet what is the extent or power of the gift these children of ours appear to be developing, but suppose they reach a point where they can easily and naturally share the totality of memory? It is not simply that among themselves there can be no lies, no deceit, no rationalization, no secrets, no guilts—it is far more than that."

Then he looked from face to face, around the whole circle of our staff. At that point we were beginning to understand him and comprehend the condition he was posing. I remember my own reactions at that moment: a sense of wonder and discovery and joy, and heartbreak too, a feeling so poignant that it brought tears to my eyes. But above and beyond all that, I felt a sense of excitement, of enormous and exhilarating excitement.

186

"You know, I see," Dr. Goldbaum said. "I think that all of you know to one degree or another. Perhaps it would be best for me to speak about it, to put it into words, and to open it up to our thinking. I am much older than any of you—and I have been through and lived through the worst years of horror and bestiality that mankind ever knew. When I saw what I saw, when I witnessed the rise of Hitlerism, the concentration camps, the abattoirs, the ovens, the senseless, meaningless madness that culminated in the use of human skin to make lampshades, of human flesh and fat to make soap, when I saw and watched all this, I asked myself a thousand times: What is the meaning of mankind? Or has it any meaning at all? Is man not, perhaps, simply a haphazard accident, an unusual complexity of molecular structure, a complexity without meaning, without purpose and without hope? I know that you all have asked yourselves the same thing perhaps a hundred, a thousand times. What sensitive or thoughtful human being does not ask this question of himself? Who are we? What are we? What is our destiny? What is our purpose? Where is sanity or reason in these bits of struggling, clawing, sick, murderous flesh? We kill, we torture, we hurt, we destroy as no other species does. We ennoble murder and falsehood and hypocrisy and superstition. We destroy our own bodies with drugs and poisonous food. We deceive ourselves as well as others. And we hate and hate and hate until every action we take is a result of our hatred.

"Now something has happened. Something new, something different, something very wonderful. If these children can go into each other's minds completely, then they will have a single memory, which is the memory of all of them. All their experience will be common to all of them, all their knowledge will be common to all of them, all the dreams they dream will be common to all of them—and do you know what that means? It means that they will be immortal. For as one of them dies, another child is linked to the whole, and another, and another. For them there will be no death. Death will lose all of its meaning, all of its dark horror. Mankind will begin, here in this place, in this strange little experiment of ours, to fulfill at least one part of its intended destiny—to become a single, wonderful thing, a whole—almost in the old words of your poet, John Donne, who sensed what each of us has sensed at one time or another: that no man is an island unto himself. Our tragedy has been that we are singular. We never lived, we were always fragmented bits of flesh at the edge of reality, at the edge of life.

Tell me, has any thoughtful man or woman ever lived life without having a sense of that singleness of mankind and longing for it and dreaming of it? I don't think so. I think we have all had it, and therefore we have, all of us, been living in darkness, in the night, each of us struggling with his own poor little brain and then dying, perishing, with all the memories and the work of a lifetime destroyed forever. It is no wonder that we achieve so little. The wonder is that we have achieved so much. Yet all that we know, all that we have done, will be nothing, primitive, idiotic, nothing compared to what these children will know and do and create. It just staggers my imagination.''

So the old man spelled it out, Harry. I can't put it all down here, but do you know, he saw it—at that moment, which was almost the beginning of it, he saw it in all of its far-flung implications. I suppose that was his reward, that he was able to fling his imagination forward into the future, the vast unrealized future, and see the blinding, incredible promise that it holds for us.

Well, that was the beginning, Harry; within the next twelve months, each one of our children was linked to all the others telepathically. And in the years that followed, every child born in our reservation was shown the way into that linkage by the children. Only we, the adults, were forever barred from joining it. We were of the old and they were of the new. Their way was closed to us forever—although they could go into our minds, and did when they had to. But never could we feel them there or see them there or go into their minds or communicate with them as they did with each other.

I don't know how to tell you of the years that followed, Harry. In our little guarded reservation, man became what he was always destined to be, but I can explain it only imperfectly. I can hardly comprehend, much less explain, what it means to inhabit forty bodies simultaneously, or what it means to each of the children to have the other personalities within him or her, a part of each of them. Can I even speculate on what it means to live as man and woman, always together, not only in the flesh, but man and woman within the same mind?

Could the children explain it to us? Did they explain it to us? Hardly. For this is a transformation that must take place, from all we can learn, before puberty; and as it happens, the children accept it as normal and natural—indeed as the most natural thing in the world. We were the unnatural ones—and the one thing they never truly comprehended is how we could bear to live in our aloneness, how we could bear to live on the edge of death and extinction and with the knowledge of death and extinction always pressing against us. Again, could we explain to a man born blind what color is, gradations of color, form, light, or the meaning of light and form combined? Hardly, any more than they are able to explain their togetherness to us who live so singularly and so alone.

As for the children's knowledge of us, we are very happy, indeed grateful, that it did not come at once. In the beginning, the children could merge their thoughts only when their heads were almost touching. This is what saved them from us, because if, in the very beginning, they had been able to touch our thoughts, they might not have been able to defend themselves. Bit by bit, their command of distance grew, but very slowly; and not until our fifteenth year in the reservation did the children begin to develop the power to reach out and probe with their thoughts anywhere on earth. We thank God for this. By then the children were ready for what they found. Earlier, it might have destroyed them.

I might mention here that the children explained to us in due time that their telepathic powers had nothing to do with brain waves. Telepathy, according to the children, is a function of time, but exactly what that means, I don't know, Harry, and therefore I cannot explain it to you.

I must mention that two of our children met accidental death— one in the ninth year and the second in the eleventh year. But the effect of these two deaths upon the other children cannot be compared to the effects of death in our world. There was a little regret, but no grief, no sense of great loss, no tears or weeping. Death is totally different among them than among us; among them, a loss of flesh and only flesh; the personality itself is immortal and lives consciously in the others.

When we spoke to them about a marked grave, or a tombstone, or some other mark that would enable us to keep alive the memory of the two dead children, they smiled sympathetically and said that we could make such a tomb or tombstone if it would give us any comfort. Their concern was only for us, not in any way for the two bodies that were gone.

Yet later, when Dr. Goldbaum died, their grief was deep and terrible, something so deep, so heartbreaking, that it touched us

189

more than anything in our whole experience here—and this, of course, was because Dr. Goldbaum's death was the old kind of death.

The strangest thing, Harry, is that in spite of all these indications and means of togetherness that I have been telling you about, outwardly our children remain individuals. Each of the children retains his or her own characteristics, mannerisms and personality. The boys and girls make love in a normal, heterosexual manner— though all of them share the experience. Can you comprehend that? I cannot; but then neither can I comprehend any other area of their emotional experience except to realize that for them everything is different. Only the unspoiled devotion of mother for helpless child can approximate the love that binds them together. Yet here, too, in their love everything is different, deeper than anything that we can relate to our own experience. Before their transformation into telepaths took place, the children displayed enough petulance and anger and annoyance; but after it took place, we never again heard a voice raised in anger or annoyance. As they themselves put it, when there was trouble among them, they washed it out. When there was sickness among them, they healed it.

After the ninth year, there was no more sickness. By then they had learned to control their bodies. If sickness approached their bodies—and by that I mean infection, germs, virus, whatsoever you might call it—they could control and concentrate the reaction of their bodies to the infection; and with such conscious control and such conscious ability to change the chemical balance of their bodies, to change their heartbeat if necessary, to influence their blood flow, to increase the circulation in one part of the body, to decrease it in another, to increase or decrease the functioning of various organs in the body—with that kind of control, they were absolutely immune to sickness. However they could go further than that. While they could give us no part of the wholeness which they enjoyed as a normal thing of their lives, they could cure our illnesses. Three or four of them would merge their minds and go into our bodies and cure our bodies. They would go into our minds; they would control the organs of our bodies and the balance of our bodies and cure them; and yet we, the recipients of this cure, were never aware of their presence.

In trying to describe all of this to you, Harry, to make it real and to make incidents come alive, I use certain words and phrases only because I have no other words and phrases, I have no language that fits the life of these children. I use the words I know, but at the same time I realize, and you must realize, that my words do not describe adequately—they do not serve the use I am trying to put them to. Even after all these years of living intimately with the children, day and night, I can comprehend only vaguely the manner of their existence. I know what they are outwardly because I see it, I watch it. They are free and healthy and happy as no men and women ever were before. But what their inner life is remains a closed thing to me.

Again and again we discussed this with various members of our group, that is, among ourselves and also among the children. The children had no reticence about it; they were willing, eager, delighted to discuss it with us, but the discussions were hardly ever fruitful. For example, take the conversation I had with one of the children, whose name is Arlene. She is a tall, lovely child whom we found in an orphanage in Idaho. She came to us as the other children did, in infancy. At the time of our conversation, Arlene was fourteen. So much, you see, had happened in the reservation during the intervening years. We were discussing personality, and I told Arlene that I could not understand how she could live and work as an individual when she was also a part of so many others, and these so many others were a part of her.

She, however, could not see that and she rejected the whole concept.

"But how can you be yourself?" I pressed her.

"I remain myself," she answered simply. "I could not stop being myself."

"But aren't the others also yourself?"

"Yes, of course, what else could they be? And I am also them."

This was put to me as something self-evident. You see, it is no easier for them to understand our concepts than it is for us to understand their concepts. I said to her then:

"But who controls your body?"

"I do, of course."

"But just for the sake of a hypothetical situation, Arlene, suppose we take this possibility—that some of the other children should want to control your body instead of leaving the control to you."

191

"Why?" she asked me.

"If you did something they didn't approve of," I said lamely, digging the hole I had gotten into still deeper.

"Something they disapproved of?" she asked. "Well, how could I? Can you do something that you yourself disapprove of?"

"I am afraid I can, Arlene, and I do."

"Now that I don't understand at all, Jean. Why do you do it?"

"Well, don't you see, I can't always control what I do."

This was a new notion to her. Even able to read our minds, this was a new notion to her.

"You can't control what you do?" she asked.

"Not always."

"Poor *Jean*," she said, "oh, poor *Jean*. How terrible. What an awful way to have to live."

"But it's not so terrible, Arlene," I argued, "not at all. For us it's perfectly normal."

"But how? How could such things be normal?"

So these discussions always seemed to develop and so they always ended. The communication between us, with all the love that the children had for us and all the love that we had for the children, was so limited. We, the adults, had only words for communication; and words are very limited. But by their tenth year, the children had developed methods of communication as far beyond words as words are beyond the dumb motions of animals. If one of them watched something, there was no necessity to describe what he or she watched to the others. The others could see it through the eyes of the child who was watching. This went on not only in waking but in sleeping as well. They actually dreamed together, participated in the same dreams.

Has it ever occurred to you, Harry, that when something hurts you, you don't have to engage in conversation with yourself to tell yourself that it hurts you? When you have a certain feeling, you don't have to explain the feeling to yourself; you have the feeling. And this was the process of communication that was perfectly natural to the children. They felt as a unit, as a body, and yet they remained individuals.

I could go on for hours attempting to describe something utterly beyond my understanding, but that would not help, would it, Harry? You will have your own problems, and I must try to make you understand what happened, what had to happen, and now what must happen in the future.

192

You see, Harry, by the tenth year, the children had learned all we knew, all we had among us as material for teaching; our entire pooled experience was now used up. In effect, we were teaching a single mind, a mind composed of the unblocked, unfettered talent and brains of forty superb children. Consider that. A mind forty times as large, as agile, as comprehensive as any mind that man had ever known before—a mind so rational, so pure, that to this mind we could only be objects of loving pity. We have among us, as a pair of group parents, Alex Cromwell and his wife. You will recognize Alex Cromwell's name; he is one of our greatest physicists, and it was he who was largely responsible for the first atom bomb. After that, he came to us as one would go to a monastery. He performed an act of personal expiation in the only manner which could give him any hope, any satisfaction, any surcease from the enormous and terrible guilt that he bore. He and his wife taught our children physics, but by the eighth year, mind you, by the eighth year of their lives, the children were teaching Cromwell. A year later, Cromwell could no longer be taught. He was now incapable of following either their mathematics or their reasoning, and their symbolism, of course, was totally outside of the structure of Cromwell's thoughts. Imagine a mind like Cromwell's, led with concern, with tenderness, with gentleness, with the greatest love and consideration that the children could give him—for he is a charming and lovable person—imagine that such a mind could not advance within the area of knowledge that these nine-year-old children possessed.

It is rather terrifying, isn't it? And when you will show this letter (and of course we want you to show this letter) to the people who command the destiny of the United States, this thing I have just written will also be terrifying to them. I think that one of the saddest aspects of our society is the fear of the child that it engenders in the adult. That is a continuing fact of our society. Each generation, as it matures, fears the coming generation, looks at the coming generation as being conscienceless and depraved. No skill of adults, no talent of adults will engender as much fear as this skill, this talent, this brilliance of our children. Remember that, Harry, and expect it.

Let me give you an example of some of the capabilities, some of the powers our children have developed. In the far outfield of our baseball diamond, there was a boulder of perhaps ten tons. Incidentally, I must remark that our children's athletic skill, their physical prowess, is in its own way almost as extraordinary as their mental powers. They have broken every track and field record, often cutting world records by one third and even by one half. I have watched them effortlessly run down our horses. Their movements and their reactions are so quick as to make us appear sluggards by comparison. If they so desire, they can move their arms and legs faster than our eyes can follow; and, of course, one of the games they love is baseball, and they play in a manner you have never seen on the outside. Now to go back to this situation of the boulder: For some years, we, the adults, had spoken of either blasting the boulder apart or of rolling it out of the way with one of our very heavy bulldozers, but it was something we had simply never gotten to. Then, one day, we discovered that the boulder was gone, and in its place was a pile of thick red dust—a pile that the wind was fast leveling.

We brooded over the matter ourselves for a while, made our usual attempt at interpretation, made our guesses, and at last, frustrated, went to the children and asked them what had happened. They told us that they had reduced the boulder to dust—as if it were no more than kicking a small stone out of one's path and just as if everyone could at will reduce a gigantic boulder to dust. Why not?

Cromwell cornered them on this one and he asked one of the children, Billy:

"But how? After all, Billy, you say you reduced the boulder to dust, but how? That's the point. How?"

"Well, the ordinary way," Billy said.

"You mean there's an ordinary way to reduce a boulder to dust?"

"Well, isn't there?" another child asked.

Billy was more patient. He sensed our difficulty and asked gently whether perhaps Cromwell did not know the ordinary way, but had to do it in some more complex way.

"I suppose I could reduce the boulder to dust," Cromwell said. "I would have to use a great deal of heavy explosive. It would take some time; it would make a lot of noise, and it would be rather expensive."

"But the end would be the same, wouldn't it?" Billy asked.

"I suppose so," Cromwell said, "if you mean dust."

"No, I mean the manner," Billy said, "the technique."

"What technique?" Cromwell asked desperately.

194

"Well, our technique. I mean to make anything dust you have to unbond it. We do it by loosening the molecular structure—not very quickly, you know, it could be dangerous if you did it too quickly—but we just loosen it slowly, steadily, and we let the thing kick itself to pieces, so to speak. That doesn't mean that it actually kicks itself to pieces. It doesn't explode or anything of that sort; it just powders away. You know, it holds its shape for a while, and then you touch it and it becomes powder—it collapses."

"But how do you do that?" Cromwell insisted.

"Well, the best way of course—directly. I mean with your mind. You understand it, and then you reject it as an understood phenomenon and you let it shake itself loose."

But the more he spoke, the further Billy traveled from Cromwell's area of comprehension; the more he used words, the less the words were able to convey, and finally, with patient and sympathetic smiles, the children dismissed the whole thing and their attempt to enlighten us as well. This was what usually happened, and this was the manner in which it usually happened.

Of course it was not always that way. They used the tools of our civilization, not because they admired these tools or because they needed mechanical things, but simply because they felt that our anxieties were eased by a certain amount of old-fashioned procedure. In other words, they wanted to preserve some of our world for our own sentimental needs. For example, they built an atomic-fusion power plant, out of which we derived and continued to derive our power. Then they built what they called free-fields into all our trucks and cars so that the trucks and cars could rise and travel through the air with the same facility as on the ground. The children could have built sensible, meaningful platforms that would have done the same thing and would have done it in a functional manner. The cars were much less functional; automobiles and trucks are not built to travel through the air. But the children had the kind of concern for the outer aspect of our world that led them to refrain from disarranging it too much.

At this point the use of thought, the degree to which they are able to use their own thoughts to influence atomic structure, is the most remarkable gift that they have beyond the power of telepathy itself. With the power of their thoughts they can go into atoms, they can control atoms, they can rearrange electrons; they can go into the enormous, almost infinite random patterns of electrons and atoms, and move things so that the random becomes directed and changes take place. In this way they are able to build one element out of another, and the curious thing of it is that all this is so elementary to them that they will do it at times as if they were doing tricks to amuse and amaze us, to save us from boredom, as an adult might do tricks for a child and so entertain the child.

So, dear Harry, I have been able to tell you something of what went on here over the years, a little bit of what the children are, a little bit about what they can do—not as much, perhaps, as I would want to tell you. I think I would like to create an hour-by-hour diary for you so that there might be a record on your side of what every day, every week of the last nineteen years has held; for, believe me, every day in the week of almost twenty years was exciting and rewarding.

Now I must tell you what you must know; and you shall tell these things to whoever you wish to tell them to. Use only your own judgment. Nothing in this document, Harry, is a secret. Nothing is for your ears alone. Nothing is to be held back. All of it can be given to the world. As for how much of it should be given to all the world, that must be a decision of the people who control the means of information. But let the decision be theirs, Harry. Do not interfere with it. Do not try to influence it; and above all, do not suppress anything that I am writing here.

In the fifteenth year of the experiment, our entire staff met with the children on a very important occasion. There were fifty-two children then, for all of the children born to us were taken into their body of singleness and flourished in their company. I must add that this was possible despite the initially lower IQ's of most of the children born to our mothers and fathers. Once the group has formed itself telepathically and has merged its powers, there is no necessity for high IQ's among the children who are brought into it. In fact, we are speculating on whether the experiment might not have proceeded almost the same way if we had chosen our first forty children at random. This we will never know.

Now, as to this meeting: It was a very formal and a very serious meeting, perhaps the most serious meeting of our experiment. Thirty days were left before the team of observers was scheduled to enter the reservation, according to the terms of our initial agreement with the Army. We had discussed that situation at great length among ourselves, the adults, and with the children, and of course it had been discussed among the children without us. But now it was discussed formally.

The children had chosen Michael to speak for them, but of course they were all speaking. Michael was simply the voice necessary to communicate with us. Michael, I might say, was born in Italy, a tall, delicate, lovely young man, and a most talented artist. Again I might mention that talent, specific talent, remained the property, the gift of the individual. This could not be communicated through the group to another child. Knowledge, yes, but a creative talent remained entirely the gift of the child who had it originally.

Michael took the floor and began by telling us how much the children loved and cherished us, the adults who were once their teachers.

I interrupted him to say that it was hardly necessary for the children ever to spell that out. We might not be able to communicate telepathically but never once was there anything in their actions to make us doubt their love for us.

"Of course," Michael said, "we understand that; yet, at the same time, certain things must be said. They must be said in your language, and unless they are said they do not really exist as they must exist in relation to you. Believe us, we comprehend fully that all that we have, all that we are, you have given us. You are our fathers and mothers and teachers—and we love you beyond our power to say. We know that you consider us something superior to yourselves, something more than yourselves and beyond yourselves. This may be true, but it is also a fact of life that in each step forward, along with what is gained, something else is lost. There is a taking and a giving, a taking on and a putting aside. For years now, we have wondered and marveled at your patience and self-giving, for we have gone into your minds and we have known what pain and doubt and fear and confusion all of you live with. But there is something else that until now you have not known."

He paused and looked at each of us in turn. Then he looked at me searchingly, wonderingly, and I nodded as if to tell him to go ahead and tell us everything and hold nothing back.

"This then," Michael said. "We have also gone into the minds of the soldiers who guard the reservation. More and more, our power to probe grew and extended itself so that now, in this fifteenth year, there is no mind anywhere on earth we cannot seek out and read. I need not tell you how many thousands of minds we have already sought out and read."

He paused, and I looked at Dr. Goldbaum who shook his head. Tears rolled down his cheeks and he whispered, "Oh my God, my God, what you must have seen. How could you do it and how could you bear it?"

"You never really knew how much we can bear," Michael said. "Always we had a child-parent relationship. It was a good relationship. Always you sought to protect us, to interpose your body, your presence, between ourselves and the world. But you didn't have to. It hurts me to say it, but you must know that long, long ago you became the children and we became the parents."

"We know it," I said. "Whether or not we spoke about it in so many words, we know it. We have known it for a long time."

"From our seventh year," Michael continued, "we knew all the details of this experiment. We knew why we were here and we knew what you were attempting—and from then until now, we have pondered over what our future must be. We have also tried to help you, whom we love so much, and perhaps we have been of some help in easing your discontents, in keeping you as physically healthy as possible, in helping you through your troubled, terrible nights and that maze of fear and nightmare and horror that you and all other human beings call sleep. We did what we could, but all our efforts to join you with us, to open your minds to each other and our minds to you, all these efforts have failed. Finally we learned that unless the necessary area of the mind is opened before puberty, the brain tissues change, the brain cells lose the potential of development and the mind is closed forever. Of all the things we face, this saddens us most—for you have given us the most precious heritage of mankind and, in return, we are able to give you nothing."

"That isn't so," I said. "You have given us more than we gave you, so much more."

"Perhaps," Michael nodded. "Or perhaps it helps for you to think that and to say that. You are very good and kind people. You have a kind of tenderness, a kind of gentle love that we can never have, for it grows out of your fear, your guilt, and the horror you live with. We have never been able, nor did we want, to know such fear, such guilt and such horror. It is foreign to us. So while we save ourselves the knowledge of these things, we are also deprived of the

198

kind of love, the kind of self-sacrifice that is almost a matter-of-fact part of your nature. That we must say. But now, our fathers and our mothers, now the fifteen years are over; now this team of observers will be here in thirty days."

I shook my head and said quietly but firmly. "No. They must be stopped. They must not come here; they cannot come here."

"And all of you?" Michael asked, looking from one to another of us. "Do you all feel the same way? Do you all know what will come after that? Can you imagine what will come after that? Do you know what will happen in Washington? This is what you must think about now."

Some of us were choked with emotion. Cromwell, the physicist, said:

"We are your teachers and your fathers and your mothers, but we can't make this decision. You must tell us what to do. You know what to do. You know that, and you know that you must tell us."

Michael nodded, and then he told us what the children had decided. They had decided that the reservation must be maintained. They needed five more years. They decided that I was to go to Washington with Mark and with Dr. Goldbaum—and somehow we were to get an extension of time. They felt that such an extension would not be too difficult to get at this point. Once we got the extension of time, they would be able to act.

"What kind of action?" Dr. Goldbaum asked them.

"There are too few of us," Michael said. "We need more. We must find new children, new infants, and we must bring them into the reservation. In other words, we must leave the reservation, some of us, and we must bring children here and we must educate the children here."

"But why must they be brought here?" Mark asked. "You can reach them wherever they are. You can go into their minds, you can make them a part of you. The children of the whole world are open to us. Why must you bring them here?"

"That may be true," Michael said, "but the crux of the matter is that the children can't reach us. Not for a long, long time. The children would be alone—and their minds would be shattered if we went into their minds. Tell us, what would the people of your world outside do to such children? What happened to people in the past who were possessed of devils, who heard voices, who heard the sound of angels? Some became saints, but many more were burned

199

at the stake, destroyed, beaten to death, impaled, the victims of every horror that man could devise and inflict upon children.

"Can't you protect the children?" someone asked.

"Someday, yes. Now, no. There are simply not enough of us. First, we must help children to move here, hundreds and hundreds of children. Then we must create other reservations, other places like this one. It cannot be done quickly. It will take a long time. For a child, even our kind of child, to grow into an effective mover, it takes at least fifteen years. It is true that when we are eight, nine, ten years old, we know a great deal, we are able to do a great deal; but we are still children. That has not changed. So you see it will take a long, long time. The world is a very large place and there are a great many children. With all this, we must work carefully, very carefully. You see, people are afraid. Your lives, the lives of mankind, are ruled by fear. This will be the worst fear of all. They will go mad with fear, and all they will be able to think about is how to kill us. That will be their whole intention: to kill us, to destroy us."

"And our children could not fight back," Dr. Goldbaum said quietly. "That is something to remember, to think about; that is very important. You see, fighting, killing, hostility—this is the method of mankind. It has been the method of mankind for so long that we have never questioned it. Can a human being kill? Can a human being fight? We simply take it for granted that this is a human attribute. Take the case, for example, of the Israelis. For two thousand years the Jews had not, as a people, engaged in any kind of war, and it was said that they had lost the will to fight to kill; but you see that with the creation of Israel this will returned. So we say that there is no place on earth where man cannot learn very quickly to become a killer. When the people of India, who were such a people of peace, obtained their freedom from England, they turned upon each other in a fratricide unbelievable, unthinkable, monstrous. But our children are different. Our children cannot kill. This we must understand. No matter what danger faced them, no matter what fate they confronted, they could not kill. They cannot hurt a human being, much less kill one. The very act of hurt is impossible. Cattle, our old dogs and cats, they are one thing—but not people, not people."

(Here Dr. Goldbaum referred to the fact that we no longer slaughtered our cattle in the old way. We had pet dogs and cats,

200

and when they became very old and sick, the children caused them peacefully to go to sleep—a sleep from which they never awakened. Then the children asked us if they might do the same with the cattle we butchered for food. But I must make one point specific, Harry, so that you will understand the children a little better: We butchered the cattle because some of us still required meat, but the children ate no meat. They ate eggs and vegetables, the fruit of the ground, but never meat. This eating of meat, the slaughtering of living things for eating, was a thing they tolerated in us with sadness. Discipline, you know, is also not a part of their being—that is, discipline in the sense that we understand it. They do not ask us not to do things. They will ask us positively to do something; but, on the other hand, if we do what to them is repulsive, no matter how obnoxious it may be to them, they will not ask us to stop doing it.)

"But not people," Dr. Goldbaum went on. "God help us, our children cannot hurt people. We are able to do things that we know are wrong. That remains one power we possess which the children lack. They cannot kill and they cannot hurt. Am I right, Michael, or is this only a presumption on my part?"

"Yes, you are right," Michael said. "We must do our work slowly and patiently, and the world must not know what we are doing until we have taken certain measures. We think we need three years more. We would like to have five years more. But, Jean, if you can get us three years, we will bear with that and somehow manage to do what we must do within that period. Now, will you go with Mark and with Dr. Goldbaum, and will you get us these three years, Jean?"

"Yes, I will get the three years," I said. "Somehow I will do what you need."

"And the rest of you," Michael said, "the rest of you are needed too. We need all of you to help us. Of course we will not keep any of you here if you wish to go. But, oh, we need you so desperately— as we have always needed you—and we love you and we cherish you, and we beg you to remain with us."

Do you wonder that we all remained, Harry, that no one of us could leave our children or will ever leave them now except when death takes us away? You see, Harry, they needed the time and they got the time, and that is why I can write this and that is why I can tell you so forthrightly what happened.

201

Mark and I and Dr. Goldbaum pleaded our case and we pleaded it well. We were given the years we needed, the additional years; and as for this gray barrier that surrounds us and the reservation, the children tell me that it is a simple device indeed. Of course that doesn't mean a great deal. They have a whole succession of devices that they call simple which are totally beyond the comprehension of any ordinary human being. But to come back to this barrier; as nearly as I can understand, they have altered the time sequence of the entire reservation; not by much—by less than one ten-thousandth of a second. But the result is that your world outside exists this tiny fraction of a second in the future. The same sun shines on us, the same winds blow, and from inside the barrier, we see your world unaltered. But you cannot see us. When you look at us, the present of our existence, the moment of time which we are conscious of at that moment of being in the universe, that moment has not yet come into existence; and instead of that, instead of reality, there is nothing: no space, no heat, no light, only the impenetrable wall of nonexistence. Of course you will read this, Harry, and you will say it makes absolutely no sense whatever, and I cannot pretend that I am able to make any sense out of it. I asked the children how to describe it. They told me as best they could, considering that they had to use the same words I use. They ask me to think of an existing area of time, of us traveling along this existing area with a point of consciousness to mark our progress. They have altered this point. And that means absolutely nothing to someone like myself.

I can only add this—from inside the reservation we are able to go outside, to go from the past into the future. After all, the crossover is only one ten-thousandth of a second. I myself have done this during the moments when we were experimenting with the barrier. I felt a shudder, a moment of intense nausea, but no more than that. There is also a way in which we return, but, understandably, I cannot spell that out.

So there is the situation, Harry. We will never see each other again, but I assure you that Mark and I are happier than we have ever been. Man will change; nothing in the world can halt the change. It has already begun. And in that change, man will become what he was intended to be, and he will reach out with love and knowledge and tenderness to all the universes of the firmament. I have written that down, Harry, and as I look upon it I find it the most thrilling idea I have ever encountered. My skin prickles at the mere thought. Harry, isn't this what man has always dreamed of? No war, no hatred, no hunger or sickness or death? How fortunate we are to be alive while this is happening! I think that we should ask no more.

So now I say goodbye to you, my dear brother, and I finish this letter.

With all my love,
Your sister,
Jean Arbalaid.

Felton finished reading, and then there was a long, long silence while the two men looked at each other. Finally the Secretary of Defense spoke, saying:

"You know, Felton, that we shall have to keep knocking at that barrier. We can't stop. We have to keep on trying to find the way to break through."

"I know."

"It will be easier, now that your sister has explained it."

"I don't think it will be easier," Felton said tiredly. "I don't think that she has explained it."

"Not to you and me, perhaps. But we'll put the eggheads to work on it. They'll figure it out. They always do, you know."

"Perhaps not this time."

"Oh, yes," the Secretary of Defense nodded. "After all, Felton, we've got to stop it. We've had threats before, but not this kind of thing. I'm not going to dwell on the fact of this immorality, this godlessness, this nakedness, this depraved kind of sexual togetherness, this interloping into minds, this violation of every human privacy and every human decency. I don't have to dwell on that. You realize as well as I do, Felton, that this is a threat to every human being on the face of the earth. The kids were right. Oh they understood this well enough, you know. This isn't a national threat; this isn't like Communism; this isn't simply a threat to the sovereignty, to the freedom of the United States, to the American way of life; this isn't just a threat to democracy; this is a threat to God Himself. This is a threat to mankind. This is a threat to everything decent, everything sacred, everything we believe in, everything we cherish. It's a disease, Felton. You know that, don't you? You recognize that—a disease."

"You really feel that, don't you?" Felton said. "You really believe what you are telling me."

"Believe it? Who can disbelieve it, Felton? It's a disease, and the only way to stop a disease is to kill the bugs that cause it. You know how you stop this disease? I'm going to say it and a lot more are going to say it, Felton: You kill the kids. It's the only way. I wish there were another way, but there isn't."

11
The Hoop

I N one of those charming expressions of candor—which were to become so well known to the television audience—Dr. Hepplemeyer ascribed his scientific success less to his brilliance than to his name. "Can you imagine being Julius Hepplemeyer, and facing that for the rest of your life? If one is Julius Hepplemeyer, one is forced either to transcend it or perish."

Two Nobel Prizes before he finally perfected the hoop attested to the transcendence. In acknowledging them, he made liberal use of what the press came to call "Hepplemeyer Jewels," as for instance: "Wisdom obligates a man to perform foolishly." "Education imposes a search for ignorance." "The solution always calls for the problem."

This last was particularly applicable to the hoop. It was never Dr. Hepplemeyer's intention to bend space, and he pinned down the notion as presumptuous. "Only God bends space," he emphasized. "Man can merely watch, observe, seek—and sometimes find."

"Do you believe in God?" a reporter asked eagerly.

"In an ironic God, yes. The proof is laughter. A smile is the only expression of eternity."

He talked that way without any particular effort, and acute observers realized it was because he thought that way. His wife was an acute observer, and one morning at breakfast, as he cracked a three-minute egg and peered into it, he explained that everything returns to itself.

It rather chilled his wife, without her knowing why. "Even God?" she asked.

"Most certainly God," he replied, and for the next two years he worked on the hoop. The Dean at Columbia cooperated with him, cutting down his lectures to one a week. Every facility was placed at his disposal. After all, it was the Hepplemeyer age; Einstein was dead, and Hepplemeyer had to remind his admirers that while "Hepplemeyer's Law of Return" had perhaps opened new doors in physics, it nevertheless rested solidly upon the basis of Einstein's work. Yet his modest reminders fell upon deaf ears, and whereas *The New York Times* weekly magazine supplement once ran no less than six features a year on some aspect of Einstein's work, they now reduced the number to three and devoted no less than seven features in as many months to Hepplemeyer. Isaac Asimov, that persistent unraveler of the mysteries of science, devoted six thousand words toward a popular explanation of the "Law of Return," and if few understood, it was nevertheless table conversation for many thousands of intrigued readers. Nor were any egos bruised, for Asimov himself estimated that only a dozen people in the entire world actually understood the Hepplemeyer equations.

Hepplemeyer, meanwhile, was so absorbed in his work that he ceased even to read about himself. The lights in his laboratory burned all night long while, with the help of his eager young assistants—more disciples than paid workers—he translated his mathematics into a hoop of shining aluminum, the pipe six inches in diameter, the hoop itself a circle of the six-inch aluminum pipe twelve feet in diameter, and within the six-inch pipe, an intricate coil of gossamer wires. As he told his students, he was in effect building a net in which he would perhaps trap a tiny curl of the endless convolutions of space.

Of course, he immediately denied his images. "We are so limited," he explained. "The universe is filled with endless wonders for which we have no name, no words, no concepts. The hoop? That is different. The hoop is an object, as anyone can see."

There came a fine, sunny, shining day in April, when the hoop was finally finished, and when the professor and his student assistants bore it triumphantly out onto the campus. It took eight stalwart young men to carry the great hoop, and eight more to carry the iron frame in which it would rest. The press was there, television, about four thousand students, about four hundred cops, and various other representatives of the normal and abnormal life of

New York City. The Columbia University quadrangle was indeed so crowded that the police had to clear a path for the hoop. Hepplemeyer begged them to keep the crowd back, since it might be dangerous; and as he hated violence almost as much as he detested stupidity, he begged the students not to get into the kind of rumble that was almost inevitable when cops and students were too many and in too great proximity.

One of the policemen lent the professor a bullhorn, and he declared, in booming electronic tones, "This is only a test. It is almost impossible that it should work. I have calculated that out of any given hundred acres, possibly a hundred square feet will be receptive. So you see how great the odds are against us. You must give us room. You must let us move about."

The students were not only loose and good-natured and full of grass and other congenial substances on that shining April day; they also adored Hepplemeyer as a sort of Bob Dylan of the scientific world. So they cooperated, and finally the professor found a spot that suited him, and the hoop was set up.

Hepplemeyer observed it thoughtfully for a moment and then began going through his pockets for an object. He found a large gray eraser and tossed it into the hoop. It passed through and fell to the ground on the other side.

The student body—as well as the working press—had no idea of what was supposed to happen to the eraser, but the crestfallen expression on Hepplemeyer's face demonstrated that whatever was supposed to happen had not happened. The students broke into sympathetic and supportive applause, and Hepplemeyer, warming to their love, took them into his confidence and said into the bullhorn:

"We try again, no?"

The sixteen stalwart young men lifted hoop and frame and carried their burden to another part of the quadrangle. The crowd followed with the respect and appreciation of a championship golf audience, and the television camera ground away. Once again, the professor repeated his experiment, this time tossing an old pipe through the hoop. As with the eraser, the pipe fell to earth on the other side of the hoop.

"So we try again," he confided into the bullhorn. "Maybe we never find it. Maybe the whole thing is for nothing. Once science was a nice and predictable mechanical handmaiden. Today two and two add up maybe to infinity. Anyway, it was a comfortable old pipe and I am glad I have it back.''

By now it had become evident to most of the onlookers that whatever was cast into the hoop was not intended to emerge from the other side, and were it anyone but Hepplemeyer doing the casting, the crowd, cameras, newsmen, cops and all would have dispersed in disgust. But it was Hepplemeyer, and instead of dispersing in disgust, their enchantment with the project simply increased.

Another place in the quadrangle was chosen, and the hoop was set up. This time Dr. Hepplemeyer selected from his pocket a fountain pen, given to him by the Academy, and inscribed *"Nil desperandum."* Perhaps with full consciousness of the inscription, he flung the pen through the hoop, and instead of falling to the ground on the other side of the hoop, it disappeared. Just like that—just so—it disappeared.

A great silence for a long moment or two, and then one of Hepplemeyer's assistants, young Peabody, took the screwdriver, which he had used to help set up the hoop, and flung it through the hoop. It disappeared. Young Brumberg followed suit with his hammer. It disappeared. Wrench. Clamp. Pliers. All disappeared.

The demonstration was sufficient. A great shout of applause and triumph went up from Morningside Heights and echoed and reechoed from Broadway to St. Nicholas Avenue, and then the contagion set in. A coed began it by scaling her copy of the poetry of e.e. cummings through the hoop. It disappeared. Then enough books to stock a small library. They all disappeared. Then shoes—a veritable rain of shoes—then belts, sweaters, shirts, anything and everything that was at hand was flung through the hoop, and anything and everything that was flung through the hoop disappeared.

Vainly did Professor Hepplemeyer attempt to halt the stream of objects through the hoop; even his bullhorn could not be heard above the shouts and laughter of the delighted students, who now had witnessed the collapse of basic reality along with all the other verities and virtues that previous generations had observed. Vainly did Professor Hepplemeyer warn them.

And then, out of the crowd and into history, raced Ernest Silverman, high jumper and honor student and citizen of Philadelphia.

In all the exuberance and thoughtlessness of youth, he flung himself through the hoop—and disappeared. And in a twinkling, the laughter, the shouts, the exuberance turned into a cold, dismal silence. Like the children who followed the pied piper, Ernest Silverman was gone with all the fancies and hopes; the sun clouded over, and a chill wind blew.

A few bold kids wanted to follow, but Hepplemeyer barred their way and warned them back, pleading through the bullhorn for them to realize the danger involved. As for Silverman, Hepplemeyer could only repeat what he told the police, after the hoop had been roped off, placed under a twenty-four-hour guard, and forbidden to everyone.

"But where is he?" summed up the questions.

"I don't know," summed up the answer.

The questions and answers were the same at Centre Street as at the local precinct, but such was the position of Hepplemeyer that the Commissioner himself took him into his private office—it was midnight by then—and asked him gently, pleadingly:

"What is on the other side of that hoop, Professor?"

"I don't know."

"So you say—so you have said. You made the hoop."

"We build dynamos. Do we know how they work? We make electricity. Do we know what it is?"

"Do we?"

"No, we do not."

"Which is all well and good. Silverman's parents are here from Philadelphia, and they've brought a Philadelphia lawyer with them and maybe sixteen Philadelphia reporters, and they all want to know where the kid is to the tune of God knows how many lawsuits and injunctions."

Hepplemeyer sighed. "I also want to know where he is."

"What do we do?" the Commissioner begged him.

"I don't know. Do you think you ought to arrest me?"

"I would need a charge. Negligence, manslaughter, kidnapping—none of them appear to fit the situation exactly, do they?"

"I am not a policeman," Hepplemeyer said. "In any case, it would interfere with my work."

"Is the boy alive?"

"I don't know."

"Can you answer one question?" the Commissioner asked with some exasperation. "What is on the other side of the hoop?"

"In a manner of speaking, the campus. In another manner of speaking, something else."

"What?"

"Another part of space. A different time sequence. Eternity. Even Brooklyn. I just don't know."

"Not Brooklyn. Not even Staten Island. The kid would have turned up by now. It's damn peculiar that you put the thing together and now you can't tell me what it's supposed to do."

"I know what it's supposed to do," Hepplemeyer said apologetically. "It's supposed to bend space."

"Does it?"

"Probably."

"I have four policemen who are willing to go through the hoop—volunteers. Would you agree?"

"No."

"Why?"

"Space is a peculiar thing, or perhaps not a thing at all," the professor replied, with the difficulty a scientist always has when he attempts to verbalize to the satisfaction of a layman. "Space is not something we understand."

"We've been to the moon."

"Exactly. It's an uncomfortable place. Suppose the boy is on the moon."

"Is he?"

"I don't know. He could be on Mars. Or he could be a million miles short of Mars. I would not want to subject four policemen to that."

So with the simple ingeniousness or ingenuousness of a people who love animals, they put a dog through the loop. It disappeared.

For the next few weeks, a police guard was placed around the hoop day and night, while the professor spent most of his days in court and most of his evenings with his lawyers. He found time, however, to meet with the mayor three times.

New York City was blessed with a mayor whose problems were almost matched by his personality, his wit, and imagination. If Professor Hepplemeyer dreamed of space and infinity, the Mayor dreamed as consistently of ecology, garbage, and finances. Thus it is not to be wondered at that the Mayor came up with a notion that promised to change history.

"We try it with a single garbage truck," the Mayor begged Hepplemeyer. "If it works, it might mean a third Nobel Prize."

"I don't want another Nobel Prize. I didn't deserve the first two. My guilts are sufficient."

"I can persuade the Board of Estimate to pay the damages on the Silverman case."

"Poor boy—will the Board of Estimate take care of my guilt?"

"It will make you a millionaire."

"The last thing I want to be."

"It's your obligation to mankind," the Mayor insisted.

"The college will never permit it."

"I can fix it with Columbia," the Mayor said.

"It's obscene," Hepplemeyer said desperately. And then he surrendered, and the following day a loaded garbage truck backed up across the campus to the hoop.

It does not take much to make a happening in Fun City, and since it is also asserted that there is nothing so potent as an idea whose time has come, the Mayor's brilliant notion spread through the city like wildfire. Not only were the network cameras there, not only the local national press, not only ten or twelve thousand students and other curious city folk, but also the kind of international press that usually turns out only for major international events. Which this was, for certainly the talent for producing garbage was generic to mankind, as G.B.S. had once indelicately remarked; and certainly the disposal of the said garbage was a problem all mankind shared.

So the cameras whirred, and fifty million eyes were glued to television screens as the big Sanitation truck backed into position. As a historical note, we remember that Ralph Vecchio was the driver and Tony Andamano his assistant. Andamano stood in the iris of history, so to speak, directing Vecchio calmly and efficiently:

"Come back, Ralphy—a little more—just cut it a little. Nice and easy. Come back. Come back. You got another twelve, fourteen inches. Slow—great. Hold it there. All right."

Professor Hepplemeyer stood by the Mayor, muttering under his breath as the dumping mechanism reared the great body back on its haunches—and then the garbage began to pour through the hoop. Not a sound was heard from the crowd as the first flood of garbage poured through the hoop; but then, when the garbage disappeared

211

into infinity or Mars or space or another galaxy, such a shout of triumph went up as was eminently proper to the salvation of the human race.

Heroes were made that day. The Mayor was a hero. Tony Andamano was a hero. Ralph Vecchio was a hero. But above all, Professor Hepplemeyer, whose fame was matched only by his gloom, was a hero. How to list his honors? By a special act of Congress, the Congressional Medal of Ecology was created; Hepplemeyer got it. He was made a Kentucky Colonel and an honorary citizen of Japan and Great Britain. Japan immediately offered him ten million dollars for a single hoop, an overall contract of a billion dollars for one hundred hoops. Honorary degrees came from sixteen universities, and the city of Chicago upped Japan's offer to twelve million dollars for a single hoop. With this, the bidding between and among the cities of the United States became frantic, with Detroit topping the list with an offer of one hundred million dollars for the first—or second, to put it properly—hoop constructed by Hepplemeyer. Germany asked for the principle, not the hoop, only the principle behind it, and for this they were ready to pay half a billion marks, gently reminding the professor that the mark was generally preferred to the dollar.

At breakfast, Hepplemeyer's wife reminded him that the dentist's bill was due, twelve hundred dollars for his new bridge.

"We only have seven hundred and twenty-two dollars in the bank." The professor sighed. "Perhaps we should take a loan."

"No, no. No indeed. You are putting me on," his wife said.

The professor, a quarter of a century behind in his slang, observed her with some bewilderment.

"The German offer," she said. "You don't even have to build the wretched thing. All they want is the principle."

"I have often wondered whether it is not ignorance after all but rather devotion to the principle of duality that is responsible for mankind's aggravation."

"What?"

"Duality."

"Do you like the eggs? I got them at the Pioneer supermarket. They're seven cents cheaper, grade A."

"Very good," the professor said.

"What on earth is duality?"

"Everything—the way we think. Good and bad. Right and wrong. Black and white. My shirt, your shirt. My country, your country. It's the way we think. We never think of one, of a whole, of a unit. The universe is outside of us. It never occurs to us that we are it."

"I don't truly follow you," his wife replied patiently, "but does that mean you're not going to build any more hoops?"

"I'm not sure."

"Which means you are sure."

"No, it only means that I am not sure. I have to think about it."

His wife rose from the table, and the professor asked her where she was going.

"I'm not sure. I'm either going to have a migraine headache or jump out of the window. I have to think about it too."

The only one who was absolutely and unswervingly sure of himself was the Mayor of New York City. For eight years he had been dealing with unsolvable problems, and there was no group in the city, whether a trade union, neighborhood organization, consumers' group, or Boy Scout troop which had not selected him as the whipping boy. At long last his seared back showed some signs of healing, and his dedication to the hoop was such that he would have armed his citizenry and thrown up barricades if anyone attempted to touch it or interfere with it. Police stood shoulder to shoulder around it, and morning, evening, noon, and night an endless procession of garbage trucks backed across the Columbia College quadrangle to the hoop, emptying garbage.

So much for the moment. But the lights burned late in the offices of the City Planners as they sat over their drawing boards and blueprints, working out a system for all sewers to empty into the hoop. It was a high moment indeed, not blighted one iota by the pleas of the mayors of Yonkers, Jersey City, and Hackensack to get into the act.

The Mayor stood firm. There was not one hour in the twenty-four hours of any given day, not one minute in the sixty minutes that comprise an hour, when a garbage truck was not backing up to the hoop and discharging its cargo. Tony Andamano, appointed to the position of inspector, had a permanent position at the hoop, with a staff of assistants to see that the garbage was properly discharged into infinity.

213

Of course, it was only to be expected that there would be a mounting pressure, first local, then nationwide, then worldwide, for the hoop to be taken apart and minutely reproduced. The Japanese, so long expert at reproducing and improving anything the West put together, were the first to introduce that motion into the United Nations, and they were followed by half a hundred other nations. But the Mayor had already had his quiet talk with Hepplemeyer, more or less as follows, if Hepplemeyer's memoirs are to be trusted:

"I want it straight and simple, Professor. If they take it apart, can they reproduce it?"

"No."

"Why not?"

"Because they don't know the mathematics. It's not an automobile transmission, not at all."

"Naturally. Is there any chance that they can reproduce it?"

"Who knows?"

"I presume that you do," the Mayor said. "Could you reproduce it?"

"I made it."

"Will you?"

"Perhaps. I have been thinking about it."

"It's a month now."

"I think slowly," the professor said.

Whereupon the Mayor issued his historic statement, namely: "Any attempt to interfere with the operation of the hoop will be considered as a basic attack upon the constitutional property rights of the City of New York and will be resisted with every device, legal and otherwise, that the city has at its disposal."

The commentators immediately launched into a discussion of what the Mayor meant by otherwise, while the Governor, never beloved of the Mayor, filed suit in the Federal Court in behalf of all the municipalities of New York State. NASA, meanwhile, scoffing at the suggestion that there were scientific secrets unsolvable, turned its vast battery of electronic brains onto the problem; and the Russians predicted that they would have their own hoop within sixty days. Only the Chinese appeared to chuckle with amusement, since most of their garbage was recycled into an organic mulch and they were too poor and too thrifty to be overconcerned with the problem. But the Chinese were too far away for their chuckles to mollify Americans, and the tide of anger rose day by day. From hero and

214

eccentric, Professor Hepplemeyer was fast becoming scientific public enemy number one. He was now publicly accused of being a Communist, a madman, an egomaniac, and a murderer to boot.

"It is uncomfortable," Hepplemeyer admitted to his wife; since he eschewed press conferences and television appearances, his admissions and anxieties usually took place over the breakfast table.

"I have known for thirty years how stubborn you are. Now, at least, the whole world knows."

"No, it's not stubborness. As I said, it's a matter of duality."

"Everyone else thinks it's a matter of garbage. You still haven't paid the dentist bill. It's four months overdue now. Dr. Steinman is suing us."

"Come, now. Dentists don't sue."

"He says that potentially you are the richest man on earth, and that justifies his suit."

The professor was scribbling on his napkin. "Remarkable," he said. "Do you know how much garbage they've poured into the hoop already?"

"Do you know that you could have a royalty on every pound? A lawyer called today who wants to represent—"

"Over a million tons," he interrupted. "Imagine, over a million tons of garbage. What wonderful creatures we are! For centuries philosophers sought a teleological explanation for mankind, and it never occurred to any of them that we are garbage makers, no more, no less."

"He mentioned a royalty of five cents a ton."

"Over a million tons," the professor said thoughtfully. "I wonder where it is."

It was three weeks later to the day, at five-twenty in the morning, that the first crack appeared in the asphalt paving of Wall Street. It was the sort of ragged fissure that is not uncommon in the miles of city streets, nothing to arouse notice, much less alarm, except that in this case it was not static. Between five-twenty and eighty-twenty, it doubled in length, and the asphalt lips of the street had parted a full inch. The escaping smell caught the notice of the crowds hurrying to work, and word went around that there was a gas leak.

By ten o'clock, the Con Edison trucks were on the scene, checking the major valves, and by eleven, the police had roped off the street, and the lips of the crack, which now extended across the entire street, were at least eight inches apart. There was talk of an

215

earthquake, yet when contacted, Fordham University reported that the seismograph showed nothing unusual—oh, perhaps, some very slight tremors, but nothing unusual enough to be called an earthquake.

When the streets filled for the noon lunch break, a very distinct and rancid smell filled the narrow cavern, so heavy and unpleasant that half a dozen more sensitive stomachs upchucked; and by one o'clock, the lips of the crack were over a foot wide, water mains had broken, and Con Edison had to cut its high-voltage lines. At two-ten, the first garbage appeared.

The first garbage just oozed out of the cut, but within the hour the break was three feet wide, buildings had begun to slip and show cracks and shower bricks, and the garbage was pouring into Wall Street like lava from an erupting volcano. The offices closed, the office workers fled, brokers, bankers, and secretaries alike wading through the garbage. In spite of all the efforts of the police and the fire department, in spite of the heroic rescues of the police helicopter teams, eight people were lost in the garbage or trapped in one of the buildings; and by five o'clock the garbage was ten stories high in Wall Street and pouring into Broadway at one end and onto the East River Drive at the other. Now, like a primal volcano, the dams burst, and for an hour the garbage fell on lower Manhattan as once the ashes had fallen on Pompeii.

And then it was over, very quickly, very suddenly—all of it so sudden that the Mayor never left his office at all, but sat staring through the window at the carpet of garbage that surrounded City Hall.

He picked up the telephone and found that it still worked. He dialed his personal line, and across the mountain of garbage the electrical impulses flickered and the telephone rang in Professor Hepplemeyer's study.

"Hepplemeyer here," the professor said.

"The Mayor."

"Oh, yes. I heard. I'm terribly sorry. Has it stopped?"

"It appears to have stopped," the Mayor said.

"Ernest Silverman?"

"No sign of him," the Mayor said.

"Well, it was thoughtful of you to call me."

"There's all that garbage."

"About two million tons?" the professor asked gently.

216

"Give or take some. Do you suppose you could move the hoop—"

The professor replaced the phone and went into the kitchen, where his wife was putting together a beef stew.

She asked who had called.

"The Mayor."

"Oh?"

"He wants the hoop moved."

"I think it's thoughtful of him to consult you."

"Oh, yes—yes, indeed," Professor Hepplemeyer said. But I'll have to think about it."

"I suppose you will," she said with resignation.

12
The Cold, Cold Box

AS always, the annual meeting of the Board of Directors convened at nine o'clock in the morning, on the 10th of December. Nine o'clock in the morning was a sensible and reasonable hour to begin a day's work, and long ago, the 10th of December had been chosen as a guarantee against the seduction of words. Every one of the directors would have to be home for the Christmas holiday—or its equivalent—and therefore the agenda was timed for precisely two weeks and not an hour more.

In the beginning, this had caused many late sessions, sometimes two or three days when the directors met the clock round, with no break for sleep or rest. But in time, as things fell into the proper place and orderly management replaced improvisation, each day's meeting was able to adjourn by four o'clock in the afternoon—and there were even years when the general meeting finished its work a day or two early.

By now, the meeting of the Board of Directors was very matter-of-fact and routine. The big clock on the wall of the charming and spacious meeting room was just sounding nine, its voice low and musical, as the last of the directors found their seats. They nodded pleasantly to each other, and if they were seated close to old friends, they exchanged greetings. They were completely relaxed, neither tense nor uneasy at the thought of the long meeting that lay ahead of them.

There were exactly three hundred of these directors, and they sat in a comfortable circle of many tiers of seats—in a room not unlike a small amphitheatre. Two aisles cut through to a center circle or stage about twenty feet in diameter, and there a podium was placed which allowed the speaker to turn in any direction as he spoke. Since the number of three hundred was an arbitrary one, agreed upon after a good deal of trial and error, and maintained as an excellent working size, half the seats in the meeting room were always empty. There was some talk now and then of redesigning the meeting room, but nobody ever got down to doing it and by now the empty seats were a normal part of the decor.

The membership of the Board was about equally divided between men and women. No one could serve under the age of thirty, but retirement was a matter of personal decision, and a reasonable number of members were over seventy. Two thirds of them were in their fifties. Since the Board was responsible for an international management, it was only natural that all nations and races should be represented—black men and white men and brown men and yellow men, and all the shadings and gradations in between. Like the United Nations—they were too modest to make such a comparison themselves—they had a number of official languages (and a system of simultaneous translation), though English was most frequently used.

As a matter of fact, the Chairman of the Board, who had been born in Indo-China, opened this meeting in English, which he spoke very well and with ease, and after he had welcomed them and announced the total attendance—all members present—he said:

"At the beginning of our annual meeting—and this is an established procedure, I may say—we deal with a moral and legal point, the question of Mr. Steve Kovac. We undertake this before the reading of the agenda, for we have felt that this question of Mr. Kovac is not a matter of agenda or business, but of conscience. Of our conscience, I must add, and not without humility; for Mr. Kovac is the only secret of this meeting. All else that the Board discusses, votes upon and decides or rejects, will be made public, as you know. But of Mr. Steve Kovac the world knows nothing; and each year in the past, our decision has been that the world should continue to know nothing about Mr. Kovac. Each year in the past, Mr. Kovac has been the object of a cruel and criminal action by the members of this Board. Each year in the past, it has been our decision to repeat this crime."

To these words, most of the members of the Board did not react at all—but here and there young men and women showed their surprise, bewilderment and unease, either by expressions on their faces or by low protestations of disbelief. The members of the Board were not insensitive people.

"This year, as in the past, we make this question of Mr. Kovac our first piece of business—because we cannot go onto our other business until it is decided. As in the past, we will decide whether to engage in a criminal conspiracy or not."

A young woman, a new member of the board, her face flushed and angry, rose and asked the chairman if he would yield for a question. He replied that he would.

"Am I to understand that you are serious, Mr. Chairman, or is this some sophomoric prank for the edification of new members?"

"This board is not used to such descriptive terms as sophomoric, as you should know, Mrs. Ramu," he answered mildly. "I am quite serious."

The young woman sat down. She bit her lower lip and stared at her lap. A young man arose.

"Yes, Mr. Steffanson?" the chairman said pleasantly.

The young man sat down again. The older members were gravely attentive, thoughtful without impatience.

"I do not intend to choke off any discussion, and I will gladly yield to any questions," said the Chairman, "but perhaps a little more about this troublesome matter first. There are two reasons why we consider this problem each year. Firstly, because the kind of crime we have committed in the past is hardly anything to grow indifferent to; we need to be reminded; premeditated crime is a deadly threat to basic decency, and God help us if we should ever become complacent! Secondly, each year, there are new members on this board, and it is necessary that they should hear all of the facts in the case of Mr. Kovac. This year, we have seven new members. I address myself to them, but not only to them. I include all of my fellow members of this Board."

Steve Kovac (the President of the Board began) was born in Pittsburgh in the year 1913. He was one of eleven children, four of whom survived to adulthood. This was not too unusual in those days of poverty, ignorance and primitive medicine.

John Kovac, Steve Kovac's father, was a steelworker. When Steve Kovac was six years old, there was a long strike—an attempt on the part of the steelworkers to increase their wages. I am sure you are all

221

familiar with the method of the strike, and therefore I will not elaborate.

During this strike, Steve Kovac's mother died; a year later, John Kovac fell into a vat of molten steel. The mother died of tuberculosis, a disease then incurable. The father's body was dissolved in the molten steel. I mention these things in terms of their very deep and lasting effect on the mind and character of Steve Kovac. Orphaned at the age of seven, he grew up like an animal in the jungle. Placed in a county home for orphan children, he was marked as a bad and intractable boy, beaten daily, deprived of food, punished in every way the ignorance and insensitivity of the authorities could devise. After two years of this, he ran away.

This is a very brief background to the childhood of a most remarkable man, a man of brilliance and strong character, a man of high inventive genius and grim determination. Unfortunately, the mind and personality of this man had been scarred and traumatized beyond redemption. A psychiatric analysis of this process has been prepared, and each of you will find a copy in your portfolio. It also itemizes the trials and suffering of Steve Kovac between the ages of nine and twenty—the years during which he fought to survive and to grow to adulthood.

It also gives a great many details of this time of his life—details I cannot go into. You must understand that while the question before us is related to this background, there are many other features I will deal with.

At this point, the Chairman of the Board paused to take a drink of water and to glance through his notes. The younger members of the Board glanced hurriedly at the psychiatric report; the older members remained contemplative, absorbed in their own thoughts. As many times as they had been through this, somehow it was never dull.

At the age of twenty (the Chairman resumed) Steve Kovac was working in a steel mill outside of Pittsburgh. He was friendly then with a man named Emery. This man, Emery, was alone, without family or means of support. A former coal miner, he suffered from a disease of the lungs, common to his trade. All he had in the world was a five thousand dollar insurance policy. Steve Kovac agreed to

222

support him, and in return he made Kovac the beneficiary of the insurance policy. In those days, insurance policies were frequently the only means with which a family could survive the death of the breadwinner.

Four months later, Emery died. Years afterward, it was rumored that Kovac had hastened his death, but there is no evidence for the rumor. The five thousand dollars became the basis for Steve Kovac's subsequent fortune. Twenty-five years later, the net worth of Steve Kovac was almost three billion dollars. As an individual, he was possibly the wealthiest man in the United States of America. He was a tycoon in the steel and aluminum industries, and he controlled chemical plants, copper mines, railroads, oil refineries and dozens of associated industries. He was then forty-six years old. The year was 1959.

The story of his climb to power and wealth is unique for the generations he lived through. He was a strong, powerful, handsome man—tortured within himself, driven by an insatiable lust to revenge himself, and his father and mother too, for the poverty and suffering of his childhood. Given the traumatic factors of his childhood, his cravings for power turned psychopathic and paranoid, and he built this structure of power securely. He owned newspapers as well as airlines, television stations and publishing houses, and much more than he owned, he controlled. Thereby, he was able to keep himself out of the public eye. In any year of the fifties, you can find no more than an occasional passing reference to him in the press.

How an individual achieved this in a time of the public corporation and the "corporation man" is a singular tale of drive and ambition. Steve Kovac was ambitious, ruthless, merciless and utterly without compassion or pity. His policy was to destroy what stood in his way, if he could; if he could not, he bent it to his will in one way or another. He wrecked lives and fortunes. He framed and entrapped his competitors; he used violence when he had to—when he could not buy or bribe what he wanted. He corrupted individuals and bribed parliaments and bought governments. He erected a structure of power and wealth and control that reached out to every corner of the globe.

And then, in his forty-sixth year, at the height of his wealth and power, he discovered that he had cancer.

The chairman of the Board paused to allow the impact of the words to settle and tell. He took another drink of water. He arranged the papers in front of him.

"At this time," he said, "I propose to read to you a short extract from the diary of Dr. Jacob Frederick. I think that most of you are familiar with the work of Dr. Frederick. In any case, you know that he was elected a member of our Board. Naturally, that was a long time ago. I need only mention that Dr. Frederick was one of the many wise and patient pioneers in the work of cancer research—not only a great physician, but a great scientist. The first entry I propose to read is dated January 12, 1959."

I had an unusual visitor today (the Chairman of the Board read), Steve Kovac, the industrial tycoon. I had heard rumors to the effect of the wealth and power of this man. In himself, he is a striking individual, tall, muscular, handsome, with a broad strong face and a great mane of prematurely-white hair. He has blue eyes, a ruddy complexion, and appears to be in the prime of life and health. Of course, he is not. I examined him thoroughly. There is no hope for the man.

"Doctor," he said to me, "I want the truth. I know it already. You are not the first physician I have seen. But I also want it from you, plainly and bluntly."

I would have told him in any case. He is not the kind of a man you can lie to easily. "Very well," I said to him, "you have cancer. There is no cure for your cancer. You are going to die."

"How long?"

"We can't say. Perhaps a year."

"And if I undergo operative procedure?"

"That could prolong your life—perhaps a year or two longer if the operation is successful. But it will mean pain and incapacity."

"And there is no cure?" His surface was calm, his voice controlled; he must have labored for years to achieve that kind of surface calm and control; but underneath, I could see a very frightened and desperate man.

"None as yet."

"And the quacks and diet men and the rest—they promise cures?"

"It's easy to promise," I said. "But there isn't any cure."

"Doc," he said to me, "I don't want to die and I don't intend to

224

die. I have worked twenty-five years to be where I am now. The tree is planted. I'm going to eat the fruit. I am young and strong—and the best years of my life are ahead of me."

When Kovac talked like that, he was convincing, even to me. It is his quality not simply to demand life, but to take. He denies the inevitable. But the fact remained.

"I can't help you, Mr. Kovac," I told him.

"But you're going to help me," he said calmly. "I came to you because you know more about cancer than any man in the world. Or so I am told."

"You have been misinformed," I said shortly. "No man knows more than anyone else. Such knowledge and work is a collective thing."

"I believe in men, not mobs. I believe in you. Therefore, I am ready to pay you a fee of one million dollars if you can make it possible for me to beat this thing and live a full life span." He then reached into his coat for his wallet and took out a certified check for one million dollars. "It is yours—if I live."

I told him to return the following day—that is tomorrow. And now I have been sitting here for hours, thinking of what one million dollars would mean to my work, my hopes—indeed, through them, to all people. I have been thinking with desperation and with small result. Only one thought occurs to me. It is fantastic, but then Steve Kovac is a fantastic man.

Again, the Chairman of the Board paused and looked inquiringly at some of the younger members. They had been listening with what appeared hypnotic concentration. There were no questions and no comments.

"Then I will continue with the diary of Dr. Frederick," the Chairman said.

January 13, (the Chairman said). Steve Kovac returned at 2:00, as we had arranged. He greeted me with a confident smile.

"Doc, if you are ready to sell, I am ready to buy."

"And you really believe that you can buy life?"

"I can buy anything. It's a question of price."

"Can you buy the future?" I asked him. "Because that is where the cure for cancer lies. Do you want to buy it?"

"I'll buy it because you have decided to sell," he said flatly. "I know who I am dealing with. Make your offer, Dr. Frederick."

I made it, as fantastic as it was. I told him about my experiments with the effects of intense cold upon cancer cells. I explained that though, as yet, the experiments had not produced any cure, I had made enormous strides in the intense and speedy application of extreme cold—or, to put it more scientifically, my success in removing heat from living objects. I detailed my experiments—how I had begun with frogs and snakes, freezing them, and then removing the cold and resuming the life process at a later date; how I had experimented with mice, cats, dogs—and most recently monkeys.

He followed me and anticipated me. "How do you restore life?" he wanted to know.

"I don't restore it. The life never dies. In the absence of heat, what might be called the ripening or aging process of life is suspended, but the life remains. Time and motion are closely related; and under intense cold, motion slows and theoretically could cease—all motion, even within the atomic structure. When the motion ceases, time ceases."

"Is it painful?"

"As far as I know, it isn't. The transition is too quick."

"I'd like to see an experiment."

I told him that I had in my laboratory a spider monkey that had been frozen seven weeks ago. My assistants could attest to that. He went into the laboratory with me and watched as we successfully restored the monkey. Seemingly, it was none the worse.

"And the mind?" he asked me.

I shrugged. "I don't know. I have never attempted it with a human being."

"But you think it would work?"

"I am almost certain that it would work. I would need better and larger equipment. With some money to spend, I can improve the process—well, considerably."

He nodded and took the certified check out of his wallet. "Here is your retainer—apart from what you have to spend. Buy whatever you need, and charge it to me. Spend whatever you have to spend and buy the best. No ceiling, no limit. And when I wake up, after a cure has been discovered, there will be a second million to add to your fee. I am not a generous man, but neither am I niggardly when I buy what I want. When will you be ready?"

226

"Considering the prognosis of your disease," I said, "we should not delay more than five weeks. I will be ready then. Will you?"

Steve Kovac nodded. "I will be ready. There are a good many technical and legal details to work out. I have many large interests, as you may know, and this is a journey of uncertain duration. I will also take care of your own legal responsibilities."

Then he left, and it was done—possibly the strangest agreement ever entered into by a doctor and his patient. I try to think of only one thing—that I now have a million dollars to put into my work and research.

The Chairman of the Board wore pince-nez, and now he paused to wipe them. He cleared his throat, rearranged the papers on the podium once again, and explained.

You see, the plan was a simple one and a sensible one too. Since Mr. Kovac's condition could not be cured, here was a means of preserving his life and arresting the disease until science had found a cure. Timidity was never one of Mr. Kovac's qualities. He analyzed the situation, faced it, and accepted the only possible escape offered to him. So he went about placing his affairs in such order as to guarantee the success and prosperity of his enterprise while he slept—and also their return to his bidding and ownership when he awoke.

In other words, he formed a single holding company for all of his many interests. He gathered together a Board of Directors to manage that holding company in his absence, making himself president in absentia, with a substitute president to preside while he was gone. He made a set of qualifying bylaws, that no president could hold office for more than two years, that the Board was to be enlarged each year and a number of other details, each of them aimed at the single goal of retaining all power to himself. And because he was not dead, but merely absent, he created a unique situation, one unprecedented in the history of finance.

This holding company was exempted from all the traditional brakes and tolls placed upon previous companies through the mechanism of death. Until Mr. Kovac returned, the holding company was immortal. Naturally, Dr. Frederick was placed upon the Board of Directors.

In other words (the Chairman of the Board concluded) that is how this Board of Directors came into being.

He allowed himself his first smile then. "Are there any questions at this point?" he asked mildly.

A new member from Japan rose and wanted to know why, if this was the case, the whole world should be told otherwise?

We thought it best (said the President). Just as we, on this Board, have great powers for progress and construction, so do we have no inconsiderable powers of concealment and alteration. The people of the United States and the United Kingdom might have accepted the knowledge that Steve Kovac brought this Board of Directors into being, but certainly in the Soviet Union and China, such knowledge might have been most disconcerting and destructive. Remember that once we had established an open trade area in the Soviet Union and had brought three of her leading government people onto our Board of Directors, our situation changed radically. We were enabled then, through a seizure of all fuel supplies on earth, to prevent the imminent outbreak of World War III.

At that point, neither the extent of our holdings nor the amount of our profits could be further concealed. I say we (the Chairman deferred modestly) but of course it was our predecessors who faced these problems. Our cash balance was larger than that of the United States Treasury, our industrial potential greater than that of any major power. Believe me, without planned intent or purpose, this Board of Directors suddenly found itself the dominant force on earth. At that point, it became desperately necessary for us to explain what we represented.

A new member from Australia rose and asked, "How long was that, Mr. Chairman, if I may inquire, after the visit of Mr. Kovac to Dr. Frederick?"

The Chairman nodded. "It was the year Dr. Frederick died— twenty-two years after the treatment began. By then, five types of cancer had already surrendered their secret to science. But there was not yet any cure for Mr. Kovac's disease."

"And all the time, the treatment had remained secret?"

"All the time," the Chairman nodded.

You see (he went on), at that time, the Board felt that the people of Earth had reached a moment of crisis and decision. A moment, I say, for the power was only momentarily in the hands of this Board. We had no armies, navies or air-fleets—all we had were a major portion of the tools of production. We knew we had not prevented war but simply staved it off. This was a Board of Directors for management, not for power, and any day the installations and plants we owned and controlled could have been torn from our grasp. That was when our very thoughtful and wise predecessors decided to embark on a vast, global propaganda campaign to convince the world that we represented a secret Parliament of the wisest and best forces of mankind—that we were in effect a Board of Directors for the complex of mankind.

And in this, we succeeded, for the television stations, the newspapers, the radio, the film and the theatre—all these were ours. And in that brief, fortunate moment, we launched our attack. We used the weapons of Steve Kovac—let us be honest and admit that. We acted as he would have acted, but out of different motives entirely.

We bought and bribed and framed. We infiltrated the parliaments of all mankind. We bought the military commanders. We dissolved the armies and navies in the name of super-weapons, and then we destroyed the super-weapons in the name of mankind. Where leaders could not be bought or bribed, we brought them into our Board. And above all, we bought control—control of every manufacturing, farming or mining unit of any consequence upon the face of the earth.

It took the Board of Directors twenty-nine years more to accomplish this; and at the end of that twenty-nine years, our earth was a single complex of production for use and happiness—and if I may say so, for mankind. A semblance of national structure remained, but it was even then as ritualistic and limited as any commonwealth among the old states of the United States. Wars, armies, navies, atom bombs—all of these were only ugly memories. The era of reason and sanity began, the era of production for use and life under the single legal code of man. Thus, we have become creatures of law, equal under the law, and abiding by the law. This Board of Directors was never a government, nor is it now. It is what it proposes to be, a group management for the holding company.

Only today, the holding company and the means of mankind are inseparable. Thereby, our very great responsibility.

The Chairman of the Board wiped his face and took a few more sips of water. A new member from the United States rose and said,

"But Mr. Chairman, the cure for all types of cancer was discovered sixty-two years ago."

"So it was," the Chairman agreed.

"Then, Steve Kovac—" The new member paused. She was a beautiful, sensitive woman in her middle thirties, a physicist of note and talent, and also an accomplished musician.

"You see, my dear," the Chairman said, lapsing into a most informal mode of address, pardonable only because of his years and dignity, "it faced us. When we make a law for mankind and submit to it, we must honor it. Sixty-two years ago, Steve Kovac owned the world and all its wealth and industry, a dictator beyond the dream of any dictator, a tyrant above all tyrants, a king and an emperor to dwarf all other kings and emperors—"

As he spoke, two of the older members left the meeting room. Minutes later, they returned, wheeling into the room and up to the podium a rectangular object, five feet high, seven feet long and three feet wide, the whole of it covered with a white cloth. They left it there and returned to their seats.

"—yes, he owned the world. Think of it—for the first time in history, a just peace governed the nations of mankind. Cities were being rebuilt, deserts turned into gardens, jungles cleared, poverty and crime a thing of the past. Man was standing erect, flexing his muscles, reaching out to the planets and the stars—and all of this belonged to a single savage, merciless, despotic paranoid, Steve Kovac. Then, as now, my dear associates, this Board of Directors was faced with the problem of the man to whom we owed our existence, the man who all unwittingly unified mankind and ushered in the new age of man—yes, the man who gave us the right and authority to hold and manage, the man whose property we manage. Then as now, we were faced with Steve Kovac!"

Almost theatrical in his conclusion and gestures, the Chairman of the Board stepped down from the podium and with one motion swept the cloth aside. The entire Board fixed their eyes on the cabinet where, under a glass cover, in a cold beyond all concept of cold, a man lay sleeping in what was neither life nor death, but a subjective pause in the passage of time. He was a handsome man, big and broad, ruddy of face and with a fine mane of white hair. He seemed to sleep lightly, expectantly, confidently—as if he were dreaming hungrily but pleasantly of what he would awaken to.

"Steve Kovac," the President said. "So he sleeps, from year to year, no difference, no changes. So he appeared to our predecessors sixty-two years ago, when they first had the means to cure him and the obligation to awaken him. They committed the first of sixty-two crimes; they took no action in the face of a promise, a duty, a legality and an almost sacred obligation. Can we understand them? Can we forgive them? Can we forgive the board that voted this same decision again and again? Above all, can we forgive ourselves if we stain our honor, break the law, and ignore our own inheritance of an obligation?

"I am not here to argue the question. It is never argued. The facts are presented, and then we vote. Therefore, will all those in favor of awakening Mr. Kovac raise their right hands?"

The President of the Board waited. Long moments became minutes, but no hands were raised. The two older members covered the cold, cold box and wheeled it out. The Chairman of the Board took a sip of water, and announced,

"We will now have the reading of the agenda."

13
The Talent of Harvey

HARVEY KEPPLEMEN never knew that he had a talent for anything, until one Sunday morning at breakfast he plucked a crisp water roll right out of the air.

It balanced the universe; it steadied the order of things. Man is man, and particularly in this age of equality, when uniformity has become both a passion and a religion, it would be unconscionable that a decent human being of forty years should have no talent at all. Yet Harvey Kepplemen was so obviously and forthrightly an untalented man—until this morning—that the label was pinned on him descriptively. As one says, He is short, She is fat, He is handsome, so they would say of Harvey: Nothing there. No talent. No verve. Pale. Colorless. No bent. No aptitude. He was a quiet, soft-spoken person of middle height, with middling looks and brown eyes and brown hair that was thinning in a moderately even manner, and he had passable teeth with good fillings and clean fingernails, and he was an accountant with an income of eighteen thousand dollars a year.

Just that. He was not given to anger, moods, or depression, and if any observer had cared to observe him, he would have said that Harvey was a cheerful enough person; except that one never noticed whether he was cheerful or not. Suzie was his wife. Suzie's mother once put the question to her. "Is Harvey always so cheerful?" Suzie's mother wanted to know.

"Cheerful? I never think of Harvey as being cheerful."

Neither did anyone else, but that was because no one ever gave any serious thought to Harvey. Perhaps if there had been children, they might have had opinions concerning their father; but it was a childless marriage. Not an unhappy one, not a very happy one. Simply childless.

Nevertheless, Suzie was quite content. Small, dark, reasonably attractive, she accepted Harvey. Neither of them was rebellious. Life was just the way it was. Sunday morning was just the way it was. They slept late but not too late. They had brunch at precisely eleven o'clock. Suzie prepared toast, two eggs for each of them, three slices of crisp bacon for each of them, orange juice to begin and coffee to finish. She also set out two jars of jam, imported marmalade, which Harvey liked, and grape jelly, which she liked.

On this Sunday morning, Harvey thought that he would have liked a crisp roll.

"Really?" Suzie said. "I never knew that you liked rolls particularly. You do like toast."

"Oh, yes," Harvey agreed. "I do like toast."

"I mean, we always have toast."

"I have toast for lunch, too," Harvey agreed.

"I could have bought rolls."

"I don't think so, because I guess I was thinking about the kind of rolls we had when I was a kid. They were light and crisp, and they were two for a nickel. Can you imagine paying only a nickel for two rolls?"

"No. Really, I can't."

"Well, no more light, crisp water rolls, two for a nickel." Harvey sighed. "Wouldn't it be nice if I could just reach up like this and pluck one out of the air?"

And then Harvey reached up and plucked a crisp, brown water roll right out of the air, and sat there, arm frozen into position, mouth open, staring at the water roll; then he lowered his arm slowly and placed the roll on the table in front of him and continued to stare at it.

"That's very clever, Harvey," Suzie said. "Is it a surprise for me? I think you did it perfectly."

"Did what?"

"You plucked the roll right out of the air." Suzie picked up the roll. "It's warm—really, you are clever, Harvey." She broke it open and tasted it. "So good! Where did you buy it, Harvey?"

234

"What?"

"The roll. I hope you bought another one."

"What roll?"

"This one."

"Where did it come from?"

"Harvey, you just plucked it right out of the air. Do you remember the magician who entertained at Lucy Gordon's party? He did it with white doves. But I think you did it just as nicely with the roll, and it's such a surprise, because I can imagine how much you practiced."

"I didn't practice."

"Harvey!"

"Did I really take that roll out of the air?"

"You did, Mr. Magician," Suzie said proudly. She had a delicious feeling of pride, a very new feeling. While she had never been ashamed of Harvey before, she had certainly never been proud of him.

"I don't know how I did it."

"Oh, Harvey, stop putting me on. I am terribly impressed. Really I am."

Harvey reached out, broke off a piece of the roll, and tasted it. It was quite good, fresh, straightforward, honest bread, precisely like the two-for-a-nickel rolls he had eaten as a child.

"Put some butter on it," Suzie suggested.

Harvey buttered his piece and then topped it with marmalade. He licked his lips with appreciation. Suzie poured him another cup of coffee.

Harvey finished the roll—Suzie refusing any more than a taste—and then he shook his head thoughtfully. "Damned funny," he said. "I just reached up and took it out of the air."

"Oh, Harvey."

"That's what I did. That's exactly what I did."

"Your eggs are getting cold," Suzie reminded him.

He shook his head. "No—it couldn't have happened that way. Then where did it come from?"

"Do you want me to put them back in the pan?"

"Listen, Suzie. Now just listen to me. I got to thinking about these rolls I ate when I was a kid, and I said to myself, wouldn't it be nice to have one right now, and wouldn't it be nice just to reach up and pick it out of the air—like this." And suiting his action to the thought, he plucked another roll out of the air and dropped it on the table like a hot coal.

"See what I mean?"

Suzie clapped her hands. "Wonderful! Beautiful! I was staring right at you and I never saw you do it."

Harvey picked up the second roll. "I didn't do it," he said bleakly. "I haven't been practicing sleight of hand. You know me, Suzie. I can't do the simplest card trick."

"That's what makes it so wonderful—because you had all these hidden qualities and you brought them out."

"No—no. Remember how it is when we play poker, Suzie, and it's my deal, and it's the big laugh of the evening when I try it and the cards are all over the table. You don't unlearn something like that."

Suzie's eyes widened, and for the first time she realized that her husband was sitting at the table in a T-shirt, with no sleeves and no equipment other than two cold eggs and three strips of bacon.

"Harvey, you mean—"

"I mean," he said. "Yes."

"But from where? Gettleson's Bakery is four blocks away."

"They don't make water rolls at Gettleson's Bakery."

They sat in silence then and stared at each other.

"Maybe it's something you have a talent for," Suzie said finally. More silence.

"Do you suppose it's only rolls?" Suzie said. "I mean just rolls? Suppose you tried a Danish?"

"I don't like Danish," Harvey answered miserably.

"You like the kind with the prune filling. I mean, when they're crisp and have a lot of prune filling and they're not all that limp, squishy kind of dough."

"You don't get them like that anymore."

"Well, you remember when we drove down to Washington, and we stopped at that motel outside of Baltimore, and you remember how they told us they had their own chef who worked in one of the big hotels in Germany, only he wasn't a Nazi or anything like that, and he made the Danish himself and you remember how much you liked it. So you could just think about that kind of Danish, full of prune filling."

236

Harvey thought about it. His hand was shaking as he reached out to a spot midway between himself and Suzie, and there it was between his thumb and his forefinger, a piece of Danish so impossibly full of sweet prune filling that it almost came to pieces in Harvey's fingers. He let it plop down on the cold eggs.

"Oh—you've spoiled the eggs," Suzie said.

"Well, they were cold anyway."

"Yes, I suppose so. I can make you some fresh eggs."

Harvey put a finger into the prune filling and then licked it thoughtfully. He broke off a corner of the Danish, ignoring the cold egg yellow that adhered, and munched it.

"There's no use making fresh eggs," Suzie observed, "because now that sweet stuff will ruin your appetite. Is it good?"

"Delicious."

Then, in a squeak that was almost a scream, Suzie demanded to know where the Danish came from.

"You saw it. You told me to get a Danish."

"Oh, my God, Harvey!"

"That's the way I feel about it. It's damn funny, isn't it?"

"You took that Danish right out of the air."

"That's what I've been trying to tell you."

"It wasn't a trick," said Suzie. "I think I am going to be sick, Harvey. I think I am going to throw up."

She rose and went to the bathroom, and Harvey listened unhappily to the sound of the toilet being flushed. Then she brushed her teeth. They were both of them very clean and neat people. When she returned to the breakfast table, she had gotten a grip on herself, and she told Harvey matter-of-factly that she had read an article in the magazine section of *The New York Times* to the effect that all so-called miracles and religious phenomena of the past were simply glossed-over scientific facts, totally comprehensible in the light of present-day knowledge.

"Would you repeat that please, darling?" Harvey asked her.

"I mean that the Danish must have come from somewhere."

"Baltimore," Harvey agreed.

"Do you want to try something else?" she asked tentatively.

"No. I don't think so."

"Then I think we ought to call my brother, Dave."

"Why."

237

"Because," Suzie said, "and I don't want to hurt your feelings, Harvey, but simply because Dave knows what to do."

"About what?"

"I know you don't like Dave—"

Dave was heavy, overbearing, arrogant, insensitive, and contemptuous of Harvey.

"I don't like him very much," Harvey admitted. Harvey disliked feelings of hostility toward anyone. "I can get along with him," he added. "I mean, Suzie, you cannot imagine how much I try to like Dave because he is your brother, but whenever I approach him—"

"Harvey," she interrupted, "I know." Then she telephoned Dave.

Dave always had three eggs for breakfast. Harvey sat at the table and watched gloomily as Dave stuffed himself and Dave's wife, Ruthie, explained about Dave's digestion. Dave had never taken a laxative. "Dave has a motto," Ruthie explained. "You are what you eat."

"The brain needs food, the body needs food," Dave agreed. "What kind of trouble are you in, Harvey? You're upset. You're down. When I see a man who's down, I know the whole story. Up and down, which is the secret of life, Harvey. It's as simple as that. Up. As simple as that. You got any more bacon, Suzie?"

Suzie brought the bacon to the table, sat down, and carefully explained what had happened that morning. Dave grinned but did not stop eating.

"I don't think you understood me," Suzie said.

Dave cleared his mouth, chewed firmly, and congratulated the Kepplemens. "Ruthie," he said, "how many times have I said to you, the trouble with Harvey and Suzie is they got no sense of humor? How many times?"

"Maybe fifty times," Ruthie replied amiably.

"It's not the biggest shtick in the world," Dave said charitably. "But it's cute. Harvey takes things out of the air. It's all right."

"Not things. Water rolls and a piece of Danish."

"What are water rolls?" Ruthie wanted to know.

"They're a kind of roll," Harvey explained uncomfortably. "They used to make them when I was a kid. Crisp outside and soft inside."

"Here is half of the second one," Suzie said, handing it to Ruthie. Ruthie examined it and nibbled tentatively. "You remember the way Pop used to dip his water rolls into the coffee," Suzie said to Dave.

"You got to butter it first," Dave told Ruthie. "Go ahead, try it."

"You don't believe one word I have said." Suzie turned to her husband. "Go ahead, Harvey. Show them."

Harvey shook his head.

"Come on, Harvey—come on," Dave said. "One lousy roll. What have you got to lose?"

For the first time that morning, Harvey felt good, really good. He reached across the table and from the airspace directly in front of his brother-in-law's nose he extracted a warm, crisp brown roll, held it for a long moment, and then placed it on Dave's plate.

"Oh, my God!" Ruthie cried.

Suzie grinned with delight, and Dave, his mouth open, stared at the roll and said nothing. He just stared and said nothing.

"It's still warm. Eat it," Harvey said with authority. It was possibly the first thing he had ever said to Dave with any kind of authority.

Dave shook his head.

Harvey broke open the roll and buttered it, the butter melting on the hot white bread. He handed it to Dave, and Dave nibbled at it tentatively. "Not bad, not bad." Dave took two large bites. He was beginning to be himself again. "You're not crapping around, are you, Harvey?" he asked. "No—no, it's impossible. You're the clumsiest jerk that ever tried to shuffle a deck of cards, so how could it be sleight of hand? Then what is it, Harvey?"

Harvey shook his head hopelessly.

"It's a gift," Suzie said.

"Did you feel it coming on, Harvey?" Dave wanted to know. "I mean, did it grow on you—or what?"

"Is it only rolls?" Ruthie asked.

"Also Danish," Suzie said.

"What's Danish?"

"Danish pastry with prune filling."

"I got to see that," Dave said, and then Harvey took a Danish out of the air. Dave stared and nodded, and he took a bite of the Danish. "Just rolls and Danish?"

"That's all I tried."

A slow, crafty grin spread over Dave's face as he reached into his pocket and took out a roll of bills. He peeled off a ten-dollar bill and pressed it flat on the table. "You know what this is, Harvey?

Harvey stared at it without comment.

"How about it?"

"It could get us into a lot of trouble," Harvey said thoughtfully.

"How?"

"Counterfeit."

"Come off it, Harvey. What's counterfeit? Are you counterfeiting rolls? Danish?"

"Rolls are different. This is larceny, Dave."

The two ladies listened and watched, their eyes wide, but said nothing. Morality had reared its ugly head, and suddenly what had been very simple was becoming most complicated.

"There never was an accountant who didn't have larceny in him. Come on, Harvey."

Harvey shook his head.

"It's a gift," Suzie explained. "It's spooky. I don't think you should talk Harvey into doing anything that he doesn't want to do. You don't want to do this, do you, Harvey?" she asked her husband. "I mean, unless you really want to."

"Listen, Harvey, level with me," Dave said. "Did you ever do anything like this before? Have you been working up to this?"

"How do you work up to it?"

"That's what I'm asking you. Because this is big—big, Harvey. If it's just a gift, you know, all of a sudden, then you got no obligations to anyone. You can take Danish out of the air, you can take a ten-dollar bill out of the air. What's the difference?"

"Counterfeit," said Harvey.

"Balls. Are the rolls counterfeit, or are they the real thing?"

"It's still counterfeiting."

"Harvey, you are out of your ever-loving mind. Look, you're sitting here in the bosom of your family—those closest to you, your own loved ones. You're protected. Suzie is your wife. I'm her brother. Ruthie is my wife. Flesh and blood. Who's going to turn you in? Myself—would I kill the goose that laid the golden egg? Ruthie—I'd break every bone in her body."

"That's right, he would," Ruthie said eagerly. "I can promise you that, Harvey. He would break every bone in my body."

"Suzie? Suzie, would you turn Harvey in? Like hell you would. A wife can't testify against her husband. That's what I have been telling you, Harvey. Flesh and blood.''

"When you think about it," Suzie said, "it's just like a parlor game, Harvey. I mean, suppose we were playing Monopoly or something like that. I mean, if you just did it for laughs. Dave says, take a ten-dollar bill out of the air. You do it. So what?"

"Maybe a dollar bill," Harvey said, for the arguments were very convincing.

"Right on," said Dave, taking a dollar bill out of his pocket. "I should have thought of that myself, Harv. Today a dollar is worth nothing. Nothing. It's like a gag." He spread the dollar on the table. "You know, when I was a kid, this could buy something. Not today. No, sir."

Harvey nodded, took a deep breath, reached for a spot two feet in front of his nose, and plucked a dollar bill out of the air. Suzie squealed with pleasure and Ruthie clapped her hands with delight. Dave grinned and took the dollar bill from Harvey, laid it on the table next to the one he had produced from his pocket, and scrutinized it carefully. Then he shook his head.

"You missed, Harvey."

"What do you mean, I missed?"

"Well, it's sort of a dollar bill. You got Washington's face all right, and it says 'one dollar,' but the color's not exactly right, it's too green—"

"You left out the little print," Ruthie exclaimed. "Here where it says that it's legal tender for all debts, public and private—you left that out."

Harvey could see the difference. The curlicues were different, and the bright green stamp of the Department of the Treasury was the same color as the rest of it. The serial numbers had been left out, and as for the reverse side, it bore only a general resemblance to a real dollar bill.

"OK, OK—don't get nervous," Dave told him. "You couldn't be expected to hit it the first time. What you have to do is to take a real good look at the genuine article and then try it again."

"I'd rather not."

"Come on, Harv—come on. Don't chicken out now. You want to try a ten?"

"No, I'll try the one again."

He reached into the air and returned with another dollar bill between his fingers. They all examined it eagerly.

"Good, good," Dave said. "Not perfect, Harvey—you missed on the seal, and the paper's not right. But it's better. I'll bet I could pass this one."

"No!" Harvey grabbed both spurious bills and stuffed them into his pocket.

"Al right, all right—don't blow your cool, Harv. We try it again now."

"No."

"What do you mean, no?"

"No. I'm tired. Anyway, I got to think about this. I'm half out of my mind the way it is. Suppose this happened to you?"

"Man oh man, I'd buy General Motors before the week was out."

"Well, I'm not sure that I want to buy General Motors or anything else. I got to think about this."

"Harvey's right," Suzie put in. "You always come on too strong, Dave. Harvey's got a right to think about this."

"And while he thinks, the gift goes."

"How do you know?"

"Well, it came on sudden. Suppose it goes the same way?"

"I don't care if it does," Suzie said loyally. "Harvey's got a right to think about it."

"OK. I'm not going to be unreasonable. Only one thing—when he thinks his way out of this, I want you to call me. I'm going to get some twenties and some fifties. I don't think we should go in for anything bigger than that right now."

"I'll call you."

"OK. Just remember that."

When Dave and Ruthie had departed, Harvey asked his wife why she had agreed to call. "I don't need Dave," he said. "You and Dave treat me like an imbecile."

"I just agreed to get rid of him."

"I'd just like to think once that you were on my side and not on his."

"That's not fair. I'm always on your side. You know that."

"I don't know it."

"All right, make a big federal case out of it. They're gone, so if you want to think about it, why don't you think about it?" And she stalked into the bedroom, slammed the door, and turned on the television.

Harvey sat in the living room and brooded. He took out the dollar bills, studied them for a while, and then tore them up and made a trip to the bathroom to flush them down the drain. Then he returned to the couch and brooded again. It had been late afternoon by the time Dave and Ruthie left, and now it was early in the evening and darkening, and he was beginning to be hungry. He went into the kitchen and found beer and bread and ham, but his inner yearning was for a hamburger sandwich, not the way Suzie made hamburgers, dry, tasteless, leathery, but tender and juicy and pink in the middle. Reflecting on the fact that he was married to a rotten cook, he took a hamburger sandwich out of the air. It was perfect. Suzie entered as he took his first bite.

"Don't think about me," she said. "I could starve to death while you sit here stuffing yourself."

"Since when do I let you starve to death?"

"Where did you get the hamburger?"

He took one out of the air and put it in front of her.

"It's full of onions," Suzie said. "You know how I hate onions."

Harvey rose and dropped the hamburger into the garbage pail.

"Harvey, what are you doing?"

"You don't like onions."

"Well, you can't just throw it away."

"Why not?" Harvey felt himself changing, and the change was encompassed in those simple words—why not? Why not? He plucked a hamburger without onions out of the air, dry and hard, the way his wife cooked them.

"Be my guest," he said coolly.

She took a bite of the hamburger and then informed him through a mouth filled with food that he was acting very funny.

"What do you mean, funny?"

"You're just acting funny, Harvey. You got to admit that you are acting funny."

"All right, it's a different situation."

"What do you mean?"

"I mean, I can take things out of the air," said Harvey. "That's pretty different. I mean, it's not something that you go around doing. For example, you want some chocolate cake?" He reached out and retrieved a piece of chocolate layer cake and placed it in front of Suzie. "How does it taste? Try it."

"Harvey, I'm still eating the hamburger, and don't think I don't realize that it's very unusual what you can do."

"It's not like I'm just a kid," Harvey said. "I'm a forty-one-year-old loser."

"You're not a loser, Harvey."

"Don't kid yourself. I am a loser. What have we got? Five thousand dollars in the bank, a four-room apartment, no kids, nothing, absolutely nothing, a great big fat zero, and I am still forty-one years old."

"I don't like to hear you talk like that, Harvey."

"I am just making the point that I got to think this through. I got to get used to the fact that I can take things out of the air. It's an unusual talent. I got to convince myself."

"Why? Don't you believe it, Harvey?"

"I do and I don't. That's why I have to think about it."

Suzie nodded. "I understand." She ate the chocolate cake and then went into the bedroom and turned on the television again.

Harvey followed her into the bedroom. "Why do you say you understand? Why do you always tell me that you understand?" She was trying to concentrate on the television screen, and she shook her head. "Will you turn off that damn box!" Harvey shouted.

"Don't shout at me, Harvey."

"Then listen to me. You watch me take things out of the air and tell me you understand. I take a piece of chocolate cake out of the air, and you tell me that you understand. I don't understand, but you tell me that you understand."

"That's the way it is, Harvey. They send people up to the moon, and I don't know any more about it than you do, but that's the way science is. I think it's very nice that you can take things out of the air. I think that if one of those computer places put it on a computer, they would be able to tell you just how it works."

"Then why do you keep saying that you understand?"

"I understand that you want to think about it."

Harvey closed the door of the bedroom and went back into the living room and thought about it. It was actually the first moment he had really thought about it, and suddenly his head was exploding with ideas and notions. Some were what his friends in the advertising agencies would have called very creative notions, and

244

some were not. Some were simply the crystallization of his own dissatisfactions. If someone had suggested to him the day before that he was a seething mass of dissatisfactions, he would have denied the accusation hotly. Now he could face them as facts. He was dissatisfied with his life, his job, his home, his past, his future, and his wife. He had never set out to be an accountant; it had simply happened to him. He had always dreamed of living in a large, spacious country home, and here he was in a miserable apartment with paper-thin walls in an enormous jerry-built building on Third Avenue in New York City. As far as his past was concerned, it was colorless and flat, and his future promised nothing that was much better. His wife—?

He thought about his wife. It was not that he disliked Suzie; he had nothing against her, nor could he think of very much that he had going for her. She was short, dark, and pretty, but he couldn't remember why or exactly how he had come to marry her. The plain fact of the matter was that he adored oversized blondes, large, tall, buxom, beautiful blondes. He dreamed about such women; he turned to watch them on the street; he fell asleep thinking about them and he awakened thinking about them.

He thought about one of them now. And then he began to grin; an idea had clamped onto him and it wouldn't let go. He sat up in his chair and stared at the bedroom door. He straightened his spine. The television blared from behind the door.

"To hell with it!" he said. It was a new Harvey Kepplemen. He stood up, his spine erect. "Tall, blond, beautiful—" he whispered, and then hesitated over the notion of intelligence. "To hell with intelligence!"

He reached out into the air in front of him with both hands now, and suddenly there she was, but he couldn't hold her and she fell with an enormous thud and lay sprawled on the floor, a blond, naked woman, very beautiful, very large, magnificently full-breasted, blue eyes wide open and very motionless and apparently lifeless.

Harvey stood staring at her.

The bedroom door opened, and there was Suzie, who also stood and stared at her.

"What is that?" Suzie cried out.

The answer was self-evident. Harvey swallowed, closed his mouth, and bent over the beautiful blonde.

"Don't touch her!"

"Maybe she's dead," Harvey said hopelessly. "I got to touch her to find out."

"Who is she? Where did she come from?"

Harvey turned to meet Suzie's eyes.

"No."

Harvey nodded.

"No. I don't believe it. That?" Now Suzie walked over to the large blonde. "She's seven feet long if she's an inch. Harvey, what kind of a creep are you?"

Harvey touched her, discreetly, on the chest just below the enormous breasts. She was as cold as a dead mackerel.

"Well?"

"She's as cold as a dead mackerel," Harvey replied bleakly.

"Try her pulse."

"She's dead. Look at her eyes." He tried the pulse. "She has no pulse."

"Great," Suzie said. "That's just great, Harvey. Here we are with a dead seven-foot-long blonde with oversized mammaries, and now what?"

"I think you ought to cover her up," Harvey suggested meekly.

"You're damn right I'm going to cover her up!" And Suzie marched off to the bedroom and returned with a blanket which just about fitted the enormous body.

"What do I do now?" Harvey wondered.

"Put her back where you got her from."

"You must be kidding."

"Try it," said a new Suzie, cold and nasty. "If you can take things like this out of the air, maybe you can put them back."

"How? Just suppose you tell me how, being such a great smart-ass about everything else."

"I'm not a prevert."

"You mean pervert. Who's a pervert? That's a hell of a thing to say."

Suzie swept the blanket aside. "Look at her."

"All right, I've seen her. Now what do we do with her?"

"What do *you* do."

"OK, OK—what do I do?"

"Lift her up and put her back."

"Where?"

"Wherever you take these damn things from, back with your lousy water rolls and Danish pastry."

Harvey shook his head. "We been married a long time, Suzie. I never heard you talk like that before."

"You never made me a present of a seven-foot dead blonde before."

"I guess not," Harvey agreed, reaching out and obtaining a prune Danish.

"What's that for?"

"I want to see if I can put it back."

"Look, Harvey," Suzie said, her voice softening a little, "it's no use putting back a prune Danish. You got to put back big Bertha there." Harvey, meanwhile, was stabbing the air with the prune Danish. "Harvey—forget the Danish."

He let go of it, hoping and praying that it would return to whatever unknown had produced it, but instead it dropped with a wet plop on one of the huge breasts, dripping its soft prune filling all over the beautiful oversized mammary. Harvey ran for a napkin, wiped frantically, and only made the situation worse. Suzie joined him with a wet sponge and a handful of paper towels.

"Let me do it, Harvey."

She cleaned up the mess while Harvey managed to heave one of the long, meaty legs into the air. "Put her back," he said. "Suzie, I could never lift her. It would take one of those hoist cranes. She must weigh two hundred and fifty pounds."

"I suppose that's what you always wanted. Do you know, she's as cold as ice."

"Do you suppose I killed her?" he asked woefully.

"I don't know. I think I'll telephone Dave."

"Why?"

"He'll know what to do."

"As far as I am concerned, your brother Dave can drop dead."

"Like this one. Sure. Wish me dead too."

"I never wished you dead. I am talking about your brother, Dave."

"At least he'd have an idea."

"So have I," Harvey said. "My idea is very simple and right on it. Call the cops."

"What? Harvey, are you out of your ever-loving mind? She's dead. You made her dead. You killed her."

247

"So I made her dead. What do we do? Cut her up and flush her down the toilet? Neither of us can stand the sight of blood. Do we dump her in an empty lot? Even with your lousy brother Dave, we couldn't lift her up."

"Harvey," she pleaded, "let's think about it."

They thought about it, and then Harvey called the cops.

A dead body, Harvey discovered, was a communal enterprise. Nine men prowled around the little apartment. Eight of them were ambulance attendants, uniformed officers, fingerprint expert, medical examiner, photographer, etc. The ninth was a heavy-shouldered man in plain clothes, whose name was Lieutenant Serpio, who told everyone else what to do, and who never smiled. Harvey and Suzie sat on the couch and watched him.

"All right, take her out," said Serpio.

They tried.

"Never saw the like of it," the Medical examiner was muttering. "She's seven feet tall if she's an inch."

"Kelly, don't stand there on your feet, give them a hand!" Serpio said to one of the uniformed cops.

Kelly joined with the ambulance attendants, and with the help of another cop they got the oversized blonde onto a stretcher. She hung over either end as they staggered through the door with her, and Suzie said to her husband:

"You're not a pervert, Harvey. You're just a lousy male chauvinist. I have been thinking about you. You are a sexist pig."

"That's great," Harvey agreed. "I never did anything to anyone, and the whole world falls on me."

"You are a sexist pig," she repeated.

"I find it hard to think of myself that way."

"Just try. You'll get used to it."

"What did she die from, Doc?" Lieutenant Serpio asked the Medical Examiner.

"God knows. Maybe she broke her back carrying that bust around. I'll go downtown and chop her up a little, and I'll let you know."

The apartment cleared out. Only Serpio and a single uniformed cop remained. Serpio stood in front of Harvey and Suzie, staring at them thoughtfully.

"Tell me again," he said.

248

"I told you."

"Tell me again. I got plenty of time. In twenty years of practicing my profesison in this town, I thought I had seen everything. Not so. This enlivens my work and gives me a new attitude. Now who is she?"

"I don't know."

"Where did she come from?"

"I took her out of the air."

"I know. You took her out of the air. I could send you down to Bellevue, only I am intrigued. Do you make a habit out of taking things out of the air?"

"No, sir," Harvey answered politely. "Only since this morning."

"What about you?" he said to Suzie. "Do you take things out of the air?"

She shook her head. "It's Harvey's gift."

"What else does Harvey take out of the air?" the Lieutenant asked patiently.

"Danish."

"Danish?"

"Danish pastry with prune filling," Harvey explained.

The Lieutenant considered this. "I see. Tell me, Mr. Kepplemen, why Danish pastry with prune filling—if it's not too much to ask?"

"I can explain that," Suzie put in. "You see, we were down in Baltimore—"

"Let him explain."

"I like it," Harvey said.

"What about Baltimore?"

"They make it very good down there," Harvey said.

"Danish pastry?"

"Yes, sir."

"Now do you want to tell me who the blonde is?"

"I don't know."

"Do you want to tell me how she died?"

"I don't know."

"The doctor says she's been dead for hours. When did she come here?"

"I told you."

"Where are her clothes, Harvey?"

"I told you. I got her just the way she was."

"All right, Harvey," the Lieutenant said with a sigh. "I am going to have to arrest you and your wife and take you downtown, because with an explanation like this, I have absolutely no alternative. Now I am going to tell you your rights. No, the hell with that. Tell you what, Harvey—you and your wife come downtown with me, and we'll let the arrest set for a while, and we'll see if the boys downstairs figured out what she died from. How does that grab you?"

Harvey and Suzie nodded bleakly.

On the way down to Centre Street, they sat in the back seat of Lieutenant Serpio's car and argued in whispers.

"Show him with a Danish," Suzie kept whispering.

"No."

"Why not?"

"I don't want to."

"Well, he doesn't believe you. That's plain enough. If you take out a Danish, maybe he'll believe you."

"No."

"A hamburger?"

"No."

Lieutenant Serpio led them into an office where there were a lot of cops in uniform and some not in uniform, and he led them to a bench and said, with some solicitude, "Both of you sit down right here, and just take it easy and don't get nervous. You want anything, you ask that fella over there by the desk."

Then he went over to the desk and spoke softly to the cop behind it for a minute or so; and then the cop behind the desk came over to Suzie and Harvey and said, "Now just take it easy, and don't get nervous, and everything's going to be all right. You want a prune Danish, Harvey?"

"Why?"

"If you're hungry. Nothing to it. I send the kid out for it, and in five minutes you got a prune Danish. How about it?"

"No," replied Harvey.

"I think we ought to call our lawyer," said Suzie.

The cop went away, and Harvey asked her whom she expected to call, since they never had a lawyer.

"I don't know, Harvey. Somebody always calls a lawyer. I'm scared."

"Either they think I am crazy or they think I am a murderer. That's the way it goes. I wish I had never seen that lousy brother of yours."

Harvey, you took the Danish out of the air before my brother set foot in the house."

"That's right, I did," said Harvey.

At which moment the Medical Examiner sat facing both Lieutenant Serpio and the Chief of Detectives, and said to them, "It is not a murder because that large blond tomato was never alive."

"I'm a busy man," said the Chief of Detectives. "I have eleven homicides tonight—just tonight on a Sunday night, not to mention two suicides. So don't confuse me."

"I'm confused."

"Good. Now what have you got on that dead blonde?"

"She is only dead in a technical sense. As I said, she was never alive. She is the incredible construction of a bewildered Dr. Frankenstein or some kind of nut. Mostly on the outside she is all right, except that whoever put her together forgot her toenails. Inside, she has no heart, no kidneys, no liver, no lungs, no circulatory system, and practically no blood, and what blood she has is not blood, because nothing she has is like what it's supposed to be."

"Then what's inside of her?" Serpio demanded.

"Mostly a sort of crude beefsteak."

"Just what in hell are you talking about?" demanded the Chief of Detectives.

"You got me," said the Medical Examiner.

"Come on, come on, I bring you a dead seven-foot blonde that makes you wish you were a single basketball player even when she's dead, and you tell me she never was alive. I seen many tomatoes that are more dead than alive, but there has to be a time when they're alive."

"Not this one. She hasn't even a proper backbone, so she could not have stood up to save her life, and I think I'll write a paper about her, and if I do I'll get it published in England. You know, it's a funny thing, you can get a paper like that published in England and it commands respect. Not here. By the way, where did you get her?"

"Serpio brought her in."

"Naked?"

"Just like she is," Serpio said. "We found her on the floor, stretched out like a lox, in the apartment of two people whose name is Kepplemen. He's an accountant. I got them upstairs.".

"Did you charge them?"

"With what?"

"Absolutely beautiful," said the Medical Examiner. "You know, you go on with this lousy job for years and nothing really interesting ever comes your way. Now did they say where she came from?"

"This Harvey Kepplemen," Serpio replied, watching the Chief of Detectives, "says he took her out of the air."

"Oh?"

"Serpio, what the hell are you talking about?" from the Chief of Detectives.

"That's what he says. He says he takes prune Danish out of the air, and he got her from the same place."

"Prune Danish?"

"Danish pastry."

"All right," the Chief of Detectives said. "I got to figure you're sane and you're not drunk. If you're insane, you get a rest cure. If you're drunk, you get canned. So bring them both to my office."

"I got to be there," said the Medical Examiner. "I just got to be there."

This time Serpio called Harvey Mr. Kepplemen. "Mr. Kepplemen," he said politely, "the Chief of Detectives wants to see you in his office."

"I'm tired," Suzie complained.

"Just a little longer, and maybe we can clear this up—how about that, Mrs. Kepplemen?"

"I want you to know," Harvey said, "that nothing like this ever happened to me before. I have good references. I have worked for the same firm for sixteen years."

"We know that, Mr. Kepplemen. It won't take long."

A few minutes later they were all gathered in the office of the Chief of Detectives, Harvey and Suzie, Serpio, the Chief of Detectives, and the Medical Examiner. The Chief of Detectives poured coffee.

"Go ahead, Mr. and Mrs. Kepplemen," he said. "You've had a

long day." His voice was gentle and comforting. "By the way, I am told that you can take Danish pastry out of the air. I can send out for some, but why do that if you can take it out of the air. Right?"

"Well—"

"Harvey doesn't really like to take things out of the air," Suzie said. "He has a feeling that it's wrong. Isn't that so, Harvey?"

"Well," Harvey said uneasily, "well—I mean that all my life I never had a talent for anything. My mother was Ruth Kepplemen . . ." He hesitated, looking from face to face.

"Go on, Harvey," said the Chief of Detectives. "Whatever you want to tell us."

"Well, she was an artist. I mean she painted lots of pictures, and she kept telling her friends, Harvey hasn't a creative bone in his body—"

"About the Danish, Harvey?"

"Well, Suzie and I were driving through Baltimore—"

"Detective Serpio told me about that. I was thinking that here we all are with coffee, and it's past midnight, and maybe you'd like to reach out into the air and get us some prune Danish."

"You don't believe me?" Harvey said unhappily.

"Let's say, we want to believe you, Harvey."

"That's why we want you to show us, Harvey," said Serpio, "so we can believe you and wind this up."

"Just one moment," the Medical Examiner put in. "Did you ever study biology, Harvey? Physiology? Anatomy?"

Harvey shook his head.

"How come?"

"We kept moving around. I just missed out."

"I see. Come on, now, Harvey, let's have that Danish."

Harvey reached out, two feet in front of his nose, and plucked at the air and emerged with air. His face revealed his confusion and disappointment. He plucked a second time and a third time, and each time his fingers were empty.

"Harvey, try water rolls," Suzie begged him.

He tried water rolls with equal frustration.

"Harvey, concentrate," Suzie pleaded.

He concentrated, and still his fingers were empty.

"Please, Harvey," Suzie begged him, and then when she realized it was all to no end, she turned on the policemen and informed them that it was their fault, and threatened to get a lawyer and to sue them and to do all the other things that people threaten to do when they are in a situation such as Suzie was in.

"Serpio, why don't you have a policeman drive the Kepplemens home?" the Chief of Detectives suggested; and when Serpio and Harvey and Suzie had gone, he turned to the Medical Examiner and said that one thing about being a cop was that if you only kept your health, you would see everything.

"Now I have seen everything," he said, "and tell me, Doc, did you lift any fingerprints off that big tomato downstairs?"

"She hasn't any."

"Oh?"

"That's the way it crumbles," said the Medical Examiner. "Every American boy's dream—seven feet high and a size forty-six bust. How do I write a death certificate for something that was never alive?"

"That's your problem. I keep feeling I should have held those two."

"For what?"

"That's just it. Are you religious, Doc?"

"I sometimes wish I was."

"What I mean is, I keep thinking this is some kind of miracle."

"Everything is, birth, death, getting looped."

"Yeah. Well, make it a Jane Doe DC, and put her in the icebox before the press gets a look. That's all we need."

"Yeah, that's all we need," the Medical Examiner agreed.

Meanwhile, back in the four-room apartment, Suzie was weeping and Harvey was attempting to comfort her by explaining that no matter how much he tried, he would have never gotten the ten-dollar-bill problem completely licked.

"Who cares about the damn bills?"

"What then, kitten?"

"Kitten! All these years, and what do you want but an enormous slobbering seven-foot blonde with a forty-six bust."

"It's just that I never got anything that I really wanted," Harvey tried to explain.

"Not even me?"

"Except you, kitten."

Then they went to bed, and everything was about as good as it could be.

254

14
The Wound

MAX Gaffey always insisted that the essence of the oil industry could be summed up in a simple statement: the right thing in the wrong place. My wife, Martha, always disliked him and said that he was a spoiler. I suppose he was, but how was he different from any of us in that sense? We were all spoilers, and if we were not the actual thing, we invested in it and thereby became rich. I myself had invested the small nest egg that a college professor puts away in a stock Max Gaffey gave me. It was called Thunder Inc., and the company's function was to use atomic bombs to release natural gas and oil locked up in the vast untouched shale deposits that we have here in the United States.

Oil shale is not a very economical source of oil. The oil is locked up in the shale, and about 60 percent of the total cost of shale oil consists of the laborious methods of mining the shale, crushing it to release the oil, and then disposing of the spent shale.

Gaffey sold to Thunder Inc. an entirely new method, which involved the use of surplus atomic bombs for the release of shale oil. In very simplistic terms, a deep hole is bored in shale-oil deposits. Then an atomic bomb is lowered to the bottom of this hole, after which the hole is plugged and the bomb is detonated. Theoretically, the heat and force of the atomic explosion crushes the shale and releases the oil to fill the underground cavern formed by the gigantic force of the bomb. The oil does not burn because the hole is sealed, and thereby, for a comparatively small cost, untold amounts of oil can be tapped and released—enough perhaps to last until that time when we experience a complete conversion to atomic energy—so vast are the shale deposits.

Such at least was the way Max Gaffey put the proposition to me, in a sort of mutual brain-picking operation. He had the utmost admiration for my knowledge of the earth's crust, and I had an equally profound admiration for his ability to make two or five or ten dollars appear where only one had been before.

My wife disliked him and his notions, and most of all the proposal to feed atomic bombs into the earth's crust.

"It's wrong," she said flatly. "I don't know why or how, but this I do know, that everything connected with that wretched bomb is wrong."

"Yet couldn't you look at this as a sort of salvation?" I argued. "Here we are in these United States with enough atom bombs to destroy life on ten earths the size of ours—and every one of those bombs represents an investment of millions of dollars. I could not agree more when you hold that these bombs are the most hideous and frightful things the mind of man ever conceived."

"Then how on earth can you speak of salvation?"

"Because so long as those bombs sit here, they represent a constant threat—day and night the threat that some feather-brained general or brainless politician will begin the process of throwing them at our neighbors. But here Gaffey has come up with a peaceful use for the bomb. Don't you see what that means?"

"I'm afraid I don't," Martha said.

"It means that we can use the damn bombs for something other than suicide—because if this starts, it's the end of mankind. But there are oil-shale and gas-shale deposits all over the earth, and if we can use the bomb to supply man with a century of fuel, not to mention the chemical by-products, we may just find a way to dispose of those filthy bombs."

"Oh, you don't believe that for a moment," Martha snorted.

"I do. I certainly do."

And I think I did. I went over the plans that Gaffey and his associates had worked out, and I could not find any flaw. If the hole were plugged properly, there would be no fallout. We knew that and we had the know-how to plug the hole, and we had proven it in at least twenty underground explosions. The earth tremor would be inconsequential; in spite of the heat, the oil would not ignite, and in spite of the cost of the atom bombs, the savings would be monumental. In fact, Gaffey hinted that some accommodation between the government and Thunder Inc. was in the process of being worked out, and if it went through as planned, the atom bombs might just cost Thunder Inc. nothing at all, the whole thing being in the way of an experiment for the social good.

After all, Thunder Inc. did not own any oil-shale deposits, nor was it in the oil business. It was simply a service organization with the proper know-how, and for a fee—if the process worked—it would release the oil for others. What that fee would be was left unsaid, but Max Gaffey, in return for my consultation, suggested that I might buy a few shares, not only of Thunder Inc., but of General Shale Holdings.

I had altogether about ten thousand dollars in savings available and another ten thousand in American Telephone and government bonds. Martha had a bit of money of her own, but I left that alone, and without telling her, I sold my Telephone stock and my bonds. Thunder Inc. was selling at five dollars a share, and I bought two thousand shares. General Shale was selling for two dollars, and I bought four thousand shares. I saw nothing immoral—as business morality was calculated—in the procedures adopted by Thunder Inc. Its relationship to the government was no different than the relationships of various other companies, and my own process of investment was perfectly straightforward and honorable. I was not even the recipient of secret information, for the atom-bomb—shale-oil proposal had been widely publicized if little believed.

Even before the first test explosion was undertaken, the stock of Thunder Inc. went from five to sixty-five dollars a share. My ten thousand dollars became one hundred and thirty thousand, and that doubled again a year later. The four thousand shares of General Shale went up to eighteen dollars a share; and from a moderately poor professor I became a moderately rich professor. When finally, almost two years after Max Gaffey first approached me, they exploded the first atom bomb in a shaft reamed in the oil-shale deposits, I had abandoned the simple anxieties of the poor and had developed an entirely new set tailored for the upper middle class. We became a two-car family, and a reluctant Martha joined me in shopping for a larger house. In the new house, Gaffey and his wife came to dinner, and Martha armed herself with two stiff martinis. Then she was quietly polite until Gaffey began to talk about the social good. He painted a bright picture of what shale oil could do and how rich we might well become.

"Oh, yes—yes," Martha agreed. "Pollute the atmosphere, kill

257

more people with more cars, increase the speed with which we can buzz around in circles and get precisely nowhere."

"Oh, you're a pessimist," said Gaffey's wife, who was young and pretty but no mental giant.

"Of course there are two sides to it," Gaffey admitted. "It's a question of controls. You can't stop progress, but it seems to me that you can direct it."

"The way we've been directing it—so that our rivers stink and our lakes are sewers of dead fish and our atmosphere is polluted and our birds are poisoned by DDT and our natural resources are spoiled. We are all spoilers, aren't we?"

"Come now," I protested, "this is the way it is, and all of us are indignant about it, Martha."

"Are you, really?"

"I think so."

"Men have always dug in the earth," Gaffey said. "Otherwise we'd still be in the Stone Age."

"And perhaps a good bit happier."

"No, no, no," I said. "The Stone Age was a very unpleasant time, Martha. You don't wish us back there."

"Do you remember," Martha said slowly, "how there was a time when men used to speak about the earth our mother? It was Mother Earth, and they believed it. She was the source of life and being."

"She still is."

"You've sucked her dry," Martha said curiously. "When a woman is sucked dry, her children perish."

It was an odd and poetical thing to say, and, as I thought, in bad taste. I punished Martha by leaving Mrs. Gaffey with her, with the excuse that Max and I had some business matters to discuss, which indeed we did. We went into the new study in the new house and we lit fifty-cent cigars, and Max told me about the thing they had aptly named "Project Hades."

"The point is," Max said, "that I can get you into this at the very beginning. At the bottom. There are eleven companies involved—very solid and reputable companies"—he named them, and I was duly impressed—"who are putting up the capital for what will be a subsidiary of Thunder Inc. For their money they get a twenty-five percent interest. There is also ten percent, in the form of stock warrants, put aside for consultation and advice, and you will understand why. I can fit you in for one and half percent—roughly three quarters of a million—simply for a few weeks of your time, and we will pay all expenses, plus an opinion.''

"It sounds interesting.''

"It should sound more than that. If Project Hades works, your interest will increase tenfold within a matter of five years. It's the shortest cut to being a millionaire that I know.''

"All right—I'm more than interested. Go on.''

Gaffey took a map of Arizona out of his pocket, unfolded it, and pointed to a marked-off area. "Here,'' he said, "is what should—according to all our geological knowledge—be one of the richest oil-bearing areas in the country. Do you agree?''

"Yes, I know the area,'' I replied. "I've been over it. Its oil potential is purely theoretical. No one has ever brought in anything there—not even salt water. It's dry and dead.''

"Why?''

I shrugged. "That's the way it is. If we could locate oil through geological premise and theory, you and I would both be richer than Getty. The fact of the matter is, as you well know, that sometimes it's there and sometimes it isn't. More often it isn't.''

"Why? We know our job. We drill in the right places.''

"What are you getting at, Max?''

"A speculation—particularly for this area. We have discussed this speculation for months. We have tested it as best we can. We have examined it from every possible angle. And now we are ready to blow about five million dollars to test our hypothesis—providing—''

"Providing what?''

"That your expert opinion agrees with ours. In other words, we've cast the die with you. You look at the situation and tell us to go ahead—we go ahead. You look at it and tell us it's a crock of beans—well, we fold our tents like the Arabs and silently steal away.''

"Just on my say-so?''

"Just on your brains and know-how.''

"Max, aren't you barking up the wrong tree? I'm a simple professor of geology at an unimportant western state university, and there are at least twenty men in the field who can teach me the right time—''

"Not in our opinion. Not on where the stuff is. We know who's in the field and we know their track records. You keep your light under a bushel, but we know what we want. So don't argue. It's either a deal or it isn't. Well?"

"How the devil can I answer you when I don't even know what you're talking about?"

"All right—I'll spell it out, quick and simple. The oil was there once, right where it should be. Then a natural convulsion—a very deep fault. The earth cracked and the oil flowed down, deep down, and now giant pockets of it are buried there where no drill can reach them."

"How deep?"

"Who knows? Fifteen, twenty miles."

"That's deep."

"Maybe deeper. When you think of that kind of distance under the surface, you're in a darker mystery than Mars or Venus—all of which you know."

"All of which I know." I had a bad, uneasy feeling and some of it must have shown in my face.

"What's wrong?"

"I don't know. Why don't you leave it alone, Max?"

"Why?"

"Come on, Max—we're not talking about drilling for oil. Fifteen, twenty miles. There's a rig down near the Pecos in Texas and they've just passed the twenty-five-thousand-foot level, and that's about it. Oh, maybe another thousand, but you're talking about oil that's buried in one hundred thousand feet of crust. You can't drill for it; you can only go in and—"

"And what?"

"Blast it out."

"Of course—and how do you fault us for that? What's wrong with it? We know—or least we have good reason to believe—that there's a fissure that opened and closed. The oil should be under tremendous pressure. We put in an atom bomb—a bigger bomb than we ever used before—and we blast that fissure open again. Great God almighty, that should be the biggest gusher in all the history of gushers."

"You've drilled the hole already, haven't you, Max?"

"That's right."

"How deep?"

"Twenty-two thousand feet."

"And you have the bomb?"

260

Max nodded. "We have the bomb. We've been working on this for five years, and seven months ago the boys in Washington cleared the bomb. It's out there in Arizona waiting—"

"For what?"

"For you to look everything over and tell us to go ahead."

"Why? We have enough oil—"

"Like hell we have! You know damn well why—and do you imagine we can drop it now after all the money and time that's been invested in this?"

"You said you'd drop it if I said so."

"As a geologist in our pay, and I know you well enough to know what that means in terms of your professional skill and pride."

I stayed up half that night talking with Martha about it and trying to fit it into some kind of moral position. But the only thing I could come up with was the fact that here was one less atom bomb to murder man and destroy the life of the earth, and that I could not argue with. A day later I was at the drilling site in Arizona.

The spot was well chosen. From every point of view this was an oil explorer's dream, and I suppose that fact had been duly noted for the past half century, for there were the moldering remains of a hundred futile rigs, rotting patterns of wooden and metal sticks as far as one could see, abandoned shacks, trailers left with lost hopes, ancient trucks, rusting gears, piles of abandoned pipe—all testifying to the hope that springs eternal in the wildcatter's breast.

Thunder Inc. was something else, a great installation in the middle of the deep valley, a drilling rig larger and more complex than any I had ever seen, a wall to contain the oil should they fail to cap it immediately, a machine shop, a small generating plant, at least a hundred vehicles of various sorts, and perhaps fifty mobile homes. The very extent and vastness of the action here deep in the badlands was breathtaking; and I let Max know what I thought of his statement that all this would be abandoned if I said that the idea was worthless.

"Maybe yes—maybe no. What *do* you say?"

"Give me time."

"Absolutely, all the time you want."

Never have I been treated with such respect. I prowled all over the place and I rode a jeep around and about and back and forth and up into the hills and down again; but no matter how long I prowled and sniffed and estimated, mine would be no more than an educated guess. I was also certain that they would not give up the project if I disapproved and said that it would be a washout. They believed in me as a sort of oil-dowser, especially if I told them to go ahead. What they were really seeking was an expert's affirmation of their own faith. And that was apparent from the fact that they had already drilled an expensive twenty-two-thousand-foot hole and had set up all this equipment. If I told them they were wrong, their faith might be shaken a little, but they would recover and find themselves another dowser.

I told this to Martha when I telephoned her.

"Well, what do you honestly think?"

"It's oil country. But I'm not the first one to come up with that brilliant observation. The point is—does their explanation account for the lack of oil?"

"Does it?"

"I don't know. No one knows. And they're dangling the million dollars right in front of my nose."

"I can't help you," Martha said. "You've got to play this one yourself."

Of course she couldn't help me. No one could have helped me. It was too far down, too deeply hidden. We knew what the other side of the moon looked like and we knew something about Mars and the other planets, but what have we ever known about ourselves and the place where we live?

The day after I spoke to Martha, I met with Max and his board of directors.

"I agree," I told them. "The oil should be there. My opinion is that you should go ahead and try the blast."

They questioned me after that for about an hour, but when you play the role of a dowser, questions and answers become a sort of magical ritual. The plain fact of the matter is that no one had ever exploded a bomb of such power at such a depth, and until it was done, no one knew what would happen.

I watched the preparations for the explosion with great interest. The bomb, with its implosion casing, was specially made for this task—or remade would be a better way of putting it—very long, almost twenty feet, very slim. It was armed after it was in the rigging, and then the board of directors, engineers, technicians, newspapermen, Max, and myself retreated to the concrete shelter and control station, which had been built almost a mile away from the shaft. Closed-circuit television linked us with the hole; and while no one expected the explosion to do any more than jar the earth heavily at the surface, the Atomic Energy Commission specified the precautions we took.

We remained in the shelter for five hours while the bomb made its long descent—until at last our instruments told us that it rested on the bottom of the drill hole. Then we had a simple countdown, and the chairman of the board pressed the red button. Red and white buttons are man's glory. Press a white button and a bell rings or an electric light goes on; press a red button and the hellish force of a sun comes into being—this time five miles beneath the earth's surface.

Perhaps it was this part and point in the earth's surface; perhaps there was no other place where exactly the same thing would have happened; perhaps the fault that drained away the oil was a deeper fault than we had ever imagined. Actually we will never know; we only saw what we saw, watching it through the closed-circuit TV. We saw the earth swell. The swell rose up like a bubble—a bubble about two hundred yards in diameter—and then the surface of the bubble dissipated in a column of dust or smoke that rose up perhaps five hundred feet from the valley bottom, stayed a moment with the lowering sun behind it, like the very column of fire out of Sinai, and then lifted whole and broke suddenly in the wind. Even in the shelter we heard the screaming rumble of sound, and as the face of the enormous hole that the dust had left cleared, there bubbled up a column of oil perhaps a hundred feet in diameter. Or was it oil?

The moment we saw it, a tremendous cheer went up in the shelter, and then the cheer cut off in its own echo. Our closed-circuit system was color television, and this column of oil was bright red.

"Red oil," someone whispered.

Then it was quiet.

"When can we get out?" someone else demanded.

"Another ten minutes."

The dust was up and away in the opposite direction, and for ten minutes we stood and watched the bright red oil bubble out of the hole, forming a great pond within the retaining walls, and filling the space with amazing rapidity and lapping over the walls, for the flow must have been a hundred thousand gallons a second or even more, and then outside of the walls and a thickness of it all across the valley floor, rising so quickly that from above, where we were, we saw that we would be cut off from the entire installation. At that point we didn't wait, but took our chances with the radiation and raced down the desert hillside toward the hole and the mobile homes and the trucks—but not quickly enough. We came to a stop at the edge of a great lake of red oil.

"It's not red oil," someone said.

"Goddamnit, it's not oil!"

"The hell it's not! It's oil."

We were moving back as it spread and rose and covered the trucks and houses, and then it reached a gap in the valley and poured through and down across the desert, into the darkness of the shadows that the big rocks threw—flashing red in the sunset and later black in the darkness.

Someone touched it and put a hand to his mouth.

"It's blood."

Max was next to me. "He's crazy," Max said.

Someone else said that it was blood.

I put a finger into the red fluid and raised it to my nose. It was warm, almost hot, and there was no mistaking the smell of hot, fresh blood. I tasted it with the tip of my tongue.

"What is it?" Max whispered.

The others gathered around now—silent, with the red sun setting across the red lake and the red reflected on our faces, our eyes glinting with the red.

"Jesus God, what is it?" Max demanded.

"It's blood," I replied.

"From where?"

Then we were all silent.

We spent the night on the top of the butte where the shelter had been built, and in the morning all around us, as far as we could see, there was a hot, steaming sea of red blood, the smell so thick and heavy that we were all sick from it; and all of us vomited half a dozen times before the helicopters came for us and took us away.

The day after I returned home, Martha and I were sitting in the living room, she with a book and I with the paper, where I had read about their trying to cap the thing, except that even with diving suits they could not get down to where it was; and she looked up from her book and said:

"Do you remember that thing about the mother?"

"What thing?"

"A very old thing, I think I heard once that it was half as old as time, or maybe a Greek fable or something of the sort—but anyway, the mother has one son, who is the joy of her heart and all the rest that a son could be to a mother, and then the son falls in love with or under the spell of a beautiful and wicked woman—very wicked and very beautiful. And he desires to please her, oh, he does indeed, and he says to her, 'Whatever you desire, I will bring it to you'—"

"Which is nothing to say to any woman, but ever," I put in.

"I won't quarrel with that," Martha said mildly, "because when he does put it to her, she replies that what she desires most on this earth is the living heart of his mother, plucked from her breast. So what does this worthless and murderous idiot male do but race home to his mother, and then out with a knife, ripping her breast to belly and tearing the living heart out of her body—"

"I don't like your story."

"—and with the heart in his hand, he blithely dashes back toward his ladylove. But on the way through the forest he catches his toe on a root, stumbles, and falls headlong, the mother's heart knocked out of his hand. And as he pulls himself up and approaches the heart, it says to him, 'Did you hurt yourself when you fell, my son?'"

"Lovely story. What does it prove?"

"Nothing, I suppose. Will they ever stop the bleeding? Will they close the wound?"

"I don't think so."

"Then will your mother bleed to death?"

"My mother?"

"Yes."

"Oh."

"My mother," Martha said. "Will she bleed to death?"

"I suppose so."

"That's all you can say—I suppose so?"

"What else?"

"Suppose you had told them not to go ahead?"

"You asked me that twenty times, Martha. I told you. They would have gotten another dowser."

"And another? And another?"

"Yes."

"Why?" she cried out. "For God's sake, why?"

"I don't know."

"But you lousy men know everything else."

"Mostly we only know how to kill it. That's not everything else. We never learned to make anything alive."

"And now it's too late," Martha said.

"It's too late, yes," I agreed, and I went back to reading the paper. But Martha just sat there, the open book in her lap, looking at me; and then after a while she closed the book and went upstairs to bed.

15
The General Zapped an Angel

W HEN news leaked out of Viet Nam that Old Hell and Hardtack Mackenzie had shot down an angel, every newspaper in the world dug into its morgue for the background and biography of this hard-bitten old warrior.

Not that General Clayborne Mackenzie was so old. He had only just passed his fiftieth birthday, and he had plenty of piss and vinegar left in him when he went out to Viet Nam to head up the 55th Cavalry and its two hundred helicopters; and the sight of him sitting in the open door of a gunship, handling a submachine gun like the pro he was, and zapping anything that moved there below—because anything that moved was likely enough to be Charlie—had inspired many a fine color story.

Correspondents liked to stress the fact that Mackenzie was a "natural fighting man," with, as they put it, "an instinct for the kill." In this they were quite right, as the material from the various newspaper morgues proved. When Mackenzie was only six years old, playing in the yard of his humble north Carolina home, he managed to kill a puppy by beating it to death with a stone, an extraordinary act of courage and perseverance. After that, he was able to earn spending money by killing unwanted puppies and kittens for five cents each. He was an intensely creative child, one of the things that contributed to his subsequent leadership qualities, and not content with drowning the animals, he devised five other methods for destroying the unwanted pets. By nine he was trapping rabbits and rats and had invented a unique yet simple mole trap that caught moles alive. He enjoyed turning over live moles and

267

mice to neighborhood cats, and often he would invite his little playmates to watch the results. At the age of twelve his father gave him his first gun—and from there on no one who knew young Clayborne Mackenzie doubted either his future career or success.

After his arrival in Viet Nam, there was no major mission of the 55th that Old Hell and Hardtack did not lead in person. The sight of him blazing away from the gunship became a symbol of the "new war," and the troops on the ground would look for him and up at him and cheer him when he appeared. (Sometimes the cheers were earthy, but that is only to be expected in war.) There was nothing Mackenzie loved better than a village full of skulking, treacherous VC, and once he passed over such a village, little was left of it. A young newspaper correspondent compared him to an "avenging angel," and sometimes when his helicopters were called in to help a group of hard-pressed infantry, he thought of himself in such terms. It was on just such an occasion, when the company of marines holding the outpost at Quen-to were so hard pressed, that the thing happened.

General Clayborne Mackenzie had led the attack, blazing away, and down came the angel, square into the marine encampment. It took a while for them to realize what they had, and Mackenzie had already returned to base field when the call came from Captain Joe Kelly, who was in command of the marine unit.

"General, sir," said Captain Kelly, when Mackenzie had picked up the phone and asked what in hell they wanted, "General Mackenzie, sir, it would seem that you shot down an angel."

"Say that again, Captain."

"An angel, sir."

"A what?"

"An angel, sir."

"And just what in hell is an angel?"

"Well," Kelly answered. "I don't quite know how to answer that, sir. An angel is an angel. One of God's angels, sir."

"Are you out of your goddamn mind, Captain?" Mackenzie roared. "Or are you sucking pot again? So help me God, I warned you potheads that if you didn't lay off the grass I would see you all in hell!"

"No, sir," said Kelly quietly and stubbornly. "We have no pot here."

"Well put on Lieutenant Garcia!" Mackenzie yelled.

"Lieutenant Garcia." The voice came meekly.

"Lieutenant, what the hell is this about an angel?"

"Yes, General."

"Yes, what?"

"It is an angel. When you were over here zapping VC—well, sir, you just went and zapped an angel."

"So help me God," Mackenzie yelled, "I will break every one of you potheads for this! You got a lot of guts, buster, to put on a full general, but nobody puts me on and walks away from it. Just remember that."

One thing about Old Hell and Hardtack, when he wanted something done, he didn't ask for volunteers. He did it himself, and now he went to his helicopter and told Captain Jerry Gates, the pilot:

"You take me out to that marine encampment at Quen-to and put me right down in the middle of it."

"It's a risky business, General."

"It's your goddamn business to fly this goddamn ship and not to advise me."

Twenty minutes later the helicopter settled down into the encampment at Quen-to, and a stony-faced full general faced Captain Kelly and said:

"Now suppose you just lead me to that damn angel, and God help you if it's not."

But it was; twenty feet long and all of it angel, head to foot. The marines had covered it over with two tarps, and it was their good luck that the VCs either had given up on Quen-to or had simply decided not to fight for a while—because there was not much fight left in the marines, and all the young men could do was to lie in their holes and try not to look at the big body under the two tarps and not to talk about it either; but in spite of how they tried, they kept sneaking glances at it and they kept on whispering about it, and the two of them who pulled off the tarps so that General Mackenzie might see began to cry a little. The general didn't like that; if there was one thing he did not like, it was soldiers who cried, and he snapped at Kelly:

"Get these two mothers the hell out of here, and when you assign a detail to me, I want men, not wet-nosed kids." Then he surveyed the angel, and even he was impressed.

"It's a big son of a bitch, isn't it?"

269

"Yes, sir. Head to heel, it's twenty feet. We measured it."

"What makes you think it's an angel?"

"Well, that's the way it is," Kelly said. "It's an angel. What else is it?"

General Mackenzie walked around the recumbent form and had to admit the logic in Captain Kelly's thinking. The thing was white, not flesh-white but snow-white, shaped like a man, naked, and sprawled on its side with two great feathered wings folded under it. Its hair was spun gold and its face was too beautiful to be human.

"So that's an angel," Mackenzie said finally.

"Yes, sir."

"Like hell it is!" Mackenzie snorted. "What I see is a white, Caucasian male, dead of wounds suffered on the field of combat. By the way, where'd I hit him?"

"We can't find the wounds, sir."

"Now just what the hell do you mean, you can't find the wounds? I don't miss. If I shot it, I shot it."

"Yes, sir. But we can't find the wounds. Perhaps its skin is very tough. It might have been the concussion that knocked it down."

Used to getting at the truth of things himself, Mackenzie walked up and down the body, going over it carefully. No wounds were visible.

"Turn the angel over," Mackenzie said.

Kelly, who was a good Catholic, hesitated at first; but between a live general and a dead angel, the choice was specified. He called out a detail of marines, and without enthusiasm they managed to turn over the giant body. When Mackenzie complained that mud smears were impairing his inspection, they wiped the angel clean. There were no wounds on the other side either.

"That's a hell of a note," Mackenzie muttered, and if Captain Kelly and Lieutenant Garcia had been more familiar with the moods of Old Hell and Hardtack, they would have heard a tremor of uncertainty in his voice. The truth is that Mackenzie was just a little baffled. "Anyway," he decided, "it's dead, so wrap it up and put it in the ship."

"Sir?"

"God damn it, Kelly, how many times do I have to give you an order? I said, wrap it up and put it in the ship!"

The marines at Quen-to were relieved as they watched Mackenzie's gunship disappear in the distance, preferring the company of live VCs to that of a dead angel, but the pilot of the helicopter flew with all the assorted worries of a Southern Fundamentalist.

"Is that sure enough an angel, sir?" he had asked the general.

"You mind your eggs and fly the ship, son," the general replied. An hour ago he would have told the pilot to keep his goddamn nose out of things that didn't concern him, but the angel had a stultifying effect on the general's language. It depressed him, and when the three-star general at headquarters said to him, "Are you trying to tell me, Mackenzie, that you shot down an angel?" Mackenzie could only nod his head miserably.

"Well, sir, you are out of your goddamn mind."

"The body's outside in Hangar F," said Mackenzie. "I put a guard over it, sir."

The two-star general followed the three-star general as he stalked to Hangar F, where the three-star general looked at the body, poked it with his toe, poked it with his finger, felt the feathers, felt the hair, and then said:

"God damn it to hell, Mackenzie, do you know what you got here?"

"Yes, sir."

"You got an angel—that's what the hell you got here."

"Yes, sir, that's the way it would seem."

"God damn you, Mackenzie, I always had a feeling that I should have put my foot down instead of letting you zoom up and down out there in those gunships zapping VCs. My God almighty, you're supposed to be a grown man with some sense instead of some dumb kid who wants to make a score zapping Charlie, and if you hadn't been out there in that gunship this would never have happened. Now what in hell am I supposed to do? We got a lousy enough press on this war. How am I going to explain a dead angel?"

"Maybe we don't explain it, sir. I mean, there it is. It happened. The damn thing's dead, isn't it? Let's bury it. Isn't that what a soldier does—buries his dead, tightens his belt a notch, and goes on from there?"

"So we bury it, huh, Mackenzie?"

"Yes, sir. We bury it."

"You're a horse's ass, Mackenzie. How long since someone told you that? That's the trouble with being a general in this goddamn army—no one ever gets to tell you what a horse's ass you are. You got dignity."

271

"No, sir. You're not being fair, sir," Mackenzie protested. "I'm trying to help. I'm trying to be creative in this trying situation."

"You get a gold star for being creative, Mackenzie. Yes, sir, General—that's what you get. Every marine at Quen-to knows you shot down an angel. Your helicopter pilot and crew know it, which means that by now everyone on this base knows it—because anything that happens here, I know it last—and those snotnose reporters on the base, they know it, not to mention the goddamn chaplains, and you want to bury it. Bless your heart."

The three-star general's name was Drummond, and when he got back to his office, his aide said to him excitedly:

"General Drummond, sir, there's a committee of chaplains, sir, who insist on seeing you, and they're very up tight about something, and I know how you feel about chaplains, but this seems to be something special, and I think you ought to see them."

"I'll see them." General Drummond sighed.

There were four chaplains, a Catholic priest, a rabbi, an Episcopalian, and a Lutheran. The Methodist, Baptist, and Presbyterian chaplains had wanted to be a part of the delegation, but the priest, who was a Paulist, said that if they were to bring in five Protestants, he wanted a Jesuit as reenforcement, while the rabbi, who was Reform, agreed that against five Protestants an Orthodox rabbi ought to join the Jesuit. The result was a compromise, and they agreed to allow the priest, Father Peter O'Malley, to talk for the group. Father O'Malley came directly to the point:

"Our information is, General, that General Mackenzie has shot down one of God's holy angels. Is that or is that not so?"

"I'm afraid it's so," Drummond admitted.

There was a long moment of silence while the collective clergy gathered its wits, its faith, its courage, and its astonishment, and then Father O'Malley asked slowly and ominously:

"And what have you done with the body of this holy creature, if indeed it has a body?"

"It has a body—a very substantial body. In fact, it's as large as a young elephant, twenty feet tall. It's lying in Hangar F, under guard."

Father O'Malley shook his head in horror, looked at his Protestant colleagues, and then passed over them to the rabbi and said to him:

"What are your thoughts, Rabbi Bernstein?"

Since Rabbi Bernstein represented the oldest faith that was concerned with angels, the others deferred to him.

272

"I think we ought to look upon it immediately," the rabbi said.
"I agree," said Father O'Malley.

The other clergy joined in this agreement, and they repaired to Hangar F, a journey not without difficulty, for by now the press had come to focus on the story, and the general and the clergy ran a sort of gauntlet of pleading questions as they made their way on foot to Hangar F. The guards there barred the press, and the clergy entered with General Drummond and General Mackenzie and a half a dozen other staff officers. The angel was uncovered, and the men made a circle around the great, beautiful thing, and then for almost five minutes there was silence.

Father O'Malley broke the silence. "God forgive us," he said.

There was a circle of amens, and then more silence, and finally Whitcomb, the Episcopalian, said:

"It could conceivably be a natural phenomenon."

Father O'Malley looked at him wordlessly, and Rabbi Bernstein softened the blow with the observation that even God and His holy angels could be considered as not apart from nature, whereupon Pastor Yager, the Lutheran, objected to a pantheistic viewpoint at a time like this, and Father O'Malley snapped:

"The devil with this theological nonsense! The plain fact of the matter is that we are standing in front of one of God's holy angels, which we in our animal-like sinfulness have slain. What penance we must do is more to the point."

"Penance is your field, gentlemen," said General Drummond. "I have the problem of a war, the press, and this body."

"This body, as you call it," said Father O'Malley, "obviously should be sent to the Vatican—immediately, if you ask me."

"Oh, ho!" snorted Whitcomb. "The Vatican! No discussion, no exchange of opinion—oh, no, just ship it off to the Vatican where it can be hidden in some secret dungeon with any other evidence of God's divine favor—"

"Come now, come now," said Rabbi Bernstein soothingly. "We are witness to something very great and holy, and we should not argue as to where this holy thing of God belongs. I think it is obvious that it belongs in Jerusalem."

While this theological discussion raged, it occured to General Clayborne Mackenzie that his own bridges needed mending, and he stepped outside to where the press—swollen by now to almost the entire press corps in Viet Nam—waited, and of course they grabbed him.

"Is it true, General?"

"Is what true?"

"Did you shoot down an angel?"

"Yes, I did," the old warrior stated forthrightly.

"For heaven's sake, why?" asked a woman photographer.

"It was a mistake," said Old Hell and Hardtack modestly.

"You mean you didn't see it?" asked another voice.

"No, sir. Peripheral, if you know what I mean. I was in the gunship zapping Charlie, and bang—there it was."

The press was skeptical. A dozen questions came, all to the point of how he knew that it was an angel.

"You don't ask why a river's a river or a donkey's a donkey," Mackenzie said bluntly. "Anyway, we have professional opinion inside."

Inside, the professional opinion was divided and angry. All were agreed that the angel was a sign—but what kind of sign was another matter entirely. Pastor Yager held that it was a sign for peace, calling for an immediate cease-fire. Whitcomb, the Episcopalian, held, however, that it was merely a condemnation of indiscriminate zapping, while the rabbi and the priest held that it was a sign—period. Drummond said that sooner or later the press must be allowed in and that the network men must be permitted to put the dead angel on television. Whitcomb and the rabbi agreed. O'Malley and Yager demurred. General Robert L. Robert of the Engineer Corps arrived with secret information that the whole thing was a put-on by the Russians and that the angel was a robot, but when they attempted to cut the flesh to see whether the angel bled or not, the skin proved to be impenetrable.

At that moment the angel stirred, just a trifle, yet enough to make the clergy and brass gathered around him leap back to give him room—for that gigantic twenty-foot form, weighing better than half a ton, was one thing dead and something else entirely alive. The angel's biceps were as thick around as a man's body, and his great, beautiful head was mounted on a neck almost two feet in diameter. Even the clerics were sufficiently hazy on angelology to be at all certain that even an angel might not resent being shot down. As he stirred a second time, the men around him moved even farther away, and some of the brass nervously loosened their sidearms.

274

"If this holy creature is alive," Rabbi Bernstein said bravely, "then he will have neither hate nor anger toward us. His nature is of love and forgiveness. Don't you agree with me, Father O'Malley?"

If only because the Protestant ministers were visibly dubious, Father O'Malley agreed. "By all means. Oh, yes."

"Just how the hell do you know?" demanded General Drummond, loosening his sidearm. "That thing has the strength of a bulldozer."

Not to be outdone by a combination of Catholic and Jew, Whitcomb stepped forward bravely and faced Drummond and said, "That 'thing,' as you call it, sir, is one of the Almighty's blessed angels, and you would do better to see to your immortal soul than to your sidearm."

To which Drummond yelled, "Just who the hell do you think you are talking to, mister—just—"

At that moment the angel sat up, and the men around him leaped away to widen the circle. Several drew their sidearms; others whispered whatever prayers they could remember. The angel, whose eyes were as blue as the skies over Viet Nam when the monsoon is gone and the sun shines through the washed air, paid almost no attention to them at first. He opened one wing and then the other, and his great wings almost filled the hangar. He flexed one arm and then the other, and then he stood up.

On his feet, he glanced around him, his blue eyes moving steadily from one to another, and when he did not find what he sought, he walked to the great sliding doors of Hangar F and spread them open with a single motion. To the snapping of steel regulators and the grinding of stripped gears, the doors parted—revealing to the crowd outside, newsmen, officers, soldiers, and civilians, the mighty, twenty-foot-high, shining form of the angel.

No one moved. The sight of the angel, bent forward slightly, his splendid wings half spread, not for flight but to balance him, held them hypnotically fixed, and the angel himself moved his eyes from face to face, finding finally what he sought—none other than Old Hell and Hardtack Mackenzie.

As in those Western films where the moment of "truth," as they call it, is at hand, where sheriff and badman stand face to face, their hands twitching over their guns—as the crowd melts away from the

275

two marked men in those films, so did the crowd melt away from around Mackenzie until he stood alone—as alone as any man on earth.

The angel took a long, hard look at Mackenzie, and then the angel sighed and shook his head. The crowd parted for him as he walked past Mackenzie and down the field—where, squarely in the middle of Runway Number 1, he spread his mighty wings and took off, the way an eagle leaps from his perch into the sky, or—as some reporters put it—as a dove flies gently.

16
The Price

FRANK Blunt himself told the story of how, at the age of seven, he bought off a larger, older boy who had threatened to beat him up. The larger boy, interviewed many years later, had some trouble recalling the incident, but he said that it seemed to him, if his memory was at all dependable, that Frank Blunt had beaten up his five-year-old sister and had appropriated a bar of candy in her possession. Frank Blunt's second cousin, Lucy, offered the acid comment that the dollar which bought off the larger boy had been appropriated from Frank's mother's purse; and three more men whose memories had been jogged offered the information that Frank had covered his investment by selling protection to the smallest kids at twenty-five cents a kid. Be that as it may; it was a long time ago. The important factor was that it illustrated those two qualities which contributed so much to Frank Blunt's subsequent success: his gift for appropriation and his ability to make a deal if the price was right.

The story that he got out of secondary school by purchasing the answers to the final exam is probably apocryphal and concocted out of spleen. No one ever accused Frank Blunt of being stupid. This account is probably vestigial from the fact that he bought his way out of an explusion from college by paying off the dean with a cool two thousand dollars, no mean sum in those days. As with so many of the stories about Frank Blunt, the facts are hard to come by, and the nastiest of the many rumors pertaining to the incident is that Frank had established a profitable business as a pimp, taking his cut of the earnings of half a dozen unhappy young women whom he had

277

skillfully directed into the oldest profession. Another rumor held that he had set up a mechanism for obtaining tests in advance of the testing date and peddling them very profitably. But this too could not be proved, and all that was actually known was his purchase of the dean. It is also a matter of record that when he finally left college in his junior year—a matter of choice—he had a nest egg of about fifty thousand dollars. This was in 1916. A year later he bought his way out of the draft for World War I in circumstances that still remain obscure.

Two years later he bought State Senator Hiram Gillard for an unspecified price, and was thereby able to place four contracts for public works with kickbacks that netted him the tidy sum of half a million dollars—very nice money indeed in 1919. In 1920, when Frank Blunt was twenty-four years old, he purchased four city councilmen and levied his service charge on fourteen million dollars' worth of sewer construction. His kickback amounted to a cool million dollars.

By 1930 he was said to be worth ten million dollars, but it was the beginning of a muckraking period and he was swept up in the big public utility scandals and indicted on four counts of bribery and seven of fraud. Frank Blunt was never one to count small change, and at least half of his ten-million-dollar fortune went into the purchase of two federal judges, three prosecutors, five assistant prosecutors, two congressmen, and one juryman—on the basis that if you are going to fix a jury, it's pointless to buy more than one good man.

One of the congressmen subsequently became a business associate, and Frank Blunt moved out of the scandal with clean hands and the receivership of three excellent utility companies, out of which he netted sufficient profit to more than replace his expenses for the cleansing.

He often said, afterward, that his Washington contacts made during that time were worth more than the expenses he incurred in, as he euphemistically put it, clearing his name; and unquestionably they were, for he got in at the rock bottom of the offshore oil development, operating with the boldness· and verve that had already made him something of a legend in the financial world. This time he purchased the governor of a state, and it was now that he was said to have made his famous remark:

"You can buy the devil himself if the price is right."

Frank Blunt never quibbled over the price. "You cast your bread upon the waters," he was fond of saying, and if he wanted something, he never let the cost stand in his way. He had discovered that no matter what he paid for something he desired, his superb instinct for investment covered him and served him.

Politicians were not the only goods that Frank Blunt acquired. He was a tall, strong, good-looking man, with a fine head of hair and commanding blue eyes, and he never had difficulties with women. But while they were ready to line up and jump through his hoop free of cost, he preferred to purchase what he used. These purchases were temporary; not until he was forty-one years old and worth upward of fifty million dollars did he buy a permanent fixture. She was a current Miss America, and he bought her not only a great mansion on a hill in Dallas, Texas, but also four movies for her to star in. Along that path, he bought six of the most important film critics in America, for he was never one to take action without hedging his bets.

All of the above is of another era; for by the time Frank Blunt was fifty-six years old, in 1952, he was worth more money than anyone cared to compute; he had purchased a new image for himself via the most brilliant firm of public relations men in America; and he had purchased an ambassadorship to one of the leading western European countries. His cup was full, and it runneth over, so to speak, and then he had his first heart attack.

Four years later, at the age of sixty, he had his second heart attack; and lying in his bed, the first day out of the oxygen tent, he fixed his cold blue eyes on the heart specialist he had imported from Switzerland—who was flanked on either side by several American colleagues—and asked:

"Well, Doc, what's the verdict?"

"You are going to recover, Mr. Blunt. You are on the road."

"And just what the hell does that mean?"

"It is meaning that in a few weeks you will be out of the bed."

"Why don't you come to the point? How long have I got to live after this one?" He had always had the reputation of being as good as his name.

The Swiss doctor hemmed and hawed until Blunt threw him out of the room. Then he faced the American doctors and specified that there was no one among the four of them who had collected less than twenty thousand in fees from him.

"And none of you will ever see a red cent of mine again unless I get the truth. How long?"

The consensus of opinion was a year, give or take a month or two.

"Surgery?"

"No, sir. Not in your case. In your case it is contra-indicated."

"Treatment?"

"None that is more than a sop."

"Then there is no hope?"

"Only a miracle, Mr. Blunt."

Frank Blunt's eyes narrowed thoughtfully, and for a few minutes he lay in bed silent, staring at the four uncomfortable physicians. Then he said to them:

"Out! Get out, the whole lot of you."

Five weeks later, Frank Blunt, disdaining a helping hand from wife or butler, walked out of his house and got into his custom-built twenty-two-thousand-dollar sports car, whipped together for him by General Motors—he was a deeply patriotic man and would not have a foreign car in his garage—told his chauffeur to go soak his head, and drove off without a word to anyone.

Blunt was not a churchgoer—except for weddings and funerals—but his flakmade image described him as a religious man whose religion was personal and fervent, and the wide spectrum of his charities included a number of church organizations. He had been baptized in the Baptist church, and now he drove directly to the nearest Baptist church and used the knocker of the adjacent parsonage. The Reverend Harris, an elderly white-haired and mild-mannered man, answered the door himself, surprised and rather flustered by this unexpected, famous, and very rich caller.

"I had heard you were sick," he said lamely, not knowing what else to say.

"I'm better. Can I come in?"

"Please do. Please come in and sit down. I'll have Mrs. Harris make some tea."

"I'll have some bourbon whiskey, neat."

Pastor Harris explained unhappily that bourbon whiskey was not part of his household but that he had some sherry that was a gift from one of his parishioners.

"I'll have the tea," said Frank Blunt.

The pastor led Blunt into his study, and a very nervous and excited Mrs. Harris brought tea and cookies. Blunt sat silently in the

280

shabby little study, staring at the shelves of old books, until Mrs. Harris had withdrawn, and then he said bluntly, as befitting his name and nature:

"About God."

"Yes, Mr. Blunt?"

"Understand me, I'm a businessman. I want facts, not fancies. Do you believe in God?"

"That's a strange question to ask me."

"Yes or no, sir. I don't make small talk."

"Yes," the pastor replied weakly.

"Completely?"

"Yes."

"No doubts?"

"No, Mr. Blunt. I have no doubts."

"Have you ever seen Him?"

"Seen who?" the pastor asked with some bewilderment.

"God."

"That's a very strange question, sir."

"All my questions are strange questions. My being here is a damn strange thing. If you can't answer a question, say so."

"Then let me ask you, sir," said Pastor Harris, his indignation overcoming his awe, "do you believe in God?"

"I have no choice. I'll repeat my question. Have you ever seen Him?"

"As I see you?"

"Naturally. How else?"

"In my heart, Mr. Blunt," Harris said quietly, with curious dignity. "Only in my heart, sir."

"In your heart?"

"In my heart, sir."

"Then, damn it, you don't see Him at all. You believe something exists—and where is it? In your heart. That's no answer. That's no answer at all. When I look into my heart, I see two damn coronaries, and that's all."

"The more's the pity for that," Pastor Harris thought, and waited for Frank Blunt to come to the point of his visit.

"Joe Jerico sees Him," Blunt said, almost to himself. Harris stared at him.

"Joe Jerico!" Blunt snapped.

"The revivalist?"

"Exactly. Is he a man of God or isn't he?"

"That's not for me to say," Harris replied mildly. "He does his work, I do mine. He talks to thousands. I talk to a handful."

"He talks to God, doesn't he?"

"Yes, he talks to God."

Frank Blunt rose and thrust out his hand at the old man. "Thank you for your time, Parson. I'll send you a check in the morning."

"That's not necessary."

"By my lights it is. I consulted you in a field where you're knowledgeable. My doctor gets a thousand dollars for a half hour of his time. You're worth at least as much."

The following afternoon, flying from Dallas, Texas, to Nashville, Tennessee, in his private twin-engine Cessna, Frank Blunt asked his pilot the same question he had asked Harris the day before.

"I'm a Methodist," replied Alf Jones, the pilot.

"You could be a goddamn Muslim. I asked you something else."

"The wife takes care of that," said Alf Jones. "My goodness, Mr. Blunt, if that was on my mind, flying around from city to city the way I do, I'd sure as hell turn into a mother-loving monk, wouldn't I?"

A chauffeur-driven limousine was waiting at the airport—not a hired car; Blunt kept chauffeur-driven custom-built jobs at every major airport—and the chauffeur, after a warm but respectful greeting, sped the car around the city toward that great, open, two-hundred-acre pasture that had been named "Repentance City."

"You're looking well, Mr. Blunt, if I may say so," the chauffeur remarked.

"What do you know about Joe Jerico?" Blunt asked him.

"He's a fine man."

"What makes you say so?"

"Take my old grandaddy. He was the dirtiest, sinfulest old lecher that ever tried to rape a nice little black girl. Truth is, we couldn't have a woman near him. That is, when he wasn't drunk. When he was drunk, he was just a mean and dangerous old devil and he'd just as soon break a bottle of corn over your head as say hello."

"What the hell has that got to do with Joe Jerico?"

"He went to one gathering—just one—and he saw the light."

"How is he now?"

"Saintly. Just so damn saintly you want to crack him across the head with a piece of cordwood."

"One meeting?"

"Yes, sir, Mr. Blunt. One meeting and he got the word."

It was dark when they reached Repentance City, but batteries of giant floods turned the vast parking area into daylight. Thousands of cars were already there, like a sea of beetles around the vast, looming white tent. Blunt respected size and organization. "How many does the tent hold?" he asked his chauffeur.

"Ten thousand."

"He fills it?"

"Every night. You wouldn't believe it, Mr. Blunt, but they drive two, three hundred miles to be here. He has a loudspeaker setup, and sometimes he has an overflow of two, three thousand can't get into the tent. So they sit in their cars, just like a drive-in movie."

"Admission?"

"Just two bits. He won't turn away the poor, but then he takes up a collection."

They parked, and Blunt then told the chauffeur to wait, while he made his way on foot to the tent. There must have been two or three hundred ushers, men and women, organizing the crowd and handing out leaflets and song sheets, the men in white suits, the women in white dresses. It was an enormous, businesslike, and well-conducted operation, and some quick arithmetic told Blunt that the nightly take, out of admission and nominal contributions, should approach a minimum of five thousand dollars. By his standards it was not tremendous, but it marked Joe Jerico as very much a man of practical affairs, however metaphysical his profession might be.

Blunt paid his quarter, entered, and found himself a seat on a bench toward the rear, sandwiched between a very fat middle-aged old woman and a very lean old man. Already the tent was almost filled to capacity, with only a rare space to be seen here and there; just a few minutes after he arrived, the meeting started with a choir of fifty voices singing "Onward, Christian Soldiers." A second and a third hymn followed, and then the house lights went down and a battery of spots fixed on stage center. The backdrop was a black cyclorama, the curtain of which parted for Joe Jerico to step into the spotlights, not a tall man, not a short man, straight, wide-shouldered, with a big head, a great mane of graying hair, and pale gray eyes like bits of glowing ice.

No introduction; he plunged right in with a voice that had the timbre of an organ: "My text is St. John, eight, twelve. 'Then spake

283

Jesus unto them, saying, I am the light of the world: he that followeth me shall not walk in darkness, but shall have the light of life.' Do you believe? So help me God, I hope not. This is no place for believers. This is for the unbelievers, for the lost, for the misbegotten, for the devil-pursued, for the lost, I say, for you come in here and you come home and you are found! Open your hearts to me . . .''

Frank Blunt listened, intent and thoughtful, less touched by emotion than by admiration for the man's masterly command of the crowd. He played them as one plays a great instrument, as if indeed he was the extension of some mighty force that operated through him. His voice, naturally deep and full timbred, magnified by the public address system, touched with just sufficient trace of a southern accent, battered his audience, grabbed them, held them and used them.

Frank Blunt observed. He listened as the charge of emotion built up; he nodded with appreciation as the sinners went forward to be saved at the urgent, pleading command of Joe Jerico, and he admired the smoothness and the fine organization of the collection, just at the right moment of emotional completion. He ignored the slotted box as it went down his row, and accepted the hostile glances of those beside him. He sat and watched thoughtfully, and when it was over and the emotionally filled crowd, so many of them in tears, filed out, he remained seated. He remained seated until he was the last person in the huge tent, and then an usher approached him and asked whether he was all right.

"My name is Frank Blunt," he said to the usher. "Here is my card. I want to see Mr. Jerico."

"Mr. Jerico sees no one now. He is understandably fatigued. Perhaps—"

"I'm here now and I wish to see Mr. Jerico. Take him my card. I'll wait here."

Frank Blunt was not easy to resist. He had issued orders for so many years and had been obeyed for so many years that people did his will. The usher took the card, walked the length of the tent, disappeared for a few minutes, reappeared, walked the length of the tent, and said to Blunt:

"Reverend Jerico will see you. Follow me."

Back through the tent, through the black curtain, and then backstage past the curious glances of the ushers, the choir singers, and the rest of the large staff Joe Jerico carried with him; and then

284

to the door of a large, portable dressing room. The usher knocked at the door. The deep voice of Jerico answered, "Come in." The usher opened the door and Frank Blunt entered the dressing room. The room was an eight-by-fourteen trailer; it had taste, it had class, and it had Joe Jerico in a green silk dressing gown, sipping at a tall glass of orange juice.

Blunt measured it with a quick glance, as he did the man. There was nothing cheap or modest about Joe Jerico; his work was no work that Blunt had ever encountered before, but the tycoon liked the way he did it.

"So you're Frank Blunt." Jerico nodded at a chair. "Sit down. Tomato juice, orange juice—we have no hard liquor—I can give you some wine."

"I'm all right."

No handshake, neither warmth nor coolness, but two men eyeing each other and measuring each other.

"I'm glad you made it this time," Joe Jerico said finally.

"Why?"

"Because it gives you time for repentance."

"I didn't come here for repentance."

"Oh?" Jerico's eyes narrowed. "What then?"

"The doctors give me a year. They're liars. It's in the nature of the profession. If they gave me less, they figure I'd fire them."

"What do you give yourself?"

"Three to six months."

"Then I'd say you need repentance, Mr. Blunt."

"No, sir. I need life, Mr. Jerico."

"Oh? And how do you propose to go about that?"

"What do you know about me, Mr. Jerico?"

"What's on the record, more or less."

"Let me fill in then. I began my career by buying a college dean. I found that if the price is right, you can buy—and there are no exceptions. I have bought judges, city councilmen, district attorneys, jurors, congressmen, and senators. I bought the governors of two states. I have bought men and women and thoroughbred horses. I took a fancy to a princess once, and I bought a night in bed with her. It cost me twenty-five thousand dollars. I bought the dictator of a European country and I once had occasion to buy a member of the Central Committee of the Communist Party of the Soviet Union. He cost less than the princess, but he was more profitable in the long run."

He said all this, never taking his eyes from Jerico's face. Jerico listened with interest.

"You're a forthright man, Mr. Blunt."

"I don't have time to crap around, Mr. Jerico."

"What do you propose?"

"I like you, Mr. Jerico. You see the point and you come to it. I want to live. I propose to buy off God."

Jerico nodded, his pale eyes fixed on Blunt. He remained silent, and Frank Blunt waited. Minutes of silence passed, and still Frank Blunt waited patiently. He respected a man who considered a proposition carefully.

"You're not dealing with the principal. You're dealing with an agent," Jerico said finally. "How do you propose to enforce the contract?"

"I'm not an unreasonable man. I'm sixty years old. I want fifteen years more. I've made arrangements with a man whose line of work is the enforcing of contracts. If I die before the fifteen years are up, he will kill you."

"That's sound," Jerico agreed after a moment. "I like the way you think, Mr. Blunt."

"I like the way you think, Mr. Jerico."

"Then perhaps we can do business."

"Good. Now what's your price?"

"How much are you worth, Mr. Blunt?"

"About five hundred million dollars."

"Then that's the price, Mr. Blunt."

"You're not serious?"

"Deadly serious."

"Then you're insane."

Jerico smiled and spread his hands. "What's the alternative, Mr. Blunt? I could suggest the reward that awaits a man who has lived well—but no one takes any money with him to that place. You want it here on earth."

"To hell with you!" Blunt snorted. But he didn't get up. He sat there, watching Jerico.

"I didn't come to you," Jerico said softly. "You came to me."

Silence again. The silence dragged on, and this time Jerico waited patiently. Finally Blunt asked:

"How much will you let me keep?"

"Nothing."

286

"A man doesn't live on air and water. A million would see me through."

"Nothing."

"Well, I've heard it said that I have more money than God. Now it's reversed. The fact is, Mr. Jerico, that you drive a hard bargain, a damn hard bargain. I don't need money; I have a credit line of twenty million. You have a deal. Suppose we let the lawyers get together tomorrow."

It took seven weeks for the lawyers to finish the legal arrangements and for the papers to be signed. On the eighth week, Frank Blunt suffered a stroke. He was taken to the Dallas Colonial Nursing Home, which Joe Jerico immediately purchased, installing his own staff of doctors, nurses, and technicians. A year later Frank Blunt was still alive. A mechanical heart had taken over the function of his own weary instrument; a kidney machine flushed his body; and nourishment was fed to him intravenously. Whether or not he was more than a vegetable is difficult to say, but the report issued by Joe Jerico, who visited him once a week, was that he lived by faith—a testimony to faith.

By the third year, Joe Jerico's weekly visits had ceased. For one thing, his home was in Luxembourg—re the tax benefits—and his fortune was increasing at so lively a pace that he abhorred the thought of airplanes. He found his eighteen-thousand-ton yacht sufficient for his travel needs. His revivals had decreased to one a year, but whenever he was in America for the occasion, he made certain to visit Frank Blunt.

Frank Blunt died in 1971—fifteen years to the day from the time in Joe Jerico's dressing room when they had shaken hands and closed their deal. Actually his death was caused by a malfunction of the artificial heart, but it was only to be expected. So much had happened; the world had forgotten Frank Blunt.

Joe Jerico received the word on his yacht, which was lying in the harbor at Ischia, where he had come to spend a few days at the Duke of Genneset's villa, and he was late to dinner because he thoughtfully took the time to compose a message of condolence to Blunt's family. Jerico, at fifty, was still a fine figure of a man, comfortable indeed, but he had by no means lost his faith. As he told the young woman who accompanied him to dinner:

"God works in strange ways."

17
The Vision of Milty Boil

NAPOLEON, Stalin, Hitler, and Mussolini all had one thing in common with Milton Boil: they were short men. But the most explosive moments in human history have often been the result of an absent six or seven inches in height, and while it is hardly profitable it is certainly interesting to speculate upon what might have been man's destiny had Milton Boil been six feet and one inch instead of five feet and one inch—with a name like Smith or Jones or Goldberg instead of Boil.

But at his maturity he was five feet and one inch, and his name had already caused him so much small suffering that no force on earth would have persuaded him to change it. All his life he had been stuck with pins, pinched and punned upon because of his name and his height; no wonder he was a millionaire before he reached thirty.

He was born in 1940 and he grew up in the time of affluence. His father was a builder of small apartment houses. Milton (or Milty, as he came to be known the world over) came out of college, spent a year learning more about his father's business than the old man ever knew, and then parted company with his father and built his first big apartment house. Milty was a genius. By 1970 he had become the largest builder of apartment houses in New York City. He married Joan Pebbleman, whose father was one of the country's largest builders of office buildings, and they had three lovely children. Joan worked in charitable efforts. Her name was in *The New York Times* at least once a week. She was only four feet and ten inches tall, so from a reasonable distance they were a very handsome couple indeed.

Milty respected money, rich people, brains, organizational drive, very rich people, the government, the church, and millionaires. In an interview, he was asked what he considered the first necessary attribute of a young man who desired to become a millionaire.

"Ambition," he replied promptly. He respected ambition.

"And after that?"

"Influence," he replied. "Proper friends."

And Milty made friends and built influence. By 1975, at the age of thirty-five, he was considered the most influential man in New York City. His influence was such that he was able to have a number of significant changes made in the building code—among them the lowering of the minimum height of the ceilings to seven feet. With this achieved, he built the first one-hundred-story apartment house in New York. In 1980, riding the crest of the wave created by the population explosion, Milty Boil managed to have the city council pass an ordinance permitting ceilings of six feet in all apartment buildings over fifty stories high.

Rival builders sneered at Milty's new house, claiming that no one would be so damn foolish as to rent an apartment with six-foot ceilings, but such was the housing shortage by then that the entire building, with its seven hundred apartments, was fully rented in sixty days.

The cash flow that passed through Milty's deserving hands had by now become so enormous that he was known throughout the business as the "golden boy" or, more often, "the golden boil"; but Milty was beyond the barbs of name-calling. His vision and imagination had lifted him to unprecedented heights, and once again he brought his influence to bear upon the lawmakers. In 1982 his workmen broke ground for a new building of one hundred stories, with ceilings five feet high. Biographers recall this as a moment of great crisis in the life of Milty Boil, and historians look back upon it as a turning point in man's destiny. Suddenly all the forces of conservatism focused upon Milty; he was called everything from a depraved profiteer to public enemy number one; he was abused in the press, in Congress, on the air. There were, of course, a handful of farsighted people who applauded Milty's courage and creativity, but mostly it was abuse that he received. And to this, at his now historic press conference, Milty replied simply and with dignity:

290

"I give people a place to live at a reasonable rent. Especially the young people, who so desperately desire an urban condition. I give them a place to live at a rent they can afford."

"Do you, sir?" demanded the representative of *The New York Times,* bold and caustic as befitting his place, leading the attack upon Milty. "How can you say that in the light of the fact that we Americans are the tallest people on earth, especially our youth?"

"I agree," Milty replied. "This height is a tribute to the American way of life. All my life I have upheld the American way of life."

"That hardly answers the question," said a CBS man.

"I intend to answer it," Milty assured them. "I have never been less than forthright about my plans. I have submitted this problem to a panel of forty-two physicians. They all agree that bending, crouching, and occasional creeping can only be beneficial to human health. Thereby a whole series of muscles formerly ignored are brought into play, and thus my own efforts coincide with the President's plan for physical fitness. As for the defense of democracy on an international scale, nothing better develops a man for jungle combat than the alertness produced by life in a five-foot-high apartment. I have here a statement from the Secretary of Defense— mimeographed copies available—which says in part: 'The constant concerns for his country's welfare which dominate the thinking of Milton Boil deserves special mention and commendation.' I also have statements from Generals Bosch and Korpulant, both of them experts—"

"Mr. Boil," he was interrupted, "are you trying to tell us that these low ceilings constitute a positive progressive feature in apartment construction?"

"They do indeed. Furthermore, an apartment is not a place where one lives vertically. We have conducted a survey of the habits of over ten thousand apartment dwellers, and the results show that ninety-two point eight percent of their hours spent in the apartment are spent in a sitting or reclining or prone position. With young married couples, the percentage is a trifle higher—"

So did Milty Boil defend himself, a man alone fighting off the forces of reaction and always contemplating the gigantic profit produced by a building consisting of five-foot-high apartments. But a day later, at his regular board of directors' meeting, Milty found that even those who shared the profits had their doubts.

"It won't work."

"Milty—you can't go on this way. I hear Washington intends to step in."

"Did you hear what *Pravda* has to say? I have the translation here—'the final step in the decadence of the United States.' Well, it gives one pause."

"I don't say it wasn't a brilliant step, Milty. I simply ask: will it work? Can it work? *Life* is not *Pravda*, but listen to its editorial: 'Has Milty finally flipped? We don't hold with those who characterize Milton Boil as a madman or public enemy. We recognize that the greatest builder of modern America does not make decisions lightly. But if Milton Boil is not mad, neither are Americans three feet tall. If—' "

"No, no!" Milty cried, finally coming to life in his place at the head of the table. "Hold it right there. Read that last sentence again."

"What last sentence?"

"You know—that business about three feet tall."

"You mean this—'But if Milton Boil is not mad, neither are Americans three feet tall—' "

"Right! Right you are! There it is!"

"There what is?" asked one of the older members, less able because of his age to follow the pyrotechnics of Milty's thought.

"The whole thing. The whole answer. The key to everything." Milty's very real excitement began to permeate the others.

"What key, Milty? Don't be so damned mysterious."

"All right. But tell me this. What is the number one problem of the world today?"

"Communism," half a dozen board members replied eagerly.

"Nuts! Communism is a word. We licked them in space and we licked them in everything else down here. Our houses are better and our roads are better and our factories are better."

"Disease," someone said hopefully.

"Did you ever hear of antibiotics? Not disease."

"War, Milty?"

"Since when is war a problem?"

"Inflation?"

"You should talk—you made millions out of inflation. Come on, come on, use your heads—there's only one number one problem in the world today, and if we lick it, it licks us, and if we destroy it, it destroys us—until now, until right this minute when your uncle

292

Milty Boil solved it, and we're going to lick it and it's not going to destroy us.''

They spread their hands hopelessly. They looked at Milty in defeat, knowing how much he enjoyed winning.

"Milty, let us in, tell us where the action is," his first vice-president pleaded.

"All right." Milty Boil leaned forward. His face hardened; his voice became precise and crisp. He was all mind now, a cold, beautiful, hard-core calculating machine. They knew that look on Milty's face; they knew it meant a breakthrough, action, action and more action. The silence at the board table became a thing in itself.

"All right. World's number one problem—over-population, namely the population explosion. Next—what is our market for anything? People. And how do you increase the market? More people. But with more people you got the population explosion. Mankind trapped. Finis. Over. The earth starves.''

"Right, Milty," the board whispered.

"But there's a way."

The board waited.

Slowly, measuring each word, Milty said, "Double the size of the earth. That's the solution. That takes care of the next hundred years.''

The members of the board relaxed, looked at each other, grinned, and then burst into laughter. Only Milty didn't laugh. His face stony-set and cold as ice, he regarded them without pleasure and waited. They saw his expression finally, and the laughter died away. Milty pointed one finger at his second vice-president, who was in charge of purchasing, and asked evenly:

"Just what in hell do you find so funny?"

"The jest, Milty. We're laughing with you."

"Why?"

"Because it's a yuk, Milty, a tribute, so as to speak. You got a sense of humor like nobody else.''

"I don't think it's funny," Milty said.

"No? But you got to be kidding, Milty. The earth is what it is. Twenty-five thousand miles in circumference. That's fourth-grade stuff.''

"And you got a fourth-grade mind."

"Milty, Milty," said the oldest member in a fatherly way, "Milty, you have a fine mind, but nobody makes the earth larger."

293

"No?"

"No, Milty, I am afraid not."

"All right," Milty said, unperturbed by the oldest member and smiling slightly. "Nobody makes the earth larger. But tell me this—suppose, just for the sake of argument, that the average man was three feet tall. Now if he kept the same scale in relation to himself, everything would be reduced by half. Six inches would be a foot, and a mile would become two miles. In other words, if the man is reduced in size to one-half, then so are all his measurements. Suddenly the world is not twenty-five thousand miles in circumference but fifty thousand miles in circumference. We have doubled the size of the earth."

"Milty, Milty," said the oldest member, still in a fatherly way, "Milty, you got a brain like a steel trap. But all you are actually doing is to buttress one impossible statement with another. To make men three feet tall is as impossible as to make the earth fifty thousand miles in diameter."

"Who says?"

"I say, Milty," continued the oldest member. "I was a friend of your father, may he rest in peace, so I have the right."

"Good," Milty said. "You got the right. Now shut up." And to the rest of the board:

"I say we can produce a three-foot man."

"How, Milty?" asked the youngest member of the board. He was with Milty all the way.

"How? First I ask this: what in hell is so great about tall? Tall, tall, tall—that's all you hear. Why? Was Adolf Hitler tall? Was Napoleon tall? Was Onassis tall? Was Willie Shoemaker tall? And do you know how much prize money he took? Over thirty million, that's all. How about art—was Toulouse-Lautrec tall? You know how tall they believe Shakespeare was? Five feet four inches. Tall is for basketball players."

"But people think tall, Milty."

"Then we change their thinking. They think tall because everywhere the propaganda says that tall is good. We change that. We show them that tall is for clods. The men who make the world go round are small. The men women prefer are small. The men who become top dog are small. It's a small man's world. That's what we show the world—that it's a small man's world, and the smaller the better."

294

"But, Milty," the older member of the board said patiently, "suppose we demonstrate all that. We still can't make men smaller."

"No?" Milty smiled. Years later, remembering that smile, some of the younger board members spoke about a "Gioconda" quality, but that was in retrospect and after Milty had gone to whatever rewards the next world provides for such genius. At the moment, then in 1982, Milty's smile was a smile of sheer superior knowledge.

"No—no, we can't make men smaller, but they can, can't they?"

"How, Milty?"

"By wanting it. Men have increased their height by over a foot in the past two hundred years. Suppose they start to decrease it—"

A month later, in the same board room, facing the representatives of the twelve largest advertising agencies in the world and the seventeen largest public relations firms, Milty Boil put his plan on its proper level.

"We are here, ladies and gentlemen," he said, "to serve mankind. In the name of mankind, its purpose and its survival, I call this meeting to order. Our goal, my friends, is to double the size of the earth."

Then, to the silent—silent, that is, until he had finished—admiration of those assembled there, Milty presented his plan; and then even those hard-bitten, cynical representatives of the one business that makes the earth turn broke into cheers and applause. Milty rose and nodded modestly; he was not egotistical, but neither was he one to hide his light under a bushel.

"Thank you," he said quietly. "And now the floor is open for ideas and questions."

No stodgy board of directors were these twenty-nine representatives of advertising and public relations. Their minds were as hard and bright as quartz. The first to rise was Jack Aberdeen, the young wonder boy of Carrol, Carrol, Carrol and Quince. Even as he snapped his fingers, Milty could see his mind crackle and snap.

"Got it, Mr. Boil. Round number one. You know the way the Kellogg Company pushes its cornflakes as the food that makes kids tall. Union Mills is our account. I see a new competitive product. *Tinies*. I got the slogan—'Small and tight.' Every company will have to fall in line. 'Are you afraid of the big bully? *Tinies* will reduce your muscles to knots of steel. Tiny knots of steel. Small and tight.' I got a tune for it—'Small and tight, small and tight, who the hell needs height, if only I am small and tight?'' Of course we got to find something like an anti-vitamin, but we represent Associated Labs, and I'll get them to work on it.''

Milty could have hugged the kid, but already Steve Johnson of Kelly, Cohen and Clark was on his feet and speaking. He represented some of the biggest airlines on earth.

"Milty," he said, "may we call you Milty?"

"Call me Milty, Steve. By all means."

"Two things. Milty, you have just kicked off the biggest chance in the history of airlines. That's number one. I got the slogan— 'Weigh less, pay less.' Why not? The small man weighs less, he pays less. Put a premium on small."

Johnson, Milty noted, was no taller than himself.

"Second thing—flights to the moon and Mars. All the airlines have been discussing the prospect of putting these flights on a tourist basis. But the cost is terrifying. We make it a bonus thing: 'Do you want to see the moon? You can't—you're too tall. But your kids can. Keep them small. Feed them anti-vitamins. So that they may have what you never dreamed of having—a flight to the moon or Mars—a step into tomorrow, a glimpse of man's glorious future. No tourist who is taller than five feet can get into outer space.' How about that—is it not beautiful?"

Cathey Brodie, public relations for Jones and Keppleman, the largest ethical drug house in the world, leaped to her feet now and cried out:

"Moon pills—does that ever send me! It means the lab boys have to really dig for something to control height, but they've found everything else. Why not? Moon pills."

"Moon pills," Milty repeated, smiling.

Tab Henderson, who managed promotion for over eight hundred large hospitals, not to mention three of the leading insurance companies, jumped right into the gap Cathey Brodie had opened.

"We could just overlook the biggest little inducement in this whole splendid project. I mean health. Long life. Added years. We have statistical charts to show that over six feet three inches, life expectancy begins to decrease. We look at it the other way. Be small and stay healthy."

There were a few sour faces, a few spoil-sports, but most of the team assembled threw their hats into the ring, and the plans came thick and fast.

"Tall, dark, and handsome—that must go. Small for tall—
'Small, dark and handsome.' "

"Beautiful."

"Get the sex angle. 'Sex is better with a small man or a small
woman.' "

" 'Try it with both—make your own decision.' That gives it a
do-it-yourself feeling."

"How about this—'Close the generation gap!' For the past three
or four generations the kids have all been bigger than their parents.
No wonder a father can't lay down the law. Now we reverse it, each
generation smaller than the one that preceded it. We reestablish the
authority of the father. The home once again becomes the sanctuary
it was in the olden times."

One after another the ideas sparkled forth, until the beginnings
of an entire world program began to take shape there in the board
room of Boil Enterprises. Rome wasn't built in a day, and neither
was the pattern of world psychology that reduced practically all the
human race to half of its size; but there the foundation was laid—
and there Milty Boil became Milty Boil, benefactor, underwriting
that first, initial effort with a cool twenty million dollars of his own
money.

For the rest of his life Milty had a goal—a reason and a meaning
for the tremendous effort that produced one of the great fortunes of
our time. Cynical people say that the first five years of the program
created a condition where Milty Boil could begin to build his
gigantic structures—one hundred floors with ceilings only four feet
and six inches high—without opposition. Others—so-called re-
formers—held that it was an indignity for man to spend his life in a
place where he could never hope to stand up straight, but Milty
answered that charge with his ringing Declaration of Purpose, a
document which takes its place in American history alongside the
Declaration of Independence and the Gettysburg Address. I quote
only the first paragraph of Milty's Declaration, for I am sure that
most of my readers know it by heart.

"Life without purpose," wrote Milty (or some unknown ghost
writer who took his inspiration from the dynamic leadership of
Milton Boil), "is neither life nor death but a dull and wretched
existence unworthy of man. Man must have a goal, a purpose, a
destination, a shining goal for which he struggles. We saw in the
hapless youth of the sixties and seventies what it meant to be
without purpose in life; but never again shall the world face that

quandary. People—shameless people—have accused me of building for profit; they charge that I reduce man with my low ceilings, that I take away his dignity. But the reverse is true. Through my splendid houses, man has found both dignity and purpose—the purpose to be small and to raise small children, so that the world may increase in size, and the dignity of men who must always fight their environment, who cannot stand in decadent comfort, who must struggle and grow through struggle.''

In the year 2010, when Milty was seventy years old, he achieved his ultimate goal. Through his ever expanding influence, he persuaded the New York City Council to pass a law cutting Central Park in half, granting all that part of it north of Eighty-second Street and south of Ninety-eighth Street to Milton Boil, so that he might fulfill his lifelong dream and build an apartment house two hundred stories tall with ceilings three feet and six inches high. Over a hundred people were killed in the riots that followed this action of the City Council, but progress is never achieved without paying a price, and Milty saw to it that no widow or child of those who had perished went hungry. Also, he guaranteed living space in his new buildings to all those made fatherless by the riots—at one-half the rent paid by the regular tenants.

After that, only fanatics and hippies would deny that Milty was the gentlest and kindest of landlords in all the history of landlordism. Indeed, after his death, the Pope instituted proceedings that would result in Milty's eventually becoming the patron saint of all landlords; but this is still in the future—with many thorns strewn on the path of sainthood, not to mention certain confusion about Milty's religion, that is, considering that he had any.

Milty died in his eighty-seventh year, and we can be pleased that he lived long enough to see his dream begin to come to fruition. His coffin was carried by eight young men, no one of them more than four feet eight inches in height, and here and there in the audience that packed the chapel were grown men and women no taller than four feet. Of course, these were the exceptions, and it was not until almost half a century later that the first generation of adults who were less than three feet tall reached their maturity.

But we must not abandon this small tribute without noting that when Milty's will was read, it disposed of no more than a few thousand dollars and a handful of things that were beloved of him.

Such was the nature of the man who earned millions only to give them away. Naturally, there are those who claim that since reading a book in his very early youth, titled *How to Avoid Probate,* Milty was never subsequently without it—that is, without this precious volume—and that eventually he memorized all of its contents and could quote chapter and verse at will.

But where is there a great man who has not suffered the barbs of envy and hatred? Slander is the burden the great must carry, and Milton Boil carried it as silently and patiently as any man.

On the modest headstone that graces his final resting place, an epitaph written by Milty himself is carved:

"He found them tall and left them small."

To which our generation, standing erect and proud under our three-foot ceilings, can only add a grateful amen.

18
Cato the Martian

THEY spoke only one language on Mars—which was one of the reasons why Earth languages fascinated them so. Mrs. Erdig had made the study of English her own hobby. English was rather popular, but lately more and more Martians were turning to Chinese; before that, it had been Russian. But Mrs. Erdig held that no other language had the variety of inflection, subtlety and meaning that English possessed.

For example, the word *righteousness*. She mentioned it to her husband tonight.

"I'm telling you, I just cannot understand it," she said. "I mean it eludes me just as I feel I can grasp it. And you know how inadequate one feels with an Earth word that is too elusive."

"I don't know how it is," Mr. Erdig replied absently. His own specialty among Earth languages was Latin—recorded only via the infrequent Vatican broadcasts—and this tells a good deal about what sort of Martian he was. Perhaps a thousand Martians specialized in Latin; certainly no more.

"Inadequate. It's obvious," his wife repeated.

"Oh? Why?"

"You know. I wish you wouldn't make yourself so obtuse. One expects to feel superior to those savages in there on the third planet. It's provoking to have a word in their language elude you."

"What word?" Mr. Erdig asked.

"You weren't listening at all. *Righteousness.*"

"Well, my own English is nothing to crow about, but I seem to remember what *right* means."

"And righteous means something else entirely, and it makes no sense whatsoever."

"Have you tried Lqynn's dictionary?" Mr. Erdig asked, his thoughts still wrapped around his own problems.

"Lqynn is a fool!"

"Of course, my dear. You might get through to Judge Grylyg on the Intertator. He is considered an expert on English verbs."

"Oh, you don't even hear me," she cried in despair. "Even you would know that *righteous* is not a verb. I feel like I am talking to the wall."

Mr. Erdig sat up—its equivalent, for his seven limbs were jointed very differently from a human's—and apologized to his wife. Actually he loved her and respected her. "Terribly sorry," he said. "Really, my dear. It's just that there are so many things these days. I get lost in my thoughts—and depressed too."

"I know. I know," she said with immediate tenderness. "There are so many things. I know how it all weighs on you."

"A burden I never asked for."

"I know," she nodded. "How well I know."

"Yes, there are Martians and Martians," Mr. Erdig sighed wearily. "I know some who schemed and bribed and used every trick in the book to get onto the Planetary Council. I didn't. I never wanted it, never thought of it."

"Of course," his wife agreed.

"I even thought of refusing—"

"How could you?" his wife agreed sympathetically. "How could you? No one has ever refused. We would have been pariahs. The children would never hold up their heads again. And it is an honor, darling—an honor second to none. You are a young man, two hundred and eighty years old, young and in your prime. I know what a burden it is. You must try to carry that burden as lightly as possible and not fight everything you don't agree with."

"Not what I don't agree with," Mr. Erdig said slowly but distinctly, "not at all. What is wrong."

"Can you be sure something is wrong?"

"This time. Yes, I am sure."

"Cato again, I suppose," Mrs. Erdig nodded.

"The old fool! Why don't they see through him! Why don't they see what a pompous idiot he is!"

"I suppose some do. But he appears to reflect the prevailing sentiment."

"Yes? Well, it seems to me," said Mr. Erdig, "that he created a good deal of what you call the prevailing sentiment. He rose to speak again yesterday, cleared his throat, and cried out, 'Earth must be destroyed!' Just as he has every session these past thirty years. And this time—mind you, my dear—this time he had the gall to repeat it in Latin: *'Earth esse delendam'*. Soon, he will believe that he *is* Cato.''

"I think that is a great tribute to you," Mrs. Erdig told him calmly. "After all, you are the foremost Latin scholar on Mars. You were the first to call him Cato the Censor—and the name stuck. Now everyone calls him Cato. I shouldn't be surprised if they have all forgotten his real name. You can be proud of your influence."

"That isn't the point at all," Mr. Erdig sighed.

"I only meant to cheer you a bit."

"I know, my dear. I shouldn't be annoyed with you. But the point is that each day they smile less and listen to him even more intently. I can remember quite well when he first began his campaign against Earth, the amused smiles, the clucking and shaking of heads. A good many of us were of the opinion that he was out of his mind, that he needed medical treatment. Then, bit by bit, the attitude changed. Now, they listen seriously—and they agree. Do you know that he plans to put it to a vote tomorrow?"

"Well, if he does, he does, and the council will do what is right. So the best thing for you to do is to get a good night's sleep. Come along with me."

Mr. Erdig rose to follow her. They were in bed, when she said, "I do wish you had chosen English, my dear. Why should *righteous* be so utterly confusing?"

Most of the Planetary Council of Mars were already present when Mr. Erdig arrived and took his place. As he made his way among the other representatives, he could not fail to notice a certain coolness, a certain restraint in the greetings that followed him. Mrs. Erdig would have held that he was being over-sensitive and that he always had been too sensitive for his own peace of mind; but Mr. Erdig himself labored under no illusions. He prided himself upon his psychological awareness of the Council's mood. All things considered, he was already certain that today was Cato's day.

As he took his place, his friend, Mr. Kyegg, nodded and confirmed his gloomy view of things. "I see you are thinking along the same lines, Erdig," Mr. Kyegg said.

"Yes."

"Well—*que serait, serait,*" Mr. Kyegg sighed. "What will be,

303

will be. French. Language spoken by only a handful of people on the European continent, but very elegant."

"I know that France is on the European continent," Mr. Erdig observed stiffly.

"Of course. Well, old Fllari persuaded me to take lessons with him. Poor chap needs money."

Mr. Erdig realized that his irritation with Kyegg was increasing, and without cause. Kyegg was a very decent fellow whom Mr. Erdig had known for better than two hundred years. It would be childish to allow a general state of irritation to separate him from any one of the narrowing circle he could still call his friends.

At moments of stress, like this one, Mr. Erdig would lie back in his seat and gaze at the Council ceiling. It had a soothing effect. Like most Martians, Mr. Erdig had a keen and well-developed sense of aesthetics, and he never tired of the beauties of Martian buildings and landscapes. Indeed, the creation of beauty and the appreciation of beauty were preoccupations of Martian society. Even Mr. Erdig would not have denied the Martian superiority in that direction.

The ceiling of the Council Chamber reproduced the Martian skies at night. Deep, velvety blue-purple, it was as full of stars as a tree in bloom is of blossoms. The silver starlight lit the Council Chamber.

"How beautiful and wise are the things we create and live with!" Mr. Erdig reflected. "How good to be a Martian!" He could afford pity for the poor devils of the third planet. Why couldn't others?

He awoke out of his reverie to the chimes that called the session to order. Now the seats were all filled.

"This is it," said Mr. Erdig's friend, Mr. Kyegg. "Not an empty seat in the house."

The minutes of the previous meeting were read.

"He'll recognize Cato first," Mr. Kyegg nodded.

"That doesn't take much foresight," Mr. Erdig replied sourly, pointing to Cato. Already Cato's arm (or limb or tentacle, depending on your point of view) was up.

The chairman bowed and recognized him.

Cato the Censor had concluded his speeches in the Roman Senate with the injunction that Carthage must be destroyed. Cato the Martian did him one better; he began and finished with the injunction that Earth must be destroyed.

304

"Earth must be destroyed," Cato the Martian began, and then paused for the ripple of applause to die down.

"Why do I go on, year after year, with what once seemed to so many to be a heartless and blood-thirsty plea? I assure you that the first time my lips formed that phrase, my heart was sick and my bowels turned over in disgust. I am a Martian like all of you; like all of you, I view murder as the ultimate evil, force as the mark of the beast.

"Think—all of you, think of what it cost me to create that phrase and to speak it for the first time in this chamber, so many years ago! Think of how you would have felt! Was it easy then—or any time in all the years since then? Is the role of a *patriot* ever easy? Yes, I use a word Earth taught us—*patriot*. A word most meaningful to us now."

"*Le patriotisme est le dernier refuge d'un gredin,*" Mr. Kyegg observed caustically. "French. A pithy language."

"English, as a matter of fact," Mr. Erdig corrected him. "*Patriotism is the last refuge of a scoundrel.* Samuel Johnson, I believe. Literary dean and wit in London, two centuries ago." Mr. Erdig felt unpleasant enough to put Mr. Kyegg in his place. "London," he went on, "largest city in England, which is an island a few miles from the European continent."

"Oh, yes," Mr. Kyegg nodded weakly.

"—not only because I love Mars," Cato was saying, "but because I love the entire essence and meaning of life. It is almost half a century since we picked up the first radio signals from the planet Earth. We on Mars had never known the meaning of *war;* it took Earth to teach us that. We had never known what it meant to kill, to destroy, to torture. Indeed, when we first began to analyze and understand the various languages of Earth, we doubted our own senses, our own analytical abilities. We heard, but at first we refused to believe what we heard. We refused to believe that there could be an entire race of intelligent beings whose existence was dedicated to assault, to murder and thievery and brutality beyond the imagination of Martians—"

"Never changes a word," muttered Mr. Erdig. "Same speech over and over."

"He's learned to deliver it very well, don't you think?" Mr. Kyegg said.

305

"—we would not believe!" Cato cried. "Who could believe such things? We are a race of love and mercy. We tried to rationalize, to explain, to excuse—but when our receivers picked up the first television signals, well, we could no longer rationalize, explain or excuse. What our ears might have doubted, our eyes proved. What our sensibilities refused, fact forced upon us. I don't have to remind you or review what we saw in the course of fifteen Earth years of television transmission. Murder—murder—murder—and violence! Murder and violent death to a point where one could only conclude that this is a dream, the being and the vision of Earth! Man against man, nation against nation, mother against child—and always violence and death—"

"He said he wasn't going to review it," Mr. Erdig murmured.

"It's rather nice to know every word of a speech," said Mr. Kyegg. "Then you don't have to listen with any attention."

But the members of the council were listening with attention as Cato cried.

"And *war!* The word itself did not exist in our language until we heard it from Earth. War without end—large wars and small wars, until half of their world is a graveyard and their very atmosphere is soaked with hatred!"

"That's a rather nice turn of phrase for Cato, don't you think?" Mr. Kyegg asked his associate. Mr. Erdig did not even deign to answer.

"And then," Cato continued, his voice low and ominous now, "we watched them explode their first atom bomb. On their television, we watched this monstrous weapon exploded again and again as they poisoned their atmosphere and girded themselves for a new war. Ah, well do I remember how calm the philosophers were when this happened. 'Leave them alone', said our philosophers, 'now they will destroy themselves'. Would they? By all that Mars means to every Martian, I will not put my faith in the philosophers!"

"He means you," said Mr. Kyegg to Mr. Erdig.

"Philosophers!" Cato repeated in contempt. "I know one of them well indeed. In derision, he dubbed me Cato—thinking to parade his Latin scholarship before me. Well, I accept the name. As Cato, I say, Earth must be destroyed! Not because of what Earth has done and continues to do to itself—I agree that is their affair—but because of what, as every Martian now knows, Earth will inevitably do to us. We watched them send up their first satellites; we did

306

nothing as they sent their missiles probing into space; and now—now—as our astronomers confirm—they have sent an unmanned rocket to the moon!''

"That seals it," Mr. Erdig sighed.

"How long must we wait?" Cato cried. "Must all that we have made of our lovely planet be an atomic wasteland before we act? Are we to do nothing until the first Earth invaders land on Mars? Or do we destroy this blight as firmly and surely as we would wipe out some new and dreadful disease?

"I say that Earth must be destroyed! Not next month or next year, but now! Earth must be destroyed!''

Cato sat down, not as formerly to a small ripple of applause or to disapproving silence, but now to a storm of assent and approval.

"Silly of me to think of myself as a philosopher," Mr. Erdig reflected as he rose to speak, "but I suppose I am, in a very small way." And then he told the assembled Council members that he would not take too much of their time.

"I am one of those individuals," Mr. Erdig said, "who, even when they cannot hope to win an argument, get some small satisfaction out of placing their thoughts upon the record. That I do not agree with Cato, you know. I have said so emphatically and on many occasions; but this is the conclusion of a long debate, not the beginning of one.

"I never believed that I should live to see the day when this Council would agree that Earth should be destroyed. But that you are in agreement with Cato seems obvious. Let me only remind you of some of the things you propose to destroy.

"We Martians never paused to consider how fortunate we are in our longevity until we began to listen, as one might say, to Earth—and to watch Earth. We are all old enough to recall the years before the people of Earth discovered the secret of radio and television transmission. Were our lives as rich then as they are now?

"How much has changed in the mere two-score of Earth years that we have listened to them and watched them. Our ancient and beautiful Martian language has become all the richer for the inclusion of hundreds of Earth words. The languages of Earth have become the pastime and delight of millions of Martians. The games of Earth divert us and amuse us—to a point where baseball and tennis and golf seem native and proper among us. You all recall

307

how dead and stagnant our art had become; the art of Earth brought it to life and gave us new forms, ideas and directions. Our libraries are filled with thousands of books on the subject of Earth, manners and customs and history, and due to their habit on Earth of reading books and verse over the radio, we now have available to us the literary treasures of Earth.

"Where in our lives is the influence of Earth not felt? Our architects have incorporated Earth buildings. Our doctors have found techniques and methods on Earth that have saved lives here. The symphonies of Earth are heard in our concert halls and the songs of Earth fill the Martian air.

"I have suggested only some of an almost endless list of treasures Earth has given us. And this Earth you propose to destroy. Oh, I cannot refute Cato. He speaks the truth. Earth is still a mystery to us. We have never breathed the air of Earth or trod on the soil of Earth, or seen her mighty cities and green forests at first hand. We see only a shadow of the reality, and this shadow confuses us and frightens us. By Martian terms, Earth people are short-lived. From birth to death is only a moment. How have they done so much in such fragile moments of existence? We really don't know—we don't understand. We see them divided and filled with hate and fear and resentment; we watch them murder and destroy; and we are puzzled and confused. How can the same people who create so splendidly destroy so casually?

"But is destruction the answer to this problem? There are two and a half thousand million people on Earth, three times the number who inhabit Mars. Can we ever again sleep in peace, dream in peace, if we destroy them?"

Cato's answer to Mr. Erdig was very brief. "Can we ever again sleep in peace, dream in peace if we don't?"

Then Mr. Erdig sat down and knew that it was over.

"It's not as if we were actually doing it ourselves," Mrs. Erdig said to her husband at home that evening.

"The same thing, my dear."

"But as you explain it, here are these two countries, as they call them, The Soviet Union and the United States of America—the two most powerful countries on Earth, armed to the teeth with heaven knows how many atom bombs and just waiting to leap at each other's throats. I know enough Earth history to realize that sooner or later they're bound to touch off a war—even if only through some accident.''

"Perhaps."

"And all we will do," Mrs. Erdig said soothingly, "is to hasten that inevitable accident.''

"Yes, we have come to that," Mr. Erdig nodded somberly. "War and cruelty and injustice are Earth words that we have learned— foreign words, nasty words. It would be utterly immoral for us to arm ourselves for war or even to contemplate war. But an accident is something else indeed. We will build a rocket and arm it with an atomic warhead and put it into space so that it will orbit Earth over their poles and come down and explode in the Arizona desert of the United States. At the worst, we destroy a few snakes and cows, so our hands are clean. Minutes after that atom bomb explodes, Earth will begin to destroy itself. Yet we have absolved ourselves—''

"I don't like to hear you talk like that, my dear," Mrs. Erdig protested. "I never heard any other Martian talk like that.''

"I am not proud of being a Martian."

"Really!"

"It turns my stomach," said Mr. Erdig.

There was a trace of asperity in Mrs. Erdig's voice. "I don't see how you can be so sure that you are right and everyone else is wrong. Sometimes I feel that you disagree just for the pleasure of disagreeing—or of being disagreeable, if I must say it. It seems to me that every Martian should treasure our security and way of life above all else. And I can't see what is so terribly wrong about hastening something that is bound to happen sooner or later in any case. If Earth folk were deserving, it would be another matter entirely—''

Mr. Erdig was not listening. Long years of association had taught him that when his wife began this kind of tidal wave of argument and proof, it could go on for a very long time indeed. He closed off her sound and his thoughts ranged, as they did so often, across the green meadows and the white-capped blue seas of Earth. How often he had dreamed of that wilderness of tossing and restless water! How wonderful and terrible it must be! There were no seas on Mars, so even to visualize the oceans of Earth was not easy. But he could not think about the oceans of Earth and not think of the people of Earth, the mighty cities of Earth.

Suddenly, his heart constricted with a pang of knife-like grief. In the old, unspoken language of Earth, which he had come to cherish so much, he whispered,

"*Magna civitas, magna solitudo—*"

The rocket was built and fitted with an atomic warhead—no difficult task for the technology of Mars. In the churches (their equivalent, that is) of Mars, a prayer was said for the souls of the people of Earth, and then the rocket was launched.

The astronomers watched it and the mathematicians tracked it. In spite of its somber purpose and awful destiny, the Martians could not refrain from a flush of pride in the skill and efficiency of their scientists, for the rocket crossed over the North Pole of Earth and landed smack in the Arizona desert, not more than five miles away from the chosen target spot.

The air of Mars is thin and clear and millions of Martians have fine telescopes. Millions of them watched the atomic warhead burst and millions of them kept their telescopes trained to Earth, waiting to witness the holocaust of radiation and flame that would signal atomic war among the nations of Earth.

They waited, but what they expected did not come. They were civilized beings, not at all bloodthirsty, but by now they were very much afraid; so some of them waited and watched until the Martian morning made the Martian skies blaze with burning red and violet.

Yet there was no war on Earth.

"I do wonder what could have gone wrong?" Mrs. Erdig said, looking up from the copy of *Vanity Fair,* which she was reading for the second time. She did not actually expect an answer, for her husband had become less and less communicative of late. She was rather surprised when he answered,

"Can't you guess?"

"I don't see why you should sound so superior. No one else can guess. Can you?"

Instead of answering her, he said, "I envy you your knowledge of English—if only to read novelists like Thackeray."

"It is amusing," Mrs. Erdig admitted, "but I never can quite get used to the nightmare of life on Earth."

"I didn't know you regarded it as a nightmare."

"How else could one regard it?"

"I suppose so," Mr. Erdig sighed. "Still—I would have liked to

310

read Caesar's *Conquest of Gaul.* They have never broadcast it."

"Perhaps they will."

"No. No, they never will. No more broadcasts from Earth. No more television."

"Oh, well—if they don't start that war and wipe themselves out, they're bound to be broadcasting again."

"I wonder," Mr. Erdig said.

The second rocket from Mars exploded its warhead in the wastelands of Siberia. Once again, Martians watched for hours through their telescopes and waited. But Mr. Erdig did not watch. He seemed to have lost interest in the current obsession of Mars, and he devoted most of his time to the study of English, burying himself in his wife's novels and dictionaries and thesaurus. His progress, as his wife told her neighbors, was absolutely amazing. He already knew the language well enough to carry on a passable conversation.

When the Planetary Council of Mars met and took the decision to aim a rocket at London, Mr. Erdig was not even present. He remained at home and read a book—one of his wife's English transcripts.

As with so many of her husband's recent habits, his truancy was shocking to Mrs. Erdig, and she took it upon herself to lecture him concerning his duties to Mars and Martians—and in particular, his deplorable lack of patriotism. The word was very much in use upon Mars these days.

"I have more important things to do," Mr. Erdig finally replied to her insistence.

"Such as?"

"Reading this book, for instance."

"What book *are* you reading?"

"It's called *Huckleberry Finn.* Written by an American—Mark Twain."

"It's a silly book. I couldn't make head or tail of it."

"Well—"

"And I don't see why it's important."

Mr. Erdig shook his head and went on reading.

And that night, when she turned on the Intertator, the Erdigs learned, along with the rest of Mars, that a rocket had been launched against the City of London. . . .

After that, a whole month passed before the first atomic warhead, launched from the Earth, exploded upon the surface of Mars. Other warheads followed. And still, there was no war on the Planet Earth.

The Erdigs were fortunate, for they lived in a part of Mars that had still not felt the monstrous, searing impact of a hydrogen bomb. Thus, they were able to maintain at least a semblance of normal life, and within this, Mr. Erdig clung to his habit of reading for an hour or so before bedtime. As Mrs. Erdig had the Intertator on almost constantly these days, he had retreated to the Martian equivalent of a man's den. He was sitting there on this particular evening when Mrs. Erdig burst in and informed him that the first fleet of manned space-rockets from Earth had just landed on Mars— the soldiers from Earth were proceeding to conquer Mars, and that there was no opposition possible.

"Very interesting," Mr. Erdig agreed.

"Didn't you hear me?"

"I heard you, my dear," Mr. Erdig said.

"Soldiers—armed soldiers from Earth!"

"Yes, my dear." He went back to his book and when Mrs. Erdig saw that for the third time he was reading the nonsense called *Huckleberry Finn,* she turned out of the room in despair. She was preparing to slam the door behind her, when Mr. Erdig said,

"Oh, my dear."

She turned back into the room. "Well—"

"You remember," Mr. Erdig said, just as if soldiers from Earth were not landing on Mars that very moment, "that a while back you were complaining that you couldn't make any sense out of an English word—*righteous?*"

"For heaven's sake!"

"Well, it seemed to puzzle you so—"

"Did you hear a word I said?"

"About the ships from Earth? Oh, yes—yes, of course. But here I was reading this book for the third time—it is a most remarkable book—and I came across that word, and it's not obscure at all. Not in the least. A righteous man is pure and wise and good and holy and just—above all, just. And equitable, you might say. Cato the Censor was such a man. Yes—and Cato the Martian, I do believe. Poor Cato—he was fried by one of those hydrogen bombs, wasn't he? A very righteous man—"

Sobbing hysterically, Mrs. Erdig fled from the room. Mr. Erdig sighed and returned to his novel.

19
Not with a Bang

O N the evening of the third of April, standing at the window of his pleasant three-bedroom, split-level house and admiring the sunset, Alfred Collins saw a hand rise above the horizon, spread thumb and forefinger, and snuff out the sun. It was the moment of soft twilight, and it ended as abruptly as if someone had flicked an electric switch.

Which is precisely what his wife did. She put on lights all over the house. "My goodness, Al," she said, "it did get dark quickly, didn't it?"

"That's because someone snuffed out the sun."

"What on earth are you talking about?" she asked. "And by the way, the Bensons are coming for dinner and bridge tonight, so you'd better get dressed."

"All right. You weren't watching the sunset, were you?"

"I have other things to do."

"Yes. Well, what I mean is that if you were watching, you would have seen this hand come up behind the horizon, and then the thumb and forefinger just spread out, and then they came together and snuffed out the sun."

"Really. Now for heaven's sake, Al, don't redouble tonight. If you are doubled, have faith in your bad bidding. Do you promise me?"

"Funniest damn thing about the hand. It brought back all my childhood memories of anthropomorphism."

"And just what does that mean?"

"Nothing. Nothing at all. I'm going to take a shower."

"Don't be all evening about it."

At dinner, Al Collins asked Steve Benson whether he had been watching the sunset that evening.

"No—no, I was showering."

"And you, Sophie?" Collins asked of Benson's wife.

"No way. I was changing a hem. What does women's lib intend to do about hems? There's the essence of the status of women, the nitty-gritty of our servitude."

"It's one of Al's jokes," Mrs. Collins explained. "He was standing at the window and he saw this hand come over the horizon and snuff out the sun."

"Did you, Al?"

"Scout's honor. The thumb and forefinger parted, then came together. Poof. Out went the sun."

"That's absolutely delicious," Sophie said. "You have such delicious imagination."

"Especially in his bidding," his wife remarked.

"She'll never forget that slam bid doubled and redoubled," Sophie said. It was evident that she would never forget it either.

"Interesting but impractical," said Steve Benson, who was an engineer at IBM. "You're dealing with a body that is almost a million miles in diameter. The internal temperature is over ten million degrees centigrade, and at its core the hydrogen atoms are reduced to helium ash. So all you have is poetic symbolism. The sun will be here for a long time."

After the second rubber, Sophie Benson remarked that either it was chilly in the Collins house or she was catching something.

"Al, turn up the thermostat," said Mrs. Collins.

The Collins team won the third and fourth rubbers, and Mrs. Collins had all the calm superiority of a winner as she bid her guests good night. Al Collins went out to the car with them, thinking that, after all, suburban living was a strange process of isolation and alienation. In the city, a million people must have watched the thing happen; here, Steve Benson was taking a shower and his wife was changing a hem.

It was a very cold night for April. Puddles of water left over from a recent rain had frozen solid, and the star-drenched sky had the icy look of midwinter. Both of the Bensons had arrived without coats, and as they hurried into their car, Benson laughingly remarked that Al was probably right about the sun. Benson had difficulty starting the car, and Al Collins stood shivering until they had driven away. Then he looked at the outside thermometer. It was down to sixteen degrees.

314

"Well, we beat them loud and clear," his wife observed when he came back to the house. He helped her clean up, and while they were at it, she asked him just what he meant by anthropomorphism or whatever it was.

"It's sort of a primitive notion. You know, the Bible says that God made man in His own image."

"Oh? You know, I absolutely believed it when I was a child. What are you doing?"

He was at the fireplace, and he said that he thought he'd build a fire.

"In April? You must be out of your mind. Anyway, I cleaned the hearth."

"I'll clean it up tomorrow."

"Well, I'm going to bed. I think you're crazy to start a fire at this time of the night, but I'm not going to argue with you. This is the first time you did not overbid, and thank heavens for small favors."

The wood was dry, and the fire was warm and pleasant to watch. Collins had never lost his pleasure at watching the flames of a fire, and he mixed himself a long scotch and water, and sat in front of the flames, sipping the drink and recalling his own small scientific knowledge. The green plants would die within a week, and after that the oxygen would go. How long? he wondered. Two days—ten days—he couldn't remember and he had no inclination to go to the encyclopedia and find out. It would get very cold, terribly cold. It surprised him that instead of being afraid, he was only mildly curious.

He looked at the thermometer again before he went to bed. It was down to zero now. In the bedroom, his wife was already asleep, and he undressed quietly and put an extra comforter on the bed before he crawled in next to her. She moved toward him, and feeling her warm body next to him, he fell asleep.

20
The Movie House

WE had an interval for popcorn and vitamins, and the projectionist came down from above. This did not happen often, and sometimes days would go by without our seeing him. His name was Matthew Ragen, and he was six feet three inches tall, and he made a most imposing presence with his great shock of white hair and his bright blue eyes. Talk had it that he was over eighty years old, but I find that hard to believe, because his stance was very erect and his walk as firm and easy as the walk of a younger man. However, there was no one who could remember a time when he was not the projectionist.

We crowded around him, delighted that he was walking among us. The children tried to touch him, and I am sure that in their fanciful minds they confused him with God. It was a great pleasure and privilege to be sought out by him, greeted by him—or even to be the recipient of his smile; and you can imagine how astonished I was when he came straight toward me, the people parting to let him through, and greeted me personally.

I had to pull myself together before I could speak, and then I simply said, "I am honored, Projectionist."

"Not at all, Dorey. It is I who am honored."

"Have I pleased you, Projectionist?"

"I think you've pleased us all, Dorey."

People listening nodded and smiled, and I think that I guessed what was coming. Was I surprised? Certainly, for no one is ever sure; but perhaps not as surprised as I might have been.

"A special treat, Dorey," the projectionist said. "A Western called *High Noon*. I am sure you remember it."

I nodded with delight, and the people around smiled with pleasure.

"I suppose it's ten years since I have played it," the projectionist went on. "It wants an occasion, you know. It's not something you throw in any old time. Well, we'll run it, Dorey, and then we'll have an interval for announcements."

"Thank you, Projectionist," I said graciously—and as modestly as I could. "Thank you, indeed."

It was something to be singled out by the projectionist; people looked at me differently. It not only gave one status, but added to the status a delicious feeling of self-importance that made one literally glow with pleasure. Jane, Clarey, Lisa, Mona—these were girls I had sat with on and off for years; suddenly their whole attitude toward me was different, and Jane tried to take possession. She was pushy; I realized that now, and how easily I could dispense with her. But more than that, I wanted to sit alone. I wanted to be by myself and within myself while I watched *High Noon*. I was sure the projectionist had a very good reason for playing it, and I wanted to concentrate and understand. I sought out a place in a rear corner of the orchestra, a place frequented mostly by the older people, and while the people around knew me, they would not bother me or intrude upon my privacy.

I relaxed in the chair and entered the world of good and evil—which was the sum and substance of our own place. Gary Cooper was good, and he slew what was evil, which was right. It was not easy. He was a leader who stood alone, because his quality was leadership—and thus I understood why the projectionist had chosen this film. The leader must see right and wrong clearly, and if death is the only solution, the leader must use death even as God would. My heart went out to Gary Cooper. I knew him. He was my brother.

The picture ended, and the deep, rich voice of the projectionist came over the stereo system:

"Let us join in silent prayer. Let us pray that God gives us wisdom in our choices."

I prayed, and then the lights came up. Everyone was alert and eager, and the old folks around me smiled at me. Sister Evelyn, in her function of chairman of the Board of Elections, came onto the

318

stage, and standing there in front of the huge silver screen—so small in front of it—she waited for the chatter of voices to cease. Then she cleared her throat, clapped her hands once or twice for attention, and then said:

"The results are tabulated."

People smiled, and heads turned, twisting around and up toward the projection booth. They wanted the projectionist to know. You must understand that we very often and quietly discussed the projectionist. If the Godhead made the film, then surely the projectionist was of the nature of God. No one actually declared this as a firm proposition; but on the other hand, neither had we ever heard of a birth date for the projectionist.

Sister Evelyn clapped her hands again. "Will Dorey please rise," she said.

I stood up. I had chosen an obscure corner, so at first people looked vainly here and there for me. Then the whispers located me, and now as I stood, every face in the theater turned toward me.

"Would you approach, Dorey," Sister Evelyn said.

I went to the aisle and walked toward the stage, and meanwhile Sister Evelyn was telling the people by what vote I had won the election. It was a very decent majority. Well, for ten years I had dreamed of being president and had prayed for the honor. Now it had come. I stood on the stage, and Al Hoppner, the retiring president, joined us, and he took off his great ribbon and medallion of honor and placed it around my neck, the broad blue band coming over my shoulders and the shining medallion bright against my breast. Then the people gave me a standing ovation, cheering and clapping for fully four minutes. I timed it surreptitiously, raising my hand in a sort of acknowledgment and noting the time on my wristwatch. I knew that Al Hoppner's ovation had lasted only two and a half minutes, so this was in the way of underwriting a change and a statement of trust in my own sense of responsibility.

I would choose two assistants, and the three of us would constitute the Committee, and the plain truth of it was that I had been mulling over my choices for more than a week—ever since the vote and the possibility that I would be elected president. Now I named Schecter and Kiley. Schecter was in his late thirties, a solid and dependable man who had worked in this post before. He was not a leader, but he was a born committeeman, and he would remain a committeeman for the rest of his life. Kiley was something else.

Kiley was only twenty-one years old, and this was the first post of responsibility that he had ever held. He had manifested leadership qualities, and he had wit and imagination. I felt proud of myself for choosing him and standing by him, even though the cheers of the audience were rather muted. Naturally, people suspect youth.

Finally we left the platform, and the projectionist began one of those splendid color spectacles—I think this was called *The Robe*—and it drew the people immediately into that part of the world known as Ancient Rome.

For myself, Schecter, and Kiley, we had work to do, and we would thereby forego this discovery. (I must mention here that the projectionist frowned on the word "film" to describe what took place on the great silver screen. He preferred to call it "discovery" in terms of a view or discovery of another part of the great world we inhabited.)

We would, instead, begin immediately to inventory and check supplies—this being one of the prime duties of the president. Coming into my administration, I had to assess the condition of place and things; and then I would make my report to the people.

Naturally, we checked the popcorn first, and then the quantity and freshness of the butter. Sadie and Lackaday and Milty were in charge of popcorn and butter, but they closed shop whenever one of the large spectacles opened. They were a bit provoked now at having to remain and watch us check out their duties and answer whatever questions we asked them; but I had decided to lay down the law immediately. I would show an iron hand and make my position on law and order plain—and thereby they would stop thinking that since I had made so radical a choice in Kiley, I would be soft and wishy-washy. In this instance I kept Kiley with me, working steadily, firmly, and in an organized fashion, so that he too could get an idea of how my administration would proceed. Meanwhile, I sent Schecter to root out the ushers and line them up in the lobby.

The ushers were prone to relax and slip into last-row seats whenever any discovery interested them, and that was one of the many slipshod things that I intended to stop. I had left Kiley to finish up with the popcorn and butter and was making my first cursory survey of the candy bars when I glimpsed the ushers marching through to the lobby.

I had not been wrong in my choice of Schecter. When I came into the lobby, the ushers were lined up in a military formation that would have done credit to West Point. I walked up and down their ranks, studying them meticulously, and I must confess that their uniforms were somewhat less admirable than their formation and posture—buttons left unbuttoned, collars open, trousers that had long lost their creases, and some even were without hats. I addressed them, stressing first how pleased I was with their military formation and posture and informing them of my high opinion of Schecter, who, among his many duties, would have that of being commanding officer of the ushers.

"However," I said, "let no one imagine that I will tolerate slovenliness or disorder. A disorderly uniform denotes a disorderly mind, and I will not have it in an organization upon which our very existence depends. Do not imagine that you can deceive or befuddle either Schecter or myself. We will parade again tomorrow morning, and I want to see you appear as ushers should appear."

For the next three days we continued to check and inventory popcorn, butter, candy bars, soda pop, and cigarettes. My choice of Kiley appeared then to be a brilliant one; for while Schecter was whipping the ushers into shape, Kiley had gone to work on three hot-drink, ice-cream, and cigarette machines that had not been functioning for months. Kiley had a really extraordinary grasp of mechanics, and he had found a room opening off the lobby that was unused and where he decided to establish a machine shop of sorts. The room had another door—one of the locked doors. Kiley was very young, and he had never actually realized that locked doors existed.

He had called me to see the room and to give him permission to use it, and he met me at the entrance to the lobby and took me there.

"Oh, yes," I said. "I know this room, Kiley. It was once called the office, although it has not been used for any purpose for years."

"For some reason I find it very exciting."

"Oh?"

"You know, I haven't looked at the screen for days, Dorey. It's very strange not to participate in the discoveries. It gives me an odd feeling. Do you know what I mean?"

"Not really, no."

"Just some silly notion," Kiley said, rather embarrassed. He pointed across the room. "Have you noticed that door? I wonder where it leads to?"

"It's a locked door."

"You mean—an actual locked door?"

"Exactly."

"Well, what do you know!" Kiley exclaimed. He was absolutely delighted. "A real locked door. Do you know, I never believed they existed."

"You never believed it?"

"No, I always thought it was some sort of metaphysical nonsense."

"Well, there it is," I said. There were a good many locked doors, and I found it rather strange that anyone should doubt their existence. However, Kiley was very young, and one tended to lose touch with what the young knew or did not know.

Kiley walked over to the door, studied it, tried the handle, and then turned to me and said eagerly, his bright blue eyes wide and excited:

"Why don't we open it, Dorey?"

"What?"

"I said, why don't we open the locked door?"

"Kiley, Kiley," I said patiently, "the door is locked."

"I know. But we could open it."

"How?"

"With a key."

"A what?"

"A key, Dorey—a key!"

"Bless your heart, Kiley, there is no such thing as a key."

"But there must be."

"No, Kiley, there is not. A locked door is a locked door, and nothing can change that."

"But a key could."

"Kiley, I told you that there is no such thing as a key. I know that the word exists, but it is only a symbol, a metaphysical symbol. I may not be a particularly devout man, Kiley, but I have always been on the side of religion, and I don't think that anyone will doubt my dedication to the religious establishment. Nevertheless, I must state that metaphysics is one thing and reality is something entirely different. I tell you flatly that a key is like a miracle. We talk of them; some even believe in them; but I have never found anyone who has ever seen one. Do you understand?"

Kiley nodded slowly.

"Then I suggest we forget about keys and set to turning this room into an adequate machine shop, and if we do, we ought to

322

have those vending machines in tip-top shape very soon. Do you agree, Kiley?"

"Yes—yes, of course."

"And quite a number of other things need repairing. Some of the chairs in the theater are absolutely unfit to sit on."

"Yes, sir," Kiley said.

The projectionist had announced a Swedish sex film for that night, and I told Schecter and Kiley that they could have the evening for the discovery, since they had been working quite hard and since it was not too often that the projectionist permitted a sex film. Schecter licked his lips with pleasure—a dirty old man if there ever was one—but Kiley said that he would prefer to tinker around in the machine shop, if I didn't mind. You can't fault devotion to duty, and of course I said that I didn't mind. I had already made my own arrangements with a delightful little blonde called Baba, and we met before the lights went off. Whenever we had a sex film, the projectionist insisted on blacking out the theater. It made a sort of sense, for the older folks are embarrassed by the close presence of younger people during a sex film, and certainly the young are made uneasy by the presence of their parents. So the auditorium was blacked out, and ushers, using tiny hand flashlights, took us to our seats.

There had been a great deal of discussion, pro and con, concerning sex on the screen; and even though the puritanical elements have considerable power, the decision was always made to continue with sex discoveries. I felt that this was because the puritans enjoyed them even more than the others; and also I might add that sex films play an important role in the reproductive activities that serve to perpetuate our society. I certainly enjoy those rare evenings, and this time I felt sorry for Kiley.

I must say that I was rather kind to him the following day. I went out of my way to compliment him on his inventories of the candy, and he in turn took me into his machine shop, which I praised highly. He was constructing a sort of lathe, which, as he explained, would enable him to reproduce elements of the vending machines.

"And do you know, Mr. President, sir," he said eagerly, "I think I could use the same machine to make a key."

"Kiley!" I said.

"Yes, sir—I know how you feel about keys."

"Not how I feel, Kiley. It's how the world feels."

"Yes, sir," Kiley said very seriously. "I know that. I am ready to accept how the world feels. I mean I don't want you to feel that I'm a radical or anything of that sort—"

"I don't Kiley. Rest assured that if I did, I never would have appointed you to the Committee. You are very young to be a member of the Committee, Kiley."

"I know that, sir."

"But I had confidence in you."

"Yes, sir."

"I had confidence in your stability, your judgment."

"Thank you, Dorey. I'm very flattered that you took such an interest in me."

"But above all, I want you to consider me as a friend."

"Oh, I do," Kiley said earnestly.

"Then as a friend, Kiley, I must ask you to give up this delusion about keys."

"Do you consider it harmful, sir—I mean to think about it or plan to make one?"

"To make something that doesn't exist?"

"But people do. I mean they make something that doesn't exist."

"Not keys, Kiley."

"Sir?"

"Why must you argue with me, Kiley? Some of the wisest men in our society have gone into this question of keys. There are no keys. There never were. There never will be."

Kiley stared at me, his honest, boyish eyes wide open.

"Yes, Kiley. I want you to promise me something."

"Sir?"

"That you will never mention this matter of keys again. Forget it. Put it out of your mind. There is no such thing as a key. There never was. There never will be."

"Yes, sir."

"Good lad." I squeezed his shoulder affectionately—to show him that I bore no ill will toward him. "Now I want you to get to work on those vending machines. You have no idea how much the people miss hot chocolate. Especially the older folks. It appears to be one of the few consolations of old age."

"I will."

324

"When might you have them?"

"Two weeks—three at the very most."

"Good. Excellent. But all work and no play makes Jack a dull boy, and I want you to take this evening off. The projectionist is showing a very rare and special piece called *Little Caesar,* which dates back to the time when organized hoodlums challenged city government. It is restricted to those who are in government today or have served in government in the past."

"Thank you, sir," Kiley answered enthusiastically.

It was Kiley's very quality of being outgoing and enthusiastic that threw me off the track. It was difficult to think of anyone with his spontaneous quality as being a creature of duplicity, but there is no other label for his subsequent actions; and five days later the whole thing exploded in my face.

Schecter came to me with it. "Dorey," he said grimly, "the devil's at work."

"Oh?"

"You know I am not prone to exaggeration."

"I know that."

"Well, I saw Kiley enter his shop today."

"What's so unusual about that?"

"I wanted a word with him."

"So?"

"I followed him. I opened the door to his office and entered. He wasn't there."

"Perhaps he left before you got there."

"I told you I saw him enter his shop. I watched the door to his shop—the door that opens into the lobby. I saw him go in. I never took my eyes off that door until I opened it. No one came out of his shop. No one."

"Then he was in there," I said calmly.

"Damn it, Dorey—am I an idiot? The room was empty."

"How could it have been empty? You said you never took your eyes off the door."

"Exactly. Still it was empty."

"All right," I sighed. "Suppose we both look into this. There are no devils, no keys, no miracles—I made all that very clear to Kiley, so suppose we just look into this."

"Good," Schecter agreed, his jaws set firmly. "Good."

He led the way into the lobby, and as we reached there, he signaled for a squad of ushers to follow us. When we reached the door to Kiley's workshop, I said to Schecter:

"Really, do we need them?"

"Alertness is the first rule of military practice! They're ushers, Dorey! This is their place, their duty! Man for man, I will match them against any dirty little subversive that ever lived!"

"Oh, come on now, Schecter—we're not going to call Kiley a subversive."

"If the name fits—"

"There's no indication that it fits or that Kiley did anything wrong. Let's have a look."

I opened the door to the workshop. I had not been inside the place in days, but Kiley's lathe was finished, and on his worktable were the bright new pieces for the vending machine. Kiley himself was not there.

"Well?" Schecter demanded.

I went out into the lobby and said to the ushers: "Did Kiley come through the lobby during the past hour?"

They shook their heads.

I went back into the workshop and closed the door behind me. Standing there now, alone with Schecter, I allowed my eyes to wander over the place again and again. It was a small room and there was no place to hide, no nook, no corner, no cranny.

"Well, sir, are you satisfied?" Schecter demanded.

"I'll let you know when I'm satisfied, Schecter."

He allowed himself a slight smile of satisfaction, and I went to the other door and tried it."

"That's a locked door, Dorey," Schecter informed me.

"I know bloody damn well that it's a locked door."

"Well, I just thought—"

"I don't give two damns what you thought, Schecter. Let's get out of here."

Schecter paraded out of the room into the lobby where the ushers were waiting, and I followed him, closing the door behind me. At that moment, I heard a sound inside the shop, and I said to Schecter, "You wait out here. I'm going back in there."

I turned and opened the door of Kiley's shop again, slipped through, and closed it behind me before Schecter could squirm

326

around and see what I was up to. Kiley was inside the shop now, grinning with delight and excitement, holding a small piece of shining metal in his hand.

"Kiley," I cried, "where the hell were you?"

"Outside."

"What do you mean, outside?"

"Through that door." He pointed to the locked door.

"What? Are you crazy? That's a locked door. No one goes through a locked door!"

"I did."

I held up my hand and pointed a shaking finger at him. "Kiley, have you gone off your nut? Have you lost your mind? You're talking crazy. You're talking so goddamn crazy even I won't be able to protect you. You talk about going through a locked door. A locked door is locked. No one goes through it."

"I unlocked it," Kiley said, almost squealing with delight.

"You unlocked it," I said with cold, deliberate scorn. "Only the greatest minds of our times have given their attention to locked doors and have proved that they can never be unlocked—but you unlocked it, all by yourself."

"And with a key!" Kiley cried. "You said I couldn't make a key, but I did. Here it is." He held up the little piece of metal, coming toward me and offering it to me.

"Keep your distance! Keep that damn thing away from me! I told you there was no such thing as a key!"

"But here it is—here it is, Dorey. Believe me, I unlocked the door and went outside—" He turned and pointed toward the locked door. "Out there, through the locked door. My God almighty, Dorey, out there the sun is shining in such a blaze of golden glory that the mind can't conceive it, and there's green grass and green trees and tall buildings, and people—thousands and thousands of people, real people who wear bright-colored clothes and the sun splashes down over them, and the girls have long, bare legs and brown and yellow and black hair, and they're real, Dorey, real! Not like those shadows that the projectionist shows us on the big screen. Do you think his discoveries are real or even discoveries? They're not. They're shadows, lies, illusions—but outside that door the world is real—"

"Enough!" I screamed at him. "God damn you, enough!"

I flung open the door to the lobby and yelled, "Schecter! Schecter—get here on the double with your damn ushers!"

Schecter and the ushers poured into the little room grabbing Kiley and overwhelming him. Kiley didn't struggle; he just stared at me in astonishment and with such hurt surprise that I said:

"Oh, for Christ's sake, Schecter, let go of him."

"What?"

"I said leave him alone and get your damned ushers out of here—now."

"Didn't you just call me?"

"You give me a pain in the ass, Schecter. Get out of here and take your ushers with you."

Aggrieved, scowling, looking hate at Kiley and me, Schecter led the ushers out of the room; and then I turned tiredly to Kiley and said:

"You certainly do louse things up, don't you? Here I go out on a limb to make you the youngest committeeman ever, and what do I get in return? A raving lunatic, that's what I get in return."

"Dorey, I'm not a raving lunatic."

"Then what in hell are you?"

"I went outside. I saw—"

"Shut up."

Kiley clenched his lips, and I said to him, "Kiley, let me make this clear. No one opens a locked door. There are no keys, and you did not go outside."

"Then what is this?" he demanded, holding up the bit of metal he had in his hand.

"A bit of metal. Nothing. There are no keys. There is no outside."

"Oh, Dorey, I went outside."

"You know what?" I said to him. "I'll tell you what, Kiley. You did not go out. You went nowhere. Now if you can get that through your head—if you can only admit that this whole thing of yours is a lie and an invention, well, then, maybe we can work something out. Maybe. Maybe not. But maybe."

"My God, Dorey, do you know what you're asking me to do?"

"To stop lying."

"You were in this room before?" Kiley demanded.

"Yes."

"Schecter too."

"Damnit, yes! So what?"

"Was I here? That's what I'm getting at, Dorey. Was I here?"

"No!" I almost shouted.

"Then where was I?"

"How the hell do I know where you were?"

"All right," Kiley said. "All right, Dorey. Then give me a chance. That's all I'm asking for. Let me open that locked door. I worked it out, and I made this key. I got it right here in my hand." He held it up for me to see. "Let me use it, Dorey. Let me open the door. Let me take you out there."

"No!"

"Why?"

"Because there is no such thing as a key and because you can't open a locked door."

"Then I will—" And he whirled and started toward the locked door.

"Kiley!" My voice hit him like a whiplash. I meant it to. He hesitated, and I snapped at him, "Kiley—take one more step and I call Schecter and his ushers."

He turned to me, pleading, "Why? Why?"

"Because there is no outside, Kiley. Because you're a twisted, pathological personality. Now, for the last time, Kiley—will you admit that you are fantasying?"

"No."

"Then you'll have to come with me to the projectionist, Kiley. Will you come willingly, or must I call Schecter?"

"Oh, God, Dorey, won't you let me open that damn door—just a crack—just so you could see the blaze of sunshine?"

"No."

"Please—must I get down on my knees, Dorey?"

"No. Now is it the ushers, or do you come peacefully?"

"I'll go with you, Dorey," Kiley said, defeated now, his shoulders hanging, the light gone from his eyes.

Somehow, word had gotten around, and there were people in the lobby who watched silently as we came through. Kiley was well liked, and only Schecter and his ushers regarded him with hate. I took Kiley into the theater and through it to the stairs. It was children's time, and today that meant a series of twelve Bugs Bunny

329

cartoons. The children were clapping and cheering, and as we passed by the back row, Kiley said:

"Why can't you think of how it would be for them outside, Dorey?"

"Still on that. What will you say to the projectionist?"

"The truth."

"Yes. He'll appreciate that."

We were outside the projectionist's booth now, far up above the second balcony. No one ever entered the booth. Instead, you pressed a button and then spoke into a speaking tube.

"I'm terribly busy now, Dorey—putting together a whole new part of the world, you know, the Fitzgerald travelogues. Thus we have not only discoveries but explorations. So if it could wait?"

"I am afraid not, Projectionist."

"Urgent?"

"Yes, Projectionist."

"If you might hint at the nature of the emergency, Dorey?"

"It's young Kiley."

"Your committeeman?"

"Yes, Projectionist. He claims to have opened a locked door."

"Of course you have told him that locked doors can never be opened—that this is the way God made the world?"

"I told him."

"Dear me. Well, go to my office. You have him with you?"

"Yes."

"Is he docile?"

"He won't give us any trouble, Projectionist."

"Good. Go to my office and wait there for me, Dorey."

"Yes, Projectionist."

I took Kiley to his office then. The projectionist's office was on the same level as the projection booth, but at the far end of the theater. We went in and sat in the leather armchairs, and while we were waiting there an usher came up with popcorn and frozen icecream balls and hot coffee. He would have brought the projectionist his supper now, and the projectionist had sent down for additional food for Kiley and myself. That was so like the projectionist, gentle and considerate of all the needs of others.

"Are you afraid?" I asked Kiley. After all, he was only a kid, and it was to be expected that he would be afraid.

"No. Well, maybe a little."

"You mustn't be. It's in the hands of the projectionist now."

"What will he do to me, Dorey?"

"I don't know, but whatever he does, it will be the right thing. You can count on the projectionist for that. He's very wise. When he makes a decision, it's a just decision, believe me."

"Yes, I guess so."

"No guessing, Kiley. Rest assured. If you will only get these damn fantasies out of your head."

Then the projectionist entered, and we both rose to our feet in respect. He nodded pleasantly and told us to be seated. He walked around to the back of his big desk and sat down in a big swivel chair, the kind that judges use on the bench.

"So this is young Kiley," he said amiably. "Fine-looking lad. I knew your father, Kiley. Good man—yes, indeed. And your grandfather. Good people, good family." And then to me, "What seems to be the trouble, Dorey?"

"I would prefer that Kiley told you himself."

"Do that, Kiley," the projectionist said.

"Yes, Projectionist," Kiley's voice trembled slightly, but that was not unusual when people first met the projectionist. "You see, Dorey let me set up a small machine shop in that unused room off the lobby. I made a lathe to cut out some new parts for the vending machines. There was a locked door in the room, and I thought I might make a key on the lathe and open the locked door—"

"I'm sure you didn't consider that," the projectionist interrupted. "You know that locked doors can never be opened. That's the nature of the world, the way God made it."

"I thought that if I made a key, Projectionist—"

"A key? Poor Kiley. There are no keys, no dragons, no unicorns, no magicians. God has ordered His world in the best of possible ways. Myths are for children."

"But I made the key and opened the door and went out into the world, Projectionist."

"Don't excite yourself, Kiley."

"But you must listen to me and believe me."

"Ah, yes. We do believe you, Kiley. Of course we do."

"Then you do! You do believe me."

"Oh, yes."

"And you know that everything in here is of shadows—without any meaning or substance, and all that is real and beautiful is outside?"

"Yes, Kiley."

"And what will we do?" Kiley asked with great excitement. "Will we go out of here? Have we been waiting only for a time, a moment—as if for God to reach down and touch us and open our eyes? Then there would be some meaning in our own life, wouldn't there? In my life? Oh, I never dreamed to be such an instrument. Thank you, Projectionist, thank you, thank you."

"It is nothing, Kiley," the projectionist said gently, while I stared at him in astonishment. "You deserve many things, and they will come to you. Now wait here for a little while. Dorey and I must step outside and have a few words in private concerning this momentous happening. You understand?"

With tears in his eyes Kiley nodded, and then he said to me, "Believe me, Dorey, I hold nothing against you. How could you know? How could anyone know without seeing it with his own two eyes? I mean anyone but the projectionist. He knew. He knew immediately. Didn't you sir?"

"Immediately," the projectionist agreed.

"God bless you!" Kiley exclaimed. "I shouldn't be saying that to anyone so superior to me as yourself, but I must say it. God bless you, Projectionist."

"Thank you, my lad. Now wait here in peace. Dorey, come with me."

"Still speechless and astonished, I followed the projectionist out into the hall, where he whispered sharply, "Get that stupid expression off your face, Dorey. You're the President."

"But I thought, Projectionist—"

"I know what you thought. I simply dissembled in front of the poor lad. His mind is gone and his disease is serious and infectious. He must be put away, you know."

"Put away?"

"Yes, Dorey—put away."

"Where?"

"In the subcellar, Dorey, deep down in the old coalpit."

"Forever?"

"I imagine so."

"Can't he be cured?"

"Not of this particular delusion, Dorey. He is like a man who believes that he has seen the face of God. The vision becomes more than the man."

"I hate to do it."

"Do you imagine I like it?"

"Is there no other possible way, Projectionist?"

"None."

The projectionist went back to his booth, and I went down to Schecter and told him what we had to do. He smiled and licked his lips with pleasure, and believe me, I could have killed him then and there, but being a President entails certain duties, and there is no way to avoid them. So I let Schecter be and instead faced the look on Kiley's face when we walked into the projectionist's office and arrested him, binding his hands in back of him.

"Dorey, you can't get away with this!" he shouted. "You heard what the projectionist said to me."

"I do this at his order," I replied dully.

"No. No, you're lying."

"I'm not lying, Kiley. God help me, I am not lying."

"But why would he go back on his own word?"

"He was humoring you."

Kiley began to weep. We took him down, balcony to balcony, and then into the basement. It was fortunate for all of us that the projectionist had begun the Fitzgerald travelogues, for everyone was in the theater now. They were of the nature of the world. How can man live and not be filled with curiosity about his world? As unhappy as I was for Kiley's fate, I was also somewhat irritated that because of him I would miss the beginning of the travelogues. Still, duty is duty.

The coalpit was the fourth level under the orchestra, a dark, low-ceilinged part of the basement. A great iron hinged cover had to be lifted, and then we untied Kiley's hands, knotted a rope around his waist, and lowered him down into the coalpit.

"It's there!" he screamed up at me. "Dorey, it's there! Do you think you can destroy it by destroying me?"

And then the iron cover clanged shut. Poor Kiley!

21
Cephes 5

THE Third Officer (in training, which meant that he was merely the aide to the regular third officer) walked through the corridor of the great interstellar ship toward the meditation room. Although he had spent four years studying the eleven classes of interstellar ships, the reality was new, awesome, and infinitely more complex—the more so since this was a Class Two ship, entirely self-sustaining and with an indefinite cruising range. Unlike other interstellar ships, it was named not for the planet of its origin but for the planet of its destination, Cephes 5, and like all medical ships, it carried clearance for any port in the galaxy.

He knew how fortunate he was to have been appointed to this ship to complete his training, and at the age of twenty-two he was young and romantic enough to doubt and bless his good fortune constantly.

The ship was only three days out of its last port of call—the port where he had come on board as an officer cadet—and since then he had been occupied constantly with medical examinations, inoculations, briefings, and orientation tours. This was his first free hour, and he very properly sought the meditation room.

It was a long, plain room with ivory-colored walls and ceiling, and lit by a pleasant golden light. Here and there were stacks of cushions, and perhaps a dozen of the ship's one hundred and twenty crew members were in the room, meditating. Each sat upon one of the thin cushions, legs crossed, body erect, hands folded, eyes cast down in a position that was more or less universal in every planet of the galaxy. The Third Officer selected a pillow and seated himself, crossing his bare legs. He was quite comfortable since he wore only a pair of cotton shorts.

He sought to lose himself in his awareness of himself, as he had learned a long time ago, to still his own wonders and doubts and fears and to immerse himself in the wholeness of the universe, his own self becoming part of an infinitely larger self; yet the process would not work. He was blocked, confused and troubled, his mind shaken and swept from thought to thought, while underneath these rushing thoughts, strange and unpleasant fantasies began to form.

He glanced at the other men and women in the meditation room, but they sat in silence, apparently untroubled by the strange and frightening thoughts that hammered at his mind.

For half an hour or so the Third Officer fought to control his own mind and kept it clear and quiet, then he gave up and left the meditation room; and he realized that he had been in this curious state of mental excitement ever since boarding *Cephes 5,* but had only become fully aware of it when he attempted to meditate.

Deciding that it was simply his own eagerness, his own excitement at being assigned to this great, mysterious interstellar cruiser, he went to one of the viewing rooms, sank into a chair, and pressed the button that raised the screen on outer space. The impression was of sitting in the midst of the galaxy, facing a blazing and uncountable array of stars. The Third Officer remembered that on his early training trips the viewing room had been a cure for almost any problem of fear or disquiet. Now it failed him, and his thoughts in the viewing room were as disquieting as they had been in the meditation room.

Puzzled and not untroubled, the Third Officer left the viewing room and sought out the ship's Counsellor. He still had four hours of free time left to him before he began his tour of duty in the engine room, and while he had hoped to devote this time to making the acquaintance of other crew members in the off-duty lounge, he decided now that the first order of importance was to learn why the ship filled him with such a sense of chaos and foreboding.

He knocked at the door of the Counsellor's office, and a voice asked him to enter, which he did gingerly, uncertainly, for he had never before gone to a Counsellor on one of the great galactic ships. The Counsellors were legendary throughout the galaxy, for in a manner of speaking they were the highest rank in all of mankind's table of organization—very old, very wise, and gifted in ways that could only fill a cadet of twenty-two years with awe and respect. On interstellar ships they ranked even above the captain, although it was rare indeed that one of them countermanded a captain's order or interfered in any manner with the operation of the ship. Legend had it that some of the Counsellors were more than two hundred years old, and certainly an age of a century and a half was not uncommon.

Now, as the Third Officer entered the small, simply furnished office, an old man in a blue silk robe turned from the desk where he had been writing and nodded at the Third Officer. He was very old indeed, a black man whose skin was as wrinkled and dry as old brown leather and whose pale yellow eyes looked at the Third Officer with pleasant inquiry. Was it true that the Counsellors were telepaths who could read minds as easily as ordinary men heard sound? the Third Officer wondered.

"Quite true," the old man said softly. "Be patient, Third Officer. There are more things for you to learn than you imagine." He pointed to a chair. "Sit down and be comfortable. There are a hundred and twelve years of difference in your age and mine, and while you may think that a matter of little account when you reach my age, it's very impressive at the moment, isn't it?"

The Third Officer nodded.

"And you were in the meditation room and you found that you could not meditate?"

"Yes, sir."

"Do you know why?"

"No, sir."

"And neither do you suspect why?"

"I have been on spaceships before," the Third Officer said.

"And you have been on this one for three days, and you have been examined, lectured to, shot full of a variety of serums and antibodies, and oriented—but never told what cargo this ship carries?"

"No, sir."

"Or its purpose?"

"No, sir."

"And quite properly, you did not ask."

"No, sir, I did not ask."

The Counsellor regarded the Third Officer in silence for perhaps two or three minutes. The Third Officer by now found his own problems submerged in his excitement and curiosity at actually sitting face to face with one of the fabled Counsellors, and finally he could contain himself no longer.

"Would you forgive me if I ask a personal question, sir?"

"I can't imagine any question that requires forgiveness," the Counsellor replied, smiling.

"Are you reading my mind now, sir? That's the question."

"Reading your mind now? Oh, no—no indeed. Why should I? I know all about you. We need unusual young men in our crew, and you are quite an unusual young man. Reading your mind would take great concentration and effort; quite to the contrary, I was looking into my own mind and remembering when I was your age. But that's a problem of the aged. We tend to be too reflective and to wander a good deal. Now concerning the meditation—it will take a little time, but once you fully understand the purpose of *Cephes 5,* you will overcome these disturbances and indeed you will find that you meditate on a higher level than before—commensurate with a new effort of will. Let that be for a moment. Do you know what the word *murder* means?"

"No, sir."

"Have you ever heard it before?"

"No, sir. Not that I remember."

The old man appeared to be smiling inwardly, and again there was a minute or two of inner reflection. The Third Officer waited.

"There is a whole spectrum of being that we must examine," the Counsellor said finally, "and thus we will introduce you to an area of being you have possibly never dreamed of. It won't damage you or even shake you over-much, for it was taken into consideration when you were chosen to be a part of the crew of *Cephes 5.* We begin with murder as an idea and an act. Murder is the act of taking a human life, and as an idea it has its origin in abnormal feelings of hatred and aggression."

"Hatred and aggression," the Third Officer repeated slowly.

"Do you follow me? Do you understand?"

"I think so."

"The words are possibly unfamiliar. Allow me to go into your mind for just a moment—and you will feel this better than I could explain it."

The old man's face became blank, and suddenly the Third Officer winced and cried out in disgust. The old black man's face became alive again, and the Third Officer put his face in his hands and sat that way for a moment, shivering.

"I'm sorry, but it was necessary," the Counsellor said. "Fear is very much a part of it, and that is why I had to touch the fear and horror centers of your mind. Otherwise, how do you explain color to a blind man?"

The Third Officer looked up and nodded.

"You will be all right in a moment. Murder is the act—the finality of what you just felt. There are other degrees, pain, torture, an incredible variety of hurts—tell me if any of these words elude you."

"Torture, I don't think I ever heard the word."

"It's a deliberate inflicting of pain, psychological pain, physical pain."

"For what reason?" the Third Officer asked.

"There you have the crux of it. For what reason? Reason implies health. This is sickness, the most dreadful sickness that man has ever experienced."

"And murder? Is it simply a syndrome? Is it something out of the past? Out of the childhood of the races of mankind? Or is it a postulate?"

"No indeed. It's a reality."

"You mean people kill other people?"

"Exactly."

"Without reason?"

"Without reason as you understand reason. But within the spectrum of this sickness, there is subjective reason and cause."

"Enough to take a human life?" the Third Officer whispered.

"Enough to take a human life."

The young man shook his head. "Incredible—just incredible. But consider, sir, with all due respect, I've had an education, a very good education. I read books. I watch television. I have kept myself informed. How can it be that I've never heard of this—indeed that I've never even heard the words?"

"How many inhabited planets are there in the galaxy?" the old man asked, smiling slightly.

"Thirty-three thousand, four hundred and sixty-nine."

"Seventy-two, since Philbus 7, 8 and 9 were settled last month. Thirty-three thousand, four hundred and seventy-two. Does that answer your question? There are thousands of planets where murder has never occurred, even as there are thousands of planets that have never known tuberculosis, or pneumonia or scarlet fever."

"But we heal these things—and almost every other disease known to man," the Third Officer protested.

"Yes, almost every other disease. Almost. We have no knowledge that is absolute. We learn a great deal, but the more we know, the wider the boundaries to the unknown become, and the one disease that defeats our wisest physicians and researchers is this thing we are discussing."

"Has it a name?"

"It has. It is called insanity."

"And you say it's a very old disease?"

"Very old."

It was the Third Officer's turn to be thoughtful, and the old man waited patiently for him to think it through. Finally the cadet asked, "If we have no cure, what happens to these people who murder?"

"We isolate them."

Realization came to the Third Officer like a cold chill. "On the planet Cephes 5?"

"Yes. We isolate them on the planet Cephes 5. We do it as mercifully, as kindly as we can. Long, long ago other alternatives were tried, but they all failed, and finally they came to the conclusion that only isolation would work."

"And this ship—" The Third Officer's voice trailed away.

"Yes—yes, indeed. This is the transport ship. We pick up these people in every part of the galaxy and we take them to Cephes 5. That is why we choose our crew with such care and concern, people of great inner strength. Do you understand now why your meditation went so poorly?"

"Yes, I think I do."

"No sensitive person can escape the vibrations that fill this ship, but you can learn to live with them and deal with them, and find new strength in the process. Of course, you always have the option of leaving the ship."

The old black man looked at the Third Officer thoughtfully, thinking rather wistfully of the precious, fleeting beauty of youth, the unfaded golden hair, the clear blue eyes, the earnest facing and assumption of the problem of life, and he remembered the time when he had been young and strong-limbed and beautiful, not with regret, but with the apparently eternal fascination in the life process that was a part of his being.

"I don't think I will leave the ship, sir," the Third Officer said after a moment.

"I didn't think you would." The Counsellor rose then, standing tall and straight and lean, his blue robe hanging from his bony shoulders, his great height and wide shoulders a quality of the black people on the Rebus and Alma constellation of planets. "Come now," he said to the boy, "we will go into this somewhat more fully. And remember, Third Officer, that we have no alternatives. This is a genetic factor in these poor souls, and had we not isolated them in this fashion, the whole galaxy would be infected."

The Third Officer opened the door for him and then followed the Counsellor down the corridor to one of the elevators. They passed other crew members on the way, men and women, black and white and yellow and brown people, and each of them made a gesture of respect to the Counsellor. They paused at the elevators, and when a door opened, they stepped in. The Captain of the ship was just leaving the elevator, and she held the door for a moment to tell the Counsellor that he looked well and rested.

"Thank you, Captain. This is Third Officer Cadet. He is with us only three days."

The Third Officer had not seen the Captain before, and he was struck by the grace and beauty of the woman. She appeared to be in her middle fifties, yellow-skinned with black slanting eyes and black hair hardly touched with gray. She wore a white silk robe of command, and she greeted the Third Officer graciously and warmly, giving him the feeling of being vitally needed and important.

"We were discussing Cephes 5," the Counsellor explained. "I take him now to the sleep chamber."

"He is in good hands," the Captain said.

The elevator dropped into the bowels of the great spaceship, stopped, and the door opened. The Third Officer followed the Counsellor out into a long, wide chamber that at first glance left him breathless and shaken—a place like a great morgue where on triple tiers of beds at least five hundred human beings lay asleep, men and women and children too, some as young as ten or twelve

341

years, none much older than their twenties, people of every race in the galaxy. In their sleep, there was nothing to distinguish them from normal people.

The Third Officer found himself whispering. "That's not necessary," the Counsellor said. "They cannot awake until we awaken them."

The old man led the young man down the long line of beds to the end of the chamber, where, behind a glass wall, men and women in white smocks were working around a table on which a man lay. A network of wires was attached to a band around his skull, and in the background there were banks of machines.

"We block their memories," the Counsellor explained. "That we are able to do, and then we build up a new set of memories. It's a very complex procedure. They will have no recollection of any existence before Cephes 5, and they will be fully oriented toward Cephes 5 and the mores there."

"Do you just leave them there?"

"Oh, no—no indeed. We have our agencies on Cephes 5; we have maintained them there for many, many years. Feeding these people into the life of Cephes 5 is a most delicate and important process. If the inhabitants of Cephes 5 were to discover this, the consequences for them would be tragic indeed. But there is very small chance of that. Indeed, it is almost impossible."

"Why?"

"Because the entire pattern of life on Cephes 5 depends on ego structure. Every person on the planet spends his life creating an ego structure which subjectively places him at the center of the universe. This ego structure is central to the disease, for given the sickness that creates the ego, each individual goes on to form in his mind an anthropomorphic superman whom he calls God and who supports his right to kill."

"I am not sure I understand," the Third Officer said.

"In time you will. It is enough to accept the fact that the people on Cephes 5 place their planet and their own selves at the center of the universe, and then they structure their lives so that no uncertainty concerning this should ever arise. This is why we have been able to continue this process for so many years. You see, they refuse even to consider the fact that mankind might exist elsewhere in the universe."

"Then they don't know?"

342

"No, they don't know."

For a while they stood there, the Third Officer watching the work on the other side of the glass panel and growing more and more uneasy. Then the Counsellor tapped his shoulder and said, "Enough. Even in their sleep, they think and dream, and you are still too new to this to suffer their vibrations for long. Come, we will go to one of the viewing rooms, sit and look at the universe, and talk a little more and compose ourselves."

In the viewing room, with the enormous, blazing glory of the stars in front of him and with the comforting presence of the Counsellor beside him, the Third Office was able to relax and begin to deal with the flood of ideas and impressions. He found that he was full of a great pity, an overwhelming sense of sadness, and he spoke of this to the old man.

"It's quite normal," the Counsellor said.

"What do they do on Cephes 5?" he wondered.

"They kill."

"Then is the planet empty?"

"Hardly. You see, these poor demented creatures are aware of their function, which is to kill, and like all creatures with a sense of function, they place the function above all else. Thus they breed like no other men in the universe, increasing their population constantly, so that while their killing mounts, their breeding remains ahead of it."

"Are they normally intelligent?"

"Very intelligent—yet their intelligence is to no effect. Their egos prevent them from ever turning it inward."

"But how can they be intelligent and continue this thing you call murder?"

"Because the intelligence is directed toward only one end—the killing of their own kind. As I told you, they are insane."

"But if they are intelligent, won't they devise ways to move through space?"

"Oh, yes. They have done so, with very crude rockets. But we chose Cephes 5 originally because it is the farthest inhabitable planet from the center of the galaxy, almost forty light-years from another inhabitable planet. They will move through space, but the problem of warping space, of moving faster than light—this will always elude them, for this is a problem that man can solve only within himself.

For some time the Third Officer sat in silence, and then he asked softly, "Do they suffer a great deal?"

"I am afraid so."

"Is there any hope for them?"

"There is always hope," the old man replied.

"We call it Cephes 5 in our table of planets," the Third Officer said. "But every planet has a subjective name for itself. What do these people call their planet?"

"They call it the Earth," the old man said.

22
Of Time and Cats

A T least, if it makes no sense at all, it explains about the cats. There was a note in the *Times* today about the pound; they have put away four times the average number of cats, and it keeps getting worse. It will continue to get worse and worse, no doubt, but cats are not as bad as some things.

To explain it, after I had convinced myself that I was in my right mind, I telephoned my wife. Some say that there is actually no way of convincing yourself that you are in your right mind, but I don't go along with that. At least I was as sane as I was a week before.

"Where are you?" my wife demanded. "Why are you telephoning—why don't you come up?"

"Because I am downtown at the Waldorf."

"Oh no—no. You are downstairs where I left you less than three minutes ago."

"That is not me—not myself, do you understand?"

"No."

I waited a while, and she waited too. Finally, I said, "No, I guess you don't."

"I also saw you dodge around the corner of 63rd Street," she added. "Were you playing games?"

"Well—"

"Yes?"

"That wasn't me either. Do you think I'm out of my mind? I mean, do you think I've had a breakdown or something like that?"

"No," my wife said. "You're not the breakdown type."

"Well, what do you think?"

"I'm reserving opinions," my wife said.

345

"Thank you. I still love you. When you saw me downstairs a few minutes ago, what was I wearing?"

"Don't you know?" She seemed shaken for the first time.

"I know. But I want you to tell me. Is that asking so much? Just tell me."

"All right. I'll tell you. The gray herringbone."

"Ah," I said. "Now I will hold the wire, and you go to my closet and tell me what you see there."

"You're not drunk. I've seen you drunk, and you don't act this way. I will not go to the closet. You come home and we'll decide whether to call a doctor or not."

"Please," I begged her. "Please. I am asking a small thing. We have been married twelve years. It has been give and take, the best with the worst. But we came through. Now all I am asking is that you go—"

"All right," she said shortly. "I'll humor you. I will go to your closet. Just hold on."

I waited while she went and returned. She picked up the phone again, but said nothing.

"Well?"

She sighed and admitted that she had gone to the closet.

"And you saw it there?"

"Your gray suit?"

"Yes?"

"Yes."

"Gray herringbone. My one gray suit. I have brown, blue and Oxford. I have two sport jackets and three pairs of flannel trousers. But only one gray suit—gray herringbone. Right?"

"Gray herringbone," she said weakly. "But maybe you bought another?"

"Why?"

"How should I know why? You like gray herringbone, I suppose."

"No, I didn't buy another. I give you my word of honor. Alice, I love you. We have been married twelve years. I'm a solid character as such things go. Not flighty. Not even romantic, as you have remarked."

"You are romantic enough," she said flatly.

"You know what I mean. I did not buy another gray suit. It is the same gray suit."

"In two places at the same time?"

346

"Yes."

"Oh?"

There was a long, long pause then, until finally I said, "Now will you do as I say, even if it makes no sense?"

She paused and sighed again. "Yes."

"Good. It is now two-fifteen. Shortly before three o'clock, Professor Dunbar will call and tell you some rubbish about his cat and then ask for me. Tell him to go to hell. Then get a cab down here to the Waldorf. I'm in Room 1121."

"Bob," she said uncertainly, "just that way—go to hell? He is the head of your department."

"Well, not in so many words. Do it your own way. Then come straight here. Yes—one thing more. If you see me anywhere, ignore me. Do you understand—no matter what. Ignore me. Don't talk to me."

"Oh? Yes—Of course. If I see you anywhere, I ignore you. And if I see you, you'll be wearing the gray herringbone?"

"Yes," I said. "And will you do as I say?"

"Oh, yes—yes. Of course."

And strangely enough, she did. There are wives and wives; I like mine. I sat in that room (the least expensive, eight dollars a day) and waited and tried to think about something no one should ever have to think about, and at exactly 3:20, there was a knock at the door, and I opened it, and there was Alice. She was a little pale, a little shaken, but still very nice to look at and standing and walking on her own feet.

I kissed her, and she returned the kiss, but told me it was only because I had the blue suit on. Not a chance with the gray suit, she said; and then asked me seriously whether we could be dreaming?

"Not both of us," I said. "Either you or me. But this isn't a dream. Why do you ask? Did you see me?"

She nodded. "Let me sit down first." She sat down and looked at me with a curious smile on her face.

"You did see me?" I asked.

"Oh, yes—yes, I saw you."

"Where?"

"On the corner of 58th Street."

"Did I see you?"

"No, I don't think so. I was in a cab. But not in the singular, either. You would have to say, 'Did we see you?' There were three of you."

"All in gray herringbone?"

"Every one of you."

I had a bottle of brandy, and I poured a tot for each of us, and I drank mine down and then so did Alice. Then she asked me what I was doing, and I told her I was taking my pulse.

"You would think the rooms would be nicer than this in the Waldorf," she said, "even for eight dollars a day. If I was hiding, I wouldn't hide in the Waldorf. I'd go downtown to a flophouse, like they do in the stories, for fifty cents a day. How is your pulse?"

"Eighty. I'm not hiding."

"Eighty is good, isn't it?"

"It's all right. It's normal," I pointed out. "We're both normal. We're plain people with common sense."

"Yes?"

"How was I? I mean, was I—"

"We. Say *we*. There were three of you. And I might as well tell you, I saw you outside the house. That makes four of you. I got the cab before you caught me, and when I looked back, there was another one of you. Five of you."

"Oh, my God!"

"Yes, indeed, and you can thank your stars that I am not the hysterical type. How many of you are there, if I may ask?"

"I don't know," I whispered. "Maybe fifty—maybe a hundred—maybe five hundred. I just don't know."

"You mean New York is full of you," Alice nodded. "When I was a little girl, I used to read *Alice in Wonderland* and pretend it was me. Now I don't have to pretend."

"No, I guess you don't. Tell me, Alice—just one or two things more—and then I'll try to explain."

I poured her another brandy and she drank it down neat, and said, "Oh, fine. I want to hear you explain about this."

"Yes, yes, naturally you do. And I'm going to—that is as much as I understand, I'm going to, I am indeed—"

"You are babbling," Alice interrupted, not without sympathy.

"I am, aren't I? Well, there you are. What I meant is—when you saw the three of me, was I—were we quarrelling, angry or what?"

"Oh, no, getting along fine. Just so deep in discussion you didn't realize you had stopped traffic. Three of you are triplets, not any kind of triplets, but bald, forty-year-old college-professor type

348

triplets, identical of course, and dressed in that gray herringbone that all of the city must be talking about—oh, yes, and the sleeveless cashmere instead of a vest and the bright green bow-tie—"

"I don't see how you can laugh at something like this."

"I have problems of my own sanity," Alice said. "Would you like another nip? Yes—I told Dunbar to go to hell, just as you advised me to."

She poured the brandy for me, and her hand didn't shake. Don't ever tell me that any man knows the woman he is married to, not in twelve years and not in twenty years—not unless something happens that can't happen, and most people live their lives without that.

"He called?"

"Yes. You said he would."

"But I didn't believe he would. What time?"

"Ten minutes to three, exactly. I checked the time."

"Yes. What did he say—for God's sake, Alice, what did he say?"

"If you had only said it was important, I would have listened more carefully."

"But you did listen—please. Alice!"

"The trouble is, he doesn't talk English even at best, and he was very excited. He's building some kind of a silly machine in his basement—a field deviator or something of that sort—"

"I know. I know what he's trying to do."

"Then perhaps you can tell me."

"I will, I will," I pleaded. "I don't quite understand it myself, to tell you the truth. He has some notion that space can be warped or bent—no, that doesn't do it, but something like that. Knotted, perhaps. A tiny corner of it twisted into a knot—"

"You're not making any sense at all, Bob. I think you're excited. I think you're upset."

"Yes, I'm upset! Going out of my mind! God damn it, Alice—what did he say?"

"That's better," Alice nodded. "I think it's good for you to get angry, a sort of safety valve."

"What did he say?"

"He said that his cat walked into the—what would it be—between two electrodes or something like electrodes?"

"A vortex?"

"Perhaps. Whatever it is, his cat walked into it and disappeared.

Poof—just like that. No cat. So he tried it on himself—he has the emotional stability of a six year old, if you ask me—and nothing at all happened. So he wants you to get in your car and get right over to his basement and let him know what you make of it."

"And?"

"I don't know," Alice frowned. "He assured me that it had nothing to do with atomic disintegration or anything of that sort or there would have been a dreadful explosion and he wouldn't have been talking to me at all. I think he thought that was a joke—he laughed. The kind of humor a professor uses with his students. Oh, I'm sorry."

"Don't mind me at all. You can't hurt my feelings now."

"And I told him to go to hell. Not in those words—I told him you were spending the night with your brother in Hartford and when he wanted your brother's telephone number, I said it had been temporarily disconnected, so he got the address and sent you a wire there, or said he would. Now it's your turn."

"Now it's my turn," I repeated, and I went over to the window and looked down.

"Looking for yourself?" Alice wanted to know.

"That's a damn poor joke."

"Sorry. Really, I am, Bob." She got up and came over to me and put her arm through mine. "I know you have trouble. Why don't you try to tell me?"

"Will you believe me?"

"I think I can believe anything, now."

"Good. Now sit down again. I want you to sit down and look at me." She did this dutifully, and rested her elbow on the arm of the chair, her chin on her knuckles, and looked at me. "I am your husband, Robert Clyde Bottman. Right?"

"I accept that."

"And all those others you saw today—they were also me, your husband, Robert Clyde Bottman—right?"

She nodded.

"What do you make of it?"

"Oh, no—not me. As soon as I try to make anything out of it, I'll go screaming mad. What do you make of it?"

"I'll tell you," I said. "This morning, at ten-thirty, you left the house to go shopping downtown. I was correcting papers. Shortly after you left, the bell rang. I opened the door—and there I was. The first one.''

"Gray herringbone, you mean.''

"Exactly. And I wasn't too surprised at first. He looked familiar, but nobody really knows what they look like to someone else. The worst moment came when I discovered that it was myself—not an imitation, not a copy, not a fraud, not proof that the devil actually exists, but myself. It was me. I was me. It was me. We both were Robert Clyde Bottman. We both were the real thing. Do you understand?''

For the first time, there was fear and horror in my wife's face as she shook her head and said, "No—I don't, Bob.''

"Listen,'' I went on. "He explained it to me. Or I explained it to me, take your choice. And while he was explaining, the doorbell rang, and I opened it, and there I was again. Three of us now. Then we began to fight it out philosophically, and the doorbell rang again. Four of us—''

"Bob, tell me!''

"Yes—now listen. Take today in terms of time. What happens to it when tomorrow comes?''

"Oh, it's yesterday, and stop that, Bob. Tell me what happened. I can't stand much more of this.''

"And I'm trying to tell you, believe me, Alice. But first we have to talk about time. What is time?''

"Bob, I don't know what time is. Time is time. It passes.''

"And I don't know any more than that, when you come right down to it. And neither does anyone else. But it's been a philosophical football for ages. I walk across this room. Time passes. I have been in a number of places just in this room, all connected by my actual physical being. What happened to me as I was two minutes ago? I was. I cease to exist. I reappear.''

"Nonsense,'' Alice snorted. "You're here all the time.''

"Because I am connected with myself in terms of time. Suppose time is an aspect of motion. No motion, no time. If you will, think of a path in terms of motion. You move along it—everything we are conscious of moves in parallel terms. But nothing disappears—it is all there always, yesterday, tomorrow, a million years from now—a reality that we are conscious of only in the flickering transition of now—this moment, this instant.''

"I don't understand that at all, and I don't believe it either," Alice said."Is this some new kismet—fate, a future ordained for us?"

"No, no," I said impatiently. "It's not that. The path isn't fixed. It's fluid, it changes all the time. But we can't sit and argue about it, because we're moving along it. And I have to tell you before we go too far. Those other myselfs—"

"Just call them gray herringbone," Alice said weakly.

"Very well, gray herringbone. They told me what happened today."

"Before it happened?"

"Before it happened and after it happened. That makes no difference. It's a paradox. That's why this sort of thing can't be handled by the mental equipment we have. There's no room for paradox. The most illogical man is still logical in terms of paradox. Today happened to me. I corrected the papers. You came home. Professor Dunbar telephoned and told me about the cat. I rushed over to his place. I took a panel of transistors with me, found where his circuit burned out, rewired it. You see, I had wired it originally. I was trembling with excitement then—"

"*You* were trembling with excitement?" Alice said.

"Yes. Well, I react to different things. You can't imagine how exciting this was—actually to warp space, even if a tiny bit of it. I wasn't thinking about time then. You see, I had picked up the professor's cat outside his door, and I brought it in with me. There were three cats there, but I didn't think twice about that. I picked up the one on the doorstep and brought it in. The professor was delighted. We decided that a space-warp had placed the cat outside the house. So when I hooked in the transistors and threw the power, I stepped between the electrode myself. What could be more natural?"

"Nothing," Alice said. "Oh—nothing at all. Very natural, only they give the younger generations to you to be taught."

"And that was five P.M., today."

"And now it's four-thirty P.M.," Alice shrugged. "Today was, but it isn't yet. For God's sake, Bob, I am a woman. Talk sense to me!"

"I am trying to. You must accept it—don't think about it, accept it. The warp was in time, maybe in space too, maybe the two are inseparable. We only had three hundred amps—a very slight effect,

352

a tiny loop or twist in time, and then it snapped back. But the damage was done. My own particular time belt now had a five hour loop in it. In other words, it was repeated, I was stranded here—no, I don't make sense, do I?''

"I'm afraid not," Alice agreed sadly. "You said it happened."

"It did. But I was pushed back to before it happened. I went straight to the apartment. I rang the bell. I opened the door and let myself in. I told myself—"

"Stop that!" Alice cried. "Stop talking about yourself. Say gray herringbone, if you must."

"All right. Gray herringbone, and he told me what had happened. Heaven knows how many times the loop had repeated already—"

"Wouldn't you know if it repeated?"

"How could I know? My own consciousness is only for now—not for yesterday, not for tomorrow. How could I know?"

Alice shook her head dumbly.

"Anyway," I continued desperately, "today, my today, our today, this morning, I decided to stop it. I had to stop it. I would go insane, the whole world would go insane if I didn't stop it. But they—the gray herringbones—they didn't want me to stop it."

"Why?"

"Because they were afraid. They were afraid that they would die. They want to live as much as I do. I am the first one, and therefore the real me; but they are also me—different moments of consciousness in me—but they are me. But they couldn't stop me. They couldn't interfere with me. When I told them to get out, they had to go. If they interfered, it might mean death for them too. So they left. But some of them watched downstairs—and some in other places, and all of them myself. Do you wonder that I am half insane?"

"All right, my dear," Alice said gently. "What did you do then?"

"I put on the blue suit, not the gray one. I climbed down the fire-escape, through the house opposite ours, hailed a cab, and checked in here at the hotel."

"But if what you say is true," Alice said, beginning to share my own fear and horror, "any one of you—of the gray herringbone—can go to Dunbar instead—"

I nodded. "I thought of that. I'm not certain it would work that way. But to make sure, I took the transistor panel with me. It would take at least ten hours of work and a good electronics shop to duplicate it. They can repair the circuit—and maybe it will be enough power for a cat, but not for a man. I can swear that. Not for a man—".

"But if they do?"

I shook my head. "I don't know. I just don't know. Nothing will ever again be the way it was. How many of me will the world contain? I don't know—"

"And if you stop it, Bob?" Whether she understood me or not, she believed me. Her eyes said that; the fear was deep and wet and sick in her eyes.

"I can't answer that," I shrugged. "I don't know. We just scraped at a great mystery. I don't know. All we can do is sit and wait. Less than a half hour to five o'clock, so it's not too long to wait."

Then we waited. At first we tried to talk, but we couldn't talk much. Then we were silent. Then, a few minutes before five o'clock, Alice came over to me and kissed me. I pushed her back and into her chair. "I've got to be alone for this." I waited for anything, more afraid than I ever have been, before that or since, and then it was five o'clock. We compared watches. We called the desk and checked the time. It was five minutes past the hour. Then Alice began to cry, and I let her cry it out. Then we decided to go home.

There was a crowd and commotion down in the lobby, but we didn't stop. Later I realized that one of them would have remembered that I liked the Waldorf and would go there, but then we didn't stop.

We got a cab. As we drove uptown, we saw seven separate crowds, accident crowds, which are unmistakable in New York. "This town is becoming a battlefront," the driver said. We didn't say anything at all. But there were no gray herringbone, not along the way, not in front of the house we lived in and not waiting for us in our apartment.

We were home less than an hour when the police came. Two plainclothes men and two men in uniform. They talked like cops and wanted to know whether I was Professor Robert Clyde Bottman.

"That's right."

"What do you do?"

354

"I teach physics at Columbia University."

"You got anything to identify yourself?"

"Well, I live here," I said. "Of course I have."

"You got pictures of yourself?"

I wanted to know if they had gone out of their minds, but Alice smiled sweetly and brought our scrapbook and our family album. That seemed to satisfy them a little; wholly satisfied, they never were. For in three places in New York, friends of mine had been talking to me when I disappeared. Just disappeared—poof, and done with.

One of the plainclothes men asked if I was twins, and the other said, "He'd have to be better than triplets."

Then they called downtown, and discovered that the number of men around town—gray herringbone suits and bald—reported to have disappeared into thin air, poof, at exactly 5:00 o'clock, had reached seventy-eight, and was mounting steadily. They stared at me without saying anything.

They argued about arresting me; one wanted to, the other didn't. They called downtown again, and then they told me not to leave town without notifying them, and then they left. A little while later, Professor Dunbar rung our doorbell.

"Ah, there you are," he said. "I turned my back for a moment, and you were gone. Really, Bob, you must trace that circuit again."

Alice smiled and promised that I would come tomorrow and fix the circuit once and for all.

As the professor was leaving, he said, "Most interesting thing, you know. There must have been two dozen cats outside when I left. All of them exactly like Prudence."

"Prudence is the Professor's cat," I explained to Alice.

"Oh, I have Prudence back—oh, yes. I'm very fond of cats. But I never realized how alike they can be."

"And I am sure we look alike to cats, Professor Dunbar," Alice said.

"Oh good. Very good indeed. I never thought of it that way. But I suppose we do. Well, tomorrow's another day."

"Thank God it is," Alice said.

We let him out and Alice made scrambled eggs for dinner, and then the press began to arrive. They were tiring, but we stuck to our ignorance and smiled disbelievingly about men in gray herringbone suits disappearing into thin air. I don't know whether it is for better or worse. For a few days, it was a bigger thing than flying saucers, and it made me rather uncomfortable at school. But Alice says it won't last.

It's her theory that I and my gray herringbone suit will be forgotten in a general problem of cats. Professor Dunbar lives in the North Bronx, and when we drove up to his house the following day, to fix a circuit once and for all and to fix it properly, we counted over a hundred cats. Those were the ones we saw. Alice says that cats that don't disappear—poof—have more lasting interest than college professors who do. Alice says if man can learn to live with the atom, he can learn to live with cats. Anyway, you can't hold science back, and sooner or later, someone else will tie a knot in time. Only I don't like to think about it.

23
The Interval

FEW will face it, but there is a beginning and an end; that's
the way it is, and after you turn fifty, it stares you in the
face. You read the obituary pages and you find that people of your
own age and people even younger than you are dying, and then it
closes in on you and you can be alone, the way I was. When you are
decently married for a long, long while you are fortunate to go first;
but if you are left behind, you keep looking at yourself and
wondering what you are waiting for.

I went up to northern Connecticut, to the foothills of the
Berkshires, to see about putting our summer place on the market;
but even as I spoke to the local real estate man, I found that I had
no feelings one way or another about the place. I was indifferent to
price or terms, and since I was so obliging a client, the broker parted
with a few pleasantries, and then said obliquely, as many New
Englanders would:

"How about them fellers up on the moon?"

These Yankees change the subject to suit them; I was talking
about the house but he wanted to talk about the moon—meaning
he had regard for me or that he was returning my favor of obliging
him, in his peculiar Connecticut manner. He didn't care what I
thought or felt about the moon; he himself felt queasy, and I
wondered whether the whole world didn't feel a bit queasy.

When I didn't answer, he said, "Fine, full moon tonight."

I nodded and left him, and then drove along Main Street to Old
Turkey Gobbler Road and then three miles to the house. The house
had stood on its knoll for two hundred years, and during that time a

357

dozen owners had cherished it and changed this and added that; and we had cherished it, too, for the nineteen years we had it.

All the time I had looked at it in the past, it had always been a house warm inside, alive, full of the past and the lives and the spirit of all the kids who had played and grown up there and the smell of the good things that had been cooked there and the passion of the sex and the love and the hate that had happened there, the hungers satisfied and unsatisfied, the longings, the fulfillment, the disappointments, the fears, the apprehensions—so it had been all the times I had seen it in the past. But now it was quiet without passion. It was only a box, and inside it was very cold, for the edge of winter had touched it already, and New England winter comes quick and hard in the Berkshires.

But this winter had an edge of icy cold that was furtive rather than literal. You felt it creeping through your bones, and before any frostbite touched your skin, you felt it at the edge of your heart. I had begun to shiver and I wanted a fire desperately, and I went out to the woodbox which I had filled with good, dry kindling the summer before. I made my fire and burned a few papers to start a blast up the chimney, and then added the kindling and put on top of that three thick old pieces of gray birch, or the silver birch, as some call it—and then indeed heat came from the big stone box. But there was still a chill in the room.

It was late afternoon and the light was beginning to fade. I prowled through the old empty house, looking for this or that to take back to the city; but there was nothing I wanted particularly, not even the first manuscripts of my very early plays and books. The battered old typewriter was a good, rare Underwood out of the thirties, but I had another in New York. Some day, perhaps, I would ship away the pictures and books, but not now. Some day when I cared more.

The moon rose, so strong and silver-bright that the day seemed not to fade or perish but only to turn color, and the moonlight turned bright the faces of the mountains to the north of me. Here and there was a thin cover of snow on the hillsides, and where the snow was you could see the distant slopes in detail.

I lit my pipe and smoked and stared at the leaping flames of the fire, and I think that in some way I knew what was coming. Because for me it was no great surprise to glance out of the window and see what I saw. I had knocked out my pipe onto the hearth, and I got

358

up and walked to the broad windows that faced north, and I saw that it was finished and that they were picking up the scenery, rolling it up, either for good and to be disposed of however they dispose of such things, or to be used again elsewhere.

I mentioned before that it was a startlingly clear night, as if they could make white, incandescent moonlight for their own needs, and I suppose I could see a long way north. In any case, I saw clearly how the forested slopes were being rolled up, the way one might roll up a thick and unusual carpet, leaving underneath the gray, sere stuff that the riders to the moon had seen and described with such loathing. The green countryside was being taken up in great pieces, miles wide, and wherever the rolling up and lifting away was finished, the dry, dead gray stuff remained.

I did not watch for long, because I felt almost immediately that I must not witness the finish of this alone. I had to be with others. I had to pass the word. I had to comment, to speculate, to bewail, perhaps, to doubt my own eyes, to plead for some explanation other than the simple obvious fact that the play was over and the curtain had come down—and because of this I bolted out of the house and into my car.

The car started easily, and I sent it plunging over the dirt road toward Route 22, over the shortest way, which would connect through the Wankhaus Overpass, a dirt road over a shoulder that linked the Old Turkey Gobbler Road with South Pike Road and so to Route 22. But they took up the Wankhaus Overpass; they had humor, and they could be bothered with small games, but I don't suppose they were vengeful. They left me alone there, and I sat in my car, staring through the windshield at the gray pumice that remained after they had taken up the road and the trees and the rocks, rolling back and away and then casting it off somewhere in the wings. I mean, they let me back up, which wasn't vengeful, while the wind blew gray powder over my car and filled my nostrils with the dry, dead smell of it. I had to back up for over two hundred yards before I was able to turn into South Pike, but with three miles more to drive than would have been the case the other way, and then they let me find my way to Route 22. They were busy to the north and the west, and there I saw a whole town, factories, motor lodges, main street, Civil War monument, new business machines plant, car dealers—everything rolled up and dragged away. But silently. Well, my windows were up and I was too far away to hear people screaming. If they screamed; I didn't know, you see, because I had not uttered a sound, never protested or wailed or prayed or pleaded.

It surprised me as I drove south along Route 22 and then onto the Saw Mill River Parkway that I saw no other cars. Was it later than I could have imagined? I felt for my watch, and then I found that I had left it behind at the house, so I really had no idea at all of what time it was.

I was impressed myself by how well I drove, how fast, and with such quiet control—all things considered—and without undue excitement and panic. The Saw Mill River Parkway is one of the older Westchester parkways, two rather narrow lanes in each direction and not built for speed, but rather meandering over the hills like an old carriage road; yet I was able to build my speed up to and past seventy miles an hour—and still in my rearview mirror I could see tracts of houses rolled up and flung aside, hillsides stripped, and even the road behind me rolled up as I left it. But not at seventy miles an hour, and by the time I reached the Hawthorne Circle I could no longer see where they were gathering up the scenery and putting it away.

Even at the circle there were no cars, and past the circle I cut into the Tappan Zee approach, and then, crossing it, down onto the Thruway. Never before had I seen the Tappan Zee approach without traffic, without the endless stream of heavy trucks thundering to and from it, yet tonight the road was empty—and I had a sudden stab of fear that they might have picked up the Thruway as they had picked up the connecting road back in the foothills. If I thought of them at all, I thought of them as stagehands with a gross, bulky physical sense of humor, stagehands who loved nothing better than the embarrassment of this or that actor; for whatever the stagehand is, he creates nothing and performs nothing, only watches with the knowledge that his only mark of superiority is that he will be there for the next show and the show after that.

But the Thruway was there, alone, empty, as if this night had seven strange hours when all the world slept; and my car alone raced down it, seventy, eighty miles an hour, the wide lanes empty and bright in the moonlight.

I braked to a screaming stop where the tollgate was, but to no purpose. The booths were empty, and there was no one to pay or

360

ask for the toll. Beyond that, where the big complex of the Cross Country Shopping Center had been, was the dry, windblown pumice of the moon; a big strip had been sliced out, rolled up and taken away, a strip that curved around to include the racetrack. But when I reached the city, nothing had been disturbed or moved. Except that mostly the city was dark. Here and there, in this apartment house or that one, a lighted window shone; yet mostly the city was dark and the Major Deegan Expressway was empty— empty all the way to the Triborough Bridge, where there was light but no cars and no toll takers. I came to the East Side Drive and drove downtown, no longer racing, but slowly and all alone, and then I left the drive and crossed through the city streets where I saw a slow-moving prowl car but nothing else alive or moving. I felt an impulse to drive up alongside the prowl car and tell them or let them tell me; but I knew it was wrong to do that.

I went where I knew I would go—to the Mummers', where I had been a member for thirty-three years. I drove down Lexington Avenue to Gramercy Park, and there was a parking space directly in front of the club. I had been so anxious that it might be dark, as almost every other building was, but no, not at all; it was well-lit, and the door was opened by old Simon, the doorman, who welcomed me gravely and took my hat and coat as if this night were no different from any other night and said very quietly:

"There are quite a few members here, sir—mostly down in the bar. We are still serving in the dining room, nothing very spectacular but sandwiches and hot soup."

"That's odd," I remarked. "Dining room at this hour."

"Well, it's an odd night, sir. You will admit that."

"Quite odd. Yes, indeed."

I went downstairs to the bar, which was quite crowded, and at the pool table half a dozen members sipped beer and seriously watched a serious game of pool. I don't know why, but it was always the thing to have beer if you watched at the pool table, only I had never remarked on it before. I did now, thinking what an excellent setting for a first act this would make. I don't remember that anyone had ever staged the first act of a play as the basement at the Mummers', yet there was no one in the theater—no male person, that is—who had not spent at least an evening here. The game was between Jerry Goldman and Steve Cunningham, both of them hustlers of a sort and good enough to make a living off it if they had to. I watched them for a moment or two, nodding to old acquaintances, and then I edged into the bar between Jack Finney and Bert Avery, the stage designer, and asked Robert, the bartender, for a double rye whiskey over ice.

"Old Overhalt?" Robert asked.

"That will do nicely."

Finney was quietly drunk. He greeted me gently and politely; he was a great Irish gentleman with the blood of kings in his veins, like all Irishmen whom one loves, and a splendid character actor. Bert Avery asked me if I had just driven down from Connecticut.

"Yes. Thank heavens I am here. It was cold and lonely up there."

"Were they taking it up?"

"Yes—from the hillsides, you know, and then behind me on the Saw Mill River Parkway. They had taken out most of New Rochelle, from the shopping center right back in."

"Irv Goldstein flew up from Miami," Finney said sadly. "His was the last flight. They had taken up most of Florida. I've had good times in Miami; some don't like it, but I always have, for it is a fine place of loose-living, easy-going people. But it is flat, you know, oh, devilishly flat, and Goldstein says that they were rolling it up from the north, just nasty and uncaring, the whole length of the state rolled up like an old piece of carpet."

"Goldstein said it looked like the moon underneath," Bert Avery added, "with craters and things like that that had been covered over, I guess the way you have a lousy floor on a stage so you carpet it, and what the hell, it's a few hundred dollars more, and that's not going to make the difference between closing first night or running for a decent while."

"You are a fine manager," said Finney. "You are a gentleman at it. It is an honor to work for you."

Robert came over with another whiskey sour for Bert Avery, listened to the last of our conversation, and then asked whether we did not think that they might be putting it away and saving it for another performance.

"Somewhere else?" I thought about it for a moment. "Then they would be changing the cast, wouldn't they?"

"That's very sad, sir."

"The kids come to the theater with joy," Finney observed, "but in all truth it's a sad profession. One day you look up at the scenery, and it looks just as shoddy as all hell, and damnit, you say to yourself, has it always been this way, or is it turning lousy or is it inside of my own aching head?''

"All of them," Avery agreed.

I finished my drink and went over to the pool table where Steve Cunningham was making one of those damned impossible cushion shots and no one was even breathing.

Of course, people never behave the way you expect them to, and these were all people who knew about it, and as a matter of fact, there was Goldstein standing very close to Cunningham, his eyes fixed upon the ball as if nothing in the whole world was as important as gauging the angle of ball to cushion and ball to side pocket; and yet they all had relatives, children, wives, brothers, sisters, mothers, fathers; but against all of that, the same thing had apparently brought them here as had brought me.

Cunningham made his shot, perfectly, ball to cushion to pocket, and there was a whisper of approval but no applause. I nudged Goldstein.

"Hungry?"

He nodded.

"They have soup and sandwiches upstairs, I hear."

"All right."

We climbed the stairs to the dining room, picking a quiet corner table. The room wasn't empty, but then neither was it crowded— oh, maybe a dozen members eating or simply relaxed and talking. One of them had lit a cigar, and I saw Goldstein frowning in disapproval. I agreed with him. There was an unwritten rule that while a cigarette or a pipe was proper at the table, cigars were to be taken to the lounge where one could have coffee or brandy or whatever one wished. I saw no reason to break the custom tonight, and I guess we were both rather pleased when one of the waiters came over and whispered something to the member, who then nodded and put the cigar out. Our own waiter said to us:

"I'm afraid there's very little choice at this point. The soup is canned. We have ham sandwiches or ham and Swiss, but only white bread, which you can have toasted. We also have some Canadian cheddar and Bath Biscuits. And the coffee is very good, sir. We keep making it freshly."

"I'll have the cheese and biscuits," I said.

"And you, Mr. Goldstein?"

"The same—yes. Would you have any Italian coffee?"

"I'm afraid not, Mr. Goldstein. You know, we make it only for dinner."

He left for the food, and Goldstein said, smiling slightly, "You know, we're good actors. All of us. Naturally, there's a difference between the dilettante and the professional, but we're all quite good, don't you think?"

"I never thought of it quite that way."

"No, of course not. But this thing of Italian coffee only for dinner—well, now!"

"Yes, oh, yes," I agreed. "I hear you flew up from Miami."

"Yes. Very good flight. Very smooth. I dislike flying, but this was very smooth."

"Vacation?"

"No, no indeed. You know, I thought I would do one of those Jewish comic-tragic things about a Miami Beach hotel. You know the kind of thing, mostly schmaltz and bad jokes and maybe two percent validity so your audience will shed a tear or two if they're in the right mood. It's very much my line, and having done one on a Second Avenue restaurant and two on the Garment District, I find it the path of least resistance. Oh, it's not playwriting in your terms, but it does want a bit of skill and a bit of staging, and there's never been a good one about Miami. I found some delicious stuff—" His voice trailed away.

"And on the way back they were rolling up Florida?"

"Yes."

"It must have been an odd thing to see. From the air, I mean."

"Damned odd. Oh, yes. I mean, it was like an old piece of carpet. You know, at twenty-five thousand feet your whole scale changes."

"I wonder what they'll do with New York?"

"I suppose it's been done already in some places—I mean Rome or London or even Boston. You drove in from New England, I hear. Boston?"

I shook my head. "We could call someone—"

"No one does. You know how you can never get at a phone on a busy day. All four of them are yours to choose from."

"I just don't like to think that they'll roll it up."

"No. I can see that."

"They might move it aside somewhere."

"I'd like to think so. You were born in Maine, weren't you?"

I nodded.

"Well, I'm the third generation born right here in the city. I hate to think that it will be all smashed up."

"We're simply being sentimental. That's no use, is it?"

"No use at all."

The waiter brought our food. The cheese was good and I've always liked Bath Biscuits, and I was hungry; but Goldstein barely touched his food. He sat in silence for a while, and then he said:

"I get a bit indignant over it, and then I remember our profession. We have no right to be indignant over it, have we?"

"You know, I read a good bit of history," I replied, "and the people of the theater always occupied a very special position. A place of privilege, you might say. Oh, I don't mean that there weren't times when they were looked down upon, and respectability was never truly a part of it; but they always had a path of privilege. They were a sort of class apart from all other classes and they hobnobbed with kings and dukes and all that sort of thing. It gave them a rather distorted view of themselves—oh, all of them, writers, scenic designers, stagehands, actors—and they would find it blurring. You know what I mean—which is the play and which is for real. Am I asleep and dreaming that I am awake, or is it the other way around?"

"Yes, I've had the feeling," Goldstein agreed.

"You've acted?"

"The coffee's delicious," Goldstein said, tasting it. "Yes—when I was a kid. I had three years of summer theater and road show. I know exactly what you mean. You look at the footlights, and there's nothing there but that blur of light, and then your eyes adjust and you see them out there and there's that moment of confusion as to place and part." He closed his eyes a moment, and then he went on, "You don't mind if I go back downstairs. I really think that Cunningham will take Jerry. It never happened before and the money on Cunningham is very attractive. Will you come along?"

I shook my head. Goldstein signed for both of us and then left, and after I sat for a while, I decided to go upstairs to the library. The Mummers' is very old, and the library is still full of overstuffed leather chairs and nineteenth-century portraits. There were five members there, all of them the older type and therefore very much like myself. Two of them nodded and the others never looked up from their reading. I dropped into one of the big chairs, trying to think of something I wanted very much to read—but my interest had lagged, and the night had been so long that now finally I felt weary and hardly able to keep my eyes open. I was dozing when I heard the kind of distant crash that might have come from a tall building shaken badly, so that its brickwork and stonework tumbles away; but in that nowhere between sleep and awakeness I might have been dreaming.

I opened my eyes then. The other members were still absorbed in their reading.

I leaned back and allowed myself to doze off again. How annoyed I would have been if anyone had done that during a scene of one of my plays! Yet I always had a nod of sympathy for the older folks, many of them lifelong devotees of the theater, who nevertheless caught forty winks during the intermission, when the set was being changed.

24
The Egg

I T was fortunate, as everyone acknowledged, that Souvan-167-arc
II was in charge of the excavation, for even though he was an
archaeologist, second rank, his hobby or side interest was the
eccentricities of social thinking in the latter half of the twentieth
century. He was not merely a historian, but a man whose curiosity
took him down the small bypaths that history had forgotten.
Otherwise the egg would not have received the treatment it did.

The dig was in the northern part of a place which in ancient time
had been called Ohio, a part of a national entity then known as the
United States of America. The nation was of such power that it had
survived three atomic fire sweeps before its disintegration, and it
was thereby richer in sealed refuges than any other part of the
world. As every schoolchild knows, it is only during the past century
that we have arrived at any real understanding of the ancient social
mores that functioned in the last decades of the previous era. A gap
of three thousand years is not easily overcome, and it is quite
natural that the age of atomic warfare should defy the comprehension of normal human beings.

Souvan had spent years of research in calculating the precise place
of his dig, and although he never made a public announcement of
the fact, he was not interested in atomic refuges but in another,
forgotten manifestation of the times. They were times of death, a
quantity of death such as the world had never known before, and
therefore times of great opposition to death—cures, serums,
antibodies, and—what was Souvan's particular interest—a method
of freezing.

Souvan was utterly fascinated by this question of freezing. It
would appear, so far as he could gather from his researches, that in

the beginning of the latter half of the twentieth century, great strides had been made in the quick-freezing of human organs and even of whole animals; and the simplest of these animals had been thawed and revived. Certain doctors had conceived the notion of freezing human beings who were suffering from incurable diseases, and then maintaining them in cold stasis until such a date when a cure for the particular disease might have been discovered. Then, theoretically, they would have been revived and cured. While the method was available only to the rich, several hundred thousand people had taken advantage of it—although there was no record of anyone ever being revived and cured—and whatever centers had been built for this purpose were destroyed in the fire storms and in the centuries of barbarism and wilderness that had followed.

Souvan had, however, found a reference to one such center, built during the last decade of the atomic age, deep underground and supposedly with compressors functioning by atomic power. His years of work were now drawing toward consummation. They had sunk their shaft one hundred feet into the lava-like wasteland that lay south of the lake, and they had reached the broken ruins of what was certainly the installation they sought. They had cut into the ancient building, and now, armed with powerful beacons, laser-cutters, and plain pickaxes, Souvan and the students who had assisted him were moving through the ruin, from hall to hall, room to room.

His research and expectations had not played him false. The place was precisely what he had expected it to be, an institution for the freezing and preservation of human beings.

They entered chamber after chamber where the refrigeration caskets lay row upon row, like the Christian catacombs of a barely remembered past, but the power that drove the compressors had failed three millenniums ago and even the skeletons in the bottom of the caskets had crumbled to dust.

"So goes man's dream of immortality," Souvan thought to himself, wondering who these poor devils had been and what their last thoughts were as they lay down to be frozen, defying that most elusive of all things in the universe, time itself. His students were chattering with excitement, and while Souvan knew that this would be hailed as one of the most important and exciting discoveries of his time, he was nevertheless deeply disappointed. Somewhere, somehow, he had hoped to find a well-preserved body, and with the

368

aid of their medicine, compared to which the medicine of the twentieth century was rather primitive, restore it to life and thereby gain at firsthand an account of those mysterious decades when the human race, in a worldwide fit of insanity, had turned upon itself and destroyed not only 99 percent of mankind but every form of animal and bird life that existed. Only the most fragmentary records of those forms of life had survived, and so much less of the birds than of the animals that those airy, wonderful creatures that rode the winds of heaven were much more the substance of myth than of fact.

But to find a man or a woman—one articulate being who might shed light upon the origin of the fire storms that the nations of mankind had loosed upon each other—that was Souvan's cherished dream, now shattered. Here and there important parts of skeletons remained intact, a skull with marvelous restoration work on the teeth—Souvan was in awe of the technical proficiency of these ancient men—a femur, a foot, and in one casket, strangely enough, a mummified arm. All this was fascinating and important, but of absolutely no consequence compared to the possibilities inherent in his shattered dream.

Yet Souvan was thorough. He led his students through the ruins, and they missed nothing. Over twelve hundred caskets were examined, and all of them yielded nothing but the dust of time and death. But the very fact that this installation had been constructed so deep underground suggested that it had been built during the latter part of the atomic age. Surely the scientists of that time would have realized the vulnerability of electric power that did not have an atomic source, and unless the historians were mistaken, atomic power was already in use for the production of electricity. But what kind of atomic power? How long could it function? And where had their power plant been located? Did they use water as a cooling agent? If so, the power plant would be on the shore of the lake—a shoreline that had been turned into glass and lava. Possibly they had never discovered how to construct a self-contained atomic unit, one that might provide a flow of power for at least five thousand years. It is true that no such plant had ever been found in any of the ruins, but so much of ancient civilization had been destroyed by the fire storms that only fragments of their culture had survived.

At that moment in his musings, he was interrupted by a cry from one of the students assigned to radiation detection.

"We have radiation, sir."

Not at all unusual in a ground-level excavation; most unusual so deep in the earth.

"What count?"

"Point 003—very low."

"All right," Souvan said. "Take the lead and proceed slowly."

There was only one chamber left to examine, a laboratory of sorts. Strange how the bones perished but machinery and equipment survived! Souvan walked behind the radiation detector, the students behind them—all moving very slowly.

"It's atomic power, sir—point 007 now—but still harmless. I think that's the unit, there in the corner, sir."

A very faint hum came from the corner, where a large, sealed unit was connected by cable to a box which was about a foot square. The box, constructed of stainless steel, and still gleaming here and there, emitted an almost inaudible sound.

Souvan turned to another of his students. "Analysis of the sounds, please."

The student opened a case he carried, set it on the floor, adjusted his dials, and read the results. "The unit's a generator," he said with excitement. "Atomic-powered, sealed, rather simple and primitive, but incredible. Not too much power, but the flow is steady. How long has it been since this chamber was last entered?"

"Three thousand years."

"And the box?"

"That poses some problems," the student said. "There appears to be a pump, a circulating system, and perhaps a compressor. The system is in motion, which would indicate refrigeration of some sort. It's a sealed unit, sir."

Souvan touched the box. It was cold, but no colder than other metal objects in the ruins. Well insulated, he thought, marveling again at the technical genius of these ancients. "How much of it," he asked the student, "do you estimate is devoted to the machinery?"

Again the student worked at his dials and studied the fluttering needles of his sound detector. "It's hard to say, sir. If you want a guess, I would say about eighty percent."

"Then if it does contain a frozen object, it's a very small one, isn't it?" Souvan asked, trying to keep his voice from trembling with eagerness.

"A very small one, yes, sir."

The Egg

Two weeks later Souvan spoke to the people on television. The people were simply the people. With the end of the great atomic fire storms of three thousand years past had come the end of nations and races and tongues. The handful of people who survived gathered together and intermarried among themselves, and out of their tongues came a single language, and in time they spread over the five continents of the earth; and now there were half a billion of them. Once again there were wheatfields, forests and orchards, and fish in the sea. But no song of birds and no cry of any beast; of those, no single one had survived.

"Yet we know something of birds," Souvan said, somewhat awed at speaking for the first time over the worldwide circuit. He had already told them of his calculations, his dig, and his find. "Not a great deal, unfortunately, for no picture or image of a bird survived the fire storms. Yet here and there we were rewarded with a book that mentioned birds, a line of verse, a reference in a novel. We know that their habitat was the air, where they soared on out-stretched wings, not as our airplanes fly with the drive of their atomic jets, but as the fish swim, with ease and grace and beauty. We know that some of them were small, some quite large, and we know that their wings were covered with downy things called feathers. But what in all truth a bird or a wing or a feather was like, we do not know—except out of the imaginations of our artists who have created so many of their dreams of what birds were.

"Now, in the last room we examined in the strange resurrection place that the ancient people built in America, in the single refrigeration cell that was still operative, we discovered a small ovoid thing which we believe is the egg of a bird. As you know, there has been a dispute among naturalists as to whether any warm-blooded creature could reproduce itself through eggs, as insects and fish do, and that dispute has still not been finally resolved. Many scientists of fine reputation believe that the egg of the bird was simply a symbol, a mythological symbol. Others state just as emphatically that the laying of eggs was the means of reproduction among all birds. Perhaps this dispute will finally be resolved.

"In any case, you will now see a picture of the egg."

A small white thing, perhaps an inch in length, appeared upon the television screens, and the people of the earth looked upon it.

"This is the egg. We have taken the greatest pains in removing it from the refrigeration chamber, and now it rests in an incubator that was constructed for it. We have analyzed every factor that might indicate the proper heat, and now having done what we can do, we must wait and see. We have no idea how long the incubation will take. The machine which was used to freeze it and maintain it was probably the first of its kind ever to be built—perhaps the only one of its kind ever to be built—and certainly its builders planned to freeze the egg for only a very short while, perhaps to test the efficiency of the machine. That a germ of living life remains now, three thousand years later, we can only hope.''

But with Souvan it was more than a hope. The egg had been turned over to a committee of naturalists and biologists, but with his privileges as the discoverer, Souvan was allowed to remain on the scene. His friends, his family saw nothing of him; he remained in the laboratory, had his meals there, and slept on a cot he had fixed up for himself. Television cameras, trained on the tiny white object in its glass incubator, reported to the world on the hour, but Souvan—and the committee of scientists as well—could not tear themselves away. He awakened from his sleep to prowl through the silent corridors and look at the egg. When he slept, he dreamed about the egg. He pored over pictures of artists' conceptions of birds, and he recalled ancient legends of metaphysical beings called angels, wondering whether these had not derived from some species of bird.

He was not alone in his fanatical interest. In a world without boundaries, wars, disease, and to a large degree without hatred, nothing in living man's memory as exciting as the discovery of the egg had ever happened. Millions and millions of viewers watched the egg through their televisions; millions of them dreamed of what the egg might become.

And then it happened. Fourteen days had gone by when Souvan was shaken awake by one of the laboratory assistants.

"It's hatching!" she cried. "Come on, Souvan, it's hatching."

In his nightclothes, Souvan raced to the incubator room, where the naturalists and biologists had already gathered about the incubator. Amid the hubbub of their voices, he heard the pleas of the cameramen to allow some space for pictures; but he ignored this as he pushed through to see for himself.

It was happening. The shell of the egg was already cracked, and as he watched, a tiny beak pecked its way free, to be followed by a little ball of downy yellow feathers. His first response was one of intense disappointment; was this then the bird? This tiny shapeless ball of life that stood on two tiny legs, barely able to walk and obviously unable to fly? Then reason and scientific training reassured him that the infant need not resemble the adult, and that the very fact of life emerging from the ancient frozen egg was more miracle than he had ever known in his lifetime.

Now the naturalists and biologists took over. They had already determined, piecing together every fragment of information they possessed and using their own wit as well, that the diet of most birds must have consisted of grubs and insects, and they had all the various possible diets ready—so that they might discover which was most congenial to the tiny yellow fluff. They worked with instinct and prayer, and fortunately they found a diet acceptable to the infant bird before it perished of indigestion.

For the next several weeks the world and Souvan observed the most wonderful thing they had ever experienced, the growth of a little chick into a beautiful yellow songbird. It moved from incubator into a cage and then into a larger cage, and then one day it spread its wings and made its first attempt at flight. Almost half a billion people cheered it, but of this the bird knew nothing. It sang, tentatively at first, and then more and more strongly. It sang its trilling little song, and the world listened with more excitement and interest than it gave to any one of the many great symphony orchestras.

They built a larger cage, a cage thirty feet high and fifty feet long and fifty feet wide, and they set the cage in the midst of a park; and the bird flew and sang and circled the cage like a darting ball of sunlight. By the millions, people came to the park to see the bird with their own eyes. They came across continents, across the broad seas—from the farthest reaches of the world, they came to see the bird.

And perhaps the lives of some of them were changed, even as Souvan's life had been changed. He lived now with dreams and memories of a world that once had been, of a world where these airy, dancing feathered things were a commonplace, where the sky was filled with their darting, swooping, dancing forms. What an unending joy it must have been to live with them! What ecstasy to look at them from one's front door, to watch them, to hear their trilling songs from morning to nightfall! He often went to the park—so often that it interfered with his work—to push his way slowly through the enormous crowds until he was near enough to see the tiny dancing bit of sunlight that had returned to the world from aeons past. And one day, standing there, he looked up at the broad blue reaches of the sky, and then he knew what he must do.

He was a world figure by now, so it was not difficult for him to get an audience with the council. He stood before the august body of one hundred men and women who managed the business of life on earth, and the chairman, a venerable, white-bearded old man of more than ninety years, said to him:

"We will hear you, Souvan."

He was nervous, uneasy—as who would not be to stand before the council—but he knew what he must say and he forced himself to say it.

"The bird must be set free," Souvan said.

There was silence—minutes of silence—before a woman rose and asked, not unkindly, "Why do you say that, Souvan?"

"Perhaps—perhaps because, without being egotistical, I can claim a special relationship to the bird. In any case, it has entered into my life and my being, and it has given me something I never had before."

"Possibly so with all of us, Souvan."

"Possibly, and then you will know what I feel. The bird had been with us for more than a year now. The naturalists I have discussed this with believe that so small a creature cannot live very long. We live by a rule of love and brotherhood. We give for what we receive. The bird has given us one of the most precious of gifts, a new sense of the wonder of life. All we can give it in return is the blue sky—the place it was meant for. That is why I suggest that the bird should be set free."

Souvan left, and the council talked among themselves, and the next day its decision was announced to the world. The bird would be set free. They gave an explanation simply, using the few words that Souvan had spoken.

Thus there came a day, not too long after this, when half a million people thronged the hills and valleys of the park where the cage was, and half a billion more watched their television screens.

Souvan was close to the cage; he had no need for one of the thousand pairs of binoculars trained upon the cage. He watched as

374

the roof of the cage was rolled back, and then he watched the bird.

It stood upon its perch, singing with all its heart, a torrent of sound from the tiny throat. Then, somehow, it became aware of freedom. It flew, first in the cage, then in circles, mounting higher and higher until it was only a bright flicker of sunshine—and then it was gone.

"Perhaps it will return," someone close by Souvan whispered.

Strangely, he hoped it would not. His eyes were filled with tears, yet he felt a joy and completeness he had never known before.

25
The Insects

PEOPLE heard about the first transmission in various ways. Although unidentified radio appeals are fairly frequent and not generally subject to any general new dissemination—being more or less of oddities and often the work of cranks—they are not jealously guarded. The interesting part of this signal was that it had been repeated at least two dozen times and had been picked up in various parts of the world in various languages, in Russian in Moscow, in Chinese in Peking, in English in New York and London, in Swedish in Stockholm. In all these various places it was on the high-frequency band, somewhat less than twenty-five megacycles.

We heard about it from Fred Goldman, who runs the monitor room for the National Broadcasting Company, when he and his wife dined with us early in May. He has his ear to things; he listens to the whole damn world breathing in half a dozen languages, and he likes to drop things, like a ship at sea pleading for help and then silence and not one word in the press, or a New Orleans combination playing the latest hard rock—if such a thing is possible—in Yarensk, which is somewhere in the tundra of Northern Siberia, or any other of a dozen incongruous daily happenings across the radio waves of the earth. But on this night he was rather suppressed and thoughtful, and when he came out with it, it was less odd than reasonable.

"You know," he said, "there was a sort of universal complaint today and we can't pinpoint it."

"Oh?"

My wife poured drinks. His own wife looked at him sharply, as if this was the first she had heard of it and she resented being put on parity with us.

"Good, clear signal," he said. "High frequency. Queer voice though—know what it said?"

There was another couple there—the Dennisons; he was a rather important surgeon—and Mrs. Dennison made a rather inept attempt at humor. I try to remember her first name, but it escapes me. She was a slim, beautiful blond woman, but not very bright; yet she managed to turn it on Fred and he retreated. We tried to persuade him, but he turned the subject away and became a listener. It wasn't until after dinner that I pinned him down.

"About that signal?"

"Oh, yes."

"You've become damn sensitive."

"Oh, I don't know. Nothing very special or mysterious. A voice said, 'You must stop killing us'."

"Just that?"

"It doesn't surprise you?" Fred asked.

"Oh, no—hardly. As you said, it's a sort of universal plea. I can think of at least seven places on earth where those would be the most important words they could broadcast."

"I suppose so. But it did not originate in any of those places."

"No? Where, then?"

"That's it," Fred Goldman said. "That's just it."

That's how I heard about it first. I put it out of mind as I imagine so many others did, and the truth is that I forgot about it. Two weeks later I delivered the second lecture in the Goddard Free Series at Harvard, and during the question period one student demanded:

"What is your own reaction, Dr. Cornwall, to the curtain of silence the Establishment has thrown around the radio messages?"

I was naive enough to ask what messages he referred to, and a ripple of laughter told me that I was out of it.

" 'You must stop killing us'. Isn't that it, Dr. Cornwall?" the boy shouted, and more applause greeted this than I had gotten on my own. "Isn't that the crux of it?" the student went on. " 'You must stop killing us'—isn't that it?"

I took a brandy afterward with Dr. Fleming, the dean, in front of the fire of his own warm and comfortable study, and he mentioned that the university did a certain amount of monitoring of sorts.

"The kids weren't too disturbing, were they?" he asked.

I assured him that I agreed with them. "We're both Establishment of sorts," I said, "so I don't want to wriggle out of it. But isn't that the radio signal? A friend of mine was telling me something about it. Did it come across again?"

"Every day now," the dean said. "The kids have taken it up as a sort of battle cry."

"But I saw nothing in the papers."

"That's curious, isn't it?" Fleming said. "I suppose some wraps are being put on it in Washington, although I can't imagine why."

"They couldn't locate the source the first day."

"We've tried on our own, and they've tried even harder over at M.I.T. It's plaintive enough, but of what import I don't know. Only the student body is very hot about it."

"So I noticed," I agreed.

A few days later at breakfast my wife informed me that she had lunched the previous day with Rhoda Goldman. The information was dropped like a small, careful bomb.

"Go on," I said with great interest.

"You'll pooh-pooh it."

"Try me."

"They have some background on the signals down at the station. Or at least they think they have."

"Oh?"

"They think they know who is sending them."

"Thank God for that. Maybe we can stop killing them—or stop whoever is doing the killing. It's the most God-awful plaintive thing I ever heard of."

"No."

"No?"

"I said no, we can't stop," my wife replied very seriously, "because it's the insects."

"What?"

"That's what Rhoda Goldman said—insects. They are sending the messages."

"I am pooh-poohing it," I agreed.

"I knew you would," my wife said.

I have been on four of the mayor's special committees, and the following day his assistant called and asked me whether I would serve on another. However, he refused to spell out the purpose, except to say that it was connected with the high-frequency messages.

"Surely you've heard of them," he said.

I agreed that I had heard of them and I agreed to serve on the committee, chiefly out of curiosity. The day I went downtown for the meeting of the new committee was the same day that General Carl de Hargod, the new chief of staff, had arrived in New York to address a dinner group at the Waldorf; and now he was being welcomed at City Hall by both the mayor and about a thousand pickets. The pickets were a conglomeration of pacifist groups and hippies, and they marched back and forth in front of City Hall in silence, carrying signs which read: "You must stop killing us."

I had arrived early enough to get inside just before the welcoming ceremonies began, and when I joined the others of the newly formed committee I listened to an apology for the mayor's absence and an assurance that he would be with us within the half hour. There were five others on the committee, three men and two women. I knew both women, Kate Gordon, who was Commissioner of Health, and Alice Kinderman, who was associated with the Museum of Natural History and newly named consultant to the Parks Department, and one of the men—Frank Meyers, a lawyer with important contacts in Washington. Meyers introduced me to the others, Basehart, who was the head of the Department of Entomology in the huge City University, and Krummer, from the Department of Agriculture in Washington.

It was the presence of the entomologist that bounced off my mind incredulously, and when Meyers asked me whether I knew what we had been gathered together for, I replied only that it had something to do with the radio signals.

"The point is, we know who is sending them."

"*What is*," Alice Kinderman amended. "*Who is* is rather disturbing."

"I don't believe it," I said. "I prefer the communists."

"We have been killing a good many communists," Basehart agreed, with that curious detachment of a scientist. "I'm sure they don't like it. Well, no one likes to be killed, do they? This time it's the insects, however."

"Fudge!" said Kate Gordon.

Then we talked about it, calmly, in a manner befitting the six middle-aged, civilized men and women that we were, and if there were doubters among us, Basehart convinced them. He convinced

380

me. He was a small, long-nosed man with electric blue eyes and an exciting smile. Anyone could see that what had happened was, so far as he was concerned, the most wonderful and exciting thing that had ever happened, and as he explained it, the preposterous disappeared and the inevitable took over. He convinced us that it had been inevitable all along. The only thing he could not persuade us to do was to share his enthusiasm.

"It's so logical," he maintained. "The insect is not a thing in itself but a fragment. The hive is the thing. Insects don't think in our terms; they don't have brains. At best they have something that might be thought of as one of these printed circuits we make for mass-produced radios. They are cells, not organs. But does the hive think? Does the swarm think? Does the city of insects think? That's the question we have never been able to answer satisfactorily. And what of the super-swarm? We have always known that they communicate with each other and with the swarm or the hive. But how? Radio? Certainly some sort of wave—and why not high frequency?"

"Power?" someone asked.

"Power. My goodness—have you any notion as to how many of them there are? Of species alone—almost half a million. Of individuals—beyond our ability to compute. They could generate any power required. Accomplish any task—if of course they come together into the theoretical super-hive or super-swarm and become conscious of themselves. And it appears they have. You know, we've always killed them, but now perhaps too many of them. They have a great instinct for survival."

"And we seem to have lost ours somewhere along the line, haven't we?" I wondered.

The mayor had too many responsibilities, too many problems in a city that was close to unmanageable, and it was difficult to say how seriously he took the plea of the insects. People in public life tend to become defensive about such things. I had lectured often enough on questions of social ecology to know how difficult it was to impress political leadership with the possibility that we may just be working ourselves out of a liveable future.

"We have just had to arrest over a hundred pacifists," the mayor said tiredly, "most of them from good families—which means I will not sleep tonight, and since I had only an hour or two last night, I think you will understand my reluctance, ladies and gentlemen, to become excited about radio messages sent by insects. I give it

381

credence only because the Department of Agriculture insists that I do—and so I ask you to please serve on this very ad hoc committee and draw up a report on the matter. We are allocating five thousand dollars for clerical assistance, and we have also been promised the full cooperation of the Ford Foundation."

The mayor could not remain with us, but we spent another half hour chatting about the matter, arranged for our next meeting, and then went our several ways. Belief in the absurd is not very tenacious, and I think that by the time our meeting broke up, we had put away the insects under a solid cover of doubt. With many pressures, I had half forgotten the matter by dinnertime, when my wife asked me pertly:

"Well, Alan—what will you do about the insects?"

When I did not answer immediately, my wife informed me that she had been on the phone that afternoon for almost an hour with her sister, Dorothy, from Upper Montclair, and that they were taking it very seriously indeed. In fact, Dorothy's son, a physics major at M.I.T., had worked out the electronics—or the physics; she couldn't say for certain—underlying the high-frequency signals.

"He's a bright boy," I said.

"And that's a very enlightening comment."

"Well, the mayor formed a committee. I have the honor to be a part of it."

"That's just what I adore most about our handsome mayor," Jane said. "He does have a committee for everything, doesn't he? I'm sure his conscience is clear now—"

"Good heavens," I said, "must he have a conscience about this too—"

I never finished my defense of a poor, harassed man. The telephone rang. It was Bert Clegmann, who was one of the editors of *The New York Times* and whom I knew slightly, and he informed me that they had decided to break the story in their morning edition, since it had already appeared in London and in Rome, and could I tell him anything about the committee?

I told him about the committee, and then I asked him my question.

"Do I believe it?" Clegmann said. "Well, thank heavens I don't have to put my own opinion on the line. There's apparently enough background now for us to quote some eminent people, and the

Russians are taking it seriously enough to raise it in the UN. Next week. Also, the little buggers have eaten three thousand four hundred contiguous acres of wheat in eastern Nebraska. Clean as a whistle. That may simply be a coincidence."

"What little buggers?"

"Locusts."

"Well, isn't that a very old business—I mean they always seem to be devouring something somewhere don't they?"

But I couldn't get any commitment from Clegmann. He always felt that he was the articulation of the *Times,* so as to speak, and very wary, but that made him no different from most. It was much too great a strain to believe.

"If you are on a committee," my wife said, "then you must believe it."

"I think that part of the work of the committee is to test the validity of the whole thing."

"Doesn't anyone on the committee believe it?"

"Basehart, perhaps. He's an entomologist."

"I feel silly," my wife said, smiling, "but I have been watching the water bugs. They're such huge, dreadful things anyway—I mean even when they don't resent being killed. But what a horrible thought! We simply take it for granted that anything not human doesn't resent being killed."

At our first formal committee meeting Krummer, the Department of Agriculture man, touched on the same theme, but he was rather acid-tongued about the humanists. After outlining the new program they had set up in Washington, a three-pronged drive, as he put it, insecticides, poison gas, and radiation, he touched on the position of those sensitive people who held that perhaps we killed too easily.

"Can anyone imagine the disaster that would strike mankind if we should give the insects a free hand! Worldwide starvation—not to mention disease and a matter of discomfort."

He went on to paint a rather ghastly picture, to which only Basehart objected, and mildly at that. Basehart pointed out that man had existed before the time of insecticides and had fed himself very nicely.

"There is a natural balance to this kind of thing—an ecological whole. Insects eat each other and birds eat insects and certain

383

animals join in, and even nature in some mysterious way restrains any part of the circle that gets out of hand. But we have killed the birds without mercy and now we are trying to kill the insects, and we keep chopping pieces out of that ecological circle and heaven knows where it will end."

But the main fact presented to the committee was that the high-frequency messages had stopped, and once that visible manifestation of so unnatural a desire as survival had ceased, the party of doubt took over and proceeded to prove that the public had been hoaxed. Since aside from the single fact of devastation in Nebraska there had been no noticeable change in insect behavior anywhere on earth, the fact of a hoax took hold very readily. We appointed Frank Meyers as a one-man subcommittee to investigate the pros and cons of the matter and to report back to us in two weeks.

"This," I explained to my wife, "is the normal process of a committee—not to find but to lose. We shall lose this crisis in very short order."

"In two weeks we are leaving for Vermont," my wife said.

"We'll adjourn for the summer," I assured her. "That too is the normal business of committees."

When we reconvened two weeks later, both Krummer and Meyers delivered reassuring reports.

With great delight Krummer told us that the Pentagon had joined forces with the Department of Agriculture to produce an insecticide so deadly that a quart of it turned into a fine spray would kill any and all insects in a square mile. However, it was almost as deadly to animal and human existence—a matter they hoped to solve in very short order. But Meyers thought it was all to little purpose.

"The people at the C.I.A.," he said, "are just about decided that the Russians are responsible for the high-frequency hoax. They have secret transmitters all over the place, and it's a part of their overall plan to sow fear and discord in the Free World. More to the point, knowing they had blown it, *Pravda* yesterday published a long article blaming it on us. I have also interviewed twenty-three leading naturalists, and all except one agreed that the notion of a collective insect intelligence on a par with the intelligence of man is preposterous."

"Of course, our work isn't wasted," Krummer said. "I mean, a new insecticide is worth its weight in gold, and since it will in its present form kill men as readily as insects, it joins our arsenal of secret weapons. It's an excellent example of how the various sciences tend to overlap, and I think we can salute it as a vital part of the American Way.''

"Who was the scientist who did not agree?" I asked.

"Basehart here," Meyers said.

Basehart smiled modestly and replied, "I don't think I can properly be counted, since I am a member of the committee. Which makes the scientific opinion unanimous. Or at least I think that is how it should go into the record."

"You still think it was the insects?" Mrs. Kinderman asked.

"Oh, yes. Yes, indeed."

"Why?"

"Only because it's logical and exciting," said Basehart, "and you know the Russians are so utterly dreary and unimaginative—they would never think of such an idea, not in a thousand years."

"But a collective intelligence," I objected. "I dislike the word preposterous—but surely rather unbelievable."

"Not at all," Basehart replied, almost apologetically. "It's a concept quite familiar to entomologists, and we have discussed it for generations. I will admit that we use it pragmatically when we run out of more acceptable explanations, but there are so many things about the social insects that do not submit to any other explanation. Naturally, we are dealing here with a far more developed and complex intelligence—but who is to say that this is not a perfectly legitimate line of evolution? We are like little children in our understanding of the manner of evolution, and as for its purpose, why, we haven't even begun to inquire."

"Oh, come now," said Kate Gordon, or snorted would be more descriptive, "you are becoming positively teleological, Dr. Basehart, and among scientists I think that is indefensible."

"Oh?" But Basehart did not desire to battle. "Perhaps." He nodded. "Yet some of us cannot help being just a bit teleological. One doesn't always surmount one's childhood religious training."

"Intellectually, one must," said Kate Gordon primly.

"Basehart," I said, "suppose we were to accept this intelligence, not as a reality, but as a matter for discussion. Should we have cause to fear it? Would it be malignant?"

"Malignant? Oh, no—not at all. That has never been my notion of intelligence. Evil is mediocre and rather stupid. No, wisdom is not a malignancy, quite to the contrary. But whether or not we have to fear them—well, that's something else entirely. I mean, we have not come back with a single response. Oh, I don't mean us on this committee. I talk of mankind. Mankind moved only in two directions, to convince itself that an insect intelligence did not exist and to make a new insecticide. But they ask us to stop killing them. What are they to do?"

"Come now"—Meyers laughed—"aren't we playing the game too well? We have a committee of sincere and interested citizens, and I don't think we have shirked the problem. I move that we adjourn now and reconvene in September."

The motion was seconded and carried.

Driving up to our summer place in Vermont, my wife, Jane, said rather sadly, "If the boy were alive, I wouldn't sleep too well. Do you know, it's three years since he died—and it seems like only yesterday."

"We are beginning a vacation and a rest," I told her, "and I will not countenance this kind of mood."

"It's just that I sometimes feel we have stopped caring. Is it a part of growing old?"

"We still care," I said sharply. But I knew exactly what she meant.

Our summer place is in a wonderful, isolated upland valley, like so many of the upland valleys in Vermont, full of sunny days and cool nights and a starry sky over the green folds of earth. It's a place where time moves differently, and after we are there for a while, we move with the time of the place.

We had occasional company, but not too often or too much, and mostly on the weekends. Town was six miles on a dirt road, and twenty miles away was a fair-sized artist colony with a summer symphony and theater and a great many people to talk to if we got lonely. But our visits there were few, two or three times a summer, and we were rarely lonely in the way people understand loneliness. Down the road about a mile lived our nearest neighbor, an old widower named Glenn Olson, who made honey in the summer and maple sugar in the winter. Both were delicious. His maples were old and strong and his bees worked among the wild flowers in the abandoned pastures.

386

I had been meaning to visit him for both honey and sugar, but put it off from day to day. On the third week the thing happened in the cities. But until then, nothing was very different, only the warm summer days and the birds and the insects humming lazily in the hot air. We could have forgotten the whole thing if only we had disbelieved; but somewhere in both of us was a nugget of belief. We had a postcard from Basehart, who was in the Virgin Islands, where he was cataloguing species and types of insects. The postcard ended with a rather sentimental good-by. Neither my wife nor I remarked on that because, as I said, we had a nugget of belief.

And of course, then, toward the beginning of the summer, the cities died.

There had been a great deal of speculation about the insects and what they might do if they were as some thought. Articles were written, books rushed into print, and even films were planned. There were nightmare things about super-insects, armies of ants, winged devils; but no one anticipated the simple directness of the fact. The insects simply moved against the cities to begin it. Apparently a single intelligence controlled all the movements of the insects, and the millions who perished made no great difference to the survival of the intelligence. They filled the aqueducts and stopped the flow of water. They short-circuited the wires and halted the flow of electricity. They ate the food in the cities and swarmed by the millions over the food coming in. They clogged the valves and intakes of motors and stalled them. They clogged the sewers and they spread disease and the cities died. The insects died by the billions, but this time it was not necessary to kill them. They imposed death on themselves, and the festering, malaria-ridden, plague-ridden cities died with them.

First we watched it happen on television, but the television went very soon. We have a relay tower, and it ceased to function on the third day after the attack on the cities began; after that the picture was so bad as to be meaningless, and a few days later it ceased. We listened to the radio then, until the radio stopped. Then there was the valley as it had always been, and the silence, and the insects hanging in the hot air and the sunlight and the nights.

My own feeling was to drive down to the town, and from day to day I felt that this had to be, but my wife would not have it. Her dread of leaving our place and going to the town was so great that it was not until our food began to run low that she agreed to my going—providing she went with me. Our own telephone had stopped functioning long ago, and it was only after days of not seeing a plane overhead that we realized no planes flew any longer.

Driving down toward town finally, we stopped at Glenn Olson's place, to ask him whether he knew how it was in the village, and perhaps to buy some honey and sugar. We found him in his bedroom, dead—not long dead, perhaps only a day. He had been stung three times on the forearm while he slept. My wife had been a nurse once, and she explained the process whereby three consecutive bee stings would work to kill a man. The air outside was full of bees, humming, working, hanging in the air.

"I think we'll go back to the house," I said.

"We can't leave him like that."

"We can," I said, thinking of how many millions of others were like that.

Olson had a well-stocked cupboard. I filled some bags with canned goods, flour, beans, honey in jars, and maple sugar, and I carried them out to my car, while Jane remained in the house. Then I pulled the blanket over Olson and took Jane by the arm.

"I don't want to go out there," she said.

"Well, we must, you know. We can't stay here."

"I'm afraid."

"But we can't stay here."

Finally I convinced her to come to the car. Her arms were covered and she held a towel over her face, but the bees ignored us. In the car we raised the windows and drove back to our summer place— and then almost ran into our house.

Yet I got over the panic and resisted the temptation to cover myself with mosquito netting. I talked to Jane and finally convinced her that this was not a thing one could avoid or take measures against. It was like the wind, the rain, the sunrise and the sunset. It was happening and nothing we could do would alter it.

"Alan—will it be everyone?" she asked. "Will it be the whole world?"

"I don't know."

"What good would it do them to make it the whole world?"

"I don't know."

"I would not want to live if it were the whole world."

"It's not a question of what we want. It's the way it is. We can only live with it the way it is."

388

Yet when I went out to the car to bring in the supplies we had taken from Olson's place, I had to call upon every shred of courage and strength I possessed.

It was a little better the next day, and by the third day I convinced Jane to leave the house with me and to walk a little. She covered herself at first, but after a while her fear began to dissipate, and then, bit by bit, it became something you live with—as I suppose anything can. The following week I sat down to write this account. I had been working on it for three days. Yesterday a bee lighted on the back of my hand, a large, fuzzy, working bumblebee. I held my hand firmly and looked at the bee, and the bee returned my stare.

Then the bee flew away, and I had a feeling that it was over and that what would happen had happened. But how we will pick it up and what we will put together, I don't know. I talked about it with my wife last night.

"I hope Basehart is alive and well," she said. "It would be nice to see him again." Which was rather curious, since all she knew about Basehart was what I had told her. Then she began to cry. She was not a woman who cries a great deal, and soon she dried her eyes and took up some sewing that she had laid aside weeks before. I lit my pipe. It was the last of the day. We sat there in silence as darkness fell.

"I lit our single kerosene lamp, and she said to me, "We will have to go down to the village sooner or later, won't we?"

"Sooner or later," I agreed.

26
The Sight of Eden

T HEY were in orbit, and it was over. They had crossed the void, leaped all the gaps of time and imagination, and bridged the unbridgeable, and they had been through the seven fires of hell. They were sane, although they had touched all the fringes of insanity. They could smile, although they had known all the profound depths of grief and suicidal profession; and they were alive, although they had flirted with all the varieties of death that boundless space can concoct.

They had come through fear and terror indescribable, and now they could speak about it and to each other. There were seven of them, three women and four men, and they had been locked away in this starship for five interminable years. They were light years from the Planet Earth beyond calculation; they had leaped their ship across the strange curves and tricks of space, played havoc with all the calculus and geometry known to men, and had flung themselves over the void to where the stars clustered thick as grapes on the autumn vines. They had done what they were ordained to do, and what no people from the Planet Earth had ever done before. And now they were in silent, flowing orbit over a planet as blue and green and lovely as the one they had left behind them.

It was something to think about and to crow about. It gave them a sense of themselves that was understandable. It made them look at each other in a certain way as they sat together in the wardroom. They had done it.

For that reason, all the words that could be said to the point were pointless; in five years, all the words had been said; all the reactions had been tested; all the tears had been wept. Now there remained only the fact, and the fact was the planet beneath them, bathed in sunshine, washed with air, and laced with rivers and lakes and lagoons. It was the proof of the universe, all they had ventured their lives and sanity to prove, that life was not limited to the Planet Earth and the Solar System, but was a part of the logic of the universe. The fact was a planet slightly larger than Earth, perhaps of somewhat less density, with a breathable nitrogen-oxygen atmosphere, well-watered and with abundant plant life. Its revolution upon its axis was thirty-two hours; its year, as well as they could calculate, was four hundred and fifteen days. Its Sun was a Sol-type sun, somewhat better than 900,000 miles in diameter and at this moment 112,000,576 miles from the planet it warmed. There were eleven other planets in the system; first this one, the other ten could wait.

Their own orbit time was five hours and sixteen minutes, and since they had gone into orbit to study the planet, their starship had made eight revolutions. This was their final meeting in the wardroom for comparative discussion. It would be a short meeting, and then they would descend.

2

Briggs, the pilot and as much the captain as anyone was captain upon the starship, looked from face to face and said, "Not very much left to talk about, unless someone can come up with a reason not to go down?"

"All the reasons," Frances Rhodes, the physician, nodded. "Bugs, germs, virus, radiation—and none of them hold water." She smiled—and she was lovely then, as they all were in the radiance of their accomplishment. "We'd go down if it was a leper colony, wouldn't we?"

They would have gone down if it were boiling lava under them, because they had endured all the confinement that is endurable and had felt all the nakedness of empty space that men can feel and remain sane.

"I'm not worried about bugs," Carrington, the agronomist, said. "Disease doesn't work that way. Not about radiation either. Something else."

392

Gene Ling, second navigator and Nobel Prize winner, nodded. She was a slender, gentle half-Chinese from San Francisco. "Yes, something else," she said. "No oceans."

"No deserts either," said Carrington.

"No lights in the cities at night," said Gluckman, the engineer.

"If they are cities," McCaffery, the navigator.

"The nights are full of starlight," Briggs thought. "Perhaps they sleep at night. It must be different. Why do we forget how different it must be?"

"They must see us," said Laura Shawn, the biologist. "Why don't they call to us, signal us, come up to us?"

"They?"

"In the scopes, it looks like fairyland," Phillips, second engineer, observed self-consciously. "I don't like that."

"Where was your childhood, Phillips?"

"I don't like it."

"Arms?" Gluckman wanted to know.

"I suppose so," said Briggs uneasily. "Sidearms anyway."

"In fairyland?" Laura Shawn smiled.

But it wasn't as light and pleasant as it seemed, and if it went on this way, Briggs realized, it could top a note of hysteria. They were clinging to reality with a thin hold, and the meeting was pointless and becoming too long.

"We go down now," Briggs said. "Go to your stations."

They were relieved, and they didn't want to talk about it. They went to their stations, and the starship slid down its electromagnetic web until it rode its anti-gravatic tensors a foot above the planet's surface. Then they opened their airlocks and went out.

3

The air was sweet as honey. When the sun shone, it was warm and beneficient and in the shade it was seventy degrees Fahrenheit. They had landed upon a broad meadow, half a thousand acres of meadow where the green grass was cropped an inch high; but when they examined it, they saw that it bent upon itself and controlled and conditioned itself. Through the meadow, winding lazily, a little river took its way, and the banks of the river were lined with a million flowers of red and blue and yellow and every other color. Bees hummed among the flowers and the air was full of their fragrance, and here and there about the meadow was a tree heavy with blue or golden fruit. About a half a mile down the river, a filigree bridge crossed it.

They had been five years in the starship, so at first they just stood and looked and breathed the air. Then some of them sat down on the grass. They all wept a little; that was to be expected. If they had faced danger or horror or the unbelievable, their reaction would have been different. It was the beauty and the peace, almost unendurable, that made them weep. They felt better when they had discharged some of their emotion.

They walked around a little, but mostly they sprawled on the grass and listened to the soft breeze blowing. No one said anything and no one wanted to say anything. A half hour went by, and Briggs said,

"We can't just stay here."

"Why not?" Laura Shawn wanted to know.

They were all thinking, as Briggs also thought, that it was a dream or an illusion or that they were dead. It was a bubble that could burst, they were thinking; and Briggs said,

"Gluckman and Phillips—go into the ship and follow us!"

Then the other five set out on foot, with the great shining starship sliding behind them on its magnetic web. They walked to the filigree bridge, which seemed to be made of crystal lace, and they crossed the river. A little road or pathway, full of dancing light and color, led up and over the brow of a low hill. On the other side of the hill was a garden and in the center of the garden a building that was like a castle in fairyland or a dream, or the laughter of children, if a building can be like the laughter of children.

If the building was like the laughter of children, then the garden was like all the dreams that city children ever dreamed about a garden. It was about a mile square, and as Briggs led them on a winding path through it, it appeared to open endless arms of delight and wonder. There were the fountains. Golden water from one, pink water from another, green water from a third, a rainbow of colors from a fourth—and there were hundreds of fountains, ornamented with dancing, laughing children carved out of stone of as many different shades as the water showed. There were nooks and corners of secret delight. There were benches to rest on that were marvels of beauty and comfort. There were hedges of green and yellow and blue. There were beds of flowers and bold beautiful birds, and there were drinking fountains to quench the thirst of those who used the garden.

Gene Ling bent to drink at one of these. They watched her, but they didn't try to stop her.

"It's water," she said. "Clean and cold."

Then they all drank. They didn't care. Their defenses were crumbling too quickly.

Gluckman brought the starship to rest in front of the building, and all seven of them went inside together. As they entered, music began, and they stopped nervously.

"It's automatic," McCaffery guessed. "Body relay or photo electric."

Their momentary nerves could not contend against the music—an outpouring of sound that vibrated with welcome and assurance and sheer delight—that filled them with a sense of innocence and purity. Wherever they went in the building, the music was with them. They went into an auditorium large enough to hold a thousand people, but empty, and with a great silver screen at one end. They wandered along empty corridors, lined with colorful and masterful murals of naked children at play. They looked into rooms full of couches, where the music made them drowsy almost immediately, and there were other rooms that were dining rooms, play rooms, classrooms—all recognizable and all different. In each case, they sensed that this was how it should be, and in each case, the memories of earth which they used for comparison became crude and senseless and ugly.

They left the building and went back to the starship.

4

With its viewplates open, the starship moved across the planet's surface, a hundred feet above the ground. They saw gardens as beautiful and more beautiful than the one they had been in. They saw forests of old and splendid trees, with colored paths among the trees. They saw mighty amphitheatres that could seat a hundred thousand people and smaller ones too. Buildings of glass and alabaster, pink stone and violet stone, green crystal. They saw groups of buildings that reminded them of the Acropolis of ancient Athens, if the Athenians had but a thousand years more to work and plan for some ultimate beauty. They saw lakes where boats were moored to docks, ready for use, but small boats, pleasure boats. They saw bathing pavilions—or so they surmised—playing fields, arbors, bowers, every structure for beauty and delight that they had ever imagined and a thousand that they had never imagined.

But nowhere did they see a living man, woman or child.

5

After nightfall, after they had eaten, they sat and talked. Their talk went in circles, and it was full of fear and speculation. They had come too far; space had enveloped them, and although their starship hung a thousand feet in the air above a planet as large as the Planet Earth, they felt that they had passed across the edge of nowhere.

"Just suppose," Carrington said, "that all our dreams had taken shape."

"All the memories and wishes of our childhoods," said Frances Rhodes.

"Taken shape," Carrington repeated. "Who knows what the fabric of space is or what it does?"

"It does strange things," Gene Ling, the physicist, agreed.

"Or what thought is," Carrington persisted. "A planet like this one—it's a fairy land—it's the stuff of dreams—all the dreams we brought with us from home, all the longings and desires, and out of our thoughts it was shaped."

"Who was it said, we will make the earth like a garden?"

"Oh, I don't buy any of that," Briggs said, more harshly than was called for, because he found himself leaning toward the madness of their theories. "I don't buy it one bit! It's metaphysical bosh, and you're all falling for it. You don't think a planet into existence."

"How do you know?" Laura Shawn asked dreamily.

"How do I know? I know. I know the fact and the substance of dreams and the fact and the substance of matter, and the two are different!"

"And we trap a curve of space and go from tomorrow into yesterday—is that real?" asked Gene Ling.

"This planet is real," Briggs insisted.

"Without people?"

"Or cities?"

"Industry? You don't spin palaces out of thin air—or do you, Briggs? Where is the industry?"

"Who cultivates it?" Carrington, an agronomist and in mental agony over this. "Who tends a million flower beds? Who fertilizes it? Who plants? Who crops the hedges?"

"And who paints the murals of earth children? And who carves the statues of earth children?"

"Why must they be earth children?" Briggs said slowly and doggedly. "Why must man be a freak of the earth, an accident on one planet out of a billion? Is the sun an accident?"

Carrington said, "I could swear by all we believe in that those flower beds were tended yesterday. Where are the people today?"

"If there is any today—"

"Enough of that," Briggs snapped. "We've seen only a tiny corner of this world. Tomorrow, we'll see more of it. Eight hours sleep won't hurt any of us, and maybe it'll clear some of the metaphysical cobwebs away."

Tomorrow came, and at the speed of five hundred miles an hour, the starship raced across the planet, a thousand feet high. They sat at the viewplates, and looked at gardens and lakes and golden, winding rivers, and palaces and all the joyous beauty that man had ever imagined and so much that he had never imagined. They watched it until it became unbearable in its glowing abundance, and then the sun set. But they saw no people. The world was empty.

That night, they talked again; and when they had talked themselves close to the edge of madness, Briggs ordered them to silence and sleep. But he knew that he was not too far from the edge of madness himself.

6

On the third day, the starship came to rest on the edge of a lake, whose shores were marked with pleasure houses and dream places.

They could think of no other names for the buildings. Phillips and Gluckman remained with the ship; Briggs led the others down to a dock that appeared to be carved out of alabaster, and he selected a boat moored there large enough to hold them all. As they took their places in the boat, it stirred to life with the strange, haunting music of the planet, and the music washed away their fears and their cares, and Briggs saw that they were smiling at some inner fulfillment.

"We could remain here," Laura Shawn said lazily.

Briggs knew what she meant. Five years in the starship had merged all their secrets, all their memories. Laura Shawn was a product of poverty, unhappiness, and finally divorce. Her scientific triumphs had left a string of emotional defeats behind her. She had never been happy before, and Briggs wondered whether any of them had. Yet they were happy now—and he himself, too, for all of his struggle to preserve in himself a fortress of skepticism and wary doubt. Doubt was an anathema in this place.

The boat had a wheel and a lever. The lever gave it motion; the wheel steered it. There was no sign of a propeller; it glided through the water by its own inner force; but this was not disturbing since their own starship rode the waves and currents of magnetism and force that pervaded the universe. So it was, Briggs thought to himself, with all the mysteries and wonders that man had faced from his very beginning; they were miracles and beyond explanation until man discovered the reason, and then in the simplicity and self-evidence of the reason, he could smile at his former fear and superstition. Was this planet any more wonderful or puzzling than the web of force that held the universe in place and order? And when the explanation came, if it ever did, he was certain it would be simple and even obvious.

Meanwhile, he steered the boat across the lake, and as they skirted the shore, building after building welcomed them with music and invited them to its own particular pleasure. He ran the boat through a canal bordered with great, flower-bearing trees, into another lake, where the water was so clear and pure that they could see all the gold and red and purple rocks on the bottom and watch gold and silver fish swimming and darting here and there. Then they entered a winding river, placid and lovely and bucolic, and they had gone a mile or so along this river, when they saw the man.

He stood on a landing place of pink, translucent stone, where there were a circle of carved benches, and he waved to them, almost casually. "Did we also think him into being?" Briggs asked caustically, as he turned the boat toward the dock. They rode to the mooring, and the man helped them out of the boat onto the steps that led up to the dock. He was a tall, well-built man, smiling and pleasant, his brown hair cut in the page-boy style of the olden times on earth. He was of indeterminate middle age, and he wore a robe of some light blue material, belted at the waist.

"Please—join me and make yourselves comfortable," he said to them, his voice warm and rich and his English without an accent. "I am sorry for these three days of bewilderment, but there were things I had to do. Now, if you will sit down here, we can relax for a while and talk about some problems we have in common."

His four companions were speechless; as for Briggs, he could only say, "Well, I'll be damned!"

7

"Call me Smith," he said. "I don't have a name in your sense of the word. Smith will make it easier for you. No you're not dreaming. I am real. You are real. The place we are in is real. There is no reason for fear, believe me. Please sit down."

They sat down on the translucent benches. He answered the thought in their minds.

"No, I am not an Earth Man. Only a man."

"Then you read our minds?" Frances Rhodes wondered, not speaking aloud.

"I read your minds," Smith nodded. "That is one reason why I talk your language so easily."

"And the other reason?" McCaffery was thinking.

"We've listened to your radio signals many years—a great many years. I'm a student of English."

"And this planet," Briggs whispered. "Do you live here, alone?"

"No one lives here," Smith smiled, "except the custodians. And when we knew you would land here, we asked them to leave for a little while."

"In God's name," Carrington cried, "what is this place?"

"Only what it appears to be." Smith smiled and shook his head. "No mystery, believe me. What does it appear to be?"

"A garden," Laura Shawn said slowly, "the garden of all my dreams."

"Then you dream well, Miss Shawn," Smith nodded. "You have places like this on your planet, parks, playgrounds. This is a park, a playground for children. That's why no one lives here. It's a place for children to come to and play and learn a little about life and beauty—you see, in our culture, the two are not separate."

"What children?"

"The children of the Galaxy," Smith nodded, waving a hand toward the sky. "There are a great many children—a great many playgrounds and parks, not unlike this one. Today, it is empty— tomorrow, five million children—they come and they go, even as they do in your own parks—"

"Our own parks," Briggs was thinking bitterly.

"No, I am not sneering, Pilot Briggs. I am trying to answer your questions and your thoughts—and to connect these things with what you know and understand."

"You're telling us that the Galaxy is inhabited—by men?"

"Why not by men? Can you really believe that man is an accident on one planet in a billion? Wherever there is life, in time man appears—and he lives now on more than a half a million planets—in our galaxy alone. And he makes places like this place for his children."

"And who are you?" Carrington said. "And why are you here alone?"

"How would you think of me?" Smith wondered. "We don't have a government in your terms. We don't have nations. I could call myself an administrator—we have a good many. And I was sent here to meet you and talk to you. We have been watching you for a long time, tracing you—yes, we've watched the earth too, for a long time."

"Talk to us—" Frances Rhodes said softly.

"Yes."

"About what?" Briggs demanded.

"About your sickness," Smith replied sadly.

8

An hour had passed. They sat silently, looking at Smith, and he watched them, and then Briggs said,

"For heaven's sake, don't pity us. We don't ask for pity—not from you or any of your breed of supermen."

"Not pity," Smith told them. "We don't have pity—it's a part of yourselves, not of us. Sorrow is a better word."

"Spare us that too," said Gene Ling.

Carrington refused to allow anger or impatience to disturb his own reasoning. He felt a compulsion to demonstrate to Smith that he could reason dispassionately, and he said quietly and firmly,

"You see, Smith—you ask a great deal when you ask us for an admission of our own insanity. You pointed out, quite properly, I think, that we were egotistical and unscientific to believe that man was limited by nature to one obscure planet on the edge of the Galaxy. I hold that it is just as unscientific for you to claim that of all the races of man on all the planets, only the people of Earth are mentally sick, emotionally unstable—yes, insane, the one word you were kind enough not to use—"

"Carrington, you're wasting your time," Briggs said sourly. "He can read our thoughts—all of them."

"Which doesn't change any of my arguments," Carrington said to Smith. "You mention our wars, our history of mass slaughter, our use of atomic weapons, our record of murdering and destroying each other—but these are the particulars and wasteful errors of our development—"

"They are the specifics of your development," Smith nodded reluctantly. "I hate to repeat that no other race of man in all the universe pursues murder as his major occupation and force of development—yet I must. Only on Earth—"

"But we are not all murderers," Frances Rhodes protested. "I am a physician. If you know Earth so well, you know the history of medicine and healing on Earth."

"A physician who carries a gun in a holster at her side," Smith shrugged.

"For my protection only!" she cried.

"Protection? Against whom, Miss Rhodes?"

"We didn't know—"

"I'm sorry," Smith sighed. "I'm sorry."

"I told you it's no use," Briggs snapped. "He reads our thoughts. He knows. God help us, he knows!"

"Yes, I know," Smith agreed.

"Then you must know that people like ourselves are not murderers," Carrington persisted, his voice still calm and controlled. "We are scientists. We are civilized people. You speak of how we are ridden with superstition, with gargantuan lies, with a love of the obscene and the monstrous. You mention half a billion Earth people who vocalize Christianity while none of them practice it. You talk about the millions we have slain in the name of freedom, brotherhood and God. You talk of our greed, our meanness, our perversion of love and sex and beauty—don't you realize that we know these things, that our best and bravest have struggled against them for ages?"

"I realize that," Smith nodded.

"He reads our thoughts," Briggs repeated stubbornly.

"We are scientists," Carrington continued. "We built this starship that brought us here. We lay in its hull for five endless years—that the frontiers of space might be conquered. And now, when we discover a universe of men—men talented and wonderful beyond all our dreams and imaginings, you tell us that this is barred to us forever—that we must live and die on our own speck of dust—"

"Yes, I am afraid it must be that way," Smith agreed.

"Everything but pity," said Laura Shawn.

Smith opened his robe, let it slip off his body to the ground, and stood before them naked. The women instinctively turned their heads away. The men reacted in shocked disbelief. Smith picked up his robe and clothed himself again.

"You see," he said.

The five men and women stared at him, their eyes full of realization now.

"In all the universe," Smith said, "there is only one race of man that holds its bodies in shame and contempt. All others walk naked in pride and unashamed. Only Earth has made the image of man into a curse and a shame. What else must I say?"

"Do you intend to destroy us?" Briggs asked harshly.

Smith looked at him with regret. "We don't destroy, Briggs. We don't kill."

"What then?"

"You have something we don't have," Smith said softly, gently. "We had no need of it, but you had to create it—otherwise you would have perished in your sickness. You know what it is."

"Conscience," Gene Ling whispered.

402

"Yes—conscience. It will help. Go back to your starship and plot your course for home. And then you must make the decision to forget. When you make that decision, we will help you—"

"If we make it," Briggs said.

"If you make it," Smith agreed.

"Hold out some hope," Laura Shawn begged him. "Don't send us away like this. We came across—we were the first—"

"You weren't the first," Smith said, the sadness in his voice unbearable. "There were others from Earth, but each time they destroyed each other and the knowledge too. You weren't the first and you won't be the last—"

"Can we hope?" Laura Shawn pleaded.

"All men hope," Smith said. "More than that—I don't know."

9

The starship circled the beautiful planet, and the seven people of Earth sat in the wardroom. Gluckman and Phillips had been told of the encounter, and by now they had all discussed it into silence and weariness. Only Briggs had said nothing—until now, and now he said,

"Why can't we remember that he reads our thoughts? He knew."

"I'm selfish," Laura Shawn whispered through her tears. "It is easier to give up all it might mean to mankind than to give up my own memories."

"Of three days of childhood?" Briggs said bitterly. "To hell with that! To hell with his damned utopia! To hell with the stars! We'll make an atmosphere on Mars and drain the poison gas from Venus! To hell with him and his gardens! We have a job of work! So set your stinking course for home, McCaffery—and the rest of you to bed. There's another day tomorrow."

That was the virtue of Briggs; for he more than any of them knew how right Smith was, and he wept his own tears into his pillow for hours before sleep came. In the morning, he was better. By then, the starship had flung itself a hundred million miles in the direction of home, and that gave Briggs a good feeling.

Like the others, he remembered only a wasteland of burning suns, and in all the galaxy, no other planets than those of the Solar System. Like the others, he knew that he was returning to a place unique and precious in its singularity—Earth, the sole habitat of man.

27
The Mind of God

"How do you feel?" Greenberg asked me.

"Fine. Lousy. Frightened. A little sick, a little stupid, empty in the stomach. Nauseous. I think I could throw up at will. But mostly afraid. Otherwise I'm fine."

"Good."

"Why is it good?"

"Because you're facing fully and acknowledging your sensations. That's very important at this moment. If you told me you were filled with noble resolve and without fear, I would be worried."

"I'm worried," I told him. "Damn worried."

"There's no contract, no commitment that's binding," Zvi Leban said slowly, his cold blue eyes fixed on me. I never saw him as the Nobel Prize winner, the brilliant physicist so often compared to Einstein and Fermi; to me he was an Israeli, the kind I respect but do not particularly like, cold as ice and full of an implacable will that appears to partake of neither courage nor cowardice, only resolution. "The door's open."

"Zvi—stop that," Dr. Goldman said quietly.

"It's all right," said Greenberg. Greenberg was many things, M.D., psychiatrist, physicist, philosopher, businessman—all of it crowded into a fat, easygoing, moonfaced man of sixty-one years who never raised his voice and never lost his temper. "It's quite all right. He has to face everything now, his fears, his hopes, his resolutions, and also the open door. The fact that he can walk out and there will be no recriminations. You understand that, don't you, Scott?"

405

"I understand it."

"We have no secrets. A project like this would be meaningless and immoral if we had secrets from each other. Perhaps it's immoral in any case, but I am afraid I have lost touch with what men call morality. We had our time of soul-searching, seven years of it, and then we came to our decision. The Sabbath of our soul-searching, I may say, and it's done. Finished. You were and are my friend. I brought you into this in the beginning, and then you placed yourself squarely in the center of it. Zvi was against you, which you also know. He thought it should be a Jew. Goldman and I thought otherwise, and Zvi accepted our decision."

"I'd like to close the door," I said. "I would not have come today if I had not made up my mind. I'm going through with it. I told Zvi that I had no hate left. The hate has washed out. I had to be truthful about that. Zvi regards it as a lack of resolution."

"You never married again," said Goldman.

"I don't quite know what that means."

"There's no point to this discussion now," Zvi said. "Scott is going through with it. He's a brave man, and I would like to shake hands with him."

He did so with great formality.

"You've thought of some questions?" Goldman asked. "We still have an hour." He was a thin wisp of a man, his brilliance honed down to knife-edge. He had an inoperable malignancy; in a year he would be dead, yet his impending doom appeared to arouse in him only curiosity and a vague sadness. They were three unusual men indeed.

"Some. Yes, I've thought of some that I haven't asked before. I don't know that I should ask them now."

"You should," said Goldman. "You go with enough doubts. If you can clear up a few of them, so much the better."

"Well, I've been brooding over the mathematics of it, and I still can't make head or tail of them, but I'm afraid an hour's no good for that."

"No."

"Still one tries to translate into images. I suppose the mathematicians never do."

"Some do, some don't," Zvi said, smiling for the first time. "I have, but it impeded my work. So I gave it up. Just as there are no words for things we do not know, so there are no images for concepts outside of our conceptual experience."

406

"Specifically, Scott?" Greenberg asked me.

"It always comes down to breaking the chain. Then the result is entirely different. For example, this project would not take place. We would not be standing here in a stone warehouse in Norwalk, Connecticut. We would not have planned what we planned. The necessity would not face us."

"Conceivably."

"Then would I take the chance of destroying you—and thousands, perhaps millions of others now alive?"

"There," said Zvi, "is where the conceptual and the mathematical part. The answer is no, but there is no way I can explain."

"Can you explain to yourself?"

Zvi shook his head slowly, and Greenberg said, "No more, Scott, than Einstein could visualize to himself his proposition that space might be curved and limited."

"But I can visualize," I protested. "Nothing as complicated as Einstein's proposition, but I can visualize sending me back twenty-four hours. At this time yesterday, the four of us were here, sitting at this same table. I was drinking a scotch and water. What then? Would there have been two of me, identical?"

"No. It would simply be yesterday."

"And if I had a bottle of wine in my hand instead of a glass of scotch?"

"Then you propose the paradox," Goldman said gently, "and so our powers of reason cease. Which is why we do not test the machine. My dear Scott—you and I both face death, and that too is a paradox and a mystery. We are physicists, mathematicians, scientists, and we have discovered certain coordinates and from them developed certain equations. Our symbols work, but our minds, our vision, our imagination cannot follow the symbols. I may brood over a death that is inevitable, the maturation of a malignancy within me; you, as a far braver man, accept the likelihood of death in your own undertaking. But neither of us can comprehend what faces us. Do you think of yourself as a good Christian?"

"Not particularly."

"Perhaps no more than I think of myself as a good Jew—if indeed either term has any meaning. But long ago I heard the legend of Moses, who could not enter the promised land. Then, standing at his side on Mount Nebo, God revealed to him all that had been and all that would be—the past and the future, all of it existent in God's time. That too is in symbols. Do you understand why we cannot take the chance of testing the machine, of sending you back even a single day?''

"Not really."

"Then you must take our word for it, as you have."

I shrugged and nodded.

"Any other questions, Scott?" Greenberg asked me.

"A thousand—plus all I have asked before. I have the questions, but you have no answers."

"I wish we had them," Goldman said. "I truly do."

"All right, let's get on with it. First, the money."

Greenberg laid it in small piles on the table. "Ten thousand dollars, American. We would have liked it to be more, but we think that this will cover every contingency. Not easy to come by, believe me, Scott. We pulled some of the largest strings we have in Washington, and if anyone tells you museum officials cannot be bribed, he is mistaken. Pay for everything in cash without any trepidation. It was the most common method in those days. There are two hundred pounds British. Just in case."

"In case of what?"

"Who knows? We simply do not wish you to have to exchange money, and thus we include these small sums in francs and lire."

"And in marks?"

"German and Austrian—about five thousand dollars in each. Strangely enough, they were easier to obtain than the dollars. We have our own sources through dealers. Indeed, most of the marks came from one man who had some sense of what we were doing. No hard money; that would only make problems."

"The revolver?"

"We decided against it. We know it was common practice at the time to carry one, but in this case you are safer with only the knife. Here it is." He placed a pearl-handled folding knife on the table. "Four blades, common gentleman's possession at the time. You will use the large one. It's honed to a razor edge."

Zvi watched me carefully, his eyes slitted. I opened the pearl-handled knife and ran my finger along the edge of the blade. I was rather relieved that they had decided against the revolver; after all, it was probably a more civilized world than the one we lived in.

Goldman brought a large cardboard box and placed it on the table. "Your clothes," he explained, smiling almost apologetically.

"You can begin to change now. Amazing how much in style they are. You may want to keep them afterwards."

"Afterwards—"

Greenberg waited, his face thoughtful.

"We are afterwards. That's what keeps tearing my gut."

"Get it out, Scott," Greenberg said.

"We are afterwards. That's all."

"Let go of it. Our minds are not made for a paradox."

" 'My ways are not thy ways; neither are my thoughts thy thoughts'," Goldman said.

"Quoting God?"

Goldman grinned, and suddenly I relaxed and began to peel off my clothes.

"Damn you, I envy you," Zvi said suddenly. "If I did not have this cursed limp and two duodenal ulcers, I would go myself. It's what no man has ever been offered, what no man has ever experienced. You step into the mind of God."

"For atheists, you Jews are the most frantically religious people I have ever known."

"That's also part of the paradox," Greenberg agreed. "The label in the suit is Heffner and Kline. They were excellent custom tailors. Imported Irish tweed, hand spun and hand woven. Your valise contains another suit, dark blue cheviot. Both of them rather heavy for May, but they didn't go in for tropicals in those days. Also six shirts, underclothes, and all the rest."

He brought the valise from where it stood by the wall, next to the strange maze of tubes and wires it had taken them seven years to build. Goldman fitted the collar to the shirt and handed it to me.

"Ever wear one of these?" he inquired.

"My father wore them." It was the first time I had thought about my father in years, and suddenly I was overwhelmed with the memory.

"No." Zvi shook his head.

"Why not?" I asked desperately. "Why not? He wouldn't know me."

"You would not know him either," Zvi said evenly. "It will be eighteen ninety-seven. You were not born until nineteen twenty. How old was he then when you were born?"

"Thirty-six."

"Then in eighteen ninety-seven he would be a boy of thirteen— to what end, Scott?" Greenberg asked.

"I don't know to what end. So help me God, I don't know. But if I could only look at him!"

Goldman walked over to me and helped me adjust the two gold buttons that held the collar to the shirt. "There, now. You will let me tie the cravat, Scott. I know exactly how it should be done. And watch me carefully, so you can do it yourself. And take our word for it. We are interfering with a schematic—a great, enormous schematic—so we must interfere as little as possible. What Zvi said before is quite true—we enter the mind of God. We are bold men, all of us. Also, perhaps, we are madmen—as the people who exploded the first atomic bomb were madmen. They tampered with the mystery, and the world paid a price. We also tamper with the mystery, and we shall also pay a price. But we must tamper as little as possible. You must not be diverted. You must speak to no one unless it is absolutely necessary. You must not touch things, you must not change things—except the single thing to which we are pledged. Now watch how I tie the cravat—very simple, isn't it?"

I had gotten hold of myself now and wanted nothing else than to get on with it. Greenberg helped me into the tweed jacket.

"Beautiful. We have not traduced the tradition of Heffner and Kline. You are a well-dressed, upper-class gentleman, Scott. Now try this hat."

He handed me a soft felt hat, which fitted quite well.

"My grandfather's," he said with pleasure. "By golly, they made things to last, didn't they? Now listen carefully, Scott—we have only ten minutes remaining to us. Here's your wallet." He handed me an oversized, bulging wallet of alligator hide. "Papers, identity, everything you need. Knife, money—change your shoes. These are hand made. Every detail. In the wallet you will find a complete and detailed itinerary, just in case you should forget some detail. This watch"—giving me a magnificent pocket watch with a cover of embossed gold—"belonged to my grandfather. Comes with the hat. Completely overhauled, it keeps perfect time."

I finished buckling on the excellent handmade Victorian boots. Soft as butter, there would be no problem of breaking them in. Greenberg went on with his instructions, precisely, rapidly.

"You have exactly twenty-nine days, four hours, sixteen minutes, and thirty-one seconds. At that time after your arrival, you must be back here in this warehouse and in the same spot. It will then have

410

been abandoned three years, and it should be as empty as when my grandfather bought the property half a century ago. Now in a few minutes I am going to mark your boots with a red pigment that will come off when you step away. No matter how nervous or startled you are upon arrival, a red outline of your boots will remain on the floor. When you return, you step into the same position. Is that clear?"

"Clear."

"You will walk to the railroad station, take the first train to New York, and buy your round-trip steamship passage immediately. From the time you arrive until the *SS Victoria* sails, you have eighteen hours. Spend them on board the ship in your cabin. On the voyage, talk to as few people as possible. Plead seasickness, if you will."

"I won't have to plead it."

"Good enough. The ship docks at Hamburg, where you buy a first-class through ticket to Vienna. But of course you know all that, and of course you have detailed written instructions in your wallet. You've brushed up on your German?"

"My German is adequate. You know that. What happens if I don't get back to the warehouse in time?"

Greenberg shrugged. "We don't know."

"I live on in a world where my father is a child?"

"You keep invoking the paradox," said Zvi. "Don't do that. It's hurtful to you, hurtful to your mind."

"My mind's all right," I assured him. "A man with one foot in hell doesn't trouble about his mind. It's my body that worries me."

"Only four minutes," Greenberg said gently. "Would you step over here, Scott. Stand precisely between the electrodes and hold the valise as close to your body as you can."

"Cigars!" I remembered. "Good God, I don't have a cigar on me."

"They were better in those days. Pure Havana. Buy some. Now take your place!"

I grabbed the valise, fixed Greenberg's grandfather's hat firmly on my head, and stood where I was instructed to stand.

"One foot at a time," said Greenberg, kneeling in front of me. He marked each sole and heel with a dab of heavy red pigment. "Now don't move."

"Three minutes," Goldman said.

"You look damned impressive in that hat and suit," Zvi admitted.

411

"How long will I be away?" I wanted to know. "I mean in your time. Here. How long do you wait until I return?"

"We don't wait. If you return, you are still here."

"That's insane."

"That's the paradox," said Zvi. "I warned you not to think about it."

"Two minutes," Goldman said.

Zvi put his hand on the switch. Goldman's lips were moving silently. Either he was praying or counting the seconds.

"Suppose something's in the way," I said desperately. "Bales, boxes. How can two objects occupy the same space? What happens to me then?"

"It won't happen. That's also part of the paradox."

"If it's such a goddamn paradox, how can you be so sure? How do you know?"

I was high-strung, frightened, despairing, and losing my nerve. In a few seconds, I would be hurtled back seventy-five years through time—riding on a set of coordinates that had come out of someone's strained logic, on an equation that had never been proved or tested—into hell or the mind of God or nothingness or the Mesozoic age, armed with a pearl-handled pocketknife and an ancient valise.

"One minute," Goldman said.

"Do you want to step out?" Greenberg asked, his voice half a plea. He too was frightened. They all were.

I shook my head angrily.

"Thirty seconds," said Goldman, "twenty, ten, nine, eight, seven, six, five, four, three, two, one, zero—"

I saw Zvi pulling the switch. When I returned, twenty-nine days, four hours, sixteen minutes, and thirty-one seconds later, his hand was still on the switch and I heard the soft vowel sound as Goldman finished saying zero. I stood there and they stood there, in a frozen tableau that appeared to go on and on.

"Zvi spoke first. "Where is the valise?"

"For heavens sake, let him sit down and rest," said Greenberg, helping me to a chair. I was shaking like a leaf. Goldman poured a glass of brandy and held it to my lips, but I shook my head.

"Are you cold?" Goldman asked.

"I'm not in shock. Just frightened. Breathless. I had to run the last hundred yards to the warehouse, and I made it by seconds. I threw the valise away."

412

"That doesn't matter."

"He failed," Zvi said bleakly. "God almighty, he failed. I knew it."

"Did you fail?" Goldman asked.

"I'll have the brandy now," I said, my hand still shaking as I took the glass.

"Let him tell it all," Greenberg said. "There will be no recriminations, no accusations. Let that be plain, Zvi. Do you understand me?"

"Seven years." There were tears in Zvi's eyes.

"And six million dollars of my money. We both learned something. Tell us, Scott—did you go back?"

I looked at Goldman, the doomed man, the man with the malignancy—and there was the slightest, thinnest smile on his lips, as if he had known all the time.

"Did you go back?"

I drank the brandy, and then I reached into my breast pocket and took out two large black cigars, handing one to Greenberg, the only cigar smoker among them. I bit off the end and lit it, while Greenberg stared at the cigar in his hand. I puffed deeply and told him it was better than anything he'd find today.

"Did you go back?" Greenberg repeated.

"Yes—yes, I went back. I'll tell you. But let me rest a moment, let me think. Let me remember. Jesus Christ, let me remember!"

"Of course," said Goldman, "you must remember. Relax, Scott. It will come back." He knew already, this withered man who was visited nightly by the Jewish angel of death. He needed no coordinates or equations; he had touched God briefly, as I had, and he knew all the terror and wonder of it. "You see," he explained to Zvi and Greenberg, "he has to remember. You will understand that in a few minutes. But he must have the time to remember."

Greenberg poured me another brandy. He didn't light his cigar. He kept looking at it and handling it. "Fresh," he muttered, sniffing at it. "Very dark. They must have cured the leaves differently."

"I went back," I said finally. "Seventy-five years. It all worked, your machine, your equations, your bloody coordinates. It all worked. It was like being sick for a few minutes—a terrible sense of being sick. I thought I was going to die. And then I was alone in the warehouse, holding my valise, standing right there. Only—" I paused and looked at Goldman.

413

"Only you could not remember," Goldman said.

"How do you know?"

"What the devil do you mean?" Zvi demanded. "What do you mean, he couldn't remember?"

"Let him tell it."

"I had no memory," I said. "I did not know who I was, or where I was."

"Go on."

"It's not that simple. Do you know what it is to have no memory, absolutely none, to be standing in a place and not know who you are or how you got there? It's the most terrifying experience I have ever known—even worse than the fear I felt when I stepped into that damn machine."

"Could you read, write, speak?" Greenberg asked.

"Yes, I could read and write. I could speak."

"Different centers of the brain," said Goldman.

"What did you do?"

"I put down the valise and paced back and forth. I was shaking— the way I am shaking now. It took a while. I had a rotten headache, but after a few minutes the pain eased. Then I took out my wallet."

"You knew what it was? You knew it was a wallet?"

"I knew that. I knew I was a man. I knew I was wearing shoes. I knew those things. As a matter of fact, I knew a great deal. I hadn't become an imbecile. I was simply without memory. I was alive and aware of today, but there was no yesterday. So I took out the wallet and went through it. I learned my name. Not my own name, but the name you gave me for the journey. I read the instructions, the timetable, the minute directions you wrote out for my journey, the warning that I must return to the exact spot in the warehouse at a specific time. And the strange thing was that never for a moment did I doubt the instructions. Somehow I accepted the necessity, and I knew that I must do the things that were written down for me to do."

"And you did them?" Greenberg asked.

"Yes."

"With no troubles—no interferences?"

"No. You see, I knew no other time than eighteen ninety-seven. There I was. Everything was perfectly natural. I could remember no other time, no other place. I walked to the railroad station, and believe me, Norwalk Station was an elegant place in those times.

414

The station-master sold me a ticket on the parlor car. Can you imagine a parlor car on the New York, New Haven and Hartford Railroad? And for less than two dollars."

"How did you know where to walk?" Zvi demanded.

"He asked directions," said Goldman.

"Yes, I asked directions. I had no memory, but I was all right, I was at home there. I booked first-class passage on the ship to Hamburg—I spent a few hours wandering around New York." I closed my eyes and remembered it. "Wonderful, wonderful place."

"And you could function like that?" Greenberg asked. "It did not upset you that you had no memory?"

"After a while—no. I simply took it for granted. You see, I didn't know what memory was. A color-blind man doesn't know what color is. A deaf man doesn't know what sound is. I didn't know what memory was. Yes, people spoke about it and that was somewhat bothersome—where did I go to school, where was I born, questions like that I avoided because my instructions were to be private. There were some questions—well, I ignored them. It was a good-sized ship, very well appointed. I could be by myself."

"Hamburg," Greenberg reminded me.

"Yes. There were no incidents that are important now. If you want me to tell you how it was then, how places were, how people were?"

"Later. There will be time for that later. You took the train for Vienna?"

"Within hours. I followed my instructions and left the train at Linz, but there was an error there. It was midnight, and I had to wait until nine the following morning to catch the train to Braunau. I was at Braunau four hours later."

"And then?"

I looked from face to face, three tired, aging Jews whose memories were filled with the pain and suffering of the ages, who had spent seven years and six million dollars to enter the mind of God and change it.

"And then my instructions ended. You know what I suffered and what my wife suffered at the hands of the Nazis. But you had not written down that I was to seek out an eight-year-old boy whose name was Adolf Hitler and that I was to cut his throat with the razor-sharp blade of my pearl-handled knife. You trusted me to remember what was the purpose of our whole task—and I had no memory of what you had suffered or what I had suffered, no memory of why I was there in Braunau. I spent a day there, and then I returned."

There was a long silence after that. Even Zvi was silent, standing with his eyes closed, his fists clenched. Then Goldman said gently:

"We have not thanked Scott. I thank you for all of us."

Still silence.

"Because we should have known," Goldman said. "Do you remember God's promise—that no man should look into the future and know the time of his own death? When we sent Scott back, the future closed to him, and all his memories were in the future. How could he remember what had not yet been?"

"We could try again," Zvi whispered.

"And we would fail again." Goldman nodded. "We are children pecking at the unknown. Because whatever has been has been. I will show you. Scott," he asked me, "do you remember where you dropped the valise?"

"Yes—yes. It was only a moment ago."

"It was seventy-five years ago. How far from here?"

"At the edge of the road at the bottom of the hill."

Goldman picked up a coal shovel that stood by an old coal stove in the corner of the warehouse and he led the way outside. We knew what he was about and we followed him, through the door and down the hill. It was late afternoon now, the spring sun setting across the Connecticut hills, the air cool and clean.

"Where, Scott?"

I found the spot easily enough, took the coal shovel from the frail man, and began to dig. Six or seven inches of dead leaves, then the soft loam, then the dirt, and finally the rotting edge of the valise. It came out in pieces, disintegrating leather, a few shreds of shirts and underwear, rotten and crumbling under my fingers.

"It happened," Goldman said. "The mind of God? We don't even know our own minds. There is nothing in the past we can change. In the future? Perhaps we can change the future—a little."

416

28
The Mohawk

WHEN Clyde Lightfeather walked up the steps of St. Patrick's Cathedral on Fifth Avenue, he was wearing an old raincoat of sorts; and then he took it off and sat down cross-legged in front of the great doors. Underneath he was dressed just like the bang-bang man in an old Indian medicine show—that is, he wore soft doeskin leggings, woods moccasins, and nothing at all from the waist up. His hair was cut in the traditional central brush style of the scalp lock, with one white feather through the little braid at the back of his neck. He was altogether a very well-built and pre-possessing young full-blooded Mohawk Indian.

A crowd gathered because it doesn't take anything very much to gather a crowd in New York, and Father Michael O'Conner came out of the cathedral and Officer Patrick Muldoon came up from the street, and the gentle June sun shone down upon everyone.

"Now just what the hell are you up to?" Officer Muldoon asked Clyde Lightfeather. There was a querulous note in Officer Muldoon's voice, for he was sick and tired of freaks, hard-core hippies, acid-heads, pot-heads, love children and flower children, black power folk, SDS, sit-ins and demonstrations-out; and while he was fond of saying that he had seen everything, he had never before seen a Mohawk Indian sitting crosslegged in front of St. Patrick's.

"God and God's grace, I suppose," Clyde Lightfeather answered.

"Now don't you know," said Muldoon, his voice taking that tired, descending path of patience and veiled threat, "that this is private property and that you cannot put a feather in your hair and just sit yourself down and attract a crowd and make difficulties for honest worshipers?"

"Why not? This isn't private property. This is God's property, and since you don't work for God, why don't you take your big, fat blue ass out of here and leave me alone?"

Officer Muldoon began to make the proper response to such talk, Mohawk Indian or not—with the crowd grinning and half disposed toward the Indian—when Father O'Conner intervened and pointed out to Officer Muldoon that the Indian was absolutely right. This was not private property but God's property.

"The devil you say!" Officer Muldoon exclaimed. "You're going to let that heathen sit there?"

Up until that moment Father O'Conner had been of a mind to say a few reasonable words that would be persuasive enough to move the Indian away. Now he abruptly changed his position.

"Maybe I will," he declared.

"Thank you," Lightfeather said.

"Providing you give me one good reason why I should."

"Because I am here to meditate."

"And you consider this a proper place for meditation, Mr.—?"

"Lightfeather."

"Mr. Lightfeather."

"The best. Do you deny that?" he demanded pugnaciously.

"What is meditation to you, Mr. Lightfeather?"

"Prayer—God—being."

"Then how can I deny it?" the priest asked.

"And you're going to let him stay there?" Muldoon demanded.

"I think so."

"Now look," Muldoon said, "I was raised a Catholic, and maybe I don't know much, but I know one thing—a cathedral is made for worship on the inside, not on the outside!"

Nevertheless, the Indian remained there, and within a few hours the television cameras and the newspapermen were there and Father O'Conner was facing no less exalted a person than the Cardinal himself. The research facilities at the various networks were concentrated upon the letter *m*—*m* for meditation as well as Mohawk. Chet Huntley informed millions not only that meditation was a significant, inwardly directed spiritual exercise, an inner concentration upon some thought of deep religious significance, but that the Mohawk Indians had been great in their time, the organizing force of the mighty Six Nations of the Iroquois Confederacy. The peace of the forests was the Mohawk peace, even

418

as the law was the Mohawk law, codified in ancient times by that gentle and wise man, Hiawatha. From the St. Lawrence River in the north to the Hudson River in the south, the Mohawk peace and the Mohawk law prevailed before the white man's coming.

Less historically oriented, the CBS commentators wondered whether this was not simply another bit of hooliganism inflicted by college youth upon a patient public. They had researched Lightfeather himself, learning that, after Harvard, he took his Ph.D. at Columbia—his doctoral paper being a study of the use of various hallucinogenic plants in American Indian religions. "It is discouraging," said Walter Cronkite, "to find a young American Indian of such brilliance engaging in such tiresome antics."

His Eminence, the Cardinal, took another tack entirely. It was not his to unravel a Mohawk Indian. Instead, he coldly asked Father O'Conner just what he proposed.

"Well, sir, Your Eminence, I mean he's not doing any harm, is he?"

"Really carried away by the notion that God owns the property—am I right, Father?"

"Well—he put it so naturally and directly, Your Eminence."

"Did it ever occur to you that God's property rights extend even farther than St. Patrick's? You know He owns Wall Street and the White House and Protestant churches and quite a few synagogues and the Soviet Union and even Red China, not to mention a galaxy or two out there. So if I were you, Father O'Conner, I would suggest some more suitable place than the porch of St. Patrick's for meditation. I would say that you should persuade him to leave by morning."

"Yes, Your Eminence."

"Peacefully."

"Yes, Your Eminence."

"We have still not had a sit-down in St. Patrick's."

"I understand perfectly, Your Eminence."

But Father O'Conner's plan of action was a little less than perfect. It was about five o'clock in the afternoon now, and the streets were filled with people hurrying home. As little as it takes to make a crowd in New York, it takes less to dispel it; and by now the Indian was wholly taken for granted. Father O'Conner stood next to Lightfeather for a while, brooding as creatively as he could, and then asked politely whether the Indian heard him.

"Why not? Meditation is a condition of alertness, not of sleep."

"You were very still."

"Inside, Father, I am still."

"Why did you come here?" Father O'Conner asked.

"I told you why. To meditate."

"Why here?"

"Because the vibes are good here."

"Vibes?"

"Vibrations."

"Oh."

"It's a question of belief. This place is filled with belief. That's why I picked it. I need belief."

"For what?" Father O'Conner asked curiously.

"So I can believe."

"What do you want to believe?"

"That God is sane."

"I assure you—He is," Father O'Conner said with conviction.

"How the hell do you know?"

"It's a matter of my own belief."

"Not if you were a Mohawk Indian."

"I don't know. I have never been a Mohawk Indian."

"I have."

Father O'Conner thought about it for a moment or two, and in all fairness he could not deny that a Mohawk Indian might have quite a different point of view.

"His Eminence, the Cardinal, is provoked at me," he said finally. "He wants me to persuade you to leave."

"So you're bringing back the fuzz."

"No, peacefully."

"Before you were with me on this being God's pad. Has His Eminence talked you out of that?"

"He pointed out that the Almighty has equal claim to the Soviet Union. I suppose wherever it is, the tenants make the rules."

"All right. Spell it out."

"I hate to be a top sergeant about it," Father O'Conner said. "How long were you planning to stay?"

"Until God answers me."

"That can be a long time," Father O'Conner said unhappily.

"Or an instant. I am meditating on time."

"Time?"

420

I always think of time when I think of God," the Indian said. "He has His time. We have ours. I want Him to open His time to me. What in hell am I doing here on Fifth Avenue? I'm a Mohawk Indian. Right?"

Father O'Conner nodded.

"I don't know," the Indian said. "We'll give it the old school try, and then you can call the fuzz. How about it? Until morning?"

"Until morning," Father O'Conner said.

"I'll do as much for you sometime," the Indian said, and those were the last words he was heard to say. The newspaper reporters came down and the television crowd made a second visit, but the Indian was through talking.

The Indian was meditating. He allowed thought to leave his mind and he watched his breath go in and out and he became a sort of universe unto himself. He considered God's time and he considered man's time—but without thought. There are no thoughts known to man that are capable of dealing even with man's time, much less God's time; but the Indian was not so far from his ancestors as to be trapped in thought. His ancestors had known the secret of the *great time,* which all white men have forgotten.

The Indian was photographed and televised until even the networks had enough of him, and Father O'Conner remained there to see that the Indian's meditation was not interrupted. The priest felt a great kinship with the Indian, but being a priest, he also knew how many had asked and how few had been answered.

By midnight the press had gone and even the few passers-by ignored the Indian. Father O'Conner was amazed at how long he had remained there, motionless, in what is called the lotus position, but he had always heard that Indians were stoical and enduring of pain and desire and he supposed that this Indian was no different. The priest was gratified that the June night was so warm and pleasant; at least the Indian would not suffer from cold.

Before the priest fell asleep that night, he prayed that some sort of grace might be bestowed upon the Indian. What kind of grace he wasn't at all sure, nor was he ready to plead that the Indian should have a taste of God's time. The notion of God's time was just a bit terrifying to Father O'Conner.

He slept well but not for long, and he was up and dressed with the first gray presence of dawn. The priest walked to the porch of the cathedral, and there was the Indian exactly as the priest had left him. So erect, so unmoving was his body that, were it not for the slight motion of his bare stomach, the priest might have thought him dead.

As for the Indian, Clyde Lightfeather, he was alert and within himself, and his mind was clear and open. Eyes closed, he felt the breezes of dawn on his cheek, the scent of morning in his nostril. He had no need for prayer; his whole being was a gentle reminder; and that way he heard a bird singing.

He allowed the sound to pass through him; he experienced it but did not detain it. And then he heard the leaping, gurgling passage of a brook. That too he heard without detention. And then he smelled the smell of the earth in June, the wonderful wet, sweet, thick smell of life coming and life going, and this smell he clung to, for he knew that his meditation was finished and that he had been granted a moment of God's time.

He opened his eyes, and instead of the great masses of Rockefeller Center, he saw an ancient stand of tulip trees, each of them fifteen feet across the base and reaching so high up that only the birds knew where they topped out. Thin fingers of the dawn laced through the tulips, and out of the great knowledge that comes with the great time, the Indian knew that there would be birch-bark canoes on the shore of the Hudson, carefully sheltered for the day they would be needed, and that the Hudson was the road to the Mohawk Valley where the longhouses stood. He waited no longer but leaped to his feet and raced through the tulip trees.

The priest had turned for a moment to regard the soaring majesty of St. Patrick's; when he looked again, the Indian was gone. Instead of being pleased that he had accomplished what the Cardinal desired, the priest felt a sense of loss.

A few hours later the Cardinal sent for Father O'Conner, and the priest told him that the Indian had left very early in the morning.

"There was no unpleasantness, I trust?"

"No, Your Eminence."

"No police?"

"No, sir—only myself." Father O'Conner hesitated, swallowed, and instead of departing, coughed.

"Yes?" the Cardinal asked.

"If I may ask you a question, Your Eminence?"

"Go ahead."

"What is God's time, Your Eminence?"

The Cardinal smiled, but not with amusement. The smile was a turning inward, as if he were remembering things that had happened long, long ago.

"Was that the Indian's notion?"

Father O'Conner nodded with embarrassment.

"Did you ask him?"

"No, I did not."

"Then when he returns," the Cardinal said, "I suggest that you do."

29
The Mouse

ONLY the mouse watched the flying saucer descend to earth. The mouse crouched apprehensively in a mole's hole, its tiny nose twitching, its every nerve quivering in fear and attention as the beautiful golden thing made a landing.

The flying saucer—or circular spaceship, shaped roughly like a flattened, wide-brimmed hat—slid past the roof of the split-level suburban house, swam across the back yard, and then settled into a tangle of ramblers, nestling down among the branches and leaves so that it was covered entirely. And since the flying saucer was only about thirty inches in diameter and no more than seven inches in height, the camouflage was accomplished rather easily.

It was just past three o'clock in the morning. The inhabitants of this house and of all the other houses in this particular suburban development slept or tossed in their beds and struggled with insomnia. The passage of the flying saucer was soundless and without odor, so no dog barked; only the mouse watched—and he watched without comprehension, even as he always watched, even as his existence was—without comprehension.

What had just happened became vague and meaningless in the memory of the mouse—for he hardly had a memory at all. It might never have happened. Time went by, seconds, minutes, almost an hour, and then a light appeared in the tangle of briars and leaves where the saucer lay. The mouse fixed on the light, and then he saw two men appear, stepping out of the light, which was an opening into the saucer, and onto the ground.

Or at least they appeared to be vaguely like creatures the mouse had seen that actually were men—except that they were only three inches tall and enclosed in spacesuits. If the mouse could have distinguished between the suit and what it contained and if the mouse's vision had been selective, he might have seen that under the transparent covering the men from the saucer differed only in size from the men on earth—at least in general appearance. Yet in other ways they differed a great deal. They did not speak vocally, nor did their suits contain any sort of radio equipment; they were telepaths, and after they had stood in silence for about five minutes they exchanged thoughts.

"The thing to keep in mind," said the first man, "is that while our weight is so much less here than at home, we are still very, very heavy. And this ground is not very dense."

"No, it isn't, is it? Are they all asleep?"

The first reached out. His mind became an electronic network that touched the minds of every living creature within a mile or so.

"Almost all of the people are asleep. Most of the animals appear to be nocturnal."

"Curious."

"No—not really. Most of the animals are undomesticated—small, wild creatures. Great fear—hunger and fear."

"Poor things."

"Yes—poor things, yet they manage to survive. That's quite a feat, under the noses of the people. Interesting people. Probe a bit."

The second man reached out with his mind and probed. His reaction might be translated as "Ugh!"

"Yes—yes, indeed. They think some horrible thoughts, don't they? I'm afraid I prefer the animals. There's one right up ahead of us. Wide awake and with nothing else in that tiny brain of his but fear. In fact, fear and hunger seem to add up to his total mental baggage. Not hate, no aggression."

"He's also quite small as things go on this planet," the second spaceman observed. "No larger than we are. You know, he might just do for us."

"He might," the first agreed.

With that, the two tiny men approached the mouse, who still crouched defensively in the mole hole, only the tip of its whiskered nose showing. The two men moved very slowly and carefully,

426

choosing their steps with great deliberation. One of them suddenly sank almost up to his knees in a little bit of earth, and after that they attempted to find footing on stones, pebbles, bits of wood. Evidentally their great weight made the hard, dry earth too soft for safety. Meanwhile the mouse watched them, and when their direction became evident, the mouse attempted the convulsive action of escape.

But his muscles would not respond, and as panic seared his small brain, the first spaceman reached into the mouse's mind, soothing him, finding the fear center and blocking it off with his own thoughts and then electronically shifting the mouse's neuron paths to the pleasure centers of the tiny animal's brain. All this the spaceman did effortlessly and almost instantaneously, and the mouse relaxed, made squeaks of joy, and gave up any attempt to escape. The second spaceman then broke the dirt away from the tunnel mouth, lifted the mouse with ease, holding him in his arms, and carried him back to the saucer. And the mouse lay there, relaxed and cooing with delight.

Two others, both women, were waiting in the saucer as the men came through the air lock, carrying the mouse. The women—evidently in tune with the men's thoughts—did not have to be told what had happened. They had prepared what could only be an operating table, a flat panel of bright light overhead and a board of instruments alongside. The light made a square of brilliance in the darkened interior of the spaceship.

"I am sterile," the first woman informed the men, holding up hands encased in thin, transparent gloves, "so we can proceed immediately."

Like the men, the women's skin was yellow, the hair rich orange. Out of the spacesuits, they would all be dressed more or less alike, barefoot and in shorts in the warm interior of the ship; nor did the women cover their well-formed breasts.

"I reached out," the second woman told them. "They're all asleep, but their minds!"

"We know," the men agreed.

"I rooted around—like a journey through a sewer. But I picked up a good deal. The animal is called a mouse. It is symbolically the smallest and most harmless of creatures, vegetarian, and hunted by practically everything else on this curious planet. Only its size accounts for its survival, and its only skill is in concealment."

Meanwhile the two men had laid the mouse on the operating table, where it sprawled relaxed and squeaking contentment. While the men went to change out of their spacesuits, the second woman filled a hypodermic instrument, inserted the needle near the base of the mouse's tail, and gently forced the fluid in. The mouse relaxed and became unconscious. Then the two women changed the mouse's position, handling the—to them huge—animal with ease and dispatch, as if it had almost no weight; and actually in terms of the gravitation they were built to contend with, it had almost no weight at all.

When the two men returned, they were dressed as were the women, in shorts, and barefoot, with the same transparent gloves. The four of them then began to work together, quickly, expertly—evidently a team who had worked in this manner many times in the past. The mouse now lay upon its stomach, its feet spread. One man put a cone-shaped mask over its head and began the feeding of oxygen. The other man shaved the top of its head with an electric razor, while the two women began an operation which would remove the entire top of the mouse's skull. Working with great speed and skill, they incised the skin, and then using trephines that were armed with a sort of laser beam rather than a saw, they cut through the top of the skull, removed it, and handed it to one of the men who placed it in a pan that was filled with a glowing solution. The brain of the mouse was thus exposed.

The two women then wheeled over a machine with a turret top on a universal joint, lowered the top close to the exposed brain, and pressed a button. About a hundred tiny wires emerged from the turret top, and very fast, the women began to attach these wires to parts of the mouse's brain. The man who had been controlling the oxygen flow now brought over another machine, drew tubes out of it, and began a process of feeding fluid into the mouse's circulatory system, while the second man began to work on the skull section that was in the glowing solution.

The four of them worked steadily and apparently without fatigue. Outside, the night ended and the sun rose, and still the four space people worked on. At about noon they finished the first part of their work and stood back from the table to observe and admire what they had done. The tiny brain of the mouse had been increased fivefold in size, and in shape and folds resembled a miniature human brain. Each of the four shared a feeling of great accomplishment, and they then proceeded to complete the

428

operation. The shape of the skull section that had been removed was now compatible with the changed brain, and when they replaced it on the mouse's head, the only noticeable difference in the creature's appearance was a strange, high lump above his eyes. They sealed the breaks and joined the flesh with some sort of plastic, removed the tubes, inserted new tubes, and changed the deep unconsciousness of the mouse to a deep sleep.

For the next five days the mouse slept—but from motionless sleep, its condition changed gradually, until on the fifth day it began to stir and move restlessly, and then on the sixth day it awakened. During these five days it was fed intravenously, massaged constantly, and probed constantly and telepathically. The four space people took turns at entering its mind and feeding it information, and neuron by neuron, section by section, they programmed its newly enlarged brain. They were very skilled at this. They gave the mouse background knowledge, understanding, language, and self-comprehension. They fed it a vast amount of information, balanced the information with a philosophical comprehension of the universe and its meaning, left it as it had been emotionally, without aggression or hostility, but also without fear. When the mouse finally awakened, it knew what it was and how it had become what it was. It still remained a mouse, but in the enchanted wonder and majesty of its mind, it was like no other mouse that had ever lived on the planet Earth.

The four space people stood around the mouse as it awakened and watched it. They were pleased, and since much in their nature, especially in their emotional responses, was childlike and direct, they could not help showing their pleasure and smiling at the mouse. Their thoughts were in the nature of a welcome, and all that the mind of the mouse could express was gratitude. The mouse came to its feet, stood on the floor where it had lain, faced each of them in turn, and then wept inwardly at the fact of its existence. Then the mouse was hungry and they gave it food. After that the mouse asked the basic, inevitable question:

"Why?"

"Because we need your help."

"How can I help you when your own wisdom and power are apparently without measure?"

The first spaceman explained. They were explorers, cartographers, surveyors—and behind them, light-years away, was their home planet, a gigantic ball the size of our planet Jupiter. Thus their small size, their incredible density. Weighing on earth only a fraction of what they weighed at home, they nevertheless weighed more than any earth creature their size—so much more that they walked on earth in dire peril of sinking out of sight. It was quite true that they could go anywhere in their spacecraft, but to get all the information they required, they would have to leave it—they would have to venture forth on foot. Thus the mouse would be their eyes and their feet.

"And for this a mouse!" the mouse exclaimed. "Why? I am the smallest, the most defenseless of creatures."

"Not any longer," they assured him. "We ourselves carry no weapons, because we have our minds, and in that way your mind is like ours. You can enter the mind of any creature, a cat, a dog—even a man—stop the neuron paths to his hate and aggression centers, and you can do it with the speed of thought. You have the strongest of all weapons—the ability to make any living thing love you, and having that, you need nothing else."

Thus the mouse became a part of the little group of space people who measured, charted, and examined the planet Earth. The mouse raced through the streets of a hundred cities, slipped in and out of hundreds of buildings, crouched in corners where he was privy to the discussions of people of power who ruled this part or that part of the planet Earth, and the space people listened with his ears, smelled with his sensitive nostrils, and saw with his soft brown eyes. The mouse journeyed thousands of miles, across the seas and continents whose existence he had never even dreamed about. He listened to professors lecturing to auditoriums of college students, and he listened to the great symphony orchestras, the fine violinists and pianists. He watched mothers give birth to children and he listened to wars being planned and murders plotted. He saw weeping mourners watch the dead interred in the earth, and he trembled to the crashing sounds of huge assembly lines in monstrous factories. He hugged the earth as bullets whistled overhead, and he saw men slaughter each other for reasons so obscure that in their own minds there was only hate and fear.

As much as the space people, he was a stranger to the curious ways of mankind, and he listened to them speculate on the mindless, haphazard mixture of joy and horror that was mankind's civilization on the planet Earth.

Then, when their mission was almost completed, the mouse chose to ask them about their own place. He was able to weigh facts now and to measure possibilities and to grapple with uncertainties and to create his own abstractions; and so he thought, on one of those evenings when the warmth of the five little creatures filled the spaceship, when they sat and mingled thoughts and reactions in an interlocking of body and mind of which the mouse was a part, about the place where they had been born.

"Is it very beautiful?" the mouse asked.

"It's a good place. Beautiful—and filled with music."

"You have no wars?"

"No."

"And no one kills for the pleasure of killing?"

"No."

"And your animals—things like myself?"

"They exist in their own ecology. We don't disturb it, and we don't kill them. We grow and we make the food we eat."

"And are there crimes like here—murder and assault and robbery?"

"Almost never."

And so it went, question and answer, while the mouse lay there in front of them, his strangely shaped head between his paws, his eyes fixed on the two men and the two women with worship and love; and then it came as he asked them:

"Will I be allowed to live with you—with the four of you? Perhaps to go on other missions with you? Your people are never cruel. You won't place me with the animals. You'll let me be with the people, won't you?"

They didn't answer. The mouse tried to reach into their minds, but he was still like a little child when it came to the game of telepathy, and their minds were shielded.

"Why?"

Still no response.

"Why?" he pleaded.

Then, from one of the women, "We were going to tell you. Not tonight, but soon. Now we must tell you. You can't come with us."

"Why?"

"For the plainest reasons, dear friend. We are going home."

"Then let me go home with you. It's my home too—the beginning of all my thoughts and dreams and hope."

"We can't."

"Why?" the mouse pleaded. "Why?"

"Don't you understand? Our planet is the size of your planet

Jupiter here in the solar system. That is why we were so small in earth terms—because our very atomic structure is different from yours. By the measure of weight they use here on earth, I weigh almost a hundred kilograms, and you weigh less than an eighth of a kilogram, and yet we are almost the same size. If we were to bring you to our planet, you would die the moment we reached its gravitational pull. You would be crushed so completely that all semblance of form in you would disappear. You can't ask us to destroy you.''

"But you're so wise," the mouse protested. "You can do almost anything. Change me. Make me like yourselves."

"By your standards we're wise—" The space people were full of sadness. It permeated the room, and the mouse felt its desolation. "By our own standards we have precious little wisdom. We can't make you like us. That is beyond any power we might dream of. We can't even undo what we have done, and now we realize what we have done."

"And what will you do with me?"

"The only thing we can do. Leave you here."

"Oh, no." The thought was a cry of agony.

"What else can we do?"

"Don't leave me here," the mouse begged them. "Anything—but don't leave me here. Let me make the journey with you, and then if I have to die I will die."

"There is no journey as you see it," they explained. "Space is not an area for us. We can't make it comprehensible to you, only to tell you that it is an illusion. When we rise out of the earth's atmosphere, we slip into a fold of space and emerge in our own planetary system. So it would not be a journey that you would make with us—only a step to your death."

"Then let me die with you," the mouse pleaded.

"No—you ask us to kill you. We can't."

"Yet you made me."

"We changed you. We made you grow in a certain way."

"Did I ask you to? Did you ask me whether I wanted to be like this?"

"God help us, we didn't."

"Then what am I to do?"

"Live. That's all we can say. You must live."

"How? How can I live? A mouse hides in the grass and knows only two things—fear and hunger. It doesn't even know that it is, and of the vast lunatic world that surrounds it, it knows nothing. But you gave me the knowledge—"

"And we also gave you the means to defend youself, so that you can live without fear."

"Why? Why should I live? Don't you understand that?"

"Because life is good and beautiful—and in itself the answer to all things."

"For me?" The mouse looked at them and begged them to look at him. "What do you see? I am a mouse. In all this world there is no other creature like myself. Shall I go back to the mice?"

"Perhaps."

"And discuss philosophy with them? And open my mind to them? Or should I have intercourse with those poor, damned mindless creatures? What am I to do? You are wise. Tell me. Shall I be the stallion of the mouse world? Shall I store up riches in roots and bulbs? Tell me, tell me," he pleaded.

"We will talk about it again," the space people said. "Be with yourself for a while, and don't be afraid."

Then the mouse lay with his head between his paws and he thought about the way things were. And when the space people asked him where he wanted to be, he told them:

"Where you found me."

So once again the saucer settled by night into the back yard of the suburban split-level house. Once again the air lock opened, and this time a mouse emerged. The mouse stood there, and the saucer rose out of the swirling dead leaves and spun away, a fleck of gold losing itself in the night. And the mouse stood there, facing its own eternity.

A cat, awakened by the movement among the leaves, came toward the mouse and then halted a few inches away when the tiny animal did not flee. The cat reached out a paw, and then the paw stopped. The cat struggled for control of its own body and then it fled, and still the mouse stood motionless. Then the mouse smelled the air, oriented himself, and moved to the mouth of an old mole tunnel. From down below, from deep in the tunnel, came the warm musky odor of mice. The mouse went down through the tunnel to the nest, where a male and a female mouse crouched, and the mouse probed into their minds and found fear and hunger.

The mouse ran from the tunnel up to the open air and stood

there, sobbing and panting. He turned his head up to the sky and reached out with his mind—but what he tried to reach was already a hundred light-years away.

"Why? Why?" the mouse sobbed to himself. "They are so good, so wise—why did they do it to me?"

He then moved toward the house. He had become adept at entering houses, and only a steel vault would have defied him. He found his point of entry and slipped into the cellar of the house. His night vision was good, and this combined with his keen sense of smell enabled him to move swiftly and at will.

Moving through the shifting web of strong odors that marked any habitation of people, he isolated the sharp smell of old cheese, and he moved across the floor and under the staircase to where a mousetrap had been set. It was a primitive thing, a stirrup of hard wire bent back against the tension of a coil spring and held with a tiny latch. The bit of cheese was on the latch, and the lightest touch on the cheese would spring the trap.

Filled with pity for his own kind, their gentleness, their helplessness, their mindless hunger that led them into a trap so simple and unconcealed, the mouse felt a sudden sense of triumph, of ultimate knowledge. He knew now what the space people had known from the very beginning, that they had given him the ultimate gift of the universe—consciousness of his own being—and in the flash of that knowledge the mouse knew all things and knew that all things were encompassed in consciousness. He saw the wholeness of the world and of all the worlds that were or would be, and he was without fear or loneliness.

In the morning, the man of the split-level suburban house went down into his cellar and let out a whoop of delight.

"Got it," he yelled up to his family. "I go the little bastard now."

But the man never really looked at anything, not at his wife, not at his kids, not at the world; and while he knew that the trap contained a dead mouse, he never even noticed that this mouse was somewhat different from other mice. Instead, he went out to the back yard, swung the dead mouse by his tail, and sent it flying into his neighbor's back yard.

"That'll give him something to think about," the man said, grinning.

434

30
The Large Ant

T HERE have been all kinds of notions and guesses as to how it would end. One held that sooner or later there would be too many people; another that we would do each other in, and the atom bomb made that a very good likelihood. All sorts of notions, except the simple fact that we were what we were. We could find a way to feed any number of people and perhaps even a way to avoid wiping each other out with the bomb; those things we are very good at, but we have never been any good at changing ourselves or the way we behave.

I know. I am not a bad man or a cruel man; quite to the contrary, I am an ordinary, humane person, and I love my wife and my children and I get along with my neighbors. I am like a great many other men, and I do the things they would do and just as thoughtlessly. There it is in a nutshell.

I am also a writer, and I told Lieberman, the curator, and Fitzgerald, the government man, that I would like to write down the story. They shrugged their shoulders. "Go ahead," they said, "because it won't make one bit of difference."

"You don't think it would alarm people?"

"How can it alarm anyone when nobody will believe it?"

"If I could have a photograph or two."

"Oh, no," they said then. "No photographs."

"What kind of sense does that make?" I asked them. "You are willing to let me write the story—why not the photographs so that people could believe me?"

"They still won't believe you. They will just say you faked the photographs, but no one will believe you. It will make for more confusion, and if we have a chance of getting out of this, confusion won't help."

"What will help?"

They weren't ready to say that, because they didn't know. So here is what happened to me, in a very straightforward and ordinary manner.

Every summer, sometime in August, four good friends of mine and I go for a week's fishing on the St. Regis chain of lakes in the Adirondacks. We rent the same shack each summer; we drift around in canoes, and sometimes we catch a few bass. The fishing isn't very good, but we play cards well together, and we cook out and generally relax. This summer past, I had some things to do that couldn't be put off. I arrived three days late, and the weather was so warm and even and beguiling that I decided to stay on by myself for a day or two after the others left. There was a small flat lawn in front of the shack, and I made up my mind to spend at least three or four hours at short putts. That was how I happened to have the putting iron next to my bed.

The first day I was alone, I opened a can of beans and a can of beer for my supper. Then I lay down in my bed with *Life on the Mississippi,* a pack of cigarettes, and an eight ounce chocolate bar. There was nothing I had to do, no telephone, no demands and no newspapers. At that moment, I was about as contented as any man can be in these nervous times.

It was still light outside, and enough light came in through the window above my head for me to read by. I was just reaching for a fresh cigarette, when I looked up and saw it on the foot of my bed. The edge of my hand was touching the golf club, and with a single motion I swept the club over and down, struck it a savage and accurate blow, and killed it. That was what I referred to before. Whatever kind of a man I am, I react as a man does. I think that any man, black, white or yellow, in China, Africa or Russia, would have done the same thing.

First I found that I was sweating all over, and then I knew I was going to be sick. I went outside to vomit, recalling that this hadn't happened to me since 1943, on my way to Europe on a tub of a Liberty Ship. Then I felt better and was able to go back into the shack and look at it. It was quite dead, but I had already made up my mind that I was not going to sleep alone in this shack.

I couldn't bear to touch it with my bare hands. With a piece of brown paper, I picked it up and dropped it into my fishing creel. That, I put into the trunk case of my car, along with what luggage I carried. Then I closed the door of the shack, got into my car and drove back to New York. I stopped once along the road, just before I reached the Thruway, to nap in the car for a little over an hour. It was almost dawn when I reached the city, and I had shaved, had a hot bath and changed my clothes before my wife awoke.

During breakfast, I explained that I was never much of a hand at the solitary business, and since she knew that, and since driving alone all night was by no means an extraordinary procedure for me, she didn't press me with any questions. I had two eggs, coffee and a cigarette. Then I went into my study, lit another cigarette, and contemplated my fishing creel, which sat upon my desk.

My wife looked in, saw the creel, remarked that it had too ripe a smell, and asked me to remove it to the basement.

"I'm going to dress," she said. The kids were still at camp. "I have a date with Ann for lunch—I had no idea you were coming back. Shall I break it?"

"No, please don't. I can find things to do that have to be done!"

Then I sat and smoked some more, and finally I called the Museum, and asked who the curator of insects was. They told me his name was Bertram Lieberman, and I asked to talk to him. He had a pleasant voice. I told him that my name was Morgan, and that I was a writer, and he politely indicated that he had seen my name and read something that I had written. That is formal procedure when a writer introduces himself to a thoughtful person.

I asked Lieberman if I could see him, and he said that he had a busy morning ahead of him. Could it be tomorrow?

"I am afraid it has to be now," I said firmly.

"Oh? Some information you require."

"No. I have a specimen for you."

"Oh? The "oh" was a cultivated, neutral interval. It asked and answered and said nothing. You have to develop that particular "oh."

"Yes. I think you will be interested."

"An insect?" he asked mildly.

"I think so."

"Oh? Large?"

"Quite large," I told him.

"Eleven o'clock? Can you be here then? On the main floor, to the right, as you enter."

"I'll be there," I said.

"One thing—dead?"

"Yes, it's dead."

"Oh?" again. "I'll be happy to see you at eleven o'clock, Mr. Morgan."

My wife was dressed now. She opened the door to my study and said firmly, "Do get rid of that fishing creel. It smells."

"Yes, darling. I'll get rid of it."

"I should think you'd want to take a nap after driving all night."

"Funny, but I'm not sleepy," I said. "I think I'll drop around to the museum."

My wife said that was what she liked about me, that I never tired of places like museums, police courts and third-rate night clubs.

Anyway, aside from a racetrack, a museum is the most interesting and unexpected place in the world. It was unexpected to have two other men waiting for me, along with Mr. Lieberman, in his office. Lieberman was a skinny, sharp-faced man of about sixty. The government man, Fitzgerald, was small, dark-eyed, and wore gold-rimmed glasses. He was very alert, but he never told me what part of the government he represented. He just said "we," and it meant the government. Hopper, the third man, was comfortable-looking, pudgy, and genial. He was a United States senator with an interest in entomology, although before this morning I would have taken better than even money that such a thing not only wasn't, but could not be.

The room was large and square and plainly-furnished, with shelves and cupboards on all walls.

We shook hands, and then Lieberman asked me, nodding at the creel, "Is that it?"

"That's it."

"May I?"

"Go ahead," I told him. "It's nothing that I want to stuff for the parlor. I'm making you a gift of it."

"Thank you, Mr. Morgan," he said, and then he opened the creel and looked inside. Then he straightened up, and the other two men looked at him inquiringly.

He nodded. "Yes."

The senator closed his eyes for a long moment. Fitzgerald took off his glasses and wiped them industriously. Lieberman spread a piece of plastic on his desk, and then lifted the thing out of my creel and laid it on the plastic. The two men didn't move. They just sat where they were and looked at it.

"What do you think it is, Mr. Morgan?" Lieberman asked me.

"I thought that was your department."

"Yes, of course. I only wanted your impression."

"An ant. That's my impression. It's the first time I saw an ant fourteen, fifteen inches long. I hope it's the last."

"An understandable wish," Lieberman nodded.

Fitzgerald said to me, "May I ask you how you killed it, Mr. Morgan?"

"With an iron. A golf club, I mean. I was doing a little fishing with some friends up at St. Regis in the Adirondacks, and I brought the iron for my short shots. They're the worst part of my game, and when my friends left, I intended to stay on at our shack and do four or five hours of short putts. You see—"

"There's no need to explain," Hopper smiled, a trace of sadness on his face. "Some of our very best golfers have the same trouble."

"I was lying in bed, reading, and I saw it at the foot of my bed. I had the club—"

"I understand," Fitzgerald nodded.

"You avoid looking at it," Hopper said.

"It turns my stomach."

"Yes—yes, I suppose so."

Lieberman said, "Would you mind telling us why you killed it, Mr. Morgan."

"Why?"

"Yes—why?"

"I don't understand you," I said. "I don't know what you're driving at."

"Sit down, please, Mr. Morgan," Hopper nodded. "Try to relax. I'm sure this has been very trying."

"I still haven't slept. I want a chance to dream before I say how trying."

"We are not trying to upset you, Mr. Morgan," Lieberman said. "We do feel, however, that certain aspects of this are very important. That is why I am asking you why you killed it. You must have had a reason. Did it seem about to attack you?"

439

"No."

"Or make any sudden motion toward you?"

"No. It was just there."

"Then why?"

"This is to no purpose," Fitzgerald put in. "We know why he killed it."

"Do you?"

"The answer is very simple, Mr. Morgan. You killed it because you are a human being."

"Oh?"

"Yes. Do you understand?"

"No. I don't."

"Then why did you kill it?" Hopper put in.

"I was scared to death. I still am, to tell the truth."

Lieberman said, "You are an intelligent man, Mr. Morgan. Let me show you something." He then opened the doors of one of the wall cupboards, and there were eight jars of formaldehyde and in each jar a specimen like mine—and in each case mutilated by the violence of its death. I said nothing. I just stared.

Lieberman closed the cupboard doors. "All in five days," he shrugged.

"A new race of ants," I whispered stupidly.

"No. They're not ants. Come here!" He motioned me to the desk and the other two joined me. Lieberman took a set of dissecting instruments out of his drawer, used one to turn the thing over and then pointed to the underpart of what would be the thorax in an insect.

"That looks like part of him, doesn't it, Mr. Morgan?"

"Yes, it does."

Using two of the tools, he found a fissure and pried the bottom apart. It came open like the belly of a bomber; it was a pocket, a pouch, a receptacle that the thing wore, and in it were four beautiful little tools or instruments or weapons, each about an inch and a half long. They were beautiful the way any object of functional purpose and loving creation is beautiful—the way the creature itself would have been beautiful, had it not been an insect and myself a man. Using tweezers, Lieberman took each instrument off the brackets that held it, offering each to me. And I took each one, felt it, examined it, and then put it down.

I had to look at the ant now, and I realized that I had not truly looked at it before. We don't look carefully at a thing that is horrible or repugnant to us. You can't look at anything through a screen of hatred. But now the hatred and the fear was dilute, and as I looked, I realized it was not an ant although like an ant. It was nothing that I had ever seen or dreamed of.

All three men were watching me, and suddenly I was on the defensive. "I didn't know! What do you expect when you see an insect that size?"

Lieberman nodded.

"What in the name of God is it?"

From his desk, Lieberman produced a bottle and four small glasses. He poured and we drank it neat. I would not have expected him to keep good Scotch in his desk.

"We don't know," Hopper said. "We don't know what it is."

Lieberman pointed to the broken skull from which a white substance oozed. "Brain material—a great deal of it."

"It could be a very intelligent creature," Hopper nodded.

Lieberman said, "It is an insect in developmental structure. We know very little about intelligence in our insects. It's not the same as what we call intelligence. It's a collective phenomenon—as if you were to think of the component parts of our bodies. Each part is alive, but the intelligence is a result of the whole. If that same pattern were to extend to creatures like this one—"

I broke the silence. They were content to stand there and stare at it.

"Suppose it were?"

"What?"

"The kind of collective intelligence you were talking about."

"Oh? Well, I couldn't say. It would be something beyond our wildest dreams. To us—well, what we are to an ordinary ant."

"I don't believe that," I said shortly, and Fitzgerald, the government man, told me quietly, "Neither do we. We guess."

"If it's that intelligent, why didn't it use one of those weapons on me?"

"Would that be a mark of intelligence?" Hopper asked mildly.

"Perhaps none of these are weapons," Lieberman said.

"Don't you know? Didn't the others carry instruments?"

"They did," Fitzgerald said shortly.

441

"Why? What were they?"

"We don't know," Lieberman said.

"But you can find out. We have scientists, engineers—good God, this is an age of fantastic instruments. Have them taken apart!"

"We have."

"Then what have you found out?"

"Nothing."

"Do you mean to tell me," I said, "that you can find out nothing about these instruments—what they are, how they work, what their purpose is?"

"Exactly," Hopper nodded. "Nothing, Mr. Morgan. They are meaningless to the finest engineers and technicians in the United States. You know the old story—suppose you gave a radio to Aristotle? What would he do with it? Where would he find power? And what would he receive with no one to send? It is not that these instruments are complex. They are actually very simple. We simply have no idea of what they can or should do."

"But they must be a weapon of some kind."

"Why?" Lieberman demanded. "Look at yourself, Mr. Morgan —a cultured and intelligent man, yet you cannot conceive of a mentality that does not include weapons as a prime necessity. Yet a weapon is an unusual thing, Mr. Morgan. An instrument of murder. We don't think that way, because the weapon has become the symbol of the world we inhabit. Is that civilized, Mr. Morgan? Or is the weapon and civilization in the ultimate sense incompatible? Can you imagine a mentality to which the concept of murder is impossible—or let me say absent. We see everything through our own subjectivity. Why shouldn't some other—this creature, for example—see the process of mentation out of his subjectivity? So he approaches a creature of our world—and he is slain. Why? What explanation? Tell me, Mr. Morgan, what conceivable explanation could we offer a wholly rational creature for this—" pointing to the thing on his desk. "I am asking you the question most seriously. What explanation?"

"An accident?" I muttered.

"And the eight jars in my cupboard? Eight accidents?"

"I think, Dr. Lieberman," Fitzgerald said, "that you can go a little too far in that direction."

"Yes, you would think so. It's a part of your own background. Mine is as a scientist. As a scientist, I try to be rational when I can.

The creation of a structure of good and evil, or what we call morality and ethics, is a function of intelligence—and unquestionably the ultimate evil may be the destruction of conscious intelligence. That is why, so long ago, we at least recognized the injunction, 'thou shalt not kill!' even if we never gave more than lip service to it. But to a collective intelligence, such as this might be a part of, the concept of murder would be monstrous beyond the power of thought."

I sat down and lit a cigarette. My hands were trembling. Hopper apologized. "We have been rather rough with you, Mr. Morgan. But over the past days, eight other people have done just what you did. We are caught in the trap of being what we are."

"But tell me—where do these things come from?"

"It almost doesn't matter where they come from," Hopper said hopelessly. "Perhaps from another planet—perhaps from inside this one—or the moon or Mars. That doesn't matter. Fitzgerald thinks they come from a smaller planet, because their movements are apparently slow on earth. But Dr. Lieberman thinks that they move slowly because they have not discovered the need to move quickly. Meanwhile, they have the problem of murder and what to do with it. Heaven knows how many of them have died in other places—Africa, Asia, Europe."

"Then why don't you publicize this? Put a stop to it before it's too late!"

"We've thought of that," Fitzgerald nodded. "What then—panic, hysteria, charges that this is the result of the atom bomb? We can't change. We are what we are."

"They may go away," I said.

"Yes, they may," Lieberman nodded. "But if they are without the curse of murder, they may also be without the curse of fear. They may be social in the highest sense. What does society do with a murderer?"

"There are socieites that put him to death—and there are other societies that recognize his sickness and lock him away, where he can kill no more," Hopper said. "Of course, when a whole world is on trial, that's another matter. We have atom bombs now and other things, and we are reaching out to the stars—"

"I'm inclined to think that they'll run," Fitzgerald put it. "They may just have that curse of fear, Doctor."

"They may," Lieberman admitted. "I hope so."

But the more I think of it the more it seems to me that fear and hatred are the two sides of the same coin. I keep trying to think back, to recreate the moment when I saw it standing at the foot of my bed in the fishing shack. I keep trying to drag out of my memory a clear picture of what it looked like, whether behind that chitinous face and the two gently swaying antennae there was any evidence of fear and anger. But the clearer the memory becomes, the more I seem to recall a certain wonderful dignity and repose. Not fear and not anger.

And more and more, as I go about my work, I get the feeling of what Hopper called "a world on trial." I have no sense of anger myself. Like a criminal who can no longer live with himself, I am content to be judged.

31
The Hunter

OF course I went out to Kennedy to greet Andrew Bell. He had sent me a wire that he was coming in on the two o'clock plane, and he had also sent a wire to Jane Pierce, his public relations girl; so practically everyone in the world knew that he was coming into Kennedy at two o'clock. My going out there was of a particular nature, because sometimes I thought that I was his friend. Otherwise, why would he have sent me a wire?

I called my wife to tell her about it, and she asked me when I thought I might see her again.

"Well, tonight," I said. "You know that."

"Do I?"

"Come off it," I said. "Andy Bell is my friend. What else do you want me to do?"

"He has ten thousand friends. He has friends in Istanbul and friends in Paris and friends in Madrid and friends in London and of course in New York. I'll bet he has friends in Albuquerque."

"All right."

"All right," she repeated, and maybe she was sorry and had pushed it too far.

"It's just a funny damn thing about friends," I told her.

"I know. And you're the only real friend Andy Bell has or ever had."

"Maybe not even me," I said. "I don't know."

445

I drove out to Kennedy, and the traffic was bad, so by the time we got there, the plane had already landed. You could not miss Andrew Bell, but neither could you get very near to him, and from the number of reporters, cameras and microphones you would have guessed an ambassador, a king or a prime minister had just landed. It was that kind of a crowd. There were civilians, perhaps twenty or thirty, but for the most part the crowd was professional and the object of the crowd was news. Andy was news. He was always news.

Jane Pierce spotted me, broke out of the crowd to grab my arm, and told me to please go to him and let him see my face. She was a tall, competent blond, middle-thirties, polite, neutral and successful, and attractive in a hard way; and I was flattered that she felt that I should be with Andy. She had that manner of authority that brings importance wherever it is directed.

"He needs a hard friend," she said in my ear. "Get over to him."

If there was a distinction between hard and soft friends, there were enough in the second category. I saw Joe Jacobs, the columnist—tomorrow he would do an entire column on Andy Bell, possibly a second one the day after that; and Frank Farrell from the *News;* and Linda Hawley, the society protocol boss and party expert, who already would be contracting for Andy's delivery here and there; and pushing hard to break through, Lucy Praise, the actress, whom he had dated half a dozen times between two wives; and just behind her, Max Golden, the millionaire, who was content to be seen within shouting distance and to pick up any check that had no other takers—Andy took most of them; and Jack Minola, the punchy, ex-heavyweight fighter, who acted as a sort of Newfoundland dog to Andy when Andy was on base in New York, and who liked to think of himself as a bodyguard, self-appointed and tolerated because Andy never got over the fact that celebrities attached themselves to him—and never really comprehended what a celebrity he himself was.

But Jane got me through, and there Andy was, big and healthy and sunburned, his massive shoulders and six feet three inches of height topped by that graying mane of hair. His blue eyes crinkled with pleasure. His face was the face of a kid, and not the face of a fifty-three-year-old who had been married four times and had won the Pulitzer Prize—the face of a kid being fussed over and praised when he might have gotten a hiding instead.

The CBS man had taken the lead in the questioning, and he had just asked Andy where the safari had been this time.

"Kenya mostly. Then we flew into Somaliland."

"Did you pilot the plane?"

"Like always."

"What kind of a plane?"

"An old Piper Cub."

"And is it true you shot a lion from the plane?"

"No. Hell, no. I'm a hunter, not a circus performer."

"But you did go after lion?"

"I never hunt in Africa without thinking of lion. He's number one. I killed three lions—all male. One was a black-maned giant—the biggest lion I ever saw, possibly the biggest ever recorded there."

"Did you shoot elephant?"

"We had a kill in elephant. We had a kill in leopard too. It was a good hunt and we had a good kill."

"And are you pleased to be back in New York?"

"I am. I like New York. I like London and Paris and Madrid and Lisbon. I liked Havana once and maybe someday I'll like Havana again. And I'm glad to be in New York."

He spoke the way he wrote, and I did not know whether to laugh or to cry. He had his entourage with him, Jose Peretz and Diva. Peretz was a small, dark, tight-muscled little man with polished hair and button eyes. He carried two knives and he had been known to use them. No one knew anything about him. Some said that he had been a bad matador and others said he had been a run-of-the-mill male whore, but no one really knew anything about him except that he spoke Spanish with a Portuguese accent—when he spoke, which was not often. That was about as much as Diva spoke. She was a tall, beautiful, black-haired woman of thirty or so, and nothing at all was known about her—that is, just a little less than was known about Peretz. That was the entourage. Somehow, they made arrangements and looked after the baggage and cleared away obstacles. Now and then a pretty and young stenographer joined them; this one, that one, the girl changed. But this time there were only two.

447

Andy saw me. "Hey, Monte!" he boomed. "Hey, Monte, god-damn you!" And then almost without pause, he was answering a question, and he said that No, he had never killed a Rocky Mountain bighorn sheep. Then he embraced me, and I could feel the iron-hard muscles of his arms biting into me. No fat and no soft. "But I will," he added, referring to the bighorn.

Some young kid who worked for one of the TV networks asked another who I was, and the reply came, "That's Monte Case, his friend."

3

I drove him back to New York in my car, just the two of us. In the time since he had last been here, the airport had changed; the roads had changed. I think it was before the Fair, and now the Fair was over; and I was not even sure that the new stadium for the Mets had been here. But he didn't notice such things, or maybe he could not admit that anything had changed since his last visit. He closed his eyes, stretched his long length, and said, oh, my God, he was tired and beat up and felt every one of his fifty-three years.

"You're young," I said inanely. I never made good or sharp conversation with him, and I was always conscious of the awkward-ness of my comments.

"Balls, Monte, I am old as the hills and goddamn tired of it. Why do I keep chasing my tail?"

"That's your problem, Andy."

"Another hunt. The chase and the kill. That's it. That's really it. That's the one sweet taste. I could give up the rest of it, the booze and the girls and all the status and celebrity horse-shit, but not that. Where are we going?"

"Where did your luggage go?"

"The hell with the luggage. That's at the Carlyle."

"The Carlyle?"

"That's right. Jane got me the suite there. It's the place, isn't it?"

"I suppose so. It's the place."

"I mean—since Jack's time. My God, I can't believe he's dead. I haven't been back since then. But the hotel is still in, isn't it?"

"Very much."

448

"But Jack is dead."

He had only met Kennedy once and briefly, but he was not name-dropping or trying to impress me. All the "great" names that flashed in and out of the press were his peers. If he was not intimate with them, it was only because time and circumstances had prevented such intimacy from developing.

"You don't want to go there?" I asked him.

"No."

"You said you were tired."

"The hell with that! I'm always tired."

"Then where?"

"Pete's—Christ Almighty, that's still there, isn't it? Pete didn't die or anything like that, did he? Or go broke?"

"It's still there, and he didn't go broke."

"Monte, let me tell you one thing—one small, crowded fact of life. Suppose I needed twenty grand. Now. This damn bloody minute. No collateral—nothing except my marker. Where would I go?"

"Make it a smaller price and come to me."

"Balls. You know goddamn well that there's only one person in the world I can go to. There's only one person in the world that will write me a check for twenty grand and never ask why or how."

"Pete?"

"That's right."

"Did you ever try it?"

"You're a cynical bastard, Monte."

"Good, we'll go to Pete's."

"You don't mind?" he asked, concerned suddenly that he might have hurt my feelings.

"Mind? My word, Andy, this is your day, your place, and it seems to me that it is maybe your city too."

4

The doorman at Pete's had only been there a year and a half or so, and he didn't recognize Andy. Afterwards, he was filled with remorse; he had the attitude of a man who wants nothing so much as to throw himself under a truck, and he pleaded for Andy's forgiveness. "You got to understand, Mr. Bell, that I'm new here.

449

That's no excuse. But that's the way it is, that's the way the cookie crumbles, that's the way it is." Andy gave him five dollars, and the doorman swore up and down that he would never forget him again, and I suppose he didn't.

But if his welcome from the doorman was less than effusive, Pete made up for it, engulfing Andy in his three hundred pounds of fat and soft muscle and kissing him. Pete was the one man in town who could kiss another man and get away with it. They embraced and hugged each other, and then Pete yelled to the bartender:

"Mike, get the hell down to the cellar and bring up that keg of black rum that has Mr. Bell's name on it. Do it yourself. I don't want any lousy, grimy busboy hands touching that keg of rum."

"You son of a bitch," Andy said, and grinned. "You kept that keg."

"They can take away my place. Not that keg."

"You fat bastard, I love you," Andy said.

"Ha! The only thing you love, Andy, are those guns of yours, which my friend Doc Schwartz holds are phallic symbols."

"Where is he? I'll put something up his ass for him to think about. Phallic symbols, huh? You've become goddamn classy for a saloon keeper."

"And how do you like this new saloon of mine—about two million dollars worth of it visible from where you stand?"

At this time of the afternoon—it was just past four o'clock now— the restaurant at Pete's place was practically empty, but there were a dozen or so people at the bar and the serious drinkers were beginning to drift in. There were two men from the Associated Press who recognized Andy and gathered around. Bernie Watts, the press agent, was drinking in a dark corner with Norma Smith, the red-headed belly dancer, who was just one inch under six feet tall and was making a sensation doing what she did best, which was belly dancing. She led him over, and Watts apologized decently for the intrusion.

"I got this broad with me and she says she'll take me apart if she doesn't meet you, Mr. Bell, and she's big enough to do it. The only claim I got on you is that Jane Pierce and I once shared an office."

Andy had an eight-ounce glass of black rum in his hand. He shook hands with Watts and grinned with pleasure at the redhead.

"My name's Norma," the redhead said. "You're my hero. Ian Fleming was my hero for a while but he's a lousy writer. You're the best writer in the world."

"God bless you! You ever tasted black rum?"

"No," the redhead said, licking her lips. "You pour it and I'll taste it. I don't mean that Ian Fleming couldn't tell a story. He's got something you can't knock, but no class. I mean he's gauche. You know what I mean?"

"I know one thing," Andy said. "You and me, we're going to talk about literature—right?"

Lieutenant O'Brian, who was the head of the detective squad at the local precinct, came in then, and he was introduced and then two Hollywood male stars and their director turned up, and then a photographer who climbed onto the bar to get a few pictures. The crowd got thicker, but Norma Smith, the big belly dancer, held her place. Andy was telling Pete about the big black-maned lion, and the hubbub died down, because when Andy told a story that way, straight and clean and simple, you didn't compete or interrupt. He had laid down the background with a few plain strokes. He had been alone at the time, quite deliberately. He had wanted to do it alone. He was in a big meadow, much of it covered with waist-high grass, with here and there an open spot. He had watched the motion of the grass defining the lion's path. It was late afternoon, and the lion had not yet made its kill; and then the lion came out of the grass and the beast stood there facing Andy.

"I was in no danger from the lion," Andy said. "There are very few animals that will go for man unprovoked. A man-eating lion has the habit, but he's old and cantankerous and incapable of running down game. This lion was young and vigorous. He was about thirty yards from me, and he regarded me with small interest and less concern, and I knew that in a moment he would step back into the grass and disappear. That was when I decided to make the kill, and everything I thought about I had to think through in a fraction of a second."

He tasted his rum and then explained that the lion had been in the wrong position.

"Head on—all I could see was his face and that great mane and his front legs. Maybe a slice of shoulder, but that kind of shot is no good. The best shot is from a parallel position, with the lion a bit ahead of you. Then you can reach the heart, and then you have time for a second shot—or your bearer has. I was alone. Only one shot and that one had to be in the brain—through the eye or the skull, and the skull can be bad. I was scared as hell. If the first shot did not kill immediately, then even a mortal wound wouldn't save

451

my life. The lion would come in like an express train—well I did it.
It was a good kill.''

"Son of a bitch," Pete said.

"You're too much," the belly dancer said. The crowd got bigger,
and I recalled that it was like the old days in Pete's old place.

5

By six o'clock, Andy had put down over a pint of black rum, and
he decided to throw a party at the suite at the Carlyle. I had no
opinions on this subject, because I knew Andy a little. He had
probably begun to drink when he boarded the plane in Africa; his
capacity was enormous and his body's ability to deal with alcohol
was little short of miraculous; and by now, underneath his controlled exterior, there was something wild and irresistible.

"All of you," he said, including a crowd of about twenty people
clustered around us and the belly dancer. "And I want the mayor,"
he said to me. "I want the mayor and the mayor's wife and the
governor and I want Monsignor Sheen—"

"You're out of your mind. And you're behind times. I think he's
a bishop now, and he sure as hell doesn't go to parties."

"Maybe he would," Lieutenant O'Brian put in. "You don't
know, Monte. You're not even a Catholic."

"And this is not even a religious matter, you will forgive me."

"And who the hell are you to say what is a religious matter?"

"Oh, wait one damn cotton-picking minute," Andy said. "You
know, I met him once maybe fifteen years ago, but we were like
brothers. There was good blood between us. We knew each other.
We broke bread and we drank wine. He said to me, 'Andy, if you
need me, call me and I'll come'." He turned to Pete. "Look,
Pete—am I stepping on anyone's toes? A man's religion is a piece of
his gut. I don't have that gut. I'm one-quarter Presbyterian,
one-quarter Methodist, one-quarter Episcopalian and I think one-
quarter Jewish and one-quarter Mormon—"

"That's five quarters," someone snorted.

"So it's five quarters," Pete said. "And if he isn't entitled to five
quarters, who the hell is? No, you're not out of line, Andy. You
were never out of line."

452

"You're too much," the belly dancer said. "I'm a Catholic. I'm a rotten Catholic, but I am a Catholic and you're not stepping on anyone's toes."

"And I want Marc Connolly and Bette Davis there, and Eva Gabor and what's-his-name, that marvelous kid who conducts the Philharmonic?"

"Bernstein, and he's not a kid any more."

"Well, I want him to come with his wife and all his friends—"

"Andy, people like that have unlisted numbers and I don't have them."

"Pete has them. Pete has the phone number of everyone on earth who matters. Even what's-his-name in the Soviet Union. You got a number for the Kremlin, Pete?"

"I got," Pete grinned, and everyone else was grinning now because they knew that the party was in the making, and that it would be a great, fabulous party that the town would remember and talk about for years to come.

"And I want the mayor and his wife."

"Andy, it's not like the old times. This is a different kind of a mayor, and he's a Republican—"

"I don't care if he's a Single-Taxer," Andy said. "Invite him. All he can do is say no." And then, to show that even if he had been away, he was as cool as any of the snotty young kids around town, Andy said to O'Brian, "Who's the lieutenant of the Nineteenth Squad? Is it still Rothschild?"

"It is."

"And how are his ulcers?"

"Rotten."

"Will you call him, lieutenant, and tell him that we will be having a drink or two with friends at the Carlyle, and that Andy Bell begs him to exhibit the quality of mercy if there is a complaint?"

Pete brought me the phone then, and I got City Hall. Everyone lapsed into a careful silence as I worked my way up to the mayor; and finally I got him and told him that Andy Bell was in town. Which he knew. And then I told him that Andy was giving a party at the Carlyle tonight and it was short notice, but would he come and bring his wife?

"I'd be delighted to come," he said. "I can't promise because it is short notice—but I'll try."

Andy and Pete hugged each other.

6

There are all kinds of parties around town. There are wild parties and lush parties, and sometimes people plan all year for a party they are going to give, and with some of the rich ones I know, a party is to be put together only by a professional party manager, like the late Elsa Maxwell. There are other parties that bear the stamp of a personality, and when Andy Bell threw a party, it grew around him, like a vine around a tree. There are parties where the host sets out to corner a few personalities and to build a certain amount of status; but if people in New York were in and important, it was up to them to know that Andy Bell was giving a party and to turn up there. It was a good thing that the suite Jane Pierce had rented at the Carlyle was a big one, because most of them turned up there.

Jane was waiting for us at the Carlyle, and she said to me, "I heard that Andy was giving a party. Was that your idea, Monte?"

"My idea? Anyway, how did you hear?"

"Because the President's kid telephoned from Texas. She wants to come. I told her to come. The hell with it. I'm going to tell the hotel to set up a bar and a table with sandwiches and junk. You know what this will cost Andy? At least two grand. And he's damn near broke."

"Why don't we get that Max what's-his-name to pick up the tab?"

"Because Andy would blow his stack."

"How can he be broke? I heard that *Life* is paying fifty thousand dollars for the story of how he shot that lion."

"He spent the fifty grand before he ever hit Africa. Take my word for it."

Andy had gone on into the suite, and now we followed him inside. Jose Peretz was explaining how he had unpacked. He had put the guns into a bedroom closet. Diva was in one corner of the big couch in the living room. She watched us silently. It was funny how no one ever asked Andy about her, who she was or what she was to any of them. Maybe she was Jose's girl, although I was inclined to think that Jose was some kind of faggot, not the ordinary kind but something esoteric; and since Diva had that lean, dry, meticulous look of a certain type of dyke about her, perhaps they matched. But no one asked about Diva, not even myself. In a way, Andy was very fond of Jane Pierce; he would embrace her and kiss her in front of Diva, and there was no reaction in the dark-haired woman that I could see. But then there was no reaction on her part to any of the play between Andy and other women—maybe because she knew that it never went beyond the opening of the game.

Andy wondered about the guns, and whether there were any laws to make things difficult.

"You don't have any pistols?" I asked him.

"Just an old Sante automatic that I use for target practice."

"Well, don't take it out on the street, and I'll call my lawyer later and see if you need any kind of a license or whether you check it downtown or what. I suppose the rest are rifles and shotguns?"

"That's right."

"I don't think it makes any difference, as long as you keep them here."

The big red-headed belly dancer came in then. She had changed clothes, from a daytime dress to a long, shimmery gown, and she told Andy that while it was a little early for the party to start, she was hungry, and she did not want to make a date with anyone else because she was going to lap on his ass like a hound dog all night.

"Don't you ever eat alone?" Jane asked her nastily.

"Honey, take a second look at me. Do you think I have to?"

The hotel waiters began to move in and set up, and I went into Andy's bedroom to call my wife. Andy came in while I was waiting for my number, and then Jose came in with Andy's tuxedo.

"I had it pressed," Jose said.

He helped Andy dress. Liz, my wife, informed me that she had heard about the party.

"How could you hear?"

"The six o'clock news. Evidently, Grand Duke Alexis is flying in from Paris as some sort of publicity stunt. He expects to make the party. Am I invited?"

"You know you are."

"Not that earnestly, but it's nice to hear it from God's right-hand man."

"Will you come?"

"I wouldn't miss it for the world—if I can fight my way in. What do you expect, a thousand people?"

When I put down the phone, I told Andy about the Grand Duke Alexis.

"Who the hell is the Grand Duke Alexis?"

"Don't you remember? He used to have a restaurant in Beverly Hills. Now he has a place on the Left Bank."

"Did I ever eat there, Monte?"

"I guess you must have, because he's flying in tonight. That's a big tab for a party. You should be flattered. Look, do you want me to go home and change?"

"What for?"

"I don't know what for. I just don't want to drag the affair down. Look, Andy, are you short of cash?"

"What?" He was provoked now. I had hit a soft spot. "What in hell ever gave you that notion?"

"All I am thinking about is this damn party. It's going to take a bundle to pay for it."

"Are you serious, Monte? You're like the oldest friend I got. Otherwise, I could get real nasty."

I let the subject drop, and Andy and I went into the living room. Two tall, distinguished, white-haired Italians greeted him with pleasure. Afterwards, I learned that they were two of the top wheels in the Mafia; Andy had met them some years before when they had helped him to arrange a wolf hunt in Sicily.

The party had started early, and now, long before post time, there were already two dozen people in the room. The buffet table had been set up, and Norma Smith, the redhead, was stuffing herself with good, nourishing food, namely toast and imported caviar.

Jane Pierce whispered to her, icily, "That, darling, is thirty-six dollars a pound."

"Then it's hardly the best, is it?" the belly dancer replied.

Max Golden arrived, with two small, blond go-go girls, one hanging on each of his arms. Their party dresses were six inches above the knee. "They're a present to you," Max said to Andy.

"What are their names?"

"Damned if I know."

Then Max saw Norma Smith, and he dropped the little go-go girls and made a beeline for the big redhead. The two kids gravitated to Jose—they thought he was "darling"; and I steered Andy over to meet the senator. You couldn't have a party like this without the senator's wife, and she had to have him with her as a door opener. The senator read books and he was really excited to meet Andy, but when he tried to talk about African politics, Andy broke away.

"He won't talk politics," I explained to the senator. "That's because he won't think politics."

"Years ago—"

"Well, that was all years ago. Things have changed."

The ambassador to the U.N. came in then, and the senator had someone to talk politics to. The management had finally produced a record player, and I had them put it out on the terrace. It was getting hot in the living room anyway, so we folded back the big double doors to the terrace and eased the increasing congestion in the living room. Jock Lewis, the radio disk jockey, was persuaded to run the phonograph, and Jose tried to teach the go-go girls some flamenco steps to the beat of rock and roll. Then I saw my wife, Liz, and I had to push people aside to reach her. She was with two pugs, one an ex-lightweight and the other an ex-heavyweight, both of them Negroes, and she yelled across to me:

"I brought some quality to your crumby party."

She was lit already. The Negro pugs embraced Andy and Jacky Minola, and they formed a little circle to talk about the fight game. The circle grew bigger.

Jane Pierce pulled me aside and demanded, "Monte—what about this? What do we do?"

"What about what?"

"This crazy party. There are already ninety-one here by head count, and look at the doorway."

It was something to think about. They were coming through the door now in almost a steady stream. I recognized two movie stars, a member of "What's My Line?" and the new parks commissioner. The quality was good.

"It's quite a party."

"If you look on it as a competition, I suppose so. I just hate to think of what the price per minute is at this moment. I didn't have time to go out and shop for bulk liquor or anything like that. It's all hotel rates, and have you ever looked at the catering sheet of this hotel?"

"No."

"You should. And where do we put them?"

"When it banks up solid, they can't get in. That's all."

"That's all?"

"Look, Jane, you can't do anything and I can't do anything. That's the way it is. Let it run its course."

"The thing that puzzles me," Jane said, "is this. A few hours ago, Andy decided to have a party. Now everyone in the world knows about it. How does that happen?"

"Word of mouth."

"You're a help."

"Well, what do you want me to do?"

"Drop dead," she said pleasantly. "When I think of something else, I'll tell you."

7

I slipped into Jose's room a little later to see whether I could make a telephone call to the manager and maybe find an adjoining suite to open up, or even a room, or maybe let the overflow into the grand ballroom or something like that; and there was Diva, sprawled on the bed and staring at me.

"Can I use the phone?" I wanted to know.

She nodded silently, and I discovered that the manager was gone for the day and the assistant manager was somewhere in the hotel— probably at the party.

"Hell with them," Diva said. I couldn't remember when I had heard her say anything else. "Let them crawl all over each other. What do you care?"

I was sitting on the edge of the bed, a few inches from where she lay sprawled out. She reached out an arm and drew me down to her, and I let myself be drawn; and then I kissed her, a wide, hot kiss, with her tongue darting in and out of my mouth like a little snake.

After that, I pulled up and away from her and said, "Whatever you want, Diva, I probably want double, but it's like trying to do it in Grand Central Station. Also, my wife is out there, and she sort of hates me and she'd love an excuse to cut my heart out."

"You afraid of her?"

I nodded. "Also, I always figured you were Andy's girl."

"Like hell you did. You are like a stinking little open book, Monte, and I read you good. You always figured me for a dyke, and you figured Jose and me, we diddled each other. Balls. I work for Andy; I'm not his girl, and I don't screw Jose backwards either. As for you, just go to hell."

458

"I'll see you later," I said, and then I went back to the party, leaving the door to the bedroom open, hoping that it might take some pressure off the living room. The living room was packed almost solid, but if you moved slowly and had some patience, you could penetrate. I got caught in a cluster of black men with fezzes and sweeping gowns, and then I saw Andy, who was trying to talk to them in Senegalese or Somali or Bantu or something like that; and he saw me and grinned and boomed:

"What a party, Monte! What a goddamn true, beautiful party!"

I grinned foolishly, and pushed on to Jane Pierce, who was out on the terrace, talking to a thin, worried-looking man in dinner clothes.

"I tried," I said. "The manager went home. The assistant manager is lost or something."

"This is the assistant manager, Monte," she replied. "This is Mr. Bell's friend, Monte Case."

"Well, are you responsible, Mr. Case?"

"Andrew Bell is a very responsible man."

"I know that. How does one find him?"

"He's right there in that group of Africans," I said.

"There are a great many people here," Jane said, smiling her best smile at him, "but I think it's a very genteel lot, don't you? We have two of the highest dignitaries in the local diocese—I can't remember their names but they are very estimable churchmen. That tall African—you can see his fez over the crowd—is the Prime Minister of Nigeria or Ghana or the Congo. Well, it's that sort of party—"

"Of course, of course. It's just a question of suffocation, simple suffocation. But if you keep the doors to the terrace open—"

"I wouldn't dream of closing them," Jane said, and she led the manager away, or rather furrowed a path for him, and I went for a drink. That was not easy. The table that had been set up as a bar was practically inaccessible, but I finally got to it. My wife, Liz, was there already and drunk, good and drunk.

"So here's Monte," she said. "The man's friend. Did all of you know that Monte is the man's friend? I'm Monte's friend too. I got news for you—when you got a friend like Monte, you don't need enemies."

People around smiled sheepishly, the way people do in such a situation. I had asked for a Scotch on the rocks but I was ready to force my way out of the place without it.

459

"Don't run away, Monte. I want you to meet my friends. Any friend of Andy's is a friend of mine, and there's no one here tonight but friends of Andy. Right? Right, Monte?"

I nodded. She put her arm around a slim, blond boy who could not have been more than twenty-three or twenty-four and who was dressed in a double-breasted mod suit of dark purple corduroy with brass buttons and skinfit trousers. "This is David Dorchester. You pronounce it Dorster, don't you lovey?"

"Oh, yes, yes—Dorster."

"He's just done the very best mod line in England and brought it over here. He's exploded into our stinking reality, haven't you, lovey?"

"Oh—yes, quite."

"Four pages in *Harper's Bazaar,* and you're a friend of Andy's—aren't you, lovey?"

"I admire him, of course. Read him and all that. Never met him. I would love to, really."

"See—he would love to, Monte. Monte is his beloved friend."

"How did you get here?" I asked him, if only to say something.

"Oh, Jerry brought me," he said, nodding at a small, fat man who stood beside him, nursing a drink and perspiring copiously. "Jerry's bought my line for America. Jerry has the mod field, and we'll all be frightfully rich out of it. That kind of opportunity in America. The old country is very stodgy, you know."

Jerry smiled and oozed perspiration, and Liz asked him, "And how did you get here, Jerry? Friend of Andy's?"

"Admiration, dear lady." He took out a handkerchief that was soaking wet and mopped his brow. "Admirer. His publisher is my brother-in-law."

I got my Scotch on the rocks and broke out of there, and pushed my way through to the terrace, where I stood and shivered. I have been married twenty-four years, if you are curious. No children. I stood and shivered and drank the Scotch. Joe Jacobs joined me there.

"Isn't this one hell of a party," he said. "You know, part of the cost ought to go on my swindle sheet. I will get three columns out of this and a couple of nights off the prowl. God bless you, Monte."

"I'm just a guest—same as you."

"Sure, sure—listen, Monte." He consulted his little notebook.

"Andy and the governor. Governor: 'What are you writing now, Andy?' Andy: 'Nothing.' (I imagine he hates that question. It's a stupid question, and I guess every writer hates it.) Governor: 'Well—I mean what are you planning?' Andy: 'Nothing. I don't plan writing. You don't plan an act of creation. It explodes inside of you and burns your gut until you rid yourself of it.' Governor: 'I never experienced quite that.' Andy: 'You're rich. You have lots of things. Why the hell should you want creation? It's pain. People don't search for pain. They're burdened with it.' How about that, Monte?"

"I don't know. I can't say that I really know what he's talking about."

"Andy?"

"Andy—yes."

"You're a little fuzzy now."

"I've had one or two."

"Sure. Anyway, thank Andy, God bless him. I will try to quote him correctly. Tell him that. When I misquote him, he wants to tear me apart."

"I'll tell him that."

My glass was empty, and I fought my way back to the bar. Liz was not there; neither was the blond boy with the mod suit. I didn't see either of them again that night, and I hoped that the kid would please her and not turn out to be the way he looked.

8

At half past four in the morning, the party was over, and except for Andy's entourage, only the red-headed belly dancer remained. She was stretched out on the couch in the living room, out cold and snoring softly. Somehow you never connect snoring with a big, sexy kid like that. Jane Pierce had kicked her way out of the debris about a half hour before, leaving me with one final look of alcoholic hostility. She had everything that a woman could want—figure, looks, brains and success—but she loved no one. Jose Peretz was beginning to clean up.

"The hell with that," Andy said. "Let the chambermaids clean up. Get yourself a nightcap and turn in."

"I am no pig to wallow in litter."

461

Andy said something in quick Spanish, and then they both laughed.

"And keep your hands off that kid," Andy said, nodding at the belly dancer. "She's twenty years old and a silly little bitch, so just let her sleep it off in peace."

He had been drinking since he opened his eyes the day before; but he wasn't drunk, and his voice was steady and easy, and he didn't appear very tired. I was tired. I was as tired as death itself, and I had the taste of death in my mouth and in my heart. I went out onto the terrace to breathe a little fresh air. Diva was there. Over in Queens, there was a bluish-pink edge in the sky. The smell of the air was clean and damp, the way it is on a New York morning.

"Well?" Diva said to me. "You have a good time at the party, Monte?"

I shrugged, and she said, "What kind of a man are you?"

"Your guess is as good as mine."

She spat on the terrace in a very expressive and Spanish gesture. Andy came onto the terrace and told her, "Leave him alone and go to bed, Diva. Haven't you any brains? Haven't you any goddamn brains at all?"

"Just be careful, hey, Andy," she whispered. "Just be careful and don't ever talk to me like this again."

Then she swirled off the terrace and we heard the door of her bedroom crash behind her. Andy looked at me and smiled thinly.

"What the hell, Monte."

I shrugged.

"So we don't do things very good. We don't write so good and we don't hunt so good and maybe we don't love so good either, and what the hell's the difference anyway! It was a hell of a party, wasn't it?"

"It was a good party."

"But you say hello too much. You give too much. You don't remember what you are—or maybe you never know. I begin to feel small and choked. Then I am lost. I want to sit down and cry. You know?"

"I know."

"Then why did you do it?" Andy asked me gently. "You didn't have to have her here tonight."

"I'm a masochist."

462

"Leave her, Monte."

"Then it hurts her and she cries and goes into a depression. I suppose I love her or something like that."

"Monte—I'm getting out of here. Tomorrow, the next day. I can choke here. Tell you what—I have a standing invitation from the Earl of Dornoch. He had seven thousand acres in the Highlands, high north—north enough so that at this time of the year there is no real night. Black Angus cattle and deer—the old English deer. Over a thousand deer run on his land. Have you ever been to Scotland?"

I shook my head.

"You can't imagine it—a tiny land with the widest vistas in the world. You stand on a mountaintop in the Highlands, and there's a kind of freedom wherever you look, an illusion of vastness. It's an old and wild and empty land, and you hunt there with a sense of others hunting before you, and it's a feeling you don't have anywhere else. It's something valid."

I shook my head.

"No. I thought not. You never hunted, did you, Monte?"

"No."

"Never wanted to?"

"No, I never wanted to, Andy."

"Why not?"

"I don't want to kill."

"On a moral basis, Monte?"

"I don't know. I never thought about it very much."

"Everything lives and dies, Monte. That's the definition of life. You're a hunter or the hunted. But in the hunt and in the kill, there is a kind of exultation. It's a moment of passion. How many moments of passion does life give you?"

"I'm just the guy to ask, Andy."

"I'm sorry. Think about it?"

"I'll think about it."

"Get some sleep. We'll talk tomorrow."

9

I walked home through a city of beginning dawn. The night workers were coming home, but the day workers had not yet appeared. Like myself, the night people were drawn and tired. I tried to remember what kind of deer one would find in Scotland. Would they be fallow deer? I seemed to recollect out of my boyhood reading that Robin Hood killed the fallow deer. Or was it the red deer? Was fallow a name of a species or simply a color? Would they be white deer or yellow deer? I made a note of that in the woolly drift of my thoughts and promised myself that I would ask Andy about it the following day.

Fortunately, we had no doorman. I let myself in with the common key, used the self-service elevator, and entered the four-room apartment that I called home. She wasn't there. I got out of my clothes, crawled under the covers and slept. It was a rotten sleep, filled with bad dreams, but I slept.

And then the phone rang. I heard Liz's voice. "Monte—for Christ's sake, will you get that phone!"

I looked at my watch: it said four o'clock, and since the room was filled with daylight, it was obviously four o'clock in the afternoon. I tried to fix the day, while the phone rang a third and a fourth time.

"Will you get that son-of-a-bitch phone!"

Andy had come in on Friday—two o'clock in the afternoon on Friday—so this was Saturday.

"God damn you!"

Usually a phone will stop after three or four rings. I picked this up on the seventh ring. I was still half asleep, but when I heard Andy's voice, I became alert. His voice was tense and hard, and he apologized for waking me, but only to get that aside.

"What is it, Andy?"

"I'm in trouble," he said. "I am in damn big trouble, Monte."

"Where are you?"

"In the phone booth at the St. Regis. In the King Cole room. You know the booth at the far end of the room?"

I couldn't see how it mattered where the phone booth was, but I told him I knew.

"That's where I am. In the phone booth."

"All right. Just take it easy." I could not have seen myself telling Andy Bell to take it easy, but neither could I have anticipated that a time would come when I would hear this kind of tension and anxiety in Andy Bell's voice.

"Monte, I'm being hunted."

464

"What?"

Suddenly, his voice became quiet and controlled. "You heard me, Monte. I am being hunted."

"How do you know?"

"Monte, goddamn it, I am a hunter. I know."

"When did it start?"

"Two hours ago—when I left the Carlyle."

"Are you all right where you are?"

"I think so. I think I broke clear. But I have to talk to you about this. I have to talk to someone I can trust. I can trust you."

"Anyone recognize you there—at the bar, I mean?"

"No. I suppose that's a blow. Funny, I sit here, and under everything else I am scared shitless the way I was never scared before, and still I can feel the bruises on my ego because no one recognized me."

"You've been away a long time."

"Yeah. The bartender looked at me twice. I didn't want anybody to spot me—not now. Then he apologized. He thought I was Burt Lancaster. Can you imagine, Burt Lancaster."

"Well, that's flattering."

"I don't want flattery, believe me, Monte. How soon can you get here?"

"I got to wash and shave—say a half hour."

"Pare it a bit. I'll stay at the bar. God bless."

I put down the phone and there was Liz at the door, not looking her best, with the day blinders around her throat like some kind of pop art necklace.

"Who the hell was that?" she asked me.

"Andy."

"Buddy-boy. What did he want?"

I never could feel hostile enough to say that it was none of her damn business. I told her that Andy was in trouble, and then I went into the bathroom and began to shave. She followed me.

"Trouble. What kind of trouble is big enough for golden boy to wake us up like this?"

"He's being hunted."

"What? Who?"

"Andy."

"Andy's being hunted? Oh, no—no, I don't believe it."

"Well, that's what it is."

"You're not pulling my leg, Monte?" I didn't reply, and after a moment, she said, "What about you?"

"He wants me. He needs me."

"He's being hunted, and you're going to him?"

"That's right."

"You're not scared?"

"I'm so scared I can't hold this razor. I've cut myself twice already."

"Schmuck," she said. It was pretty ethnic for a woman who was part Irish, part Polish and a little Presbyterian. She could come up with the right word. I could not.

10

I found Andy at the bar in the St. Regis, and he took his drink to a table. He was holding a brandy, and mostly he was holding it and not tasting it.

"I can't drink," he said. "Do you want to order something?"

The waiter was hovering over us, so I sent him away for a dry vermouth on the rocks.

"The thing is," Andy said, "that I can't bear to have it on my tongue or my stomach. I tried. I figured I would get drunk."

"That's not easy for you."

"No, it's not."

"I've been thinking about it," I said. "I've been trying to work something out. I even thought of calling Jose and telling him to meet us here with one of your guns—or maybe that pistol you talked about."

"That would be stupid!" he snapped.

"I didn't do it."

"All right. I'm sorry. I'm tense and as I said, I am scared shitless. I wouldn't have said anything like that to you otherwise, Monte. You know that."

"I know that."

The waiter came with my drink. We were silent until he was gone, and then Andy said gently, "You see, Monte, it's no damn good to have a gun or anything like that. That's for the hunter. I'm the hunted."

"You're sure, Andy?"

466

"Oh, so right, Mr. Bell."

He nodded.

"I thought of something else."

"Oh?"

"Obvious. Not like some stupid notion about a gun, but just obvious."

Andy waited.

"Get away," I said. "You make a run for it. Out of the city. A long, clean run."

He was silent for a while, and then he shook his head.

"You said you were clear—you said you broke clean. This may be the only moment."

"I know."

"I got six hundred and change in my pocket. They know me at the desk. I could cash another two—three hundred there. It's no great stake, but along with a couple of charge cards, it can take you a long way."

He shook his head again. "Thanks."

"Why not?"

"I don't know. Pride."

"You're going to be brave," I said. "Jesus Christ. Andy, you're being hunted and you're going to be brave. You got to make a big score in opinion. For what?"

"It's hard to explain, Monte."

"You have to prove you're brave. I'm scared. I don't want to prove anything."

"I'm scared, Monte."

"And you won't run. My God, Andy," I begged him, "what else is there? What's the alternative?"

"I don't know. Maybe it was just too much for me alone. Maybe I don't know how to be alone. Maybe I don't know how to be hunted. Maybe it's something you have to learn. You don't have to stay with me, Monte."

"Go to hell."

A slim kid with heavy black glasses came over to the table and said, "I recognized you, Mr. Bell." He was so nervous from his own presumption that he could hardly speak. "I'm a researcher for *Life*. If I could get some kind of exclusive interview with you, it might be the turning point in my career. I know I got no call coming over and barging in on you like this. My name is Harry Belton. I guess you can see how scared I am—"

"I can see." Andy nodded, smiling slightly.

"But, you know—"

"I hate to send you away," Andy said.

"It's just a set of circumstances," I told the kid. "It's impossible now."

"I understand."

"Some other time. Not now."

"I understand," the kid repeated. "I just want to say that I am a great admirer of yours, Mr. Bell. I read one of your books when I was nine years old. I don't know whether I understood everything in it, but I read it through. I was only nine."

11

About Andy and myself—I met him in 1938 in Spain—I mean the first time that I ever met him and knew him, although I had heard about him. Moving back from a tour of the front lines, I was in a car with five other correspondents and one of them was Andrew Bell. The car was a big, yellow Buick touring car, a 1934, which was one of the best and most enduring Buicks ever built, and it took us east from the front over some of the worst roads I ever traveled. At one point, where the road was too narrow and too curved to pass another car, we found ourselves tailgating an old truck loaded with Republican soldiers back for leave. The truck appeared to have no springs left; it was a platform truck with gate sides and a couple of pieces of old rope backing it, and possibly good for two tons when new. Now there must have been thirty-five or forty soldiers packed into it—men full of laughter and pleasure at being alive and returning from the front, standing, most of them, swaying gaily with the truck's motion and singing the Spanish round about the farmer, the sheep and sodomy.

And then the truck driver, trying to demonstrate he could go along as briskly as we in the touring car, took a curve too fast and the truck went over. One moment a truckload of singing, happy soldiers on leave, and the next moment a hillside covered with broken, bleeding bodies, a burning truck, and the kind of horror that you do not want to witness twice.

The correspondent driving the Buick came down on the brakes very hard, and we skidded to a stop; and then we tumbled out of the car, and Andy raced to the scene of horror, myself behind him. He went to work with his first-aid kit, with torn shirts for bandages and tourniquets, with whatever he could put to use in stopping bleeding or holding a broken bone in place. I was behind him, and then I found myself assisting him and responding to his instructions; but when we turned back to the touring car for a moment, we discovered that the four other correspondents were standing at the edge of the road, watching, and preserving their bright, expensive Abercrombie uniforms in pristine spotlessness, free of nasty blood-stains and soot stains.

"Lousy bastards," Andy said. Those were the first words he ever addressed to me. That was how I met him.

Now he was still talking to the kid, because he didn't know how exactly to brush him off, and he couldn't say to the kid, "Look, kid, I'm being hunted. I'm not the hunter any more. I'm the quarry. I'm the game. Have you ever seen a fox run? Have you ever watched them beat the brush for hares? Have you ever watched a line of naked black men with drums run the lions? I'm being run—that way, and now I have gone to earth, and I am hiding for a little while." No, he could not say that or anything like that, so he continued to answer the kid's questions.

I got up and went to the phone. Andy hardly noticed. "Phone call," I said. He nodded. I closed the door of the booth behind me and then I dialed Pete's number. The bartender answered. I asked for Pete and then waited and cracked my knuckles and tried to get more control of myself and watched Andy talk to the kid. Finally, Pete's voice came through the phone, and I said to him:

"Pete, this is Monte—Monte Case. Andy's friend."

"Sure. Check. That was one hell of a party! Oh, Lord, that was a party! Where is my buddy-boy, sleeping?"

"No, he's awake."

"Oh, Jesus, he's nursing a head. Right?"

"No—not exactly."

"There's a man who can hold his liquor."

"Pete—he's in trouble."

"Who? Andy? Balls. If Andy wants the city, the mayor will give it to him. What kind of trouble can Andy have? He ain't sick, is he?"

"He's not sick. Pete, this is confidential, between us. You and me. I'm swearing you to a confidence."

469

"Horse-shit! Andy knows me. He can trust me with his last dollar. Tell me he's a Russian spy. It dies with me."

"Listen to me, Pete," I begged him, feeling how enthralled he was becoming with the sound of his own voice. Pete was a man who loved best to listen to himself. He was talking to himself now and listening to himself. He had no idea what I was trying to say to him, until I put it flatly.

"Pete—Andy is being hunted."

"I say you can trust me with anything. With his life. I say Andy can trust me with his life, if it comes to that."

"Pete, did you hear me?"

"I heard you."

"I said that Andy is being hunted."

"Hunted? Who, Andy?"

"That's right."

"Crazy. It's crazy. You putting me on?"

"I am trying to make you understand that Andy is being hunted."

"But he's the hunter."

"Not now. Now he's the game."

"Andy? Andy Bell can take care of himself."

"No! Why don't you listen to me, Pete? Why don't you stop being a goddamn fool."

"Who the hell are you to—"

"All right, all right. I apologize. But, my God, I'm here with Andy and we've gone to ground, and maybe we've shaken loose and maybe we haven't, but we have to have a place to lay in and someone to cover us—"

"What are you suggesting, Monte?" He understood me now. His voice was suddenly cold and flat.

"Give us cover."

"Here?" Pete asked evenly.

"That's right. You have an apartment there. You got food and liquor—"

"Why don't Andy get out of town?" he interrupted.

"You know Andy. Andy can't run."

"Why don't he get it through his head that he's not the hunter any more?"

"Will you give us cover, Pete?"

"What is this *us?*"

"I'm staying with him."

470

"You're a big hero, Monte. I am no hero. You know how much it cost to run up this little shack of mine. Two and a half long miles. Two million, five hundred thousand dollars—American. And not my dough. I never saw that kind of dough. This is stockholders' money. I'm a public corporation—listed on the American Stock Exchange. Look me up some day if you want to buy a nice investment. Suppose you do—so I got a responsibility to you same as I got to my other investors. It's not my place. It's a public responsibility. I'm not some kind of stinking louse that's pulling any rug from under you. I got responsibility—"

I spoke a four-letter word and hung up, and then I went back to where Andy was still talking to the kid.

"Son," I said to the kid, "please blow. This is a lousy night for what you want."

"I got more than I hoped for," the kid said.

"Good. Will you leave us alone then?"

"Sure," the kid said. He shook hands with Andy and thanked him, and then he walked over to the bar to scribble what he remembered into his notebook.

"Nice kid," Andy remarked.

"What made you come to a place like the St. Regis?" I asked him. "It's the one place in town where you got to be recognized. It's a wonder you haven't gathered a crowd already. You know that sooner or later a columnist or a *Variety* guy or one of the news guys cases the King Cole Room."

"I don't think that way any more. It's a long time since I've been to this city."

"All right. Where now?"

"Why don't we go over to Pete's," he said. "I hear that he keeps a six-bedroom apartment over the place. He could give us cover, and if we get there clean—well, maybe I'd have a chance."

"No."

"Why not?"

"It's a lousy idea," I said. "You're running scared. That's the only reason you come up with such a lousy idea."

"You're out of your mind, Monte."

"Sure."

"We go to Pete's. Suppose you go out and snare us a cab—"

"No!"

He stared at me strangely, and finally I said, "I just spoke to Pete. That's what I went to the phone for."

471

"Oh."

"We'll go back to Carlyle," I said. "As long as you got to be so stinking brave and stay here, we'll go back to where you got some clothes and friends and guns."

Staring at the table top, he muttered, "Guns are no damn good. How many times do I have to tell you that?"

"I know. I just think in patterns."

"I'm sorry. I keep jumping on you. Why don't you spit in my face and walk out of here?"

"Sure." I looked at him newly and said, "I'll do that some time. Remind me."

12

We walked north on Madison Avenue. It was Saturday, too early for dining and too late for strolling, and the shoppers had gone home too. The streets were empty. I glanced at Andy, and he was tense, alert, his eyes darting here and there.

"The game isn't brave," he said.

"The hunter is brave."

"Crap," he said. "Just pure crap, Monte."

Then we ran for cover, and we found the entrance to the subway under the front doorway of Bloomingdale's. In the subway, it was better. People in the subway didn't recognize Andy, and the subway was covered over, dark, a place to run to ground.

"But when you run to ground," Andy said to me, "that's it, isn't it? Then it's over. Then you got a hole in the earth, and you stay there. You put your face on the ground. Do you remember what the ground feels like against your cheek, Monte, cold and wet?" A train pulled in and we got on, going uptown, north. The car was almost empty, and we sat down slowly, like strangers.

"I remember," I said.

At 77th Street, Andy got up to leave. I followed him. We stood on the platform until the train roared away uptown, and then the only sound was the grumbling distant noise that a subway always makes.

"What in hell is in it for you, Monte?" Andy asked me harshly.

"You wouldn't write it that way," I said to him. "You'd call me names and burn my ass a little, so I walk out on you. We don't want to go in for that kind of thing."

"I suppose not," he said. "If you want to stay, Monte, let's try to stop being afraid."

"We can try," I agreed.

13

At the hotel, outside of Andy's suite, a press delegation bigger than the one that had met him at the airport was waiting. The worried manager had told us that there were reporters upstairs, but we hadn't anticipated anything like this. A big feeder cable lay on the hallway floor, and maybe forty – fifty other wires as well, and there were TV cameras from the three big networks. There were newsreel cameras, hand cameras and a flock of reporters; and the moment Andy came in sight, the take began. The reporters crowded around, with the CBS microphone shoved close in, ABC and NBC flanking, and the NBC man alternating the questions with Frank Brady from *The New York Times,* and everyone else made notes and sparked the excitement. I didn't make any notes there, but it was pretty much as follows, checked against the *Times* story:

"When did you discover that you were being hunted, Mr. Bell?"

Andy could have told them to go to the devil and be damned, and what difference would it have made at that point? But instead he stood there, his hands in his pockets, towering over the lot of them and slouching slightly, and informed them quietly and politely that he had become aware of being the quarry only a few hours ago, early in the afternoon.

"And what did you do then, Mr. Bell? What steps did you take?"

"I hid my trail as well as I could. I was in a snare of sorts then, but I broke out and found cover."

"What kind of cover?"

"It doesn't matter. I needed a place where I could sit and think."

"And how did you get back here?"

"Simple evasion. Nothing very clever."

"Will you be leaving New York now?"

"No."

"Why not?"

"I don't choose to."

"Then doesn't it follow—"

"It follows."

"How does it feel to change places, Mr. Bell?"

"Lousy."

"But don't you feel that your skill as a hunter—?"

"No."

"But surely you don't consider yourself in the same position as any other man being hunted?"

"I do."

"Do you have any feelings of fear, Mr. Bell?"

"If it interests your readers, yes."

"Your reputation for courage—"

"A lie, like all other reputations."

"To get back to the question of evasion as a tactic, Mr. Bell— doesn't it follow that the only evasion that makes any sense is to leave the city?"

"I never was very sure of what makes sense."

"Yet you state emphatically that you will not run?"

Andy shrugged.

"Have you ever been hunted before?"

"No, this is the first time."

"Tiny Joe was on the air less than an hour ago, charging that this whole thing is a publicity stunt. Have you any comment to make about that, Mr. Bell?"

"No."

"Won't you please make a statement?" the NBC man pleaded. "Any kind of a statement. People want to know how you are taking this."

Andy shook his head.

"You have an obligation to the public, Mr. Bell."

"I am very tired," Andy said. "I think that's all for now."

I maneuvered him toward the door of the suite. Jose had the door open. We both slipped in, and Jose drove the door closed behind us. Andy flopped into a chair in the living room, and said to Diva, who was standing tensely at one side of the room:

"Diva, call the manager and tell him to clear them out of the hall. That's his obligation. I don't care how he does it, and I don't give a damn how they feel about it. I want to be able to come and go without fighting that line-up out there."

Diva nodded and went into the bedroom to make the call. Jose poured Andy a glass of brandy and said:

474

"Trouble—damn big trouble, hey Monte?"

"You can say that."

Andy stared at the brandy for a long moment; then he gulped it down and almost choked on it. He flung the glass away from him.

"I understand," Jose nodded.

"This crap that it's easy to die," Andy said. "This filthy crap that it's easy to die."

Diva came out of the bedroom. "I spoke to the manager. He'll do his best. He wants to stop by later and have a word with you. I tell him is all right—yes?"

"No. I don't want to talk to him."

"Have a word with him, Andy."

"You had a word with Pete."

"Then I'll talk to him," I said.

"No—the hell with that. I'll see him when he comes up."

"You want anything, Andy?" Diva asked him.

"No."

I walked out onto the terrace, and Diva followed me. The sun was setting over Queens. The city was quiet and lovely and full of shadows.

"I am a bitch, Monte," Diva said. "You are married to one. You need me like I need what happened today. I suppose you tell your wife. Oh, you shouldn't have, Monte. That's how they know."

"Maybe not. I had to tell Pete."

"Pete is a pig," she whispered. "Don't you know Pete is a pig?"

"He's Andy's friend."

"Oh, that's a stinking lie, number one. Friends! Andy has no friends. Jose and me—we are servants. That's better. And you—"

"Yeah—and me?"

"I don't know what you are. You asked Pete for shelter? You asked Pete for life?"

"He's a public corporation."

"You know what he is."

The doorbell rang, and Diva went inside to open the door. I followed. Andy sat in his chair without moving. It was the hotel manager. Diva let him in and closed the door quickly behind him. Jose pulled up a chair for him. He nodded at me and sat down facing Andy.

"I manage the place," he said to Andy. "It's a job."

"Why don't you tell me that you admire me?" Andy asked.

"I have too much respect for you to say that."

"Thank you," Andy said.

"Still—well, what do you say, Mr. Bell?"

"I don't think any harm will come to the hotel."

"Can you guarantee that?"

"You know better than to ask me that." Andy smiled.

"I have to ask it."

"I was a hunter," Andy said. "A hunter waits until the game moves into the open. Even when he spots the lair."

"Unless he becomes impatient."

"I'll make my run," Andy said. "I have to rest a little. I'm tired now. But I'll make my run."

"I heard you won't leave the city."

"I don't have to leave the city to make a run."

The manager watched Andy for a moment, saw him and appraised him. I liked the manager. "What the hell," the manager said, "it's only a job. Get your rest."

Then he left.

Andy closed his eyes. I went out onto the terrace, where the night was washing in. I stayed there for fifteen or twenty minutes, and then Andy called me.

14

"Sit down, Monte," he said.

I sat in the chair facing him.

"None of that crap I tried before. This is very simple and direct. I am going to make a run for it. Get out and get clear."

"Tonight?"

"Tonight." Jose and Diva stood by the doors to the terrace, and Andy told them to clear out of the living room. "I want to talk to Monte alone." They went into their respective rooms, and I suppose they stood there with their ears against the doors.

"Why tonight?"

"I like the manager. I don't know what to say to you, Monte. I don't know how to thank you."

"For what?"

"Ah—I don't know. The hell with it. You get sentimental with someone like Pete. Right now sentiment would be offensive. It would offend you, wouldn't it?"

"It would offend me," I agreed.

"Then take off, Monte. For Christ's sake, take off."

Then I got up and left—without looking behind me and without saying anything else. Down in the lobby, I ran into the manager, and he said to me:

"Could I buy you a drink, Mr. Case?"

"If we don't talk about Andy Bell."

"I'll talk about running a hotel."

"You got me," I said.

I had three drinks and I learned a lot about running a large, posh, uptown eastside hotel, and then I shook hands with the manager.

"He'll make a run for it tonight, won't he?" the manager said.

"I guess so."

Out on the dark street there was a cool breeze. The summer was almost done. It was a pleasant night. I thought about getting drunk, but the thought was not too pleasant. I thought about calling someone to have dinner with me, but first I called Liz. She wasn't home. Then I called a few people, but everyone knew about Andy being the quarry, and I was close enough to Andy for the people I knew not to desire closeness with me. Not on that evening anyway. I walked downtown and then I went into one of the flicks on Third Avenue, and I sat through a picture without knowing what went on in front of me and without being able to remember any of it; and then I walked over to the Oak Room at the Plaza and had a few more drinks and hoped that someone would happen by, but no one did. I went home then.

15

I slept badly. I dreamed and the dreams were not good, and then I woke up and lay in the dark and heard Liz come in; and then I must have dozed a little, because the telephone woke me at about six in the morning. It was O'Brian, from the Twenty-third Squad, and he told me about Andy.

"When?"

"Maybe twenty minutes ago. On Fifth Avenue, just south of the 56th Street corner."

"I'll be there."

"Good. That's good. I'll wait for you."

"What son of a bitch—" Liz began.

I put away the telephone and told her that Andy was dead.

"Oh my God—"

It was no use to hurt her, and anything I would have said would have hurt her. It was never any use to hurt her; the world hurt her too much, and you would have to be a psychopath to add to it. I dressed and got down to 56th Street, and then I was sorry that I had been in such a damned hurry.

The hunt had finished there, and there was nothing recognizable left of Andy. What had been him was spread in a bloody smear halfway across Fifth Avenue, and the men from the morgue were trying to gather it up and make something in the way of remains out of it.

At this hour, on a Sunday morning, Fifth Avenue was all but deserted. The one or two citizens who came by did not stop. The smear was not something that anyone would want to stand around and look at.

O'Brian, who was supervising things, spotted me and came over with a handkerchief filled with a few possessions that had survived Andy—keys for doors I had never stepped through, some bills and some change, a crushed card case, a penknife, cufflinks bent shapeless, a broken pen—what could have belonged to Andy or to any other mortal man.

"I'm going to throw up," I said to him.

O'Brian nodded and led me over to a cardboard container that was conveniently waiting. Evidently, others had felt the same way.

"Too much to drink last night."

"Sure," O'Brian said. "When did you see him last, Monte?"

"Last night at the Carlyle. At about eight or so, I guess."

"Did you know he would make a run for it?"

"He told me."

"Did you try to stop him?"

"Andy?"

"All right, but why did he stay in the city? Why didn't he break clear?"

I shook my head.

"Who are the next of kin, Monte?"

"One wife is dead. Another lives in Paris. The third lives in San Francisco and hates his guts."

"How about that Spanish dame and the little creep with the black polish hair?"

"They worked for him."

"Well someone has to come over to the precinct with me," O'Brian said, "and sign papers and then go to the morgue and make arrangements."

"I'll do that."

"Funeral arrangements?"

"I'll start the ball rolling. I'll do what I can."

"My God," O'Brian said, "Andy Bell had enough friends. We certainly won't have any trouble in that department."

16

We didn't. Andy had been part Episcopalian, and the Rector of St. John the Divine suggested that the services be held there. Over three thousand people turned up, and the front part of the Cathedral contained about five percent of the best names in *Who's Who*, not to mention the *Blue Book*. Liz and I patched things up, and I dutifully put out two hundred and twenty-five dollars for the black ensemble she wore. She looked very attractive. I suppose a hundred people mentioned to me how attractive Liz looked. Diva and Jose were not there. They took off the same day Andy died, and no one ever saw them again or heard of them again, and the talk around was that they had robbed Andy of every nickel he had. But the truth of it was that every nickel he had was on him when he died, and his estate was deeply in debt, even though the royalties would pay off the debts in due time and show a handsome income eventually.

Andy's third wife's father had established a family plot in an Episcopalian cemetery out in the Hamptons. Strangely, with all that great crowd at the cathedral, only a handful drove to the cemetery: his third wife, her mother, myself and some cameramen. It was a pleasant day, and the cemetery was on a high, pretty, windy knoll. Liz was going to go out with me, but at the last moment she developed a migraine headache and had to go to bed.

Afterword

TOO much has been written about Zen, but of course not enough; and so it will continue and properly so. The flashing bit of light, flame, and color in the sunlight of a garden has very little relationship to the specimen pinned in a glass case. The first is a butterfly; the second is a specimen. That interesting old Zen man, Paul Reps, wrote that "Zen carries many meanings, none of them entirely definable. If they are defined, they are not Zen." But then he went on to put together a marvelous little book about Zen called *Zen Bones, Zen Flesh,* and that too was quite proper within the context of what he had said.

Conclusions about the childishness of non sequitor, the fallacy of the contradiction, and the unshakable validity of logic and reason are not a part of Zen thinking, if indeed there is such a thing as Zen thinking. Zen has been defined and explained over and over, a thousand times, and while I have not counted all the books that have been written about Zen, I am sure that there are more than a thousand of them—which does not mean that Zen has been defined or explained.

Of all the thousands of definitions of what Zen is, I like best the one given by the Zen master who was asked by a Western person to tell him the difference between his own belief and the belief of Zen. "To your way of thinking," the Zen master replied, "your skin is a thing which separates and protects you from the outside world. To my way of thinking, my skin is a thing which connects me and opens me to the outside world, which in any case is not the outside world."

But while I like it, I must assure you that it is hardly a definition of Zen.

481

Literally, Zen means to sit cross-legged in a position of meditation, being the Japanese transliteration of the Chinese word *ch'an*. But beyond that, it has many other meanings; it is a name for a philosophy, a religion, a way of life, a way of seeing, a way of being, a way of connection. It is these and many other things, and, perhaps most importantly, it is a way of self knowledge. It assumes that in the normal course of life and growth, human beings set up barriers between themselves and reality, and Zen is a way of breaking down these barriers.

When the time came in my life that I had to know about Zen, I looked for a teacher. It was not a simple matter, nor are the series of events that finally led me to him pertinent to what I write here, but eventually I found him and persuaded him to instruct me. It was no easy matter; he looked upon me dubiously, as poor material for accomplishment. Eight years later, he finished his instruction, and in the years since then I have marveled at his patience and persistence. In the course of his teaching, he told me many stories about Professor Daisetz Teitaro Suzuki, who was his teacher, and who, in a manner of speaking, became my own teacher since I read and reread so much of his writing.

Once (my teacher told me) I asked Professor Suzuki, who was one of the wisest men on earth, about his name.

"But it is not my name," he replied.

"Oh?"

"They changed my name," he explained.

"May I ask why?"

"Oh, yes. Of course. You see, when I left the Buddhist monastery in Japan, my master—"

"Your master?"

"In the Zen sense, my teacher, who was a great Zen master, but then there is always trouble with words when we go from my language into yours. You see, it was understood that my mission would be to go to America, and my master thought I should change my name."

"Why?"

"Because it was inappropriate. So he changed it to Diasetz," Professor Suzuki said apologetically.

"And may I ask what Diasetz means?"

"It means Great Stupid," Professor Suzuki replied.

482

Naturally, the meaning of the story was plain, and therefore my teacher never bothered to explain it to me, and in this he was absolutely right. They say of Zen that one who speaks of it does not know and that one who knows does not speak. At the same time, millions of words have been written about Zen and tens of millions spoken, and I add these to them.

Firstly, Zen is a religion, not in the Western sense, not in the anthropomorphic sense, not in the sense that invokes a god or defines a god or ever speaks of a god; indeed, not in the sense that ever admits of a god in the terms of Western religion or accepts such usages as prayer, sacrifice, invocation, or repentance. Zen is a religion in the sense that it admits of a mystery, a reality from which human beings separate themselves, and which reality, if perceived, will contain both the question and the answer. For both the question and the answer are within us and outside of us, inseparable and identical. Zen offers nothing, and the person who comes to Zen must ask for nothing; for in the sense that we comprehend giving, it has nothing to give. The story is told of the seeker who came to the Zen teacher and asked him, "Master, why should I study Zen?" And the master answered, "So that when the time comes, you will not be afraid to die."

Zen is also a philosophy, but again not in the Western sense; for Zen does not instruct one in a set of ethics and demand that one live by them. Zen holds instead that if you can open your eyes and see the reality of being, both within yourself and outside of yourself, then you will live life with purpose and love and apart from the monster of good and evil and right and wrong that men have created. Zen attempts neither to define nor explain the world; it is a way of changing oneself, so that one may see the reality of the world. It is a way of being, rather than a way of thinking, a way of seeing rather than a way of judging. It is a way without a scripture, without a premise, without a dogma, without reward and without punishment.

Zen is also a way of life. There is no intellectual approach to Zen, no way of instruction as applies to religion, no way of teaching as is used in the various disciplines of Western practice. To find Zen, one must live Zen, one must practice it, in terms of meditation and in terms of everyday existence. I have in my study a whole shelf of books on Zen, and most of them are worth reading. But in the final analysis, Zen cannot be found in books. What can be found is the interest and excitement that will lead a person to think about Zen and to make some steps toward it. But even if those steps are taken, the way is neither easy nor of short duration. There is no instant Zen, no capsule Zen, and few things in life are more demanding and more difficult to master than the art of Zen meditation.

What then has all this to do with this strange collection of improbable stories that I have chosen to call, quite arbitrarily, Zen stories? Is there such a thing as Zen writing, Zen art, Zen literature? The question falls apart when we reflect on the usual definitive labels pinned onto art, such as ancient art, modern art, Renaissance art, ethnic art, English art, French art—and so forth and so on. Yet if you are aware of the place of Zen in Japanese culture, you will counter with the argument that there is a form of art in Japan that is called Zen art. It is found in brush painting, in writing, in flower arrangement, and even in such formal courtesies as the serving of tea. These are the outgrowth of a culture that has—at least in some minor part—practiced Zen Buddhism for centuries, and there is nothing quite comparable in Western civilization. Therefore, I would hardly presume to relate the stories in this book to the Zen art which exists in Japan.

At the same time, I would say that they partake of something of the Zen spirit and were certainly written by a person deeply under the influence of Zen thinking. Nevertheless, they are western stories, contrived in a form that is specific to the heritage of the short story in English and American literature. If they entertain and amuse the reader, they do so in the Western fashion, and if they happen to instruct, their instruction is particular to the form of our literature. Only when they pose an answer to which there is no question, or a question to which there is no answer, do they depart from the above formalities. Nevertheless, I do not think I have taken liberties in calling them Zen stories since all of them touch, to one degree or another, on the relationship of subject to object. I do not refer to this relationship in the Western manner of thinking, for out of that mode would come the contention that all of human activity partakes of the relationship of subject to object.

In the Zen manner of thinking and seeing, the relationship of subject to object is another thing entirely—which is not to say that this idiom is the preserve of the Eastern philosopher and has never been uttered in the West. I speak of broad patterns of thought and existence, and just as this manner of thought, which I call Zen thought, is absent in much of the Orient, so has it been present in many Western people who have never heard of Zen. When John Donne wrote, in one of his "Devotions," "No man is an Iland, intire of it selfe; every man is a peece of the Continent, a part of the maine; if a clod bee washed away by the Sea, Europe is the lesse . . . . . .," he was making a statement not unrelated to Zen thought, and, indeed, the experience of all Western mystics is related to the Zen experience. In the relationship of subject to object, there is, even among these extraordinary souls, a difference. And since this difference is terribly important and very central to the Zen fact, I will take the liberty of quoting at some length from a remarkable little book, called *The Method of Zen,* written very simply yet profoundly by Eugene Herrigel. Speaking of the Western mystic, he says:

> In Zen, man does not have the central position he has in European mysticism, where the *unio mystica* appears as the overwhelmingly blissful privilege to which he, as a human being, is entitled. He alone, of all living creatures, is destined for this experience, and by attaining it he steps out of the state of being-in-the-world. This stepping out he calls "ecstasy" *(ek-stasis)*; it is losing himself and finding himself again, dying and being born again. What he finds again is his true center, his inalienable self, which is canceled out and yet preserved in the *unio mystica.* In God, in the Godhead, or whatever else European mystics term that with which and in which the union is accomplished, the self is not finally extinguished, but is saved, reprieved, and its fate sealed forever. Only temporarily, only for the sake of the ultimate atonement which tolerates no duality, is "dying of self" demanded, because God is born only into those souls that have offered up "being themselves" as the final and supreme sacrifice. But once the birth is accomplished, the soul becomes the divinely empowered center from which to be itself forever, evolving out of itself like Nietzsche's ever-rolling wheel.
>
> In Zen, on the other hand, human existence as such is "ek-static" and "ek-centric," whether we are aware of it or not. The more a human being feels himself a self, tries

to intensify this self and reach a never attainable perfection, the more drastically he steps out of the center of being, which is no longer now his own center, and the further he removes himself from it.

For the Zen Buddhist everything that exists, apart from man—animals and plants, stones, earth, air, fire, water—lives undemandingly from the center of being, without having left it or being able to leave it. If man, having strayed from this center, is to know security and innocence of existence as they live it, because ultimately they live without purpose, there is no alternative for him but a radical reversal. He must go back along the way whose thousand fears and tribulations have shown it to be a way of error, must slough off everything that promised to bring him to himself, renounce the seductive magic of life lived on his own resources, and return home to the "house of truth" which he wantonly left in order to chase phantoms when he was scarcely fledged. He must not "become as a little child," but like forest and rock, like flower and fruit, like wind and storm.

The *unio mystica* in Zen therefore means homecoming, restoration of an original state now lost.

Have we made more of an enigma of the particular relationship of subject to object that is Zen, or have we clarified it somewhat? I think the few paragraphs quoted above put it beautifully and clearly, but like most Zen statements, it mystifies by its very simplicity. It might well be read two or three times. No matter how sophisticated Western thinking on the subject of God becomes, it never really departs from the incredible vulgarism of "the Man upstairs," a kind of anthropomorphic infantilism that even the most primitive "savage," living in a community of nature, would be forced to reject. Zen never speaks of God, which has led many Western commentators to refer to it as a philosophy and not a religion. But we have put our own narrow stigma on "religion," divorcing it from compassion, love, mercy, humanity; bending it toward the support of every abomination, prejudice, bigotry, ignorance, hatred, and, of course, that ultimate vileness which men call war.

Zen does not judge. It abhors the trap of right and wrong, good and bad, for these are tools and definitions which men fashion to their own ends, and which always make the unity of subject and object impossible. Yet it is precisely this unity of subject and object which is at the core of Zen.

I have never read a commentary by a Zen authority on the art of the short story from the Zen point of view, yet the short story is an ancient and well-loved form of Zen instruction; and Zen literature abounds in hundreds of remarkable short stories. Some of them are told in the marvelous economy of just a few lines, some of them longer, but all of them leave the impression of a brush stroke that strikes true and correctly. However, they are in the tradition of Japanese and Chinese culture, which should be understood. If we speak of Zen in the broadest sense, it must be thought of as a thing which has always been and will always be. When a human being expresses it, lives it, or thinks in such terms and transmits his thinking to whatever he practices, the product will be the result of his own experience, in the shape of his own culture and tradition; and since Zen is neither exclusive nor parochial, there are any number of stories in our own culture that might well be considered as Zen.

I think immediately of O. Henry's lovely tale, "The Gift of the Magi." Here was a young married couple, very poor, very much in love. Each had a single treasured possession: the girl had a head of long, splendid hair, the boy a watch. She cut her hair and sold it to a wigmaker to buy him a watch-chain; he sold his watch to buy her a set of combs for her hair. Probably O. Henry never heard of the word Zen, since there was no knowledge of the practice in America then, yet I can't think of anyone who put the essence of it much better than he did in the last paragraph of his story:

And here I have lamely related to you the uneventful chronicle of two foolish children in a flat who most unwisely sacrificed for each other the greatest treasures of their house. But in a last word to the wise of these days let it be said that of all who give gifts these two were the wisest. Everywhere they are wisest. They are the magi.

What is meant by this is not to be explained, for indeed there is no proper explanation of wisdom. It is another thing than logic and intelligence, both of which are pliable and diverting instruments of modern existence, and it abhors the separation of subject and

487

object. Yet is seems to me that this quesiton of subject and object is most pertinent to the best of short stories, and when the two come together in a circle, the art of the short story is fulfilled.

There is little interest today in the writing or the publication of short stories. Where once, half a century ago, more than a thousand magazines in America published short stories, today the market is limited to a handful, and publishers most often look upon the publication of books of short stories as favors done to otherwise successful writers. And the reading public in America concurred in this and dismissed this ancient and wonderful art with hardly a glance of regret. But perhaps this too will change, for the short story is too essential an ingredient of art to disappear.

Of course, when I speak of the short story as a literary form so expressive of a Zen point of view, I do not refer to all short stories and certainly not to all of mine; but rather to the possibility of a flash of illumination not unlike the clean brush stroke of a Zen artist. It is a direct simplicity that does away with complexity, or, perhaps better said, it assures one that the apparent complexity is an illusion. It is not possible to expand such a story without destroying it. Yet if the story succeeds, it contains a nugget of truth that makes rejection difficult.

The old Zen masters were fond of understatement, sometimes to a point that can be utterly provoking and frustrating to anyone who attempts to find Zen in the written word. When asked what was the nature of Zen, a Zen master of long ago replied, "I eat when I am hungry, I drink when I am thirsty, and I sleep when I am tired," which is one way of saying it, and as directly true as it is difficult to comprehend. The old Zen man simply omitted the sorrow, the tragedy, and the complexity of human life. He was not asked what is not Zen or how is Zen to be found; he was asked a specific, and he replied with a specific, quite aware of the fact that had he gone on talking all day, the question would have been answered no better. This must be understood in terms of the short story, that is, the short story which illuminates in the Zen manner. Either it poses a question to which there is no answer, or an answer to which there is no question; for again in the Zen sense, each—the question, the answer—must contain the subject and the object for the circle to be complete, and if it is complete, there is nothing to add, nothing to subtract. The illumination has taken place.

488

An example is a very old story out of the Bible. It tells how Jephthah, who was a judge over Israel, led his people into battle against the Ammonites. If victory were granted him, Jephthah pledged to his God that he would sacrifice to God that which came forth to meet him on his return home. His daughter came forth to meet him.

I would ask my reader to reflect on the above without prejudice— and I refer to the specific prejudice that regards ancient man as a barbarian. A barbarian he was not, certainly not in our sense of the word, and, in many ways, he was closer to the center of things than we are. By that center, I mean the reality both within and outside of ourselves that Zen seeks to reveal or illuminate. Reflecting upon it, wonder why God required the life of Jephthah's daughter? What did the writer of this tale have in mind?

The question contains the answer. One cannot elaborate. One could say that sacrifice, as such, is always to and of oneself, since there is no other reaching out to God—if indeed the word God is capable of meaning, comprehension, or definition. Those who call Zen simply a philosophy are quick to point out that there is no word equivilent to God in Zen thinking or terminology, and that the word God cannot be translated into Buddhist terms. But such argumentation is antrhopomorphic in content and without any serious weight. Yet even if one plays with notions of God and sacrifice, the story of Jephthah does not yield to inquiry, either rational or mystical; and even the argument that the myth has basis in history does not help to clarify things. The answer is there, yet it is not there. It is seen, yet unseen.

In the above sense, it is Zen, a whiplash commanding one to see not the apparent, but that which is imminent yet clouded by what is apparent. Such stories, stories in the Zen manner and out of Zen thinking, reject the judgmental. If they offer a flash of illumination, the bit of bright light commands the reader to see what is and not be trapped in the morass of right and wrong and good and evil.

I must make note again of the fact that I am not trying to explain Zen or to comment upon it, but simply to tell why I chose to call the stories you have just read Zen stories; and perhaps to suggest that the short story form is particularly suited to project the Zen outlook. Some of them, previously published, were called science-fiction, for want of a better category to place them in, but there is so little science in these stories that I hardly have to argue that the label is inappropriate. Nor are they fantasy, but rather answers for which I invented questions. If an angel falls to earth, I must have a question, namely, what happens when an angel falls to earth? And rather than argue the existence of angels, it is simpler to reply that nothing at all happens. This is the way it is, and not a very bad way if we ever learn to open our eyes and see.